GLYNDŴR BOOK 2

Glorious Shall Their Dragon Be

CATRIN COLLIER

First published in Great Britain in 2020 by Catrin Collier

Copyright © Catrin Collier 2019

The right of Catrin Collier to be identified as the author of this work has been asserted by her in accordance with the Copyright, Designs and Patents Act 1988. All rights reserved. No part of this publication may be reproduced, stored in a retrieval system, or transmitted, in any form or by means, electronic, mechanical, photocopying, recording or otherwise, without the prior permission of the copyright owner, catrincollier@aol.com

The story contained within this book is a work of fiction. Names and characters are the product of the author's imagination and any resemblance to actual persons, living or dead, is entirely coincidental.
All film and television rights are the property of Tanabi Films, Swansea.

GLORIOUS SHALL THEIR DRAGON BE

Welsh legend prophesied that a messianic leader, The Foretold Son, "Y Mab Darogan" in Welsh, would appear to drive the English from the lands of Britain and reclaim it for the Celts. His banner would bear the golden dragon of Uther Pendragon. And, it did shine glorious. For a while.

CONTENDERS

KING ARTHUR

Late 5th to early 6th century AD – (possibly? details of his life dissolved in the mists of time before being embroidered by bards). Lies asleep on his shield in a hidden cave alongside his knights awaiting a call to fight for Wales when he is needed.

LLEWELYN THE GREAT

(Llewelyn ap Iorwerth) 1173 – 1240 – ruled as Prince of Gwynedd and later Prince of Wales, possibly assisted by King John after he married John's bastard daughter, Joan. Died in Aberconwy Abbey (rumoured as the result of a paralysing stroke) and was buried there. His coffin was later moved to St Grwst's church, Llanrwst.

LLEWELYN THE LAST

(Llewelyn ap Gruffydd) 1223 -1282 – killed by English soldiers who decapitated his corpse after discovering his identity post mortem. Portions of his mangled remains were buried in the Abbey of Cwm Hir by the monks of the Cistercian Order, his head was despatched south and displayed on London bridge for over twenty years.
After Llewelyn's death, Edward I proceeded to eradicate Llewelyn's royal Welsh bloodline. Llewelyn's brother Dafydd was hung drawn and quartered in Shrewsbury, the punishment invented and refined by Edward as fitting for high treason.

Llewelyn's daughter, Gwenllian, was incarcerated in a convent from the age of eighteen months until her death 53 years later. Dafydd's daughter, 13 year old Gwladys, was sent to a separate nunnery, to be held until her death at the age of 66. Dafydd's two sons were imprisoned in cages at Bristol castle for the remainder of their lives. Other men and women related to the Welsh royal house of Gwynedd were imprisoned, murdered, died in mysterious circumstances or simply disappeared.

Over 500 Welsh bards were rounded up and slaughtered by Edward I so they could not pen poetry, songs, stories or otherwise venerate the fate of the Welsh Royal family. When Henry IV usurped Richard II he not only made it illegal for Welsh bards to ply their trade but illegal for anyone to employ them. The bards were not only entertainers and poets but the keepers of the history and legends of the Welsh people.

The silencing of the bards effectively stole both their past and identity from the Welsh, but the persecution of the Welsh bards became known in Europe and celebrated in poetry and legend. As late as the nineteenth century Hungarian poet, Janos Arany wrote of the silencing of the medieval Welsh bards

"But high above all drum and fife
And trumpets shrill debate,
Five hundred martyred voices chant
Their hymn of deathless hate . . . "

Proof, if it is needed, that truth is seldom silenced forever.

OWAIN OF THE RED HAND

(Owain Lawgoch) 1330 – 1378 – assassinated in Poitou, France on the order of King Edward III who continued Edward I's eradication of the Welsh royal line of Llewelyn the Great and Llewelyn the Last. Owain Lawgoch was buried in the chapel of St Leger, which was his HQ while conducting the siege of Mortagne-sue-Gironde for the French.

A military genius Owain attracted mercenaries from as far afield as Wales and the Prussian Teutonic knights to his banner.

And one who would have changed the face of Britain had he succeeded

OWAIN GLYNDŴR 1359 – ?

Owain was the direct descendent and link between three Welsh royal houses.
Powys through his grandfather, Gruffydd ap Madog and father Gruffydd Fychan.
Deheubarth through his mother, Elen ferch Tomas ap Prince Llewelyn of Deheubarth.
And Gwynedd through Elen's mother, Elinor Goch, the daughter and heir of Catherine, an illegitimate daughter of Llewelyn II. As the last direct survivor of the house of Gwynedd she had been concealed from the English after the murder of her father.
Provoked by Reginald de Grey, Baron Ruthyn's theft of his land and Henry IV's anti Welsh edicts, as the surviving heir of three Welsh Royal houses, Owain Glyndŵr felt it his duty to fight for Welsh Independence.

The history of his revolt was written by monks in monasteries the content of the manuscripts they penned dictated by King Henry IV and King Henry V.

If the siege of Harlech Castle was documented the account did not survive.

If his death and final resting place was chronicled beyond dispute, the account has been lost – or deliberately concealed.

DEDICATION

For Mary Loring, my editor and friend of decades, with more gratitude than I can express for her incisive comments, corrections and suggestions which have improved so many of my books.

Without her magic touch my work would be very much the poorer.

Thank you, Catrin Collier June 2020

God cannot alter the past, though historians can.

Samuel Butler – "Prose Observations."

PROLOGUE

Snowdonia May 30th 1421
'Have we many more miles to cover before nightfall?' the young traveller asked his companion as their mounts picked their way along the sheep track that wound upwards to the mountain pass.

'No.' The old man's voice was rough from disuse.

The young man's horse slipped, dislodging small stones that sent scree rattling down the steep slope to their right.

'Dismount!'

The traveller obeyed the old man's order. He trailed behind his guide, leading his mount and packhorse by the reins. The sun was sinking somewhere above the pewter clouds and such light as there was, faded as darkness rose from the ground. The temperature dropped and the air fell cold, heavy with moisture, coating their faces with a translucent film.

When the old man reached the pass he pointed silently down to their left.

The young man drew alongside him 'If the light was right we'd see the cave opening from here?' he suggested.

The old man nodded.

The young man peered into the mist. 'I've heard a thousand descriptions of this place.'

The old man recognised nostalgia in the traveller's voice. A longing for days of adventure followed by evenings when warriors gathered around campfires inside the cave, to eat, drink, argue, plot and plan campaigns that would lead to that most elusive of prizes, freedom!

He closed his mind to memories riddled with grief, squared his shoulders and began the descent. When the first heavy drops fell, he brushed the back of his hand across his face. He could have been wiping rain away, but the young man thought otherwise.

Twenty-one years ago, seven men had spent a freezing, snow-filled, dark winter holed up in a cave in the hidden valley they were about to enter. Seven men who'd whiled away their confinement by plotting a rebellion they hoped would transform the destiny of a nation.

Each had treasured their memories and the stories they had to tell about that season and the years that followed. But both travellers knew it was a story that still awaited an ending.

***

A hollow in the hillside had been fitted out as a stable, with a primitive but serviceable wooden manger, buckets of rainwater, stalls and a stout gate at the mouth of the opening. After both men had seen to their horses, the old man led the way outside along a path marked by boulders before ducking into a cave.

The young man waited while the old man struck a flint and held it to a handful of dried kindling in an iron bowl. When it caught, the old man took a stick from a pile coated with rancid mutton fat and lit it. An effective, if odorous torch, the flames set grotesque shadows flickering on the walls and ceiling.

'The passage is behind the stone pillar?' the young man questioned.

'I see you listened to your elders.' The voice was still gruff, but slightly warmer.

The traveller followed his guide, bending almost double when he negotiated the low tunnel that turned back on itself. When they reached a large open "room" it also proved too low for him to stand upright.

'Your sire could also only sit in here.'

The young man thought he detected a trace of humour. 'Father must have found that irksome.'

'He did. The minute darkness fell he went outside. When he wasn't on watch, he frequently used to ride or walk all night.'

More primitive torches were suspended in crude metal brackets hammered into the walls. The old man lit them and the fires laid in hearths of stones either end of the cave.

The traveller looked around. Despite the lack of light, fresh air and cold damp walls it was a home - of sorts. Shelves carved in the rock walls displayed an odd collection of objects. Blankets were heaped on the pressed dirt floor below them, along with old saddlebags and saddles. He walked to the deepest shelf and picked up a curiously shaped, worn, scratched stone.

'Tudor Glyndŵr's whetstone. He used it to sharpen his dagger and short sword until he replaced it with a better one he found in the river bed.'

'And this?'

The old man smiled. 'What's left of Rhys Fierce's favourite dagger. He broke the blade on Reginald de Grey's leg. Most of it was left in the baron's calf. It would have been better in his heart, but your sire would never allow bloodletting in revenge, only what he referred to as "God's justice".'

The traveller picked up a small bard's lyre. Some strings were loose and sadly out of tune. 'Do you play?'

The old man kicked the logs that had begun to burn, re-arranging them so they'd send out more warmth. 'That was Crab's.' His voice softened when he spoke her name.

'She was here?'

'More than once, or so I heard, but never when I was. Many of us sought refuge here when the king's men were at our heels.'

'Did the English ever find this cave?'

'They never found the valley, which is why I choose to live here.' The old man pointed to an array of flat stones covered in charcoal sketches. 'Your sire's battle plans. He spent hours sketching them that first winter after we sacked the Marcher towns.'

'And this?' The young man ran his fingers over the scales of a beautifully carved serpent that ornamented an unfinished hawk perch.

'David left that in the spring of 1401. He said he'd finish it when he returned.'

'Did he return?'

'Not that I heard.' The old man's terse reply, didn't invite further comment. He indicated two wooden crates filled with iron pots and cooking utensils. 'Llewelyn ap Gruffydd Fychan's field kitchen. He left it for future occupants.'

'It looks like you've made use of it.'

'I have but we've no need of it tonight. The good wife packs me enough bread and cheese to last four days whenever I visit the tavern.'

The young man picked up a heavily scarred wooden box, covered with carvings and symbols he recognised as Roman.

'Don't . . . '

The old man's warning came too late. He'd already opened the lid. He looked down on a cloth of stained silk that had had once been white, ornamented with tarnished gold embroidery. He unfolded it and the breath caught in his throat. 'Y Ddraig Aur,' he whispered.

'Torn, bloodied and battle singed but never captured. Arthur's standard and his.'

Below it was a simple gold circle crown.

'How did these come to be here?'

'That's a long story.'

'We face a long night.' When the old man hesitated, the young man added, 'and a long journey ahead.'

CHAPTER ONE

Owain Glyndŵr's "call to banner" camp Carmarthenshire April 1401
Maredydd and David Glyndŵr pulled the ropes taut and glanced up at the standard to ensure they'd raised it the right way before securing the knot. Y Ddraig Aur - the Golden Dragon embroidered on the ancient white silk banner danced again in the breeze that ruffled the tented roof of his father's pavilion.

Volunteers who'd answered Glyndŵr's call for men to fight to free Wales from the subjugation of Henry IV flooded the clearing and the woods behind them. The conversation and laughter were deafening, but one voice carried above the din.

'God and all the saints bless the Prince of Wales.'

'I think they've already done that, Llewelyn ap Gruffydd Fychan, given the number heaven has sent to join our army.' Owain Glyndŵr emerged from the pavilion and embraced the old man. 'I wasn't expecting to see you again so soon.'

'I dare say.' Llewelyn slapped Owain's back and whispered low in Owain's ear.

Owain smiled and raised his voice. 'So your good wife drove you from your door?'

'The moment I dismounted in my stable yard she ordered me back on my horse. There was no keeping her or the girls in Caeo. They'd already packed their best gowns . . . '

'Girls?' Maredydd interrupted.

'Sioned invited a houseful to stay with her this winter. She said she was lonely without me. As if Jonnet, Hova and Lowri aren't enough for her. But then Hova and Lowri haven't wanted any company other than one another's since they married. You know what young people are when they believe they've invented love. As for Adam, he's been haring around the country with your brother Gruffydd all winter . . . '

'You said girls. Has Lady Sioned brought anyone besides Jonnet and Lowri?' Maredydd dropped the rope he'd used to haul up the Golden Dragon without checking if it would hold.

'Lowri is in a delicate condition so Hova stayed in Caeo with her.'

'So Lady Sioned has only brought Jonnet?'

'And if she has?' Llewelyn teased.

'I was just wondering . . . '

Llewelyn took pity on the boy. 'Your sister Catrin was visiting Jonnet so naturally she travelled with us, and as your cousin Elwy . . . '

'Elwy's here!' Maredydd demanded.

Owain, David and Llewelyn burst into laughter.

'Never allow a girl to see how hard you're chasing her, boy,' David advised with all the authority of a married man of four years. 'Especially when you deserve a mouthful of ale after a morning spent putting up pavilions.'

'Ale and I think a taste of gwisgi to chase it down.' Llewelyn suggested as he and Owain led the way past the pavilion towards the field.

'Where is Elwy now?'

'All in good time, boy,' Llewelyn wrapped his arm around Maredydd's shoulders and steered him towards the makeshift market that the traders were setting up.

***

'Not that I'm grumbling about heaven's gift of volunteers for father's army, but there was more room to move on Michaelmas Fair Day in Oswestry than here,' David complained. Owain and Llewelyn had been side-tracked by their uncles and he and David were elbowing their way through a throng of Oxford students recognisable by their distinctive caps.

'I didn't know Wales could hold this many people,' Maredydd grumbled. 'Uncle Tudor said earlier he thinks over four thousand have rallied to father's call. He also commented that a quarter look as though they've never seen a sword or a bow, let alone used one.'

'That's because most of that quarter are useless women.'

'Sour, because you were hoping to see your wife here with your sons?' Maredydd suggested archly.

'God's tooth no!' David protested. 'When I visited Enfys in Valle Crucis Abbey, to see if she'd recovered from de Grey's men burning our home, I ordered her to stay there with the boys until either our house or her parents' mill could be rebuilt.'

'And she was happy to obey?' Maredydd was sceptical. David's "differences" with his wife were legendary.

'I gave her enough money to re-hire servants, so with luck she'll be too busy re-settling herself and the children to think of joining me.'

The "re-settling herself and the children" wasn't lost on Maredydd. He gave David a searching look. 'Is it really that bad between you?'

'Worse,' David tried to sound cheerful, but the word had an acidic edge.

'If there's anything I can do . . . '

'I may need a witness to testify to my exemplary and faithful behaviour as a husband. How's your lying?'

'Not as good as yours.'

'I can see you need a few lessons from the way you run after Elwy.'

'I love her . . . '

'Now that's something you should never say to a woman.'

'But it's true.'

'Especially if it's true, because she'll take advantage of you. Which is something Enfys never dares do with me.'

'Because she knows "when the tomcat's away the tomcat will play" and she's afraid if she complains the tomcat won't return to her hearth?' Maredydd suggested.

'She's so house proud she prefers a clean hearth to one with a tomcat in it. Besides, it really doesn't matter if Enfys is in Valle Crucis or Pont Gweni or wants to complain to me or not, the important thing is she's not here and that leaves this tomcat fancy free.'

David caught the widowed seamstress Morfel's eye and gave her a broad wink. She blew back a kiss before the crowd surged and carried her from sight.

'Father's cornered.' Maredydd pointed to where Owain stood head and shoulders above a crowd of students who'd hemmed him in between a gwisgi booth and beer "tavern" set up on a trestle. 'Do you want to rescue him?'

David shook his head. 'He won't die of thirst or want for company there, and I'm in desperate need of a spiced pie after a winter spent chewing Llewelyn's solid trenchers and gristly mutton.'

'Count yourself fortunate to have been given food you didn't have to cook, you ungrateful boy.' Llewelyn had reached the pie vender's cart ahead of them.

'Sorry, Llew,' Maredydd apologised. 'But that was a comment on the quality of the meat you had to cook not your ability to roast it. The flesh of mountain sheep is never fat and juicy only tough and stringy.'

'Good to see you honing your diplomatic skills, boy. Your father might find a use for them.'

Maredydd stepped behind the cart and looked around for girls, or rather one in particular. Bright spring sunshine puddled down between the trees, flooding the meadow and the shadowy fringes of woodland that encircled it, and everywhere teemed with people.

Veteran soldiers in full and part armour were advising well-dressed gentlemen on the restoration of hand-me-down weapons, wrought decades, and in some cases, centuries before. Crossbow and longbow archers had gravitated together to organise impromptu target-shooting competitions inside the wood away from the melee. Young squires swore at one another as they struggled to erect campaign tents on the perimeter of the field, short-tempered because they wanted to practise swordplay not organise accommodation. Women, girls and young boys were busy building and tending cook fires.

Tradesmen who'd brought in handcarts and packhorses laden with food, wine and beer were unharnessing donkeys, carthorses and ponies and setting up a market on their wagons and trestles. Blacksmiths were sharpening and repairing old blades and selling new. Saddlers were stitching broken tack and harnesses next to cobblers resoling shoes and boots that were more patches than leather.

'As you're near the pie man, Maredydd, bring me one please,' Dewi the blacksmith called out before turning back to a splintered blade he was examining for an optimistic squire.

A young student inched his way forward until he succeeded in worming close to Owain.

'My prince, if I may speak?'

Amused by the boy's mixture of temerity and subservience Owain broke off his conversation with the gwisgi seller to return the smile of the personable young man. 'You may.'

'Thank you, my prince. I'm Joshua ap Hova.'

'Pleased to meet you, Joshua,' Owain shook the boy's hand.

'It's an honour, sir.' Overwhelmed, the boy spoke at speed. 'I wanted to tell you, my prince, the minute news reached Oxford that an heir to two Royal Welsh Houses had declared himself Prince of Wales and ordered the English king to rescind those – ' The boy glanced around to make sure no women were close enough to hear him swear – 'damnable new laws he's drafted to enslave the Welsh, we – that is most of the students - decided to leave Oxford to join you.'

Owain marvelled at the speed and inaccuracy of rumour. Henry's anti-Welsh laws were damnable but he was hardly in a position – yet - to demand the king repeal them.

'I'm grateful for your support, Joshua. Which part of Wales do you hail from?' he asked, picking up on a hint of a Flemish accent.

'Pembroke, my prince.' Joshua hadn't joined Owain to talk of his home county. 'We stayed in Oxford only as long as it took us to notify your supporters of the day and time we were leaving so we could travel together.'

'I'm Peter ap Geraint, also from Pembroke, my prince,' one of Joshua's fellow students introduced himself. 'Over a hundred of us marched out of Oxford in my group and I know of at least five other parties headed here.'

'Before we set out we "borrowed" weapons to send the English running back over the border.' Joshua pulled a rusty sword from his scabbard.

'"Borrowed?"' Owain raised an enquiring eyebrow.

'Some men are careless with their weapons, my prince. They leave them lying around pothouses and lodgings where they're can be lost or stolen.' Peter made Owain formal obeisance.

'Pleased to meet you, Peter. Can I trust you not to "borrow" any of my men's weapons.'

Peter blushed at Owain's admonishment. 'The borrowing was necessary, my prince. Our need for instruments of war is great.'

'Not as great as the need of my men at arms.' Realising he'd pricked the pride of academics who'd abandoned their education to trudge over muddy roads from Oxford to Wales in the depth of April's rains to join his force, Owain attempted to make amends. 'I know how much you've sacrificed to answer my call.'

'No sacrifice, my prince. I'd rather die a beggar fighting for Welsh freedom, than live a rich man in England,' Peter boasted. 'May I introduce you to my companions, you've met Joshua, this is . . . '

Given the number of young men surrounding them Owain held up his hands in a gesture of defeat. 'I look forward to getting to know all of you in time, but forgive me. I'll never remember your names now.'

'Is it true you intend to build two universities in Wales, my prince?' Joshua asked.

Owain was moved by the earnest expressions on their youthful faces. He knew from the way they wore their caps they were proud of their academic status. From their travel stained dress he determined the professions they hoped to follow; the church, the law, soldiering. They were precisely the calibre of educated Welshmen he'd hoped to recruit to administer his government and assist him to rule.

'It's true, I dream of founding universities in North and South Wales as soon as we have won our freedom. Henry Bolingbroke has replaced every Welshman in authority in our land with Englishmen loyal to him. That is a situation that needs rectifying.'

'And fast, my prince,' Peter re-joined.

'Agreed,' Owain smiled. 'When we've reinstated the Welsh Henry has dismissed, and appointed our own people to the remaining vacancies, we will have taken the first step towards self-government. But the real test will come when we create a Church in Wales, build a Welsh Parliament as well as universities and assign our ablest men to run them.'

'But first we must destroy the English and drive them from our land. And we are here to help you do it, my prince,' Joshua said.

Peter shouted, 'God Bless Owain Glyndŵr, Prince of Wales.' The cry was taken up and repeated, echoing over the clearing and through the woods.

Owain found the attention embarrassing. When he saw his brother Tudor making his way through the crowds he beckoned to him. The students looked from him to his brother, and back.

Tudor saw the quizzical glances and called out above the hubbub. 'You're not seeing double even if you've had a glass or two of gwisgi, boys. Everyone knows that I, the prince's younger brother, Tudor, am the handsome one because the Prince of Wales, has a blemish above his eye.

When you become better acquainted with us you'll also discover the Prince is a saint. I'm a sinner.'

'Never a truer word was spoken by a rogue.' Owain's captain Rhys Black's declaration prompted a burst of good humoured laughter.

'I'll see you later, Rhys Ddu,' Tudor threatened. 'We all agree we have to fight for our country, but today is not for fighting but for friends and feasting.' He pointed to the carts. 'Meat, bread, wine, beer and for those who can boast strong Welsh heads, gwisgi.'

'The first rule of soldiering is "scavenge while you can because if there's more than one of you, it won't be for long." Go to it, boys,' Rhys advised.

Dewi took two of the four pies Maredydd had bought, and thrust one at Tudor.

'If you'll excuse us, my prince,' Peter apologised.

'The inner man drives the outer man and his needs come first.' Owain watched the tide of students ebb towards the food carts.

'Are you going to use the same tactics you employed after Ruthyn for the spring campaign?' Llewelyn asked.

'We need to make plans. Bolingbroke will march his army into Wales any day now spring has arrived. That's if he isn't here already.' Owain looked around at the crowd and realised how vulnerable some of the untried volunteers were.

The Rhys among Owain's captains, Rhys Ddu or Black in English, Rhys Coch or Red in English, Rhys Gwilym and Rhys Gethin, known as Fierce, who'd all fought with Owain in Scotland and the Channel sauntered over from the bakers' carts, their hands and mouths full of pies.

'I'm calling a meeting in my pavilion right away,' Owain announced.

Tudor pushed half a pigeon pie into his mouth chewed it twice and swallowed. 'This isn't a good time to call a council with everyone eating, drinking, and getting acquainted, my lord. We'll confer in . . . ' Tudor looked at the carts, then the sky. 'An hour, Rhys?' Tudor addressed the captains without differentiating between them. 'Will you warn all the officers that the prince has called a council then?' He turned back to Owain. 'That will give us time to rest and collect our thoughts.'

Owain narrowed his eyes. 'We've done nothing but rest all winter.'

'Except today. I rose early and you were already up and talking to Trefor so I doubt you slept last night.' Tudor gripped Owain's shoulder and walked him to the edge of the field. 'Here,' he lifted a flagon of wine from Dewi's clutches. 'We'll take this with us.'

'You need wine to rest?' Owain enquired sceptically.

'Can you think of a better soporific?' Tudor asked.

Owain's pavilion had been erected inside the wood. He noted the pickets stationed around the perimeter.

'Gruffydd in charge of sentry duty?'

'Who else?'

'You trained my son well, brother.'

'That's the inner circle. The outer ones are well hidden. I'll know the minute an Englishman draws breath within a five-mile radius of this spot,' Tudor boasted.

'Where did these come from?' Owain asked his brother-in-law Philip Hanmer who was checking the officers' tents for tears and holes.

'My brother John,' Philip Hanmer answered. 'He raided the attics in our brother Hanmer's barns. When we picked them up Hanmer told us to tell you that you're welcome to use his house in Plynlimmon, . But a word of caution, no one's checked the manor in years. There's a steward there, or at least Hanmer pays a man to watch the place, but Hanmer couldn't recall his name and no one's heard news of the place in years.'

'Neither has anyone erected these tents in years by the look of them,' Owain commented.

'Family legend has it they were made for our great grandfather's, great grandfather. But as John said, ancient and threadbare is better than nothing. He also likes his comfort. It wouldn't surprise me if he's carted a full sized feather bed here to furnish his own campaign tent. But in honour of your rank, my prince, I've spread clean blankets over the felt that floors your private quarters.'

'Thank you. A clean blanket, will be luxury after the flea infested sheepskins in the cave.'

'We've probably brought the fleas with us,' Philip warned.

'Not me, I washed in the river this morning and they don't like cold water. We confer in an hour,' Tudor said loudly as he passed Philip. The curtain that divided the interior into Owain's public and private quarters opened and Owain's wife smiled at them.

'Hello, Tudor.'

'Hello, Margaret. Have you made it a home yet?'

'Almost.' She emerged from the inner chamber. 'I'll be back when I've tracked down the chests I asked Enyd and Hova to pack with our clothes.'

Owain stepped inside the pavilion. He pushed aside the inner curtain to reveal a low pallet of sheepskins wide enough to accommodate two people. It was covered with linen sheets and a blue, white and black wool blanket he recognised from Sycharth. It reminded him of every home Margaret had made for them since their marriage and he wondered if she'd spent the winter planning the domestic arrangements for his spring campaign.

'My sleeping pallet is half that size.' Tudor was at his elbow.

'As there's only one of you, that sounds fair.'

'I'm not complaining just reminding myself that I'll have to cuddle up close if I find an amenable companion. I'm loathe to look for a thin one because they make cold bedfellows.'

'Given your vast experience of bed mates I'll take your word for it.'

'Vast experience as opposed to yours?' Tudor raised his eyebrows but he knew better than to make further comment when Margaret could be within earshot.

'Considering the way my bones are aching after sleeping in a freezing cave all winter, I could lie on that right now.'

'No, you couldn't, because I'd haul you from it.' Owain changed the subject. 'Was that Morfel I saw earlier talking to Crab?'

'It was,' Tudor smirked. 'It was kind of Margaret to bring her.'

Owain scowled. 'Are there any women in my household you haven't slept with?'

'Several, including your wife and daughters.'

'As they're family you had no choice but to leave them alone.'

'In my defence I would like to say I only make love to women who let me know they welcome my attentions.'

'You left out "pretty" before women, Tudor, which is why your brother Gruffydd married a grim-faced miserable scold of a wife in the hope that you wouldn't seduce her.' Philip Hanmer walked in behind two squires who were carrying a trestle table.

'Margaret's not a grim-faced scold of a wife and I haven't tried to seduce her,' Tudor protested.

'She'd geld you if you tried.' Philip's comment was followed by an outburst of laughter.

'We need benches,' Tudor reminded the squires.

'Everyone will be here in an hour, my lord,' Philip checked the table was stable.

'Why do we have to wait?' Owain complained.

'To give you time to congratulate the bride and groom.' Margaret entered with Owain's liege man, Xian, a Seres or in common tongue, a Chinese man of arms who'd been introduced to Owain by their mutual friend Hotspur. Behind them were Owain's children by his mistress, Gweni, who'd been murdered by Reginald de Grey's men when they'd attacked her village last autumn.

Fascinated by the similarities between his family banner and Owain's, Xian had offered his services to the house of Glyndŵr. Owain had accepted, although he'd suspected the knight had been more attracted by the charms of his illegitimate daughter Gweni, than his desire to fight for a free Wales.

Owain looked from Gweni to Xian. 'You two are married?'

'You gave me permission to ask Gweni for her hand when we last spoke, my lord.' Xian reminded.

'So I did. You accepted, Gweni?'

'I did, father.'

'Judging by the look on your faces you're both happy in the choice you made. I trust that was a good flask of wine you took from Dewi, Tudor?'

'The best, my lord,' Tudor opened it, filled the goblets Gweni's brothers David and Ieuan had brought in and handed them around.

Owain raised his cup. 'To the newest member of the Glyndŵr family, Xian. Your good health, long life and happiness with Gweni.'

A small shadow darkened the doorway before Owain drained his cup.

'My apologies for interrupting, my prince.' Crach Ffinnant hovered at the entrance.

'It's not an interruption when it's you, Crach. Please join us in a toast to the bridal pair.' Owain filled another goblet and handed it to his chief ambassador and soothsayer Crach Ffinnant.

Crach took it and lifted it to Xian and Gweni. 'Long life, good health and many sons.'

'And daughters,' Gweni added.

Crach emptied his cup and bowed before opening his hand and placing a coin on the table in front of Owain. There was a deep gouge in the coat of arms on the back.

'He's here?' Owain asked Crach.

'His messenger, my lord. A woman who carries words in her head. She awaits you in my tent.'

***

The woman's black hair was streaked with grey and there were lines around her mouth carved deep enough to owe more to grief than laughter but her dark eyes were bright and questioning.

'You have a message for me?' Owain whispered. Crach had stationed himself outside the tent to deter eavesdroppers but he was conscious only a thin layer of cloth separated them from the outside, and Crach could only watch one side.

'Several if you match the coin I gave the dwarf,' the woman answered in Welsh.

Owain pulled two identical groats from a pocket in his cotte and held them out to her. Both were scarred by deep gouges that marred the coat of arms stamped on one side.

'Then you are the Prince of Wales?' She rose from the camp stool and curtsied.

'Please don't, good wife. We leave ceremony to the English.' Owain answered her in Welsh, 'and you are?'

'Flur, my prince.'

'How long have you carried messages from the English to the Welsh?'

Flur waited until Owain sat on a box before returning to her stool 'This is my first, my prince. I was married to an English captain who fought for Lord Hotspur. He died of plague at the siege of Conwy Castle a week ago.'

'I am sorry.'

'Thank you, my lord, that is kind of you.' She brushed aside a tear before continuing. 'Being Welsh I no longer felt welcome in a camp of English soldiers. Lord Hotspur heard I was thinking of leaving Conwy. He sought me out and employed me to bring you a message. He also asked if I would carry any messages you had for him on a return journey.'

'Would you?' Owain asked.

'Willingly, my prince. I have no children and now my husband is dead, no home. The only home I knew in the twenty years of our marriage was the tent my husband pitched in Lord Hotspur's camp.'

'After I've heard what you have to say you will be free to remain here or go as you wish. My wife will find you a bed for the night or longer should you stay. I have no doubt I will have need of your services once you are rested.'

'Lord Hotspur said he will be at Cader Idris at the end of May and God willing, meet you there. There is much more that I didn't understand and one phrase in a strange tongue that he stressed was more important than all the rest.' She lowered her voice and spoke.

Owain made her repeat the phrase three times, only then did he recognise her whisper as phonetically learned Latin. From the way she spoke it was obvious the woman had no idea what the words meant.

He opened the small box he'd brought with him and removed a quill, a used parchment, which was clean on one side and a leather flask of oak gall ink. He uncorked the flask, rested the parchment on top of the box and dipped the quill in ink. Only then did he write, *Beware the limping man* at the head of the page.

'Let's see if I can make sense of your other messages, Mistress Flur. Start with what you can recall, please.'

CHAPTER TWO

Owain Glyndŵr's pavilion and camp April 1401
Owain sent Flur to Margaret before calling Crach Ffinnant into the tent. Even before Crach sat down they heard footsteps outside. Owain asked Crach his opinion of the army he'd attracted, speaking loudly for their unseen audience, while they conducted a second written conversation on the vellum.

They left the tent together and Owain returned to his pavilion. Crach looked around the outside of his tent and saw Dafydd Gam close by, cleaning his boots in a patch of rough grass. He beckoned to him and waited for the man to hobble to him with the aid of his stout walking stick. It took some time as Gam's left leg was considerably shorter than his right and too weak to bear his weight.

'I find myself in need of help, Gam,' Crach said. 'Do you have half a dozen trustworthy men in your retinue?'

'I do,' Gam replied warily.

'The prince asked me to check our weapons. He believes we have sufficient to arm half of our number.'

'I saw Glyndŵr's armourer bring in a cartload of weapons, but not enough to arm two thousand men,' Gam said.

'You think we have four thousand men here?' Crach stroked his chin thoughtfully.

'So I heard someone say. But I haven't counted either weapons or men,' Gam protested unconvincingly, knowing that Crach had caught him spying out Owain's strength.

'The weapons are stored in a barn half a mile from here. Llewelyn ap Gruffydd Fychan and the prince's brother in law John Hanmer have offered to check them but I could do with another head and some strong sober men to move the crates they've been stored in since we ransacked the Marcher towns last autumn.'

'I can vouch for the strength of my retinue if not their sobriety,' Gam said.

'It's their muscle I need.' Crach looked down pointedly at his own diminutive stature.

'When will the prince distribute the weapons?' Gam asked.

'Tomorrow.'

'And then?'

Crach looked around to ensure no one was within listening distance. 'Those fortunate enough to have been given a blade, can practice with it until we leave for Conwy the day after.'

Gam could barely contain his excitement at the revelation. 'So the prince will join the Tudors' rebellion?'

'Ssh . . . ' Crach hissed. 'The prince doesn't want his plans spread abroad. But it makes sense. Why go looking for Bolingbroke in the field when there's an English army waiting to be vanquished in Conwy.'

'I'll get my men and order them to saddle our horses.'

'I'll meet you there with Llew and Hanmer.'

***

Owain entered his pavilion to find Margaret and Gweni supervising the men carrying chests into the sleeping area. When they left, Margaret blew him a kiss before dropping the curtain.

John Hanmer and Maredydd entered with armfuls of maps they piled on the table. Tudor, followed with Owain's captains and lieutenants. Owain's squire Dafydd and the blacksmith Dewi were the last to enter. Dafydd shouldering a barrel of ale, Dewi carrying four flagons of wine and a sack of wooden cups.

'Hova will send in mutton from the cookfires as soon as it's roasted, my lord,' Dafydd set the barrel on a stool.

Maredydd unrolled the largest map, weighed it down with his dagger and short sword, climbed on a bench, set his elbows on the table and studied it.

'Is this a formal war council?' Tudor took a stool, sat on it, pushed a cushion behind his back and leaned against one of the posts that supported the pavilion.

'We have an army awaiting orders. We need to decide priorities, and how best to train those inexperienced in warfare.' Owain unrolled another map and set it beside the cup Dafydd had poured for him.

A hubbub of young voices rose outside the tent and died when the group of students walked on. Although he only had to step out to see them Owain was finding it difficult to comprehend the number of volunteers he'd attracted. He turned to his son and brother-in-law.

'As some of us spent the winter in isolation, John Hanmer, Gruffydd, will you enlighten us as to recent events?'

Tudor suddenly realised why Owain had insisted Gruffydd and John over-winter with his wife's eldest brother. Given Hanmer's wealth, connections and position in the upper echelons of English as well as Welsh society, his household would be in receipt of the latest news from Henry's court.

'Hotspur and Bolingbroke's son, young Hal, are still besieging Conwy Castle with five hundred men,' John began. 'Rhys and Gwilym Tudor continue to hold it. The castle is proving impregnable, the Tudors obdurate.'

'It's a family trait we've inherited.' Tudor and Owain were the Tudors' first cousins as their respective mothers had been sisters.

'Prince Hal is ostensibly in charge,' John continued, 'but he's fourteen and it's his first command, so I'd say Hotspur is issuing the orders. From what I've heard, there's no discord. Young Hal is content to listen and learn, but the siege has reached stalemate.'

'I'd say the Tudors and Hotspur are evenly matched when it comes to waging warfare and digging in their heels,' Tudor commented.

'The English have artillery and attack engines. Not that they've proved an advantage. They've attempted to storm

Conwy Castle four times without result. Hanmer heard that Hotspur is running out of patience and money. He's appealed repeatedly to Bolingbroke for coin to pay his troops,' John asserted, 'but the king ignores his petitions.'

'As the English soldiers lack the means to pay Conwy tradesmen, they've been reduced to looting,' Rhys Coch added. 'But the Welsh are adept at hiding their stores, which means Hotspur's troops are starving.'

'And dispirited,' Gruffydd added. 'The ones I met were threatening mutiny.'

'You talked to English soldiers in Conwy?'

Gruffydd switched to a credible English court accent. 'You know me, Uncle John. I'll talk to anyone.'

'Why were you in Conwy and what were you doing there?'

'What news of the Tudors?' Owain changed the subject. 'How are they faring inside the castle?'

'They have deep wells and full storerooms. If they find themselves in need of anything they shout over the walls and the locals deliver it at night,' Gruffydd replied.

'Are there underground passages out of the castle?' Owain asked.

'According to legend,' John answered, 'as is said of every castle, but when the Tudors expect a delivery they lower a rope on the seaward side. The locals take a boat out and tie whatever's needed to it so it can be hauled in over the battlements. Rumour has it one of the Tudors was missing his wife, so he had her pulled up one moonless night.'

'Moonless lest her shining face attract an archer. It's true, I had it from a Tudor squire in a tavern,' Gruffydd confirmed.

'No hot-blooded Welshman can live without the fair sex,' Tudor quipped.

'Does that smile honour a memory or is it anticipation?' Philip Hanmer enquired.

Gruffydd interrupted his uncles' banter. 'Uncle Hanmer heard that Hotspur's men are deserting in droves. No soldier enjoys a siege inside or outside the walls but between hunger, thirst . . . '

'Thirst can be a terrible thing,' Tudor broke in.

'I'm surprised you have experience of that, Tudor.' Philip watched Tudor refill all the cups on the table.

' . . . and the locals harrying Hotspur's men every chance they get,' Gruffydd continued when he could wedge a word into his uncles' repartee, 'the English appear to be having a worse time of it than the Welsh.'

'Does Hanmer think Hotspur will admit defeat and call off the siege soon?' Owain asked.

John shrugged. 'That depends on Hotspur, Prince Hal and how many of their men are prepared to stick it out until one or the other capitulates. From what I heard it already feels like forever for the poor beggars outside the walls.'

'I've heard your cousins' supporters take delight in slipping out on cloudy nights and slitting the throats of Hotspur's watchmen.' Rhys Ddu took a shield loaded with sliced baked mutton folded on bread trenchers from Gwilym when the steward entered the pavilion.

'I'm surprised Hotspur allows the Welsh to get close to his guards.' Tudor helped himself to meat and bread.

'He tries to keep them at a distance, but you know soldiers and women, especially patriotic Welsh women. They can appear seductive and charming, but in my experience, most carry daggers in their garters and aren't shy about using them.' Rhys handed the platter to Maredydd.

'Garters or daggers?' Tudor enquired.

'Both.'

'Just what kind of women do you sleep with, Rhys Ddu?' Tudor asked.

'Ones with the blood of Cymru in their veins.'

'Ah, I understand.'

'Understand what?' Rhys questioned.

'Everything.' Tudor nodded through a mouthful of hot mutton.

'Does anyone know how many have answered our call?' Rhys asked.

'They didn't stand still for me, Tudor and Gruffydd to count them but as a rough estimate we agreed it has to be close to four thousand but I'd say a fifth of those are traders, women and camp followers too young to fight and a tenth of the remainder keen, eager, but untrained in weaponry,' John Hanmer answered.

'I doubt Bolingbroke will bring as numerous an army into Wales,' Tudor m used.

'I'm not relying on your doubts when Bolingbroke has all England to draw on for mercenaries to add to those already in his pay.' Owain eyed the meat on the trencher Gwilym had handed him but made no attempt to eat.

'Will you face the king across a field?' Tudor asked

Owain looked into the eyes of his assembled officers before answering.

'What I'm about to say, stays within this group. We have too many untrained men to risk them in battle. A head on clash between English mercenaries and our mix would work in Bolingbroke's favour.'

The light was fading. Dafydd, ever mindful of Owain's needs, left and returned with a pair of oil lamps that he set on the table.

The faces of the men sitting around Owain were thrown into relief by the flickering flames that darkened the shadows, lending them a gaunt, skeletal appearance. Owain studied them. It was an instant in time he sensed he'd remember and return to, if for no other reason than this moment, even more than his attack on Ruthyn, would mark the onset of their war for Welsh Independence.

'I impress the need for security. Bolingbroke watches our every move and has chests full of gold to reward traitors who are prepared to betray those who fight to free Wales.' He held up his hand at a hubbub of voices. 'We must all be on our guard.'

All the men looked around the pavilion. Absences were noted, but they knew better than to comment.

'So, no fixed major battle. We repeat the tactics we used after Ruthyn?' Tudor prompted.

'With a few variations,' Owain returned to planning tactics. 'I want all of you to talk to the volunteers. Any men with battle experience you know to be loyal . . . '

'Surely their presence here speaks for their loyalty,' Rhys Fierce said.

'There are snakes in every meadow,' Tudor murmured.

'Not all are poisonous,' Rhys reminded.

'Perhaps, but they may have crawled from Bolingbroke's preserves and that is enough to cause concern.'

'When you've quite finished, Tudor, Rhys,' Owain reprimanded. 'Pick out a few trustworthy men and women, from every town, village and locality in Wales. Look for those respected by their neighbours, who are anxious to help but too old or weak to fight. Tell them you've earmarked them for a special task.'

'Unfit men?' Tudor asked in surprise.

'And women,' Owain added. 'List their names and bring them here. We'll meet in the morning and chose those most likely to succeed in fermenting rebellion against the crown.'

'You expect old, infirm men and women to rouse shepherds, farmers, bakers and butchers, to battle Henry's men at arms?' Philip Hanmer was astounded.

'Not to fight, but mount challenges to civil authority and encourage their neighbours to withhold the taxes, fines and debts the English crown levies on the Welsh. If Henry can't collect coin, his treasury will run dry. He needs money to pay his mercenaries. His soldiers are not volunteers, like ours. They fight for gold, not freedom. I know this plan won't have immediate effect, but once in place, given time, it will garner results.'

'I can see that it might, provided enough are prepared to brave prison for non-payment. But we have men anxious to fight out there . . . ' Philip began.

'And they will, but not until they're ready, and then we'll use them on our terms not those dictated by Bolingbroke,' Owain broke in. 'Gruffydd, talk to the students. Tell them each will be assigned to an experienced man at arms who will train them in combat. Warn them it will be impossible to assign more than six to any single band. Persuade them it's for their own good.'

'I agree,' Tudor concurred. 'If we send half trained men against Henry's mercenaries they'll be cut to pieces in the first skirmish and we'll pay the price not only in their lives, but those of the men who'll sacrifice themselves to protect them.'

'For the first time we have an army to equal Henry's. Are you sure you want to break it up?' Rhys Fierce asked.

'The least we can give the volunteers is good leadership after they've sacrificed their education and livelihoods to join us.' Owain said. 'I know you burn to face Henry across an open field, but Bolingbroke will break us if we meet his army head on or attack his castles. We have no cannon, or ships to ferry men and supplies. Nor do we have streams of gold to pay mercenaries.'

'So we hold back?' John Hanmer's disapproval was evident in his tone.

'We could "borrow" some English siege engines and use them to batter the walls of the castles from the landward sides,' Rhys Fierce suggested.

'Even if we managed to take them from the English, it would be nigh on impossible to haul them up and down the hills and valleys. They'd become bogged down and then we'd end up sitting ducks like Hotspur in Conwy,' Tudor countered.

'Tudor's right about siege engines. They'd only slow us down,' Philip agreed. 'We proved after Ruthyn that small bands of mounted men at arms, supported by archers who can ride swiftly and unexpectedly into a target area, hit hard, fast and pull out before the opposition have time to saddle their mounts, gain the best results.'

'Exactly, and that's how we'll win this war.' Tudor picked a choice piece of seared lamb from the platter.

'So, it's decided, we continue using the tactics we developed when we fired Ruthyn and the marcher towns?' Owain looked around the table for dissenters. There were none.

'Time to recreate a few mounted bands and more Owain Glyndŵrs to lead them?' Rhys Ddu speared a piece of lamb Tudor was eyeing.

'It is, gentlemen.' Owain straightened the dagger he'd placed on the map and turned the blade to point North.

Tudor squinted over his bread and lamb. 'Plynlimmon?'

'Wild mountainous country,' Owain said. 'A man can travel miles without seeing a living soul.'

'Apart from sheep and the odd ox,' Tudor confirmed.

'It has hidden valleys, caves large enough to conceal a sizeable force and a few strategically placed small ones to house lookouts who can give notice of an impending English invasion. An abundance of rivers to provide fresh water for stock, mounts and men, and it's as good a central point as you will find in Wales to set up our headquarters. A day's hard ride will take you to the English border. A day and a half to the heart of the North or South of the country and two days to Fleming controlled Pembrokeshire. All lands with towns garrisoned by the English, awash with full warehouses of goods, grain, well stocked livestock pens, and men with fat purses worth ransoming.'

'Waiting for us to swoop down and make a collection,' Tudor grinned.

'Ripe for the picking,' Rhys Fierce unsheathed his dagger and polished the blade between his leather gloved fingers.

'So, you want us to decamp to Plynlimmon, my lord?' Rhys Ddu suggested.

'Not all of us. I propose Tudor take an advance party of three hundred men at arms and their retinues to set up our main camp plus a few smaller ones with look-out posts to ensure none of our forces are caught unawares.'

'So, I end up doing the donkey work again,' Tudor grumbled good naturedly.

'You'll have plenty of men to call on for help. I give you leave to pick out as many as you need in addition to the soldiers and archers but I suggest you restrict the number of camp followers. Two thousand men is a large body to lose even in Plynlimmon. Take a look at Hanmer's manor and see if we can use it to accommodate the officers. Gruffydd?' Owain turned to his son. 'Do you want to ride with your uncle?'

'It's not that I don't want to ride with you, father . . . '

Owain waved his hand in dismissal. 'We've had that discussion, Gruffydd. Ride with Tudor with my blessing and hopefully God's. Tudor, avoid engaging the enemy but should conflict prove inevitable, wear my tabard over your Glyndŵr armour and keep your visor down, not that there's a likelihood of anyone determining the difference between us, but if they have seen one of the other Glyndŵrs they may wonder at the change in stature. Gruffydd, keep my tabard and armour in reserve if, God forbid, Tudor should be taken . . . '

'The Englishman has yet to be born who can trap me in a snare.'

'I pray you're right, Tudor. Gruffydd, don't wear your Glyndŵr tabard or armour while Tudor wears his but keep it close. We don't need to set our enemies wondering. While they see one Glyndŵr at a time, they'll continue to attribute stories of my appearance in two or more places at the same time to sorcery. When Tudor heads to Plynlimmon, Rhys Fierce, you scout the area to the South East around Abergavenny.' Owain outlined the area of the country he wanted Rhys to target with the point of a Scottish dirk he'd "liberated" from a Highlander a decade before. 'I received a message that John Charleton . . . '

'The King's man, Lord of Powys?' Rhys questioned.

Owain nodded. 'Him. Henry has ordered him to search for me.'

'So you can be hung, drawn and quartered and your head sent to Westminster as a decoration for London Bridge.' Tudor muttered between mouthfuls of mutton.

'A friend told me that the Abbot of Cwmhir has ordered ancient religious artefacts of inestimable power and value to the Welsh, be moved from the Abbey and given to Bolingbroke.' Yonge drained his cup and handed it to Gwilym for a refill.

'Given to the king where?' Tudor asked.

'My friend was unaware of the designated destination.'

'If they are being taken to Bolingbroke you can be sure he intends to purloin the power they possess. He must have put pressure on the church. It's unlike the Abbot to relinquish anything of value belonging to him or his Abbey,' Bishop Trefor observed.

'If these Welsh treasures exist beyond rumour, Bolingbroke and the Abbot could be using them as bait to trap you, Owain. If they succeed they'll end the rebellion before it's begun,' Tudor said.

'Bolingbroke will have heard that the Cross of Neith and the Crown of Elisig were displayed at your coronation.' Trefor shook his head at Gwilym when he offered him more meat. 'It's possible he believes the Welsh crown jewels that aren't in his possession or yours, are in Cwmhir.'

'Do you want me to attack Cwmhir Abbey, my lord?' Rhys Fierce asked Owain.

'No. I don't trust the Abbot but I have no proof of his treachery. Should I discover otherwise I'll reconsider.' Owain set his cup down. 'Pick out sixty men at arms with experienced archers, squires and pages in their retinue. Allow no more than four students to ride with you.'

Rhys nodded assent.

'Scour the towns and villages around Abergavenny. Should you find John Charleton, pick off and worry his rear guard, take out the stragglers from his army . . . '

'As Owain Glyndŵr in your armour?'
'Of course,' Owain confirmed.
'Chevauchee inside the walled towns?'
'If you can enter the gates with the element of surprise and little risk to yourselves. Burn everything you can't carry off. Leave the English no recourse other than to turn to their lords for succour and support. We need to show Henry that his isn't the only army who knows how to use the devastation of chevauchee as a weapon. Show mercy and quarter to all English civilians, but not soldiers. When you fight, leave the students with your baggage. Take the spoils ... '

'To the abbeys?' Rhys suggested.

'To Tintern. Abbot John Wysbech is a just and Godly man who'll see the goods distributed to the Welsh in need.'

'Where do I return when I'm done with Charleton?' Rhys asked.

'If you capture him, show mercy and ransom him. If he escapes and goes to ground don't waste time chasing his shadow. Join Tudor in Plynlimmon.'

'We should have set up our camps by then,' Tudor said. 'I'll look for a nice cosy spot for you and your men.'

'Away from muddy river banks and mosquitoes?'

'Of course,' Tudor winked.

Owain moved the dirk further South. 'Philip Scudamore you ride for Ceridigion.'

'Can I take Dewi?'

'He'll be needed along with Hunith in the blacksmith workshops to repair and forge new weapons.'

'Rhodri ... '

'War is hard on horses, he'll be busy breaking in new mounts.' Owain stroked his chin.

'Harri ... '

'Will be training new recruits in Glyndyfrdwy while it's still mine. But Yonge is keen to ride.'

'A churchman!' Philip exclaimed in disgust, avoiding Yonge's eye.

'Who trained alongside me in warfare and can fight as well as any man at arms,' Owain looked from Philip to Yonge. 'Follow the rules I laid down for Rhys, chevauchee inside the walled towns when you can attack without risk, show mercy and quarter to all English civilians but not soldiers. When you fight, leave the students with your baggage. Take the spoils . . . '

'To Strata Florida?' Philip suggested.

'Yes. Philip Hanmer, you take Pembrokeshire but steer clear of the Flemings, take your spoil to the Abbey at St Clears or St Dogmaels.'

'Can I take David, not as my lieutenant but equal, my prince?'

Owain knew his son had great regard and respect for Philip. 'Gladly, Philip. Same applies to you and David with your Glyndŵr armour. Take turns to wear it in battle. John Hanmer, you take Gower.'

'And your son Madog?' John asked. 'I know he's young . . . '

Owain interrupted John. 'Margaret and I trust you to take care of the boy. You'll hold him in reserve until he's ready for full battle?'

'You have my word on it, my prince.'

'Thank you.' Owain looked to his other lieutenants 'Rhys Coch, Poulson?'

Rhys Coch glanced at Owain's sister's husband, Poulson. 'We take North Wales, my lord?'

'You know the estates to avoid?'

'We know exactly whose estates to avoid,' Rhys Coch confirmed.

'You'd best give Conwy a wide berth,' Owain advised.

'We don't need to be told, my prince. I've seen Hotspur angry. It reminded me of a wildcat stung by a wasp.' Rhys Coch upturned a flagon and emptied it into his cup.

'That leaves you and me, Rhys Ddu.' Owain stared at the map. 'We accompany Maredydd, Ieuan, and Xian to Glyndyfrdwy but only for a day or two.'

'Why such a short time, my prince?' Rhys asked.

'Because the king has sequestered my estates, forfeiting them to the crown. I'd like to take a last look around my ancestral manors before the English take up residence in one or both.'

'You're expecting Henry to seize your homes?'

'He's gifted them to his half-brother John Beaufort the Earl of Somerset. Beaufort won't move in until he's milked enough money from Henry to pay mercenaries to protect him. But to return to our plans, we have six bands of armed men ready to ride out and storm English strongholds in Wales. We should be safe here for two or three days. That gives us enough time to advise and prepare them. When you've chosen your men, Harri, Gwilym, Rhodri, and Hunith will take those in need of training to Glyndyfrdwy, and there they will stay until they are fit to join our battle ready forces. It's harsh terrain around Glyndyfrdwy. From vantage points on the hills you can see an army coming for miles. I can't think of a better place to exercise and instruct our volunteers.'

'It's a good choice, my lord,' Tudor endorsed. 'With Harri to train them and the blacksmiths to supply weapons, they should make usable fighting men in a few months.'

'Rhys Coch, John Hanmer and Poulson, split the remainder of the volunteers between you. I'll send a small but strong force to Snowdonia from Glyndyfrdwy.'

'To your hunting lodge, my prince?' John asked.

'It won't accommodate many so they'll have to haul tents and pavilions. There's enough stone in the area to enlarge the house and barn and build a few watchtowers. It will make a sizeable stronghold once we've set up enough outposts to give fair warning of advancing forces. It's also as good a place as Glyndyfrdwy to train troops.'

'How much longer do you think we can use Glyndyfrdwy?' John asked.

'Until Beaufort has enough mercenaries to take it by force. As Sycharth is built of wood and easily burned, I consider the manor already lost.'

41

'Given the pressure the king is under from us, the Tudors in Conwy and the troubles in Scotland I doubt he'll be in a hurry to lend Beaufort troops any time soon,' Trefor commented.

'I agree, and even if Scotland and the North quieten, a large party of soldiers travels slowly. A few judiciously placed scouts will give our men in Glyndyfrdwy enough time to pack and head for Snowdonia.'

'You don't intend to defend your estates?' Philip Scudamore asked.

'I knew the price I would pay when I placed the crown on my head,' Owain answered. 'My lands and manors were lost from that moment, but I see no need to leave my stone built house until Beaufort batters down the doors. Meanwhile, I need to set up a network of couriers and stables so news and messages can be sent between our camps.'

'I'll do that, and liaise with the abbeys and religious houses that are willing to pass on messages.' Trefor offered.

'I tender my own services and those of my fellow friars to help Bishop Trefor in any way we can, my prince,' Friar Brown said eagerly.

'Seems you have found work for all of us, my prince,' Tudor scratched his chin thoughtfully, 'excepting yourself.'

'I will join the party travelling to Glyndyfrdwy and from there to Snowdonia. When I'm satisfied everything that needs to be done to secure our people's safety has been undertaken I'll join you in Plynlimmon, brother. Don't expect me soon. I'll be breaking my journey to talk to a few people who might be persuaded to assist us.'

'You're not thinking of travelling alone.'

'Rhys Ddu, Maredydd and four men at arms will act as my escort.'

'Then our plans are made.' Tudor looked for and received general assent before picking up the empty wine skins. 'Good, just in time for a second supper.'

'Uncle Tudor . . . '

'Nephew Ieuan,' Tudor smiled.

'Can I have a word?'

'Several if you've a mind.'

'I saw Dafydd Gam . . . '

'We all have, boy.'

'But . . . '

'There are more way of killing a cockroach than by stamping on it. Patience, boy,' Tudor cautioned.

Tudor turned to Owain as the men filed out and asked, 'Margaret?'

The inner curtain opened and Margaret joined them. 'Will be at her husband's side.'

'Whether he is in Glyndyfrdwy or Snowdonia. You may stay at either place.' Owen wrapped his arm around her waist.

'May I?' she queried, crossing her arms and glaring at Owain. 'I gave you fair warning, there'll be no leaving me behind. Not again. From this moment on I'm travelling with you wherever you go. You'd find it easier to escape the king's guard than me, but that's not to say I wish to see you in the custody of Bolingbroke.'

Owain's eyes shone with humour. 'That's good to hear, but surely you're not expecting to ride with me into battle.'

'I'll stay with the baggage carts, students and apothecary. But mark my words, there'll be no gainsaying me. Not this time.'

Owain recognised the fire flashing in Margaret's eyes. He kissed her hand.

Crach entered. 'My prince.'

'We left you some meat, Crach,' Tudor handed him a wooden platter of scraps.

Crach sniffed disparagingly. 'Barely enough for a puppy.'

'Come, Gweni,' Margaret said, 'let's find this poor man a supper worthy of him.'

Crach waited until the flap swung shut to speak to Owain. 'The bait has been laid. '

43

'You've set a trap?' Tudor asked.

'One we're hoping the prey won't be able to resist,' Owain answered.

CHAPTER THREE

Owain Glyndŵr's pavilion and camp April 1401
'Now work's done for the day we're free to play.' Tudor checked the wine flasks were empty before abandoning them. He stepped out of the pavilion, walked past the scattering of small tents and headed for the camp fires.

'Isn't that what you do every night, brother,' Owain fell into step beside him, while Crach went ahead to join Crab who was already singing to a rapt audience.

'I try on the rare occasions you don't find work for me.'

'Work?' Owain repeated in amusement.

'Shush!' Margaret was sitting at the campfire with Llewelyn, Sioned, Catrin, Gweni and the girls, listening to Crab sing of the exploits of Hwyel Dda.

Gweni turned, saw Xian behind Tudor and Owain, returned his smile and left the fire.

'Young love,' Tudor murmured, watching them embrace. 'They must have been apart for at least two hours.'

'Mockery?' Owain asked.

'Jealousy.' Tudor confessed, following Owain when he stepped back out of earshot. 'Xian reminds me I'm no longer as young as I was.'

'You're not,' Owain agreed. 'Although there aren't that many years between you.'

'Every year feels like a score.'

Owain's smile broadened as Gweni kissed Xian. 'What it is to be young.'

'Which makes the twinges of encroaching old age all the harder to bear.'

'I would call you a poor old man, if you weren't two years younger than me.'

'So, where and when will you be meeting Hotspur?' Tudor changed the subject.

'Who told you I'm meeting Hotspur?' Owain asked suspiciously.

'I saw the groat Crach flicked you.'

'Hotspur gave it to a messenger to prove the message she carried was from him.'

'He wanted you to know that he's about to march his soldiers north and leave Bolingbroke to do his own dirty work in Conwy?' Tudor suggested.

'It's no secret Hotspur considers doing just that every day that passes without Henry sending him coin to pay his men,' Owain answered.

'You're not going to tell me what Hotspur said, are you?'

'Hotspur will acquaint us with his intentions, when he's ready.' Owain looked to the fire where the younger people had congregated 'Gruffydd reached manhood this winter.'

'He did that a few years ago when you weren't looking,' Tudor chided. 'If he and Maredydd grow much taller we'll have to search out a larger breed of horse lest their stirrups drag on the ground.'

'Margaret regrets the loss of the children they were and I'm in danger of developing the same sentimental streak. Not even the youngest of my sons, likes to be reminded I regard them as children.'

'I remember what we were like at their age.'

'I recall our fellow squires refusing to allow their fathers to watch them the first time they raised a sword.'

'We never had that concern,' Tudor said softly.

'No.' Owain's voice carried regret and the reverence every mention of the man who'd sired him warranted. 'I've often wondered how we would have felt had our father lived long enough to see us fight.'

'He would have lectured us on ways to improve our technique and we would have resented him for it, as our fellow squires felt aggrieved by their fathers' well-intentioned advice. Just as your eldest sons do every time you point out their failings.'

'You're probably right.'

'When am I ever wrong?'

'I'd rather not discuss that,' Owain replied.

'Do you intend to help the Tudors by attacking Hotspur's forces in Conwy?' Tudor asked.

'No.' Owain was decisive. 'The Tudors have taken Conwy Castle. It's for them to decide the fate of the town.'

'I can't see them willingly handing it over to Hotspur.'

'I doubt they intend to, but Conwy is the Tudors' concern. Plynlimmon is ours, and you'll need more lieutenants than Gruffydd if you're going to keep control of your men.'

'I've an eye out for likely candidates.' Tudor smiled when he saw Margaret glance at Owain. 'Your wife wants you.'

'How do you know?'

'You two don't need words to talk.'

'Neither do you when you eye one of your paramours, but with both here, I suggest you turn your back on one while you look at the other,' Owain warned.

'Both here!' Tudor sounded surprised. 'Which two?"

'I saw the widows Morfel and Abertha gossiping, possibly about you, when I was talking to the students.'

'Ah, Morfel and Abertha?' Tudor smiled.

'Who did you think I was talking about?'

'Ask no questions and I'll tell you no lies.' Tudor tapped his nose.

'Do you have anyone besides those two visiting your bed?'

'And, if I do?'

'You're incorrigible.'

'I never take on more than I can handle, brother.' Tudor left Owain and joined a group of women. Within seconds of his arrival, their laughter escalated.

***

Owain offered Margaret his arm and they walked from fire to fire greeting old friends and introducing themselves to those they didn't recognise.

'I wish people wouldn't thank me, when I've done nothing,' Owain complained as they moved on from a group of labourers who'd been glad of an excuse to leave their plague decimated village.

'Nothing?' Margaret reiterated. 'Only had Bishop Trefor endorse your coronation as Prince of Wales to give the Welsh a leader worthy of the name prepared to stand up to the English. Nothing!' she repeated, 'when you rode out with your men, risking life and limb to raze Reginald de Grey's Ruthyn in the name of justice after he burned Pont Gweni and kidnapped and slaughtered innocent men, women and children. You might think you did nothing, Owain, but it was you who organised the attacks on the Marcher towns to warn the English the Welsh are rising, and will continue to rise until they receive the same treatment as the English in their own land. Look around you. For a man who's done nothing you've attracted an army of volunteers the like of which has never been seen in Wales.'

'So speaks the devoted wife. I'm one man, not a miracle worker.'

'But what a man.'

'Enough.' He kissed her to take the sting from his reprimand. Margaret rested her head on his arm and smiled at their eldest sons, who were sitting close to David and Ieuan.

'It's good to see the boys such firm friends,' she said. 'I wish I could help Ieuan. When he spoke of his betrothed it was obvious he loves and misses her very much.'

'He does,' Owain agreed.

'Gweni told me Lizzie disappeared when Reginald de Grey's men sacked Pont Gweni but someone must know something of her whereabouts.'

'Not that I or the boys have heard and we've asked enough people. David searched for her after Ieuan was wounded and forced to keep to his bed. He found a few women who'd been taken by de Grey's men but not Lizzie. He looked for her again after we sacked Ruthyn, but met no one who owned to having seen her after she'd been taken into the castle.'

'If the apothecary hadn't fed Ieuan a soporific draught I think he would have left his sickbed in Sycharth and crawled to Ruthyn,' Margaret said. 'Gruffydd told me when he rescued Lizzie's oldest sister from de Grey's soldiers' brothel, she told him she'd arranged for Lizzie to be taken into de Grey's steward's household.'

'I know it's what Llibio told Gruffydd, but I doubt it's the truth. I don't believe any man of de Grey's would take advice from a convicted thief and whore. I suspect Llibio recommended Lizzie as a virgin in the hope of gaining favours.'

'Aren't you being harsh on Llibio?'

'No,' Owain said. 'Lizzie was a sweet innocent girl as was her younger sister Efa before she ended up in the brothel. The older sisters, Grug and Llibio were cut from different cloth, but saying that, Grug didn't deserve to die at the end of a de Grey rope. All we can be sure of is no one has heard anything of Lizzie since she entered the castle. I pray the girl still lives and will eventually find her way back to Ieuan - that's if he still wants her after de Grey's steward has finished with her.'

'Do you hold out any real hope of her returning?' Margaret asked.

'David, Gruffydd and Maredydd were with me when de Grey hung his Welsh servants from the battlements of his Castle. We feared Lizzie might be among them, but none of the victims resembled her. However, given de Grey's temper I doubt he excluded Lizzie from kindness.'

'You think he'd already killed her?'

'It's possible,' Owain said.

I can't imagine what you suffered having to watch those executions.'

'Not just us, everyone who fought with us.' Owain's hands tightened into fists at the memory. 'De Grey raised his drawbridge to keep us out, then killed them simply because he could. He knew their deaths would devastate the Welsh. They died bravely, even the children. I have no idea if Lizzie escaped their fate. De Grey has no compunction about hanging women or children, but she was young and pretty. Just the sort to catch the eye of de Grey, or one of his captains if he didn't take her for himself.'

Margaret shuddered. 'I can't bear the thought of the girl suffering.'

'Given time, Ieuan may find another girl to help him forget his Lizzie.'

'Some loves can never be forgotten.' Margaret wrapped her arm around Owain's waist as far as it would go. 'I wouldn't have wanted to live if you'd disappeared during the Scottish wars.'

'I wouldn't have wanted you to waste your life grieving for me. Ieuan is a boy . . .'

'Age has nothing to do with love.'

Owain glanced back at his sons. 'I won't argue with you, sweetheart, especially when I look at Ieuan.'

'It's late. You'll want to talk to the boys. I'll say goodnight to Sioned and the girls and walk back to the tents with Gweni.'

'I'll go with you,' Owain offered.

'There's no need. Not with the number of pickets Tudor and Gruffydd have posted.' Margaret left him, and joined the women at the campfire. Owain beckoned to Maredydd and Xian. They left the circle and joined him.

'When will we be ready to set out for Glyndyfrdwy?' Owain pitched his voice below a raucous burst of laughter at another of Tudor's jokes.

'Uncle Tudor aims to break camp here at dawn the day after tomorrow,' Maredydd answered. 'I've picked out our men at arms and four students, including the two you spoke to earlier, Joshua and Peter. I told them to make ready to join us.'

'I've found something else for them to do.'

'I thought you liked them.'

'I do, which is why I've a special use for their talents. Crach is giving them instructions now.'

Maredydd knew better than to question his father when he was reluctant to volunteer information. 'Hunith and Dewi said they'll check the weapons and armour of those who travel with us.'

'Good. You'll find replacements for Joshua and Peter?'

Maredydd nodded. 'I will.'

'I know you haven't seen your brothers in a while but we all have to work tomorrow, so don't talk all night.'

'We won't,' Maredydd answered, although he suspected his father knew how little he meant it. 'Good night, father.'

'Sleep well, Maredydd.' Owain watched him walk over to his brothers. 'Do you have enough Flying Fire to allocate a supply to each of the captains?' he asked Xian.

'I do, my lord,' Xian confirmed. 'I'd also like to discuss the best use that can be made of it with you, Tudor and the captains tomorrow. Konrad's organised a demonstration which will be best seen in the dark. Flying Fire is more versatile than most of your men at arms realise, even after using it in our attacks on the Marcher towns last autumn.'

'A demonstration is a good idea,' Owain agreed.

'I suggest we meet in the woods to the east of the camp an hour before dawn. I'll ask Konrad to apportion supplies based on the size of each captain's band, and to give any extra we may have after distribution to Tudor to take to your new headquarters, my lord. Which group would you like me to join?'

'You or you and Gweni?' Owain questioned.

'Gweni is your daughter, my lord. Do you think she'll allow herself to be left behind?'

'No more than my wife,' Owain frowned. 'It might be best if you go to Glyndyfrdwy. You can take charge of the house, oversee Harri's training of the volunteers and pack the remaining Flying Fire and materials and tools you need to manufacture more. When Tudor finds a suitable base in the Berwyn Mountains I'll ask him to send word so you can inspect it before you go to the trouble of relocating your workshop.'

'How much time do you think we'll have before the king attacks your estates?'

'If we're fortunate a month or so . . . '

'You have two years, my lord.'

Owain recognised Crach's voice. He peered into the darkness and spotted him sitting on a log barely a foot away.

'You creep quietly through the night, Crach.'

'And as low and unseen as a worm,' his soothsayer answered, 'attributes I use to your advantage, my lord.'

'I thank God and you for them. Henry confiscated my estates last November. What makes you think Beaufort won't claim them for another two years?'

'Lack of fighting men and fear of what he'll meet if he tries, my lord. Bolingbroke and Beaufort are aware of the lengths your supporters are prepared to go to ensure your lands remain with your family.'

'You've spoken to Crab?' Owain asked.

'I have, my lord. We agreed on the two years grace you'll have to call your manors your own. Given the pressure the Tudors are exerting on Hotspur, coupled with Scottish unrest and the size of your new army neither of us needed the sight to foretell Bolingbroke's reaction.'

'You know what he'll do?'

'Details are clouded by the king's indecision, my lord. Bolingbroke has little sense, but he knows better than to poke a bear with a stick.'

'Who will you and Crab travel with tomorrow, Crach?'

'You're not assigning us to a party.'

'I know better than to try.'

Crach laughed. 'Rhys Fierce will have need of me, my lord, but I'll re-join you again soon, and when I do I won't leave your side for a while.'

'And Crab?'

'She will go to the mountains with Lord Tudor.'

'I'll move out the same time as Tudor and Gruffydd so we'll travel part way together. Rhys Fierce and Yonge will also journey with the Glyndyfrdwy party until their roads diverge.'

'I was going to suggest they do,' Crach mused.

'You've foreseen trouble?' Owain suggested.

'Nothing your soldiers won't countermand although they travel with untrained volunteers.'

Maredydd re-joined them. 'Will mother be travelling with you, or with Uncle Tudor to the new headquarters, father?'

'Tudor sent you to ask me?' Owain guessed.

Maredydd supressed a smile. 'He said he didn't want to get caught in an argument between you and mother.'

'Tell him he's safe. Your mother will be travelling with me. You can also tell him I'm not happy with her insistence as I know it will lead to every woman wanting to travel with her husband.'

'As if any husband can stop his wife from doing what she wants,' Xian said.

'For someone who only married at Christmastide you've learned quickly, Xian. As for Gweni, remind her when the fighting starts, we have to ride swiftly and that means abandoning any luggage,' Owain said.

'We both know that, my lord,' Xian replied.

'A raiding party is no place for a woman,' Owain warned.

'It's preferable to a separation between husband and wife. Gweni knows she'll have to stay with the baggage train.'

'She agreed to that?' Maredydd had trained in arms alongside his half-sister and knew how stubborn she could be.

'She agreed.' There was a hint of steel in Xian's voice neither Owain nor Maredydd had heard before.

***

'You look as though marriage agrees with you,' Margaret said to Gweni as they walked towards the tents.

'It does. I've never met anyone like Xian, he's different from other men ... ' Gweni fell silent as she realised how her words could be construed as a slur on Owain. 'Not that father wasn't very good to us ... '

'King Richard commanded his services in the army when we were at war, and the law courts when we were at peace. He would have liked to have given more of his time to your mother, brothers and you, as he would have us, but it wasn't possible,' Margaret said tactfully when she sensed Gweni floundering.

'We always knew he had another more important family.'

They reached the pavilion and the sentry on duty held back the curtain for them to enter. Margaret thanked him and offered Gweni a seat.

'You were never of secondary importance to your father, Gweni. He loves all his children equally and I hope your mother knew I never resented her. Your parents met and loved one another long before your father married me.'

'I didn't expect you to accept me.'

'Why ever not, Gweni? You and your brothers are Owain's children. You bear his name. I hope you'll come to regard me, not as a mother because no one could possibly replace Gwyneth in your affections, but a kind of aunt. Remember, I also love your father very much and as you and your brothers are very like him it follows that I love you and them too.'

'Mother used to speak highly of you. She told me you'd met,' Gweni ventured shyly.

'In Sycharth,' Margaret smiled at the memory. 'She visited your brothers when she thought I was away. We shared an afternoon together. Gwyneth was a kind and exceptional woman and you and your brothers are a credit to her. I'm glad I met her and I'm glad that you and I are friends now.'

They heard voices outside and Owain entered the tent. 'I regret to put an end to this ladies' evening but it's past my bedtime.'

'I was just leaving, father.'

'Xian is waiting for you.' He kissed the top of Gweni's head. 'I take it from that smile on your face you're happy in your marriage. So happy in fact you intend to accompany your husband wherever he goes. Even into battle?' Owain raised a disapproving eyebrow.

'I will go wherever he goes, father,' she insisted defiantly.

'You're welcome on condition you don't put yourself or any of my men in danger and obey my orders, exactly as my men have to.'

Gweni's smile broadened. 'I will, father.'

'So, you've given Xian permission to take Gweni with him "wherever he goes"?' Margaret said after Gweni left.

'You gave me little choice when you demanded to travel with me. You knew perfectly well once word reached the other wives they'd ask insist on travelling with their husbands as well.'

'They fought their battles as I had to fight mine.' Margaret allowed herself a small smile of triumph.

'You and Gweni won't be the only women accompanying their menfolk, but aside from your maids I suspect you'll be the only ones who'll conduct yourselves like ladies.'

'That is a thoughtful warning, Owain. Do you believe Gweni and I have been so carefully secluded, that we've never extended our acquaintance among our own sex beyond our maids and ladies of our own class? Or we're unaware of the existence of bawdy houses and bawds?'

'A lady ... '

'Is supposed to be blind deaf and dumb?'

'Didn't you see ... '

'The prostitutes in the camp? Of course I did. I recognise a yellow or striped hood when I see one, and I know what it means. When you called for fighting men did you expect to attract only soldiers? Girls reduced to selling their bodies because it's all they have of value, flock to armies, and that's what you have here. An army to rival Bolingbroke's. And should the women choose to call themselves cooks or laundresses that is their prerogative.'

'If you're telling me you're acquainted with the ways of the world, I'm painfully aware of the fact.' Owain frowned at Margaret before pulling off his cotte and looking around.

'There are no hooks in the wall of a tent but there is a chest,' Margaret pointed to where his stood in the corner of the pavilion.

'Do you approve of Xian taking Gweni with him?' Owain asked.

'Why shouldn't he when I've told you that I'll not be left behind again.'

'You will remain with the baggage train when we fight?'

'Where else would we women sit and wait while you men try to kill one another? I've asked Master Rhys to teach me to cut and roll bandages and mix potions so I can be of some use after the bloodletting.'

Owain knew she was being sarcastic, but couldn't resist asking, 'Do you intend to assist the blacksmith and grave diggers as well?'

'I'm serious, Owain.'

'So am I - my love,' he added in the hope of soothing her irritation.

'I told you I'll not be abandoned again and I meant it.'

'This is not how I intended us to live out what's left of our lives, Margaret.'

'I knew when you rode out of Sycharth at the head of your men after de Grey attacked Pont Gweni, my dream of ending our days peacefully was over. But, in truth, it was never your dream was it, Owain?'

'When a man takes up arms he loses the right to dream. The Bible says "live by the sword, die by the sword." It's a soldier's fate. I've never expected mine to be different. But you deserve better.' He took her hand into his and looked down at the ruby he'd placed on her finger on their wedding day. 'If I'm killed, you'll have no choice but to leave me.'

'You won't be rid of me that easily. I'd order your corpse to be strapped to your horse and lead it to Valle Crucis where I'd ask Abbot David to bury you among your sires. There I would live out the remainder of my days tending to your grave and paying for masses for your soul.'

'And if Bolingbroke takes what's left of my head to decorate London Bridge?'

'I'd rescue it or die trying.'

'Margaret . . . '

She laid her finger over his lips. 'The Bible teaches us our earthly bodies are clay but our souls live on. Either one of us could die at any moment and not only by the sword. Abbot David told me there's been two outbreaks of plague this winter that have taken a dozen men, women and children in Valle Crucis.'

'He told me the same thing.'

'No one knows why it returns every few years or why a second outbreak takes fewer than the first, only there is no avoiding it. And if plague doesn't kill us, God could will that I fall from my horse, trip over my skirt or choke on a crumb of bread.'

He tried to give her a stern look but it proved impossible when he saw her mouth curl upwards at the corners. 'I've agreed you can come, but you and every other woman remain with the rear guard.'

'How many times do I have to agree to do just that?'

'As many as it takes for you remember you promised to do so.'

She lifted his hand to her lips and kissed it.

'Drop the display of mock subservience,'

'I wouldn't dare mock you, even subserviently.'

'Yes, you would.' He leaned over and kissed her. 'The bed looks comfortable.'

'I've done my best to make it so.'
'Is it too cold to undress?' he asked.
'It is unless you promise to keep me warm.'
'I can but try.' He pulled his tunic over his head.
'My lord.'

Owain recognised the voice. He made a face as he looked apologetically at Margaret.

'A prince can't afford to ignore their soothsayers,' Margaret warned as Crach reiterated "my lord".

'Apparently not.' Without bothering to dress, Owain drew back the curtain.

Crach was standing next to the table which was still covered by maps.

'You've paid the merchants and venders' bills?'
'I have, my lord.'
'There were no problems?'
'None, my lord, but perhaps you should consider sacking another Marcher town or two before hosting a second gathering this size.'
'Then it's our snake in the grass?' Owain guessed.
'He passed down orders among his men to have their horses saddled and waiting at moonset.'
'Have you embedded spies in every faction in Wales, Crach?'
'And England, my lord,' Crach replied seriously. 'Shall I order them to be detained?'
'No, just followed. But at a distance. We both know where he'll be heading.'

CHAPTER FOUR

Owain Glyndŵr's pavilion and camp April 1401
Tudor winked at Abertha and nodded in the direction of his tent as people began to drift away from the campfire. He headed in the opposite direction and walked along the picket line to check that every man he'd posted was awake. After exchanging a few words with each one, he discovered Abertha had reached his quarters ahead of him.

He closed the tent flap, wrapped an arm around her waist and pulled at the ribbons that fastened her sleeveless surcoat with his free hand. 'Did you run all the way here?' He dropped her surcoat on to his saddlebags and set to work on her tunic.

'I asked your squire to point out your tent earlier.'

Tudor flicked back the woollen cover on the bed and pulled her down. She fell, laughing on top of him. He slid his hands beneath her gown and shift and closed his mouth over hers.

'Did you miss me?' she pulled away from him to take a breath.

'Every minute of every day and every night through an endless dark winter starved of female company. I would have gone mad if I hadn't had memories of you to keep me warm.'

There'd been a passable and accommodating shepherd's daughter a two-hour ride from the cave where Tudor had wintered with his brother and six followers. He'd long perfected the art of lying.

'You thought of me?'

'Constantly.' He lifted her skirts to her waist.

'Tudor?'

Realising she was fishing for another compliment, he murmured, 'and now you're in my bed, I can see you're twice as pretty as my memories.'

'That's no accident. Have you any idea how difficult it is to dress my hair in plaits?'

He silenced her by placing his mouth over hers but she refused to be quietened.

'Or the trouble I took to make myself a new shift and embroider it with your favourite daisies?'

Tudor couldn't recall mentioning daisies, but he didn't want to get embroiled in a discussion about needlework. 'I'd like your shift even more if was off your back.' He sniffed and smiled. 'You stole your mistresses' violet water?'

'A drop . . .'

'Or two,' he added.

'You won't tell her, will you?' She slipped her hand beneath his tunic, unfastened his belt and pulled his shirt free from his braies, heaving them down together with his hose before kissing his erection.

'Don't stop,' he groaned when she moved away.

'You know my rules.'

'We'll discuss them later.'

'Give me what I want, or I'll leave,' she threatened.

'You, Madam, are a bully.' He sat up and lifted the edge of her gown to her waist exposing her buttocks. She lay across his lap and watched as he removed one of his leather wrist guards.

'What's that for?' she asked.

'Jam it between your teeth, to muffle your cries. It's either that or you entertain the entire camp with your penchant for punishment.'

She took it from him and placed it between her teeth.

He brought his hand down as hard as he could on her buttocks. The result was a muffled squeak from her, the plop of the wrist guard falling to the floor followed by a sharp intake of breath.

'Ow! That hurt!' she moaned.

'You asked me to do it.'

'Not that hard.'

Feeling guilty because he'd been irritated enough to inflict real pain he massaged her naked flesh. He could see the imprint his hand had left in the light of the lamp his squire had lit. 'Enough?'

'Yes.' She moved from his lap, wincing when her back hit his bed.

He kicked off his hose and lifted her on top on him. As he entered her he found himself contrasting their self-centred relationship with the loving intimacy his brother shared with Margaret and Xian with Gweni.

He couldn't wait for Abertha to leave so he could look for Crab. It had been over six months since he had spoken to her. And all he wanted to do was sit next to her and hold her hand.

***

'You're on edge tonight. Is your shoulder paining you?' David asked his brother.

'I'm fine.' Ieuan snapped.

David suddenly realised what was wrong with Ieuan. 'I'm sorry. I'm being stupid. You're thinking of Lizzie.'

'It's odd to be surrounded by people from Pont Gweni and not know where she is,' Ieuan admitted. 'Sometimes, I think I'll go mad from not knowing. I picture her. . . no . . . it's bad enough I imagine it, without inflicting my nightmare thoughts on anyone else.'

'I'm sorry,' David murmured impotently in the absence of anything more comforting to say.

'Efa met a brother from Valle Crucis who visited Ruthyn Castle. He told her Lizzie is carrying the steward's child.'

'Efa could be lying in the hope you'll see her as a replacement for Lizzie.'

'Efa knows she could never replace Lizzie in my affections.' Ieuan was mortified when he felt his cheeks flush from more than the heat of the fire.

'If you pardon my bluntness, brother, it's obvious Efa has replaced Lizzie in your bed.'

'Lizzie was never in my bed,' Ieuan bit back sharply.

'That explains a lot.'

'Like what?' Ieuan demanded.

'Why you're having trouble forgetting her. If you'd bedded her, you'd have consigned her to history by now. Anticipation is always better than reality.'

'I couldn't bed Lizzie because her father . . . '

'Wanted all his girls to remain pure and virtuous until they married,' David broke in. 'He wanted but didn't get. The two eldest were born whores. I smile every time I recall him warning me off Llibio when he caught me winking at her before Enfys dug her claws into me. Are you sure Lizzie didn't develop the same appetite for men as Llibio and Grug?'

'I'm sure!' Ieuan was vehement.

'Gruffydd told me Efa took to a whore's life like a duck to water. He also noticed she set her sights on you the moment he delivered the whores Abbot David threw out of Valle Crucis to Glyndyfrdwy. He was afraid Efa would see you as a soft touch.'

'Efa was a virgin before she was taken by de Grey's men. A soldier raped her when she was captured, and she was forced to enter the soldiers' brothel in Ruthyn at the point of a blade. If she'd refused, she'd have been murdered along with the Welsh servants Baron de Grey hung from his battlements.'

'Are you sure she had no choice about the brothel?' David questioned. 'Because that's not what I heard. Her customers said she was not only willing but revelled in her profession and proved expert at servicing her clients.'

'Efa didn't choose to wear the yellow hood,' Ieuan retorted angrily. 'She was as innocent as Lizzie until Mrs Swive and Llibio got their hands on her.'

'Is that what she said when you took her into your bed?'

Ashamed to reply after what he felt was his betrayal of Lizzie and their love for one another, Ieuan didn't answer.

'Llibio wasn't the only whore in that family. I should know,' David continued.

'As do I after the number of times I watched you sneak off with Grug when her husband wasn't looking,' Ieuan snapped.

'Grug invited, I accepted. It's no different to you with Efa and the only person blaming you for taking what Efa offered, is you.'

'I hate myself for it,' Ieuan cut in sharply.

'Grug was a whore before and after she married. From what Gruffydd said, Efa's no different from Llibio and Grug. Be careful, brother. The only way a man can be certain the children who bear his name were sired by him is to marry a virtuous, honest woman.'

'I had one,' Ieuan said mournfully.

'If it's any comfort. it's not just you who's been asking about Lizzie. Gruffydd has, and he met more people this winter, than Maredydd, Father or me. No one has heard anything of her since she was taken into Ruthyn Castle. I asked around Ruthyn's pothouses before I joined father this winter. Between them they know all the bawds in the town but no one had seen anyone who resembled Lizzie.'

'It's good news that Lizzie's not been forced into a brothel, isn't it?' Ieuan asked eagerly. 'And it's understandable she should be taken into the castle. She reads and writes a fair hand, so the steward would find her useful, and as she wasn't hung along with the other Welsh servants it's likely the steward didn't want to lose her and either hid her or argued her case.'

David recognised his brother's need for reassurance and limited his response to a nod.

'That's it, isn't it? That and you're right about Efa making up the story that Lizzie is carrying the steward's child. She's his clerk . . . nothing more.'

David couldn't bring himself to listen to any more of Ieuan's excuses. 'Only Efa can tell you whether her story is true or not.'

'I'll ask her again, but the more I think about it, the more I think you're right about Efa hoping to take Lizzie's place as my wife, not that Lizzie was ever my wife,' he added mournfully.

David was reluctant to give his brother false hope but he heard the eagerness in Ieuan's voice and couldn't take away his hope. 'Given the public way de Grey hung the others, he would have killed Lizzie with them if he'd laid hands on her.'

'Do you think someone is hiding her inside the castle?'

'It's possible. It's a large castle.' He hesitated. 'You do know there are plenty of girls here. I saw Lady Sioned's high-born ward watching you earlier, and there's . . . '

'How can I look at another girl when I love Lizzie?'

David was tempted to mention Efa but managed to keep quiet. He glimpsed movement from the corner of his eye and saw Morfel walking up from the river. 'I'm married and I find it easy to look at another girl.'

Morfel blew David a kiss.

'I don't know how you can sleep with another woman after making vows before God to Enfys in church,' Ieuan reproached.

'Everyone knows the "faithful vows" are only meant to be kept by women, so men can be sure who fathered the children they clothe and feed.'

'But Enfys is sweet tempered she's . . . '

'She can nag and scold better than any fishwife on Chester market.' David rose to his feet.

Ieuan didn't give up. 'You have three sons you must have loved Enfys once.'

'Enough to fulfil my duty as a husband the three times necessary and more to sire my sons and heirs. But I would have found more excitement and tenderness in a log. That's something that's impossible to explain to a man who sleeps in the bed of a schooled whore. Word of advice, baby brother. Before you take a wife, try her well. If you're not satisfied, or you think marriage will dull her appetites, go elsewhere, or - forget the wedding and keep to your whore.'

Ieuan watched David take Morfel's hand and lead her into the woods. He couldn't help sympathising with Enfys. Given the way David constantly wandered from her bed she had sound reason to scold and nag him.

***

'Elwy, Catrin and Jonnet, it's time to retire to our tent.' Sioned called the girls away from her son, Adam, and Maredydd who was gazing at his cousin Elwy the way a monk would look at an angel. Or to quote David, "like a starving man eyeing a leg of roast lamb". A comment she pretended she hadn't heard.

'I have to go.' Elwy tried to extricate her hand from Maredydd's, but he refused to relinquish it.

'Aunt Sioned, please give us a few more minutes. Crab is going to sing *The dream of Rhonabwy* next.' Catrin linked her arms into Jonnet's and Adam's. 'I promise you, hand on heart, I'll chase Elwy and Jonnet into our tent with our chaperones and lace it tight the moment Crab finishes.'

Sioned couldn't help smiling at the solemn look on Catrin's face. 'You're every bit as persuasive as your mother, Catrin, but in the absence of Elwy's mother I stand as her guardian. I couldn't face her parents if I allowed anything untoward to happen to her.'

'It won't.' Jonnet added her pleas to Catrin's. 'Adam is here . . .'

'Your brother is too busy admiring Catrin to notice what you, Elwy and Maredydd are doing.' She looked around. 'I don't see Gruffydd . . . '

'He's helping our uncle with the pickets,' Maredydd lied. He knew exactly where Gruffydd was and who he was with. He also knew how angry Sioned would be if she suspected the truth. Gruffydd and Jonnet had been betrothed for years, but like their brother David, Gruffydd's eye along with the rest of him tended to rove.

'Rest assured I won't allow the young ladies out of my sight, Mistress Fychan.' Ina, the elderly maid Margaret had appointed to keep a close eye on Catrin, promised Sioned.

'You will escort the girls to the tent the moment the song is finished?'

'I will, Mistress Fychan.'

'You agree you'll all be in the tent directly the last note dies away?' Sioned looked at the girls.

'We will, I promise, Aunt Sioned.'

'That look on your face suggests that you are up to something, Catrin Glyndŵr, but one of our tenants' wives is about to give birth to a child before term. I told the midwife I'd attend the woman with her, not that there's a great deal I can do other than hold the poor woman's hand.'

'Don't worry, Mistress, I will take good care of the young ladies.'

'I believe you will, Ina.' Sioned frowned at Jonnet. The girl appeared crestfallen, and she wondered if Gruffydd's absence was the cause. But even if it was, she had no time to talk to her. Later - she'd find time then.

***

'As you look at your tent from the outside, where is your bed?' Maredydd whispered to Elwy as they were ostensibly listening to Crab sing.

'Back right corner, but don't . . . '

He saw Ina watching them and turned his attention back to Crab who was singing the last notes.

'Ladies,' Ina rose from the tree trunk she'd been sitting on and motioned the girls closer.

'We'll escort you to your tent, Mistress Ina.' Maredydd offered her his arm.

'No you won't, Lord Maredydd. The pickets will give us all the protection we need.' Ina tapped him sharply with her walking stick before herding Elwy in front of her.

Preoccupied with keeping Elwy away from Maredydd, Ina neglected Jonnet and Catrin who lagged behind with Adam. He wormed his way close enough to Catrin to whisper, 'May I have your permission to speak to your father?'

Choosing to misunderstand him, she replied, 'of course. He doesn't stand on ceremony with anyone. He encourages people to talk to him.'

'Catrin . . . '

'Ina's about to shout at me.'

'How do you know?'

'Because she's eying me with her, "I know what you're thinking, Catrin," look. She watches me even more than she watches Elwy. I must go.'

Catrin dived into the tent behind Elwy and Jonnet leaving Adam standing in front of it.

***

Ieuan didn't expect to find David in their tent after seeing him disappearing into the woods with Morfel. He wasn't, but neither did he expect to see Efa there. David's words echoed in his mind.

Gruffydd told me Efa took to a whore's life like a duck to water. He also noticed she set her sights on you the moment he delivered the whores Abbot David threw out of Valle Crucis to Glyndyfrdwy. He was afraid Efa would see you as a soft touch.

Angry, he growled. 'What are you doing here?'

'I came to see if you wanted anything,' she said softly.

More annoyed by her gentle tone than he would have if she'd shouted at him, he snapped, 'I want for nothing.'

She rose from his blanket. 'Then I'll leave.'

He wanted to hurt her, the way Lizzie's absence from his life hurt him. 'When I find Lizzie I'll have no more use for you, in or out of my bed.'

'I know.'

David's words echoed through his mind. *"Efa could be lying in the hope you'll see her as a replacement for Lizzie."*

'You'll never take Lizzie's place in my heart or my bed,' he added viciously.

'I realised that the first time I slept with you.'

'Have you no pride?' he demanded. 'To allow me to use you the way a man uses a whore . . . '

'Before you took me into your bed, many men used me and it wasn't pleasant, Ieuan. So if anyone is using anyone it's me using you.'

Rendered speechless by the thought, he stared at her.

'I know you consider me a poor substitute for my sister and the moment she returns you'll order me to leave you. It's all right. You've done me a kindness in allowing me to stay with you this long. If it wasn't for you I'd have had to live with Llibio and the other whores and please any man who offered to pay me for my services. Thanks to you I can say, I am no longer a whore because I serve only one man . . .'

'When I find Lizzie . . . '

'I'll be an encumbrance and I'll have to find another place or another man to keep me. In the meantime, such status as I have in your father's army comes from you Ieuan. You are kind and I like sleeping with you. But if you no longer want me I'll go.' She reached for the tent flap. He grabbed her hand.

'When I find Lizzie . . . ' he began.

'She'll never know what happened between us from me.'

'You promise?'

'I swear it.' She looked at him for what seemed like a long time.

He broke the silence between them. 'Undress and get on my mattress, Efa. But . . . '

'Yes?' she prompted when he didn't continue.

'No whore's tricks.'

'It's for you to tell me what you want me to do, Ieuan.' She unfastened the shoulder clips on her gown and stepped out of it.

***

'Sniffing the air for a trace of Elwy's rose water?'

Adam's question shattered Maredydd's day-dream. He'd imagined himself sitting at Elwy's feet . . . reaching up and unrolling a stocking from her leg. The fantasy had been so immediate - so real he'd felt as though he were actually stroking his fingers along the white, translucent skin on her thigh . . .

Startled, he looked around and realised he was standing, staring blankly at the girls' tent. Odd behaviour that would incite ribald comments from men and a scolding from any woman who suspected his thoughts.

'I wasn't thinking of Elwy,' Maredydd muttered.

'No?' Adam raised a sceptical eyebrow. 'Crab's still singing, there was ale left the last time I looked, and although the chaperones have shepherded the good girls' to their beds, the naughty ones are still out.'

'You're like David and Gruffydd . . . ' Maredydd fell silent when he realised he was talking to Jonnet's brother.

'Where is Gruffydd - really ?' Adam looked around.

'Where I told Ina he was, helping my uncle with the pickets,' Maredydd snapped.

'No, he's not, Tudor is sitting at Crab's feet.'

'Then he sent Gruffydd to check the pickets for him,' Maredydd's colour heightened. He hated lying.

'Well, I've more pressing things to worry about than the whereabouts of my future brother-in-law, like beer, or gwisgi if I can find it and wayward girls.'

'I'm for bed.'

'Please yourself and sweet dreams.'

Maredydd watched Adam turn towards the fire. He headed back to his tent, saw the unmistakable shadows of Gruffydd and his visitor inside, walked on and proceeded to do what he'd told Ina and Adam that Gruffydd was doing. Checking that the pickets posted around the camp were awake.

***

Owain's head was too full of questions that had no answers for him to sleep. Carefully, so as not to disturb Margaret, he stole from the bed and dressed, stopping when Margaret stirred.

He held his breath while she stretched her arm across the bedcover. He sensed her searching blindly for him. Her hand came to rest on his pillow, she pulled it close to her cheek, sighed and relaxed back into sleep.

When he was certain she slept, he lifted the curtain and left the tent. Nodding to the pickets he headed out of the woods to the camp fires.

Most of the stalwarts who'd stayed to hear the last songs had fallen asleep where they'd sat. Wrapped in their cloaks they lay on the ground in between the logs they'd used as benches. Those on guard duty were drinking small beer and eating rye bread and soft cheeses. To his surprise he saw Xian among them.

Xian poured a second cup of small beer and carried it over to Owain. 'You couldn't sleep either, my lord?'

'I keep mulling over the decisions we made earlier.'

'We made the correct choices,' Xian reassured.

'So sayeth the loyal man at arms.'

'We did,' Xian smiled.

Owain stood back and studied Xian in the firelight. 'You look even happier than you were earlier.'

'I've a great deal to be happy about. I promised Gweni I wouldn't say anything . . . but . . . '

'She's going to have a child?' Owain guessed.

'You won't tell her I told you?'

'I promise I'll wait for her to break the news to me.'

'This is the first time I've fathered a child.'

Given the number of women who'd turned up on his doorstep ten months to a year after he'd made love to them asking him to contribute to the upkeep of their baby, Owain almost said, "that you know about," but the happiness that Xian radiated stayed his tongue.

Used to congratulating his sons by slapping them soundly across the shoulders, he did the same to Xian who winced, although he did manage to stand his ground.

'I'm sorry,' Owain apologised. 'I'm accustomed to patting my sons on the back.'

'And they, like you, are giants, not man sized like me,' Xian commented.

Owain asked 'Do you want a boy or a girl.'

'A miniature Gweni would be perfect.'

'She would, but if she's anything like my sons and daughters she wouldn't remain small for long. Are you returning to your tent?'

Xian held up a bowl. 'I am. Gweni had a sudden craving for a slice of salty bacon.'

'I'd forgotten that husbandly duty. When Margaret was carrying Gruffydd it was green apples. Gwyneth craved syllabub with Gweni.'

'Salty bacon is easier to find than green apples out of season.' Xian hesitated as they approached the back of the tent Sioned was sharing with the girls and their chaperones. He peered into the darkness. 'Is that who I think it is?'

'It is. But given that he's outside the tent, and the girls inside, their virtue appears to be safe.' Owain took a last look at Maredydd wrapped in his cloak, asleep while leaning leaned against the back corner of the girls' tent.

Moonlight shone down on his arm, but his hand appeared to be tucked inside and Owain wondered if Maredydd had cut a hole in the cloth so he could hold Elwy's hand.

'Such is the power of love and the need to be together even when separated by a tent wall.' Xian shook his head fondly.

'There is nothing as strong as the first flush of passion,' Owain agreed.

'The need for sleep perhaps.' Xian squinted up at the stars. We have two hours until we meet.'

Owain nodded and walked back towards his pavilion. 'Until then.'

***

Inside the tent, Jonnet gripped the hand she believed to be Gruffydd's tighter and held it against her breast. Maredydd stirred in his sleep caressed her nipple and planted a kiss on the canvas that covered Jonnet's face.

***

Owain stepped out of his pavilion before dawn to find Tudor, Xian and his captains waiting for him next to the dying embers of the camp fire.

'Thank you, my lord, and gentlemen for forgoing sleep leaving your beds early. This shouldn't take much of your time.' Xian pulled a torch from the ground, lit it on the last flickers of flame, and led the way into the woods.

***

'"Won't take much of your time",' Tudor grumbled after ten minutes of stumbling over tree roots. 'If I wanted a ten-mile trek I would take one in daylight so I could see where I was going.'

'I thought it best to put a safe distance between the flying fire and the volunteers. We're nearly there.'

Xian stopped when he saw torches rammed into the ground ahead of them. They illuminated a small clearing that housed a burning brazier and stationary cart.

Xian's squire Konrad was feeding the brazier with dead wood, his body servant, Ulrich, was sitting on the driver's bench of the cart and his page, Franz, was perched on the back on an array of boxes.

'You've finished the preparations?' Xian asked Konrad.

'Everything is ready, my lord. We waited only on your arrival.'

Xian went to the back of the cart, opened a box and removed an object the size of a rolled hedgehog.

'Two or three of these are light enough to carry in a bag hooked on a saddle. Each has a flax tail.' He tossed the ball to his squire.

Konrad held the fuse in the flames of the brazier. It caught, flared, and he tossed it as far as he could throw.

'Nothing,' Tudor sighed after a few seconds crawled past, an eternity to the men waiting for a reaction.

Xian held up his finger as an explosion tore through the bushes, scattering sparks, burning twigs and branches, trailing flames that licked the undergrowth.

Konrad took a bucket of water from the back of the cart and quenched the fire.

'You've made enough of these to furnish every man at arms, Xian?' Owain asked.

'Enough to give everyone who rides for our cause, two - maybe three, my lord. I lost count when we were making them. They're good for starting fires, and unnerving enemy horses. I've also filled barrels with flying fire powder.' Xian went to the back of the cart, lifted the lid on a barrel, picked up a handful of fine black powder and ran it through his fingers. 'It has many uses, including laying a trail to more barrels when you want to blow a wooden building or door, or given sufficient quantity a hole in a stone town or castle wall.'

Xian trickled a line of powder along the edge of the clearing, and dipped a length of flax into the brazier. When it flared he set a flame at the end. Fire darted swiftly, travelling along the line at speed as though it were living creature before dying, leaving a pungent odour in its wake.

'That stinks.' Tudor wrinkled his nose.

'It does,' Xian agreed cheerfully.

'How much do you have?' Owain asked Xian.

'Of the powder? Stored in Glyndyfrdwy, enough barrels to blow a dozen holes in five castle or town walls, decimate an enemy's cavalry charge, and destroy an enemy camp.'

'How quickly can you replenish your stock should we need more?'

'Now Crach has helped me source the materials, I can make as much as you require but I'd appreciate a few days' notice if you want a large amount.'

'I'll take a couple of waggon loads,' Tudor rubbed his hands together in anticipation.

'Before you pack all Xian's stock into your baggage train I dare say the rest of us can find a use for it too,' Owain warned Tudor.

'There's enough to supply every party for the moment,' Xian answered tactfully.

'Can you make it anywhere?' Tudor asked.

'Glyndyfrdwy has the advantage of stone buildings with sound walls and roofs. Damp kills Flying Fire and prevents it burning. I can make it in any dry space that's large enough. As can my apprentices.'

'You've instructed others how to make it?' Tudor asked.

'Gweni, Ieuan, Master Rhys the apothecary and his daughter Joan as well as my retinue.'

A regular workshop full,' Tudor commented.

'I'm on the lookout for more workers. It would be my pleasure to instruct you in its composition.'

Tudor slapped Xian across his shoulders so soundly he sent him reeling. 'As soon as we've driven the English over the border I'll be knocking on your door.'

'The idea, Lord Tudor is to knock on my door beforehand so you can send them back with fire tickling their heels.'

'Well said, Xian. I'll set aside some time to talk to you.'

'I look forward to our conversation.' Xian stared thoughtfully at the last tenacious speck of fire as it flickered out beneath the undergrowth.

'I need a volunteer to put a bucket of that black powder beneath Bolingbroke's throne or Reginald de Grey's chair.' Tudor wrapped his arm around Xian. 'You're more of an asset to this family than I thought you'd be and well worth the price of a niece's affections, nephew through marriage.'

CHAPTER FIVE

Countryside on the outskirts of Cwdweli Wales, en route to Cadair Idris early June 1401

The sun broke free from the clouds. Its rays beat down, uncomfortably warm after days of cool winds and rain. Friar Brown's wool habit clung close to his body, warm and damp, prickling his legs, and hampering his movements as he lumbered through the woods. His laboured breath sounded a drumming in his ears and his heart beat frantically, driven more by fear than exertion.

Was the camp further up-stream than he recalled? Or had the captains ordered it moved?

He'd left early that morning to look for a village to gather information, or so he'd told Rhys Ddu. Driven by his stomach he'd been more preoccupied with thoughts of pies he might find at the nearest tavern than news.

He halted when he saw his party's horses tethered close to the river bank. He dived into a patch of bracken, held his breath and listened hard for following footsteps. After a few minutes during which he heard only birdsong, he crawled forward and fell exhausted beside Ieuan who was sitting on the riverbank with Maredydd and Rhys Ddu.

'Is the ghostly Bwda of legend chasing you Friar Brown? I thought he only came out at night,' Maredydd cast a fishing line baited with bread into the shallows.

The Friar shook his head, lay back on the bank, gasped for air and started coughing. Ieuan slipped his arm behind his back and helped him sit up.

'Breathe before you talk, friar,' Rhys advised.

'Gam . . . ' the friar heaved out the word.

'Dafydd Gam?' Maredydd was instantly alert.

The friar nodded.

'You were followed?' Rhys asked urgently.

Unable to speak, the friar shook his head again. All four sat still and listened hard for a few minutes. Even then

Ieuan rose and walked around the area twice to ensure they were alone.

'Last I heard of Gam, he'd left Carmarthen to show his true colours by re-joining Hotspur and Hal's command in Conwy,' Rhys said when Ieuan returned.

'He's . . . not . . there . . now,' the friar gasped, finding his voice.

'Evil bastard!' Ieuan declared. 'The first time I set eyes on him he threatened to kill me and David for hunting on Uncle Gruffydd's land. If Uncle Tudor hadn't arrived, I think Gam would have run us through with his blade. I was furious when he turned up at father's call to arms. I wanted to have a go at him but Uncle Tudor wouldn't let me.'

'We have to tell your father . . . '

'He warned us not to expect him for two or three days,' Maredydd reminded Rhys.

Owain had ridden off with Margaret, Dafydd and Enyd in the early hours, leaving Maredydd and Rhys Ddu in command. He'd told them he was hoping to meet "someone who might be persuaded to support Welsh freedom."

He hadn't given any clues as to the identity of the "someone" but Maredydd and Rhys suspected he was visiting Henry Dwn in Cwdweli Castle. Dwn was a long standing friend of the Glyndŵrs, and along with Owain had supported King Richard II until Bolingbroke had deposed him.

After days in the saddle, Owain's men had welcomed the opportunity to rest and indulge in fishing and hawking to supplement their campaigning diet of twice baked bread and cheese. But after hearing the friar utter "Gam" Maredydd was already reeling in his twine and bread bait.

'Was Gam alone?' Ieuan handed the friar his water bottle.

Friar Brown drank before vigorously shaking his head. 'He leads a band of thugs. Every one as evil as Bolingbroke's hangman or so the taverner I spoke to said.'

'Evil?' Rhys queried.

Friar Brown rested his back against a stone. 'They've been raiding the local farms and villages, killing, stealing and raping in the name of the king who's given Gam an official badge, along with a commission and authority to collect "taxes" and "fines" for him.'

'No doubt as a reward for reporting every man who attended father's call to arms at Carmarthen, so Bolingbroke can arrest, and hang draw and quarter them as traitors.' When Maredydd had learned of Gam's treachery after the man had left the camp, he was furious he hadn't been told of it earlier so he could have challenged the man to single combat.

'Every man at Carmarthen knew that in responding to father's call they ran the risk of having their head ornament London bridge.' The friar handed back Ieuan's water bottle and produced a gwisgi flask from under his cloak.

'Bolingbroke has probably given Gam permission to take a percentage of what he collects,' Maredydd said.

'It's well known Gam will lick Bolingbroke's arse clean if commanded,' Rhys mocked.

'The taverner took me within sight of Gam's camp. He's bivouacked an hour's walk outside the nearest village - if you call four hovels and a ramshackle barn a village.'

'How many men are with him?' Maredydd questioned.

'I counted fifty, including fifteen archers in Gam's livery and fifteen constables sporting Bolingbroke's insignia. I heard one of the archers address Gam as "colonel" when Gam shouted for someone to bring him a woman.'

'They have women with them?' Ieuan asked eagerly, thinking of Lizzie.

'Local women and children. The taverner recognised them. They've taken no men - alive. Although they've killed at least three the taverner knew of who were trying to protect their women.' The friar shrugged off his cloak and loosened the rope belt on his robe. 'They stole a couple of carts and filled them with the peasants' stores, leaving them to starve until the next harvest.'

'Bastards!' Ieuan cursed.

'Where Gam's men find nothing of value they take people. They snatched a farmer's two daughters in Llansaint. They told him they'll sell them to a brothel but you know soldiers. They're probably using them already. There was talk in the tavern of trying to free the girls, but that's all it was, talk.'

Ieuan recalled de Grey's raid on his village, how helpless he'd felt pitted against men at arms. 'Farmhands with pitchforks are no match for soldiers,' he murmured.

'How many girls are with the soldiers?' Rhys asked.

'I saw six,' the friar answered. 'I'd stake my purse none were there willingly. All sported bruises and three were tied hand and foot.'

'Are the constables armed as well as the soldiers and archers?' Maredydd filled a wooden cup with water.

'They have weapons, but their blades and armour are rusty and the constables have run to fat. Their tunics are grease stained, their hands and faces unwashed,' the friar replied.

'Sloppy soldiers are undisciplined. They don't fight well,' Maredydd mused.

'We could inflict some serious damage if we hit them when their guard is down,' the friar declared,

Maredydd allowed the "we" to pass. He'd never seen the friar in the front line of his father's attacks on the Marcher towns, but he'd noticed him on battlefields at the victory "pickings" stage. 'Do you think father would approve of us attacking Gam's party?' he asked Rhys.

'He left us in charge, which means he trusts us to make his decisions for him,' Rhys reminded. 'If we free the women, and retrieve and return stolen goods to their rightful owners, we might gain your father more supporters. And if we injure Gam or his thugs?' Rhys shrugged. 'Some men deserve injury.'

'And should we fail?' Ieuan didn't want to play devil's advocate but their father had warned them not to attract attention while he was away.

'We won't,' Maredydd and Rhys Ddu chanted simultaneously.

'Supper time would be best, after they've prepared their food, before they've had time to eat it,' the student, Elias, mumbled, wary of speaking his mind in front of Rhys and Maredydd.

'A voice from the bushes, Elias. I didn't see you there,' Maredydd said. 'Thank you for your contribution but when you said "best", best for what?'

'To strike the enemy camp.'

'You don't want to cook this evening, Elias?' Rhys suggested in amusement.

'We always raided rival university halls in the early evening when we knew the students would be preoccupied by thoughts of their meal, especially on days when meat was permitted. And when our raids were successful, our reward was eating their meal in front of them.'

Maredydd laughed. 'Are you driving the students too hard, with your insistence that they cook for the men, Rhys?'

'Not at all, lord,' Elias answered. 'Lord Rhys has been most helpful to those of us unversed in warfare. We all knew before we volunteered that the last to arrive would be given the worst jobs, but with respect, Lord Rhys, we joined to fight, not prepare food.'

'You need a deal more practice before I'll allow you to draw a sword on the enemy,' Rhys warned. 'Go, gut the rabbits we snared this morning and get them ready for the pot.'

Elias left but Maredydd and Ieuan noticed he was careful to remain within earshot.

'How long would it take us to reach the camp of these "tax collectors"?' Maredydd drained his cup.

'I'd say less than three hours including preparation time, lord,' Friar Brown answered,

Maredydd looked up at the sky. 'If we rest for an hour before we saddle our horses and check our weapons, we'll have light to get there and dusk to hit them.'

'I hope the troops have made a tasty stew for their supper to go with the fresh bread I saw in their grain cart.' Friar Brown beamed at the thought.

'Fifteen constables, fifteen archers and twenty troops, how many of our men do you want to lead into the camp?' Ieuan asked.

'Thirty mounted swordsmen,' Maredydd answered decisively looking to Rhys Ddu for confirmation. 'Anymore and we'll trip over one another. Twenty archers, half longbow, half crossbow, will ride with us and fire a volley of arrows before we go in but they'll remain outside the camp within calling range should we need them. Bowmen to fire their arrows first, crossbow archers to follow with their quarrels, both to pick out their targets from a safe distance.'

'Given the accuracy of our archers our thirty won't be going in outnumbered.' Rhys laid his hand on Elias's shoulder. 'You'll stay with the rear-guard and take care of the women, horses and supplies.'

'Of course. When will I be ... '

'Fit to fight?' Ieuan finished Elias's question for him. 'I suggest you ask Dafydd that after you've beaten him in sword practice.'

'That will never be, lord.' Elias was crestfallen.

'When Dafydd thinks you're ready he'll allow you win,' Ieuan consoled, 'but he won't allow you to face the enemy half trained.'

'Ieuan?'

Consumed by envy for the authority their father had placed in his half-brother, Ieuan struggled to subdue his resentment. 'You want me to stay with the students, Maredydd?'

'Father watched our last sword practice. He saw you give as many blows as you received but only you know if your shoulder is up to combat.'

'It is,' Ieuan replied resolutely. 'I won't let you down.'

'Then you'll ride into the camp alongside Rhys Ddu and follow his lead and command.'

'I would rather ride next to you.'

'The first lesson a soldier learns, is to obey orders.'

Irritated with himself for risking the permission to ride into battle he'd been waiting for, Ieuan murmured, 'it appears I have yet to learn it.'

Maredydd gripped Ieuan's arm. 'You know I ride alone and you know why?'

'Because you'll be wearing father's armour which makes you a target.'

'As father says, a captain has no business placing any soldier other than himself in danger. Check your weapons and armour and saddle your horse.' Maredydd looked at Rhys. 'You have Xian's bag of tricks.'

'I do,' he grinned.

'I leave their use to your discretion. You have oil soaked twine?'

'I have the fuses in hand, lord.'

***

While Rhys Ddu and Maredydd were passing orders and flasks of gwisgi around the camp, Ieuan went to the rope the squires had slung between the trees to tether their mounts. Elias was watering the archers' horses.

'May I speak, Lord Ieuan?'

'Be my guest, and there's no need to call me lord.'

'Before I joined the rebellion, I expected there to be discussion and challenges to authority when orders were passed down, as there are after tutors' lectures in Oxford. But everyone listens to the officers, even the low ranking ones, and obeys their directives without question.'

'Soldiers have more sense than to invite chaos by disobeying orders. Are you disappointed by the lack of protest and discussion?'

'No, but I expected more excitement to soldiering.'

'According to my older brothers, soldiers get enough excitement to last ten years in ten minutes of battle.' Ieuan glanced at the crossbow archers who were checking their stocks of quarrels and the longbow men their flights.

'I'd like to experience that for myself.' Elias returned the horses he'd watered to the rope, untied two more and led them to the stream where Ieuan was saddling his horse. 'What's it like having the Prince of Wales as your father?' Elias asked.

'As I have no other father to compare him with, I can't answer that question.'

'You must think me a fool for asking.'

'No.' Ieuan glanced over his shoulder and saw Rhys Ddu giving last minute instructions along with a gwisgi flask to the archers. 'I was six before I realised my father was the lord of our manor. My brothers, sister and I looked forward to his visits, as did my mother. Not that we ever knew when he was coming. But he never forgot our birthdays, sending something to mark the day when he couldn't come himself, and he always made sure we had enough clothes and the village enough food when the harvest failed. Later, when I joined my brother at Glyndyfrdwy to train as a squire, our father never treated us any differently from his legitimate children.'

'You're illegitimate?'

'Unlike the English the Welsh accord their bastards the same rights in law and society as the children of their marriages.'

'I didn't realise.'

'There are many differences between English ways and those of the Welsh.'

'So my mother kept telling me. She was born in Carmarthen. These are the last two horses that need watering. Would you like me to help your squire strap on your armour?' Elias ventured.

'You're offering in the hope that I'll consider taking you on as my squire when my squire is promoted to swordsman?'

Elias shrugged. 'If you don't want me as a squire you could always use me for sword practice.'

'You're good?'

'I've beaten my ten year old brother.'

'Even I can beat my younger brother, but Robert's only five. My older brother David and my twin sister Gweni,' he gave a grim smile. 'They're invincible.'

'Your sister fights?'

'Viciously and pays no heed to rules.'

'Is she the one married to the foreign knight?'

'Xian, yes.'

'I saw her at the meeting place. Does she fight alongside him?'

'Not if he or my father can stop her. But Gweni is headstrong. According to our mother,' he suppressed a catch in his voice, 'we were born fighting one another.' Ieuan saddled his mount and tightened the girth. 'Thank you for your offer, I'll take you up on it when you can tell the difference between one piece of armour and another.'

'I can't at the moment,' Elias confessed, 'but I'm a quick learner.'

'There's not much to it besides buckles, ties and endless polishing. Here, I'll show you now if you like,' he offered.

***

The archers, longbow and crossbow were mounted by the time Elias finished helping Ieuan don his armour. Like his brothers before him, Ieuan had raided the armouries at Sycharth and Glyndyfrdwy during his training. The chainmail hauberk that covered his arms and torso from neck to hips had been new when his great grandfather had fought his first battle. Hunith had riveted steel plates on the leather base of his brigandine which had belonged to a great uncle. The two garments worn together offered protection but at the cost of considerable, uncomfortable weight.

He carried his helmet along with his gauntlets, in a bag attached to his saddle. They were new, presents from his father, as were his long and short sword and the scabbards that hung from his belt.

'Ieuan?' Rhys Ddu called.

'I'm there.' Ieuan mounted with his squire's help and looked down on Elias. 'Thank you for your assistance.'

'Good luck.' Elias watched Ieuan ride into the first ranks behind Maredydd.

He envied him, yet was terrified by the thought of leaving the baggage train and rear guard and joining him.

There had been no fatalities among Owain's men in any of the dozen or so skirmishes they'd fought since leaving Glyndyfrdwy and Snowdonia. But the first thing the battle hardened men did after uttering a prayer to St David, or St Martin, depending which saint they sought protection from, was to agree the first death among their numbers could only be a matter of time.

He hoped it wouldn't be Ieuan. The only friend he'd made, as yet, outside of the students from Oxford.

Carmarthenshire countryside, June 1401
Maredydd set a slow but steady pace. They travelled quietly for a large group of armed men, but Maredydd found himself tensing at every clink of harness, thud of hoof and snap of twig. When he saw the smoke of cook fires curling above the tree tops, he reined in his destrier and passed down a whispered order to dismount.

The wind brought a mouth-watering scent of roasting hog and mutton and he realised he was hungry. No bad thing before a battle. Experience had taught him fighting was best done on an empty stomach.

He sent out scouts. When they returned to report no sightings of pickets he blessed Gam's lack of foresight and continued to lead the way on foot, forging a path through the woodland that encircled the village fields.

What had been arable land before the plague had decimated the population half a century ago, was now reclaimed by nature. Towering weeds, brambles and self-seeded saplings had reshaped the landscape and as twilight thickened, the wilderness heightened the atmosphere of dereliction. He called a second halt when he was close enough to hear men's voices.

Rhys waited for Maredydd's signal before reaching for his horn and nodding to Ieuan. They both dismounted, and lay full length on the ground before slithering forward, and disappearing into the undergrowth.

Rhys reappeared ten minutes later and signalled to Maredydd who raised his hand and waved to the longbow men. They handed the reins of their horses to their squires and followed Rhys. Maredydd counted silently to two hundred before alerting the crossbow archers who stepped forward and followed the path of the longbow men.

The sound of conversation and laughter from the encampment grew louder as dusk thickened. Maredydd recognised Gam's men need to make a noise. When night blanketed the woods it created shadows capable of hiding terrifying monsters, including the evil beasts the bards depicted in their tales which had populated his nightmares since childhood.

That quick movement barely espied from a corner of his eye could be "Y Gwillgi" the legendary black dog with red eyes whose glare could kill a man with a single glance. And that bubble in the reed bed beside the bank of willows, a Ceffyl Dŵr about to rise to the surface and once it did, the evil water horse would open its mouth to reveal its sharp teeth, steal up on him and . . .

A single musical note echoed through the trees, preceding a whirring rush of wind. Arrows flew thick and fast westwards from the longbows, blotting out the dying glimmers of light from the sliver of setting sun.

The screams of the wounded and dying drowned the shrill cries of birds as they rose from the trees and scattered. As a second musical note rang through the air Maredydd lifted his hand and brought it down sharply.

Crossbows fired and steel quarrels slammed upwards on a lower path than the flights from the longbows.

Before the last quarrel fell to earth squires were assisting their lords to mount and don their gauntlets and helmets. Maredydd gripped his reins in one hand and dropped his visor with the other.

Three notes resounded in quick succession followed by a deafening roar of "Havoc"! Men at arms spurred their destriers and galloped into the English camp.

Caught unarmed and unaware the swiftest of Gam's men fled into the woods. The slower ones were crushed beneath Welsh hooves and the weight of horseflesh. Behind them a sergeant stood his ground in a vain attempt to rally the remnants of the English soldiery and constables. He remained alone, a solitary figure to emphasise the success of the surprise Welsh onslaught.

Ieuan was aware of Maredydd drawing his blade as he galloped ahead of him. He pulled his short sword from his scabbard with his left hand and hauled his sword out with his right, using his knees to guide his horse into the centre of the camp.

His mount stumbled, lost its footing, staggered and regained it. Ieuan knew without needing to look that his horse was trampling over the bodies of the English fallen.

The distinctive Glyndŵr helmet adorned with three crimson flamingo feathers towered above the thick of the fighting. Maredydd swung his great sword right and left as he hacked his way through the enemy that surrounded him.

Light flashed in brief loud cacophonies as Xian's flying fire balls exploded. Behind Maredydd, Rhys's mount, schooled to ignore noise, was making steady progress through the ranks of the English who were retreating on foot. Ieuan saw none of the men he thought of as "enemy" on horseback and presumed the surprise attack had left them no time to saddle their mounts.

Spurring his horse he drew alongside a constable and struck out with his sword. The man turned his back and ran. A hand reached out of the melee and grabbed his ankle. He lifted his sword arm and swivelled in the saddle. A broad shouldered man, hair cropped to his ears hurled himself on his stirrup. Without hesitation, training superseding thought, Ieuan raised his sword high and brought it down on the man's arm with all the force he could muster. The man screamed and fell back clutching the stump of his severed elbow.

A second soldier gripped the reins of Ieuan's mount, forcing it to a standstill. Ieuan leaned back in the saddle and kicked out, catching the man under the chin, His assailant staggered back on to Rhys and his sword.

'Behind you!' Rhys's voice cut through the screams and clamour of clashing blades. Ieuan pulled on his freed reins and turned. A constable had sliced down on the rump of his horse drawing blood. Ieuan leaned sideways and caught the man with his short sword, bringing it up beneath the constable's armpit. The man fell beneath Rhys's horse.

Ieuan gripped hard with his thighs to maintain his balance and lashed out with his weapons, cutting and thrusting his way through the thicket of English soldiers and constables. The discordant clashing of blades, the screams and moans of the injured and dying barely penetrated his consciousness. He was beset by the oddest sensation of detachment, as though he wasn't really there, only watching the fight from a distance.

He wasn't sure where he was but he knew he was with his mother. He not only pictured her, he could feel her touch as she gently ruffled her fingers through his hair, which was ridiculous when the weight of his helmet pressed down on his head.

She loved him – he loved her - yet he was in the midst of violence and chaos created by men who hated enough to kill strangers.

He knew about hatred, but only the kind borne from personal pain. If he'd been strong enough he would have killed de Grey's soldiers for murdering his mother, burning Pont Gweni and taking his Lizzie. Were the men under Dafydd Gam's command the same as the murdering brutish louts that de Grey employed?

He thought of Elias as he thrust his sword into a constable's neck. The student had said he wanted excitement. Was this what he hoped for?

Exhausted, summoning his remaining strength, he watched the constable fall to the ground, lifted his sword, froze and stared. The only enemy left standing was Gam's sergeant, ignored by everyone he was still shouting rallying cries. Gam himself was running, blade outstretched, towards Maredydd.

Ieuan shouted a warning but Maredydd was ahead of him. His brother lifted his leg over his saddle and slid from his destrier. His blade parried Gam's blow and bounced back as they squared up to one another, side-stepping over and around the bodies of the wounded and those too weak to rise from the ground.

Gam feinted. Maredydd lunged. Gam aimed for the leather padding Maredydd wore beneath his breastplate. Before he could slice into it, Maredydd counter moved hitting Gam's sword with sufficient force to splinter the blade.

His weapon rendered useless, Gam fell to his knees. 'Mercy, Glyndŵr!'

Maredydd signalled to Ieuan. 'See to him.'

Rhys sounded a final note on his horn. It was over. Ieuan watched Maredydd walk away, keeping his identity to himself, just as their father had ordered.

CHAPTER SIX

Carmarthenshire, June 1401
Trembling too much to trust his feet on the ground Ieuan called to a group of archers and ordered them to bind Gam. They stretched out Gam's arms and fastened his wrists to a stout section of silver birch they jammed between his elbows. When Gam was trussed like a chicken for market they marched him off to an English tent along with the other captives who were capable of walking.

Rhys stationed men around the perimeter of the tent before joining Ieuan, who'd remained mounted, lest the men see just how shaken he'd been by the battle.

The glade the English had occupied was littered with bodies. Some groaned and twitched, most were still and silent and it was obvious they would never move again. The spring grass was trampled, sodden and crimson with blood that had pooled in places and stood proud on patches of rock.

Maredydd returned without his Glyndŵr armour, tabard or battle banner. 'Your horse is bleeding, Ieuan.'

'I know.' Ieuan wrenched open a saddlebag and pulled out his spare tunic. Hoping Maredydd wouldn't see how unsteady he was, he dismounted and slid to the ground. He pressed his tunic against his horse's rump.

Maredydd was at his elbow. 'You're lucky. It's not that deep. Your squire can stitch it. Are, you, all right?'

Ieuan stared uncomprehendingly at his brother. He could see his lips moving, he could hear him, but he couldn't understand a word he was saying.

Maredydd gripped his arm. 'It's all right to feel sick.'

That Ieuan understood. He nodded.

'I couldn't eat for days after my first battle. I was fine when I was fighting. Afterwards I couldn't walk straight, think straight, or talk sense, and I'm not feeling too good now.'

'You're not saying that to make me feel better?'

Maredydd shook his head. 'Aside from making me vomit, fighting leaves me shaking, confused and asking questions that have no answer. Such as, "how did I survive when better men didn't?"'

Ieuan turned aside and retched.

'But sick and confounded as I undoubtedly was and am, Ruthyn and Denbigh taught me the dead need to be piled for burying or burning, the wounded tended and any enemy in one piece identified in case they're worth ransoming.' Maredydd helped Ieuan to stand upright. 'I also need to ensure that the ropes that bind Gam have been tied tightly.'

The battle hardened archers had lit torches in the enemy campfires and were already moving among the enemy dead, searching the bodies and stripping them of coins, shoes, weapons, shields, uniforms, arm bands, and everything useable worth scavenging.

Maredydd entered the prison tent, Ieuan remained where he stood, lifted his visor and looked up at the sky. The sun had dropped below the trees, leaving only the faintest rim of cold light.

'My lord,' Rhys walked over to him with a priest. 'This is father Wyn.'

The priest bowed to Ieuan who acknowledged him.

'May I speak to you on behalf of the villagers, lords?' Father Wyn asked.

'Of course,' Rhys answered.

'When we saw you heading for this camp, a few of us followed. More will be on their way to retrieve those taken captive by the English,' the priest began. 'But there's a problem. If the women have been defiled, some of their families won't take them back.'

'Whatever happened to them, is none of their doing.' Ieuan's worst fear was that he'd never see Lizzie again in this life, but he couldn't stop hoping. And if he was fortunate enough to find her, he was sure he'd still love her, no matter what she'd done, or what had been done to her.

'I agree.' Maredydd returned and led Ieuan and Rhys aside. 'Now is not the time to argue right from wrong with the villagers, Ieuan. Rhys and I have to question the English captives and determine which ones are worth ransoming.'

'And which, if any, hold information we can use.' Rhys ran his forefinger down his blade, slicing the skin, opening a shallow cut that dripped blood.

'Go with the priest, Ieuan, do what you can for the captives and help return the goods and livestock to the villagers. If they refuse to accept the girls, we'll have to take them with us,' Maredydd said. 'We may pass farms looking to employ workers.'

'And if we don't?' Ieuan asked.

'There are always nunneries and brothels looking to recruit,' Rhys answered. 'Women generally suit one or the other.'

Ieuan followed the priest to where the girls were sitting. A middle-aged man in a beer stained tunic was screaming at one of them.

'You're no wife of mine, whore! I'd rather see you dead than the state you're in.' He kicked her, lifting her skirts with the toe of his boot. Her bare legs were streaked with filth and blood. He cleared his throat and aimed a streak of spittle at her.

The girl glared at him, ran her hands over the gob of phlegm that had landed in her hair scooped it up and flung it back at him.

The priest raised his hand between the man and his wife. 'Mair has been through enough ... '

'You should be fighting the English, not your wife or the priest,' Ieuan admonished.

'And who are you to tell me what to do, pup!' The man squared up to Ieuan.

'He fought to rescue our women, Maldwyn. The boy has earned our gratitude and respect,' the priest reminded him gently.

'He,' Mair pointed to her husband, 'told the soldiers they could take me if they left him and his stock alone . . .'

'You lying, swiving . . . '

'You're a coward who thinks more of your sheep, goats pigs and hens than your wife,' she shouted furiously.

'Christianity is founded on forgiveness,' the priest intoned. 'Mair has suffered enough. Maldwyn, remember your marriage vows.'

'I'd as soon take a snake to my bed than her. She's soiled, filthy . . . '

When half a dozen men from the village muttered noisy agreement with Maldwyn, Ieuan stepped in front of Mair.

'If anyone wishes to claim their relatives, please do so. If the "tax collectors" took your livestock or property and you recognise it here, ask one of the Prince of Wales's captains to help you retrieve what is yours.'

Ieuan's prompt had the desired effect. Most men went to the carts. The girls who'd been taken captive stayed where they were.

One brave woman ignored her husband, stepped forward and embraced her daughter. She released her, and looked to her husband who eventually gave a grudging nod. Slowly, gradually, others followed suit. Eventually the only woman left was Mair.

Feeling sorry for the girl Ieuan said, 'if you have nowhere to go, you're welcome to travel with us.'

'I'll not be your whore.'

He gave a wry smile. 'I have one woman in my bed. Another would crowd it.' It was the first time he'd publicly admitted to sleeping with Efa, and he felt more relieved than shamed by the confession.

'If not your whore, then what would I be?' Mair demanded.

'A friend?' he suggested. 'We'll be passing farms and villages that need workers to do an honest day's work for an honest day's pay. If none suit, you can search until something does. In the meantime you look as though you could eat.'

The girl stared at him for a moment before rising to her feet.

Glyndŵr's camp, the lower slopes of Cadair Idris June 1401

'I'm proud of Maredydd,' Owain's whisper sounded loud in the darkness of his pavilion as he opened the chest that held his clothes, 'but being proud doesn't blind me to the risk he took in attacking Gam's party.'

'You left him and Rhys Ddu in charge. It was you who gave them the authority to make decisions.' Margaret moved closer to the warmth he'd left in their makeshift bed.

'I thought Rhys Ddu was of a more cautious mind than Maredydd. I was wrong.'

'So you blame Maredydd . . . '

'Only a petty minded fool would blame the boy for success. I'm not angry but I am afraid for him. He weighed the risks, fought valiantly and coolly and led the men well. But I can't deny he was reckless. Every time I think of the risks he took in attacking Gam's camp I imagine the worst outcome. I tremble at the thought of losing him or any one of my sons in battle. Just the thought is enough to . . . '

'What, Owain?' Margaret prompted when he stopped speaking.

'In twenty years of fighting in the king's service, I've seen too many men - good men, close friends I loved, die.' He closed the chest and tossed the clothes he'd removed on top of it. 'But they were men not children.'

'Your sons are men.'

'I find it hard to accept that they are old enough to make their own choices when it comes to life and death.'

'Yet you mock me for thinking of them as boys.'

'Gentle mocking, and I won't do it again.' He leaned over the bed and kissed her lips.

'I'll hold you to that,' she smiled, watching as he stepped into his braies.'

'That girl Maredydd rescued and Ieuan is so fond of talking to . . . '

'Mair?' Margaret interrupted.

'Do you know she's refused offers of work from farmers, brewers and bakers, in every village we've passed through?'

'Yes, but Enyd and I are keeping her busy. '

'Doing what?' Owain asked suspiciously.

'Helping where help is needed.'

'You're a soft touch. I believe if Satan himself turned up at this pavilion hungry you'd offer him a meal in exchange for stoking the cook fires.' Owain turned up the wick in the oil lamp. The flame flared, shedding light into the corner where he kept his blades.

Although he was turned away from Margaret, Owain sensed her looking at him from the bed and waited for her to speak.

'You'll watch your back?'

'Maredydd will do it as closely as you are now, which is why I'm taking him with me.' Owain buckled on his sword belt. 'I intend to return before nightfall but don't worry if I don't. Should our friend keep faith, we'll have a great deal to discuss and I'm leaving you in good hands. Dafydd will see to everything here.'

'If Maredydd will be watching your back, who's watching his?'

'We'll watch one another's. It's an opportunity for me to talk to him. It's time he was given a grounding in diplomacy and statesmanship.'

'Rebellion and trouble making more like,' Margaret amended lightly.

'History teaches us that today's rebels are tomorrow's rulers. I need to tell him about Henry Dwn's support.'

'Dwn's a good man and good friend,' Margaret lay back on the pillows but continued to watch him.

'I'm sorry I disturbed you. Go back to sleep.' Owain lowered the wick in the oil lamp and bent to kiss Margaret again. He missed her mouth in the gloom and hit her nose with his forehead.

'Ow!'

'Forgive my head for being harder than yours,' he apologised.

'In more senses than one as I've discovered over the years.' She reached up and stroked his cheek.

He held her hand for a moment. 'Please, go back to sleep, my love.'

***

Owain brushed aside the curtain that separated their private quarters from the rest of the pavilion and opened the flap. It was a clear, star studded night. The moon hung low in a lapis lazuli sky, a rich golden orb that illuminated the rocky slopes of Cadair Idris that towered over their camp.

'My lord.' Dafydd's stocky silhouette rose from the ground next to the campfire. 'Maredydd is waiting for you at the outer pickets, but I would rest easier if you would allow me to accompany you.'

'I need you to keep my lady and everyone here safe in my absence, Dafydd. But even if that wasn't the case, my son would think I didn't trust him to watch my flank if you were with us.'

'Then God go with you, my lord.'

'And be with you and all here, Dafydd.' Owain strode off.

Maredydd was at the outer guard post. He fell in step beside his father. Together they began the steep climb up the stone strewn terraces that bordered the Nant Cadair river that flowed from the summit.

They walked in silence, treading carefully on the loose gravel, avoiding the larger boulders lest they send them tumbling to the foot of the mountain and alert hidden watchers. The river dropped suddenly when the cliff face sheared, creating foaming falls that drowned the sound of their steps, and formed shallow pools that reflected star and moonlight in between the rocks.

Owain smiled when he remembered Margaret christening them "glimpses of heaven" when she'd seen them during a night visit they'd made to the mountain the year of their marriage.

He felt at home and at ease, as he always did in the wilderness of his homeland. Neither the night nor the majesty of Snowdonia held any terrors for him. Even as a boy he'd sought solitude and solace in night walks in the hills and mountains.

Familiar sounds closed around him. The scampering of hares over grass and stony ground. The heavier hooves of stray sheep and goats. The eerie mating calls of vixens, so like children's cries, were joined by the whoop of an owl as it swooped over the slope in search of prey.

After two hours of steady climbing they stopped to drink, stretch their aching legs and rub their protesting calf muscles. Owain lay back on a moss covered stone and studied the sky. The moon was fading, losing its light as it sank beneath a peak, allowing the stars greater prominence.

'Are we going as far as the summit?' Maredydd's question broke his train of thought.

'No.' Owain spoke softly. 'And you've reached the end of your climb. There's a fork in the path ahead.'

'I know it. One track leads to Mynydd Moel and Pen y Gadair the other to Llyn Cau lake.'

'I'm heading for the lake. No matter what you hear, don't follow. The land can be treacherous.'

'Boggy marsh,' Maredydd said. 'The last time I was here Gruffydd showed me the stones that mark a safe route.'

Owain shivered as the last vestige of moon disappeared behind the mountains. A breeze blew moist and chill. 'We may not be as alone as we intend to be. '

'All the more reason for me to follow you.'

'I know the mountain, and I'm not too old to defend myself or run and hide, and neither is the one I hope to meet.' Owain dug into the leather bag he carried on his shoulder and pulled out a waxed linen bag. 'Food. Take the empty bag back to Enyd, or you'll have your mother to answer to.' He handed it to Maredydd. 'You have your flask?'

'Filled with small beer, yes.'

'No gwisgi?'

Maredydd sheepishly produced a smaller flask.

'Wrap your cloak closer. It won't rain, but the morning mist is damp here.'

'You're leaving now, in the dark?'

Owain pointed upwards and Maredydd saw a pale silver streak haloing the rim of the mountain. He looked at his boots and realised the approaching dawn had already lifted the light from dark to pale grey at ground level.

'Remember, no matter what you hear, don't follow me. If I don't return by mid-afternoon go to the camp. Tell Dafydd I was heading for the south side of Llyn Cau.'

Before Maredydd could answer, Owain was swallowed by the mist that rolled down the mountain.

Cadair Idris, Snowdonia early June 1401
Owain continued climbing, trusting to memory more than his eyes. The fog grew gradually denser until he could no longer see his feet when he stepped forward. The world was cloaked in a thick shimmering grey that resembled sea water more than waterlogged air, making it impossible to decipher landmarks or gauge distances.

He found himself ankle deep in the lake before he realised he was close to it.

'Are you drowned,' drawled a familiar voice.

'Most of me is above water. Where are you?'

'Where we agreed.'

'Where am I standing?'

'By the sound of your voice, north of south.'

Owain stepped gingerly forward and found himself on the bank.

He followed the direction of the voice. The mist splintered and he saw Hotspur's slim figure perched on a boulder at the water's edge.

'Gwisgi?' Hotspur handed him a leather flask. 'It won't dry your boots but it will do wonders for your blood and stomach.'

'Thank you.' Owain took it and pulled the stopper.

Hotspur removed a sealed parchment from his leather satchel and handed it to Owain. 'Don't read it now, but later, when you receive news of the battle our forces fought so valiantly when they met this day on the slopes of this mountain. Your friend and mine, John Irly, bore witness to the action. He will give Bolingbroke a first-hand account when he next sees him.'

'Who won?'

'Me of course, but it was close and there was fierce hand to hand combat between your men and mine. Long and bloody.'

'I protest the outcome. My volunteers have better reason to fight and are vastly superior to your mercenaries.'

'As they're not likely to meet again, even in our imagination, you can tell your volunteers they won.'

'That's generous of you. No doubt I'll hear rumours of the clash soon, just as I've heard that you've left Conwy to the Tudors?'

'I've left Conwy but not to the Tudors. They're surrounded by Prince Hal's forces and stuck in the castle but not for much longer. They sent an emissary who visited Prince Hal and me secretly. He carried papers that bore the signatures of Rhys and Gwilym Tudor pleading with us to negotiate a surrender they could live with. When I rode away Prince Hal was discussing terms with them.'

'I imagine the Tudors would like to walk away, if only out of sheer boredom. There are only so many things you can do in a besieged castle.'

'Prince Hal and I wanted to offer the Tudors and their followers a full pardon on surrender, but the tradesmen and people in Conwy would have none of it. When they heard we were considering allowing them to leave the castle without punishment, they screamed for compensation for their goods and buildings.'

'Understandable, if half of what my brother told me about the damage our cousins wrought was true.'

'Knowing your brother, I doubt he exaggerated. Especially as according to the people I spoke to, a fair amount of that damage was inflicted by him. I also heard your son Gruffydd was with him.'

Owain shrugged. 'You English can't tell one Welshman from another. It's your standard excuse whenever we prove you've hung an innocent man.'

'Prince Hal wrote to his father and suggested we offer the Tudors and their followers inside the castle six months immunity from prosecution followed by a fair trial with mixed Welsh and English jurors.'

'That would be a compromise.' Owain lowered himself on to a large boulder close to Hotspur's.

'Bolingbroke didn't think so. He insisted 300 archers and 120 men at arms remain in Conwy to hold the siege and mete out, "just desserts" to the miscreants when we lay our hands on them.'

The mist cleared enough for Owain to see Hotspur raise an eyebrow.

'That sounds ominous.'

'The king's steward, Arnold Savage wants blood and won't be satisfied with anything less. Unfortunately, he has Bolingbroke's ear. Savage demands the Tudors and a dozen of their supporters be drawn, disembowelled, hanged, beheaded and quartered in front of the castle walls in full view of the populace.'

'No doubt Savage believes taking a hard line with the Tudors will win him Bolingbroke's favour.' Hoping to send the blood circulating to his wet and frozen feet, Owain reached for the gwisgi flask again.

'Young Hal and I pleaded for the Tudors' lives on the grounds that public torture and executions would be more likely to incite further rebellion among the Welsh than quell it. As the rising son who will one day occupy Bolingbroke's throne, Hal was better placed than me to argue for leniency, but unfortunately he was just as unsuccessful.'

'Did you really expect Bolingbroke and Savage to show compassion?'

'We hoped reason would win. But Savage is out for blood which is why I left Hal to deal with the details of the Tudors' surrender. If I'd stayed any longer I'd have happily hung, drawn, disembowelled and quartered Savage.'

'What chance do my cousins have of escaping with their lives?'

'Better than they deserve after the problems they've caused. Their emissary said Rhys and Gwilym have received offers from several followers who are willing to suffer the ultimate punishment in their place. Some are old, some sick, but even those who aren't, are ready to sacrifice their lives for their lords.'

'Knowing my cousins, whoever the volunteers, their families will be well cared for after their execution. I bow to their bravery after watching Thomas Usk suffer the ultimate punishment at Tyburn in March 1388. It took thirty strokes of the axe to sever his head.'

'So I heard.'

Owain shuddered as though he were trying to shake off the memory.

'Have you heard much news of late?' Hotspur continued.

'Plenty. What news were you thinking of?' Owain asked.

'The 1500 strong army of Flemish mercenaries the English settlers in Pembroke have recruited and paid to kill you, destroy your army and end the Glyndŵr raids on their county.'

'Sounds like Philip Hanmer and my son David have had some success in looting the Pembroke farms,' Owain smiled.

'They made the Fleming farmers angry enough to put their hands in their purses, which in Fleming terms is very angry indeed.'

'Did your news say which way this army of Flemish mercenaries is headed?'

'Elenydd.'

Hotspur's revelation shook Owain but he was too well schooled to allow his emotions to show. "Elenydd" was the ancient name for the heartlands of the Cambrian mountains. Someone had betrayed him, either one of the men Tudor had recruited to help him set up their headquarters or one of his captains who'd received his confidences at Carmarthen. 'I thought they'd head for Snowdonia,' he said casually.

'Here! Is that where . . . no don't tell me. I don't want to know.' Hotspur drank from the gwisgi flask Owain returned to him.

'And you, my friend?' Owain asked.

'What about me?' Hotspur answered warily.

'You are here and not in Conwy. Do you intend to return there?'

'Not unless the devil sends me back. God would be more forgiving of my sins.'

'You're heading for London?'

'To do more of Bolingbroke's bidding. No, damn him,' Hotspur was vehement.

'Then what?' Owain asked.

'Peace, if I can find it. I've had enough of arguing with Bolingbroke and emptying my treasury to pay men to wage his wars when he's proved himself more unjust than Richard ever was. After a surfeit of fighting and bloodshed enough to last a dozen lifetimes, I'm for Northumberland.'

'Home to your wife and family?' Owain experienced a rare taste of envy when he realised anew, that the peace, familiarity and comfort of Sycharth and Glyndyfrdwy was lost to him and forever relegated to his past.

'God knows how I hunger for the sight of my wife, and to feast my eyes on her and my children and hold them close. Elizabeth will be six in October and young Henry is eight. I can count on one hand the number of quiet days I have spent at home with them and my wife.'

'I'd hazard it's about the same number I've spent with my family.'

'You and I have grown old fighting the wars of kings, Owain. But age has caught up with us. It's time to hang up our blades.'

'I'd agree with you if I didn't have one last war to fight.' Owain looked across the lake. The mist had gathered on the opposite bank forming a wall of impenetrable grey that appeared as solid and substantial as that of a castle keep.

'Do you believe you can win?' Hotspur asked suddenly.

'I wouldn't be fighting if I didn't.' Owain took another sip of gwisgi from Hotspur's flask and handed it back to him. 'You don't?' he asked.

'I know your skill and admire your determination as a soldier. I believe your cause to be a just one, and if heaven allows good to triumph over evil you will win. But I have lived too long and seen too many wrongs that have violated God's and man's laws to expect right to win simply because it deserves to.'

'The outcome for the house of Glyndŵr and the Welsh nation is in God's hands.'

Hotspur narrowed his eyes. 'That sounds like an answer you give to a question you don't wish to think about.'

'If I don't wish to think about it, it's because I've staked all I possess including my family's lives and my sons' inheritance on the outcome of this war. The money, land, manors and estates are nothing, but my family and friends' wellbeing are beyond price.'

'Beyond price indeed. Yet the king has placed a high one on your head.'

Owain's smile was sardonic. 'In gold or so I've heard.'

'Doesn't it concern you?'

'For myself, no. For my family and friends, yes. After watching Arundel lose his head on an executioner's block I know the price a king exacts when he seeks to assuage his anger in blood. Which is why I tremble for my Tudor cousins.'

'You do not fear betrayal?'

'Not from my countrymen and women.'

'And you will carry on fighting?' Hotspur persisted.

'It's the only course open to me.'

'You'll be meeting Bolingbroke soon?'

'In one guise or another,' Owain answered.

'But not in drawn battle?'

'We Welsh fight in other ways.'

'More devious ones as I've discovered to my cost.'

'Which is why I'll say no more than I already have of my plans.' Owain stretched out his hand to Hotspur. 'Good journey, my friend, and my respects to Elizabeth and your children. May you find the peace and solace you seek with them.'

'And mine to Margaret and your children.' Hotspur linked his arm into Owain's as they gripped their hands in farewell. 'Take care my friend. My brother in arms.' Hotspur's voice was thick with supressed emotion.

'May we meet again and soon, but never swords drawn against one another.'

'Amen to that. Tell your men to keep a look out for Welsh women who carry messages in their heads. You have your coin?'

Owain produced his groat, as did Hotspur. They exchanged them, yet again.

'God go with you to Northumberland.'

'And you to your camp - don't tell me where it is,' Hotspur warned.

'I didn't intend to.' Owain turned, and retraced his steps, when he looked back Hotspur's silhouette had faded into the mist. He shuddered . . . a reaction to the ice that had caused the haze . . . or a premonition of what lay ahead?

Glyncoch Valley Berwyn Mountains, Wales third week of June 1401

Owain and Margaret reined in their horses at the top of the pass and waited for their escort to catch up. A cleft in the rocks gave a panoramic view of the wooded slopes that led down to the river that meandered over the valley floor. Hills boxed it in on all sides except for two narrow passes. One in the northern hills, the other between two hills in the south west.

Owain compared it to the valley in Snowdonia where he'd over wintered in a cave. Miles apart, yet surprisingly similar and for his and his army's purposes, reassuringly secluded.

'You could search these hills for months and not find this valley,' Margaret commented.

'That's the idea,' Owain said.

A rough built, square stone house, its slate roof inexpertly patched with green thatch stood in a horseshoe bend in the river. Men and women were working around it, repairing a sprinkling of primitive stone and wood "cot" houses.

No fields had been marked off but scores of cattle were grazing on the lush grasslands of the valley floor. Sheep and goats had been herded on to the higher slopes by shepherds and their dogs.

'Looks like someone has been busy collecting livestock.' Rhys Ddu drew his horse to a halt alongside Owain's.

'It looks like we won't be going hungry, but the houses need work before the autumn rains sweep in,' Owain eyed them critically. 'The weather here can be cold, cruel and wet.'

'You've attracted plenty of volunteers to carry out the repairs, but I'll not answer for their building skills,' Rhys Ddu commented.

'We have time on our side.' Maredydd joined them and pointed to the head of the valley behind the house. The tents Philip and John Hanmer had scavenged had been set up in military style formation.

'I hope they're expecting guests for dinner.' Dafydd kicked his heels into his mount's flanks. 'I could eat one of those beasts without any help.'

'You may have to earn your supper, Dafydd.' Owain narrowed his eyes as he looked to the north. A lone horseman stood on the crest of the hill. As he watched, the sun's rays glinted on his breastplate sending a flash of light across the valley, as a line of riders drew in their mounts alongside him.

CHAPTER SEVEN

Glyndŵr's Headquarters Glyncoch Valley Berwyn Mountains, Wales June 1401

Gwilym was waiting at the door of the house for Owain and ran out to meet him before he'd dismounted.

'I've tried to make the house comfortable, my lord but it's not Sycharth or Glyndyfrdwy ... '

Owain interrupted his steward's apologies. 'There are men on the hills ... '

'I know, my lord.'

'Has Tudor ridden out to meet them?' Owain demanded.

'They are Tudor's men, my lord. He left here to scout the hills two days ago. He sent a messenger this morning to inform us that he was riding in from the north with guests, and they'd be here by supper time.'

'Did Tudor say who the guests were?'

'No, my lord, but the cooks are doing their best to produce a feast.' '

'Are you sure they're Tudor's party? They carried no banner?' Owain commented.

'Tudor passed down an order that no identifying banners, flags or livery are to be worn or carried within these hills, my lord.'

'Which only makes sense if we know the whereabouts of our men at all times. Otherwise we run the risk of killing our own.' Owain dismounted and lifted Margaret from her palfrey.

Gwilym followed Owain and Margaret inside the building. 'I apologise, my lord, my lady, this house is sadly wanting.'

'The house may be wanting, Gwilym, but not for hard work on your part.' Margaret looked around the hall and staircase.

'It's ancient, damp and mouldering, my lady.'

'Given the amount of rain that falls on Wales find me a dwelling in this land that isn't waterlogged, and I'll move into it, Gwilym.' Margaret unlaced her woollen cloak and handed it to Enyd who'd followed her into the ante chamber.

'I've managed to accommodate most of the officers in the outbuildings, cottages and tents within easy distance of the house,' Gwilym continued. 'Dewi sent stonemasons to repair the shepherds' huts on the mountains for the lookouts. They'll start work as soon as they finish this place.'

'What prompted Tudor to lead a scouting party?' Owain asked Gwilym.

'A shepherd told us he'd sighted a score of armed men heading this way. Lord Tudor left to intercept them before they reached here.'

'The shepherd was sure it was a small party?' Owain checked.

'He was most insistent he'd counted every one of them, my lord.'

'What of Glyndyfrdwy and Sycharth?' Margaret asked.

'Both manors have been stripped as far as possible, my lady,' Gwilym assured her. 'All the tapestries on these walls have come from one house or the other. I didn't order them to be hung to improve the look of the place. I've never known such a cold and windblown building. The hangings haven't stopped all the draughts but they've muted the whistling.'

'We had more than these. What happened to them and the rest of the furnishings?' Margaret asked.

'Regrettably we had to leave some of the larger items in the houses, my lady, including the tables, chairs, beds, dressers and clothes presses. Lords Hanmer, Llewelyn ap Gruffydd Fychan and Gruffydd Glyndŵr sent carts to ferry the smaller items, to their houses. They will store them until you have need of them again.'

'That was good of them,' Owain commented.

'Pray we need them again soon,' Margaret added. 'You brought all our personal items here?' she asked Gwilym.

'Of course, my lady. You will find your books, jewels and garments in your chamber. I don't doubt Enyd is improving my arrangement of them this minute.'

'We all have our own ways, Gwilym. Thank you for transporting them.'

'Your silver and pewter plate, goblets, and knives are in the kitchens and great hall, my lady.'

Owain glanced around the cramped ante-chamber that held a table, two benches, a chair, and pile of logs that left little space in which to move. A fire smouldered in the hearth sending more smoke than warmth into the room. Wooden and metal candlesticks stood on the mantelshelf above it.

To his knowledge Hanmer had never lived in, or visited the manor. After days spent travelling to reach Glyncoch - the red glen - possibly named after a forgotten battle, he understood why. A long ride across rough country from the nearest road, the valley wasn't a place a casual traveller would stumble across, or someone acquainted with it would want to revisit. The house itself, had been sorely neglected.

The chamber they were in, like the outer hall was freezing cold with condensation running down the inside walls. He was grateful to his brother-in-law, but he would have been more grateful if the building had possessed a sound roof, walls, and the luxury of modern chimneys.

The front door opened and voices echoed in.

'Tudor and Gruffydd,' Margaret smiled. 'I'm not critical of anything you've done, Gwilym, but could you show me the bedrooms please? I'd like to keep as many family as close as possible.'

'I'll give you a tour, my lady.'

'At least we have a table to lay out our maps,' Maredydd commented.

'There are larger tables in the great hall, lord, although the chamber should be referred to as the "small hall." It's the most inadequate "great" hall I've seen and not what you're used to.' Gwilym couldn't have been more apologetic if he was personally responsible for its shortfalls.

He opened a door concealed in the panelling of the ante chamber. It led into a chamber less than a third the size of Glyndyfrdwy's hall. Tudor and Gruffydd strode in from the outer porch making it seem even smaller than it was. Three young girls entered behind them.

Owain knew his brother had an eye for young women, but these appeared to be barely out of childhood. Then he recognised Lewellyn ap Gruffydd's, dark eyed and haired, eldest daughter Jonnet who was betrothed to Gruffydd. One he didn't recognise was slender with brilliant green eyes and loose auburn hair. The third was his daughter Catrin.

'And pray may I ask what you ladies are doing here?' Owain demanded of Catrin.

Catrin tilted her chin and looked him directly in the eye. Owain stifled a smile. He'd seen the same look of bravado and defiance on the faces of twelve year old squires facing their first battle.

'It's not our fault, father,' Catrin replied. 'Uncle Hanmer had a letter from . . . '

Tudor gave her a warning look before taking control of the conversation. 'Rhys Coch and Poulson stopped off at Hanmer on their return journey from the north. Catrin was missing you . . . '

'. . . And mother,' Catrin interrupted, sidling up to Margaret seeking support. 'So I asked Uncle Hanmer if I could travel back here with Uncle Poulson. I knew you'd want me to travel with an armed escort and Uncle Hanmer kindly agreed to allow Elwy to keep me company.'

'Rhys and Poulson broke their journey from Hanmer at Caeo,' Tudor continued. 'A messenger arrived there from Rhys Fierce in Powys, requesting assistance. Rhys Coch went to his aid and Llew loaned Poulson men at arms so he, Catrin and Elwy . . . '

'Could continue our journey here. Jonnet begged her father's permission to travel with us. Uncle Llew agreed, and here we are,' Catrin finished gleefully.

'Elwy,' Owain studied the girl he'd failed to recognise as his younger brother Gruffydd's daughter. 'I apologise, you've grown somewhat since I last saw you.' He kissed his niece's cheek.

'It comes to something when you don't recognise your own flesh and blood, brother.' Tudor chided Owain,

'How lovely to see you, Elwy. You've grown half a head taller since I saw you at Christmas,' Margaret kissed the girl, Catrin and Jonnet.

'So mother said. But I rather not grow any taller if I can help it. I already tower above my brothers.'

'Give them a few more years and it will be the other way around. In the meantime we could always tie a large stone to your head,' Tudor joked. 'But I'm pleased to see you don't bear the slightest resemblance to your father.'

'Is that meant to be a compliment, Uncle Tudor?' Elwy asked.

'It is. You only have to look at me to see I'm the best looking brother, not that your uncle Owain is ugly, but your father.' Tudor shook his head. 'He wasn't only last in line in age but also looks. That's not to say you resemble your mother either.'

Tudor's remark earned him a frown from Margaret.

'By that I mean you look very like your grandmother Elen,' Tudor added hastily. 'And she was very beautiful.'

'She certainly was,' Margaret agreed.

'I heard a small but well-armed party of men was heading this way so I went out to meet them expecting foes and finding friends,' Tudor explained to Owain. 'Poulson was leading them and he agreed that as you and Margaret were expected here, the girls should be entrusted to you as soon as possible.' Tudor went to a table that held a row of goblets.

'I have missed you, father, mother.' Catrin gave her parents a bright artificial smile.

Margaret shook her head at Maredydd who was staring open eyed and mouthed at Elwy. 'You are most welcome, Elwy and Jonnet for your own as well as your families' sake. Catrin, I trust your Aunt Hanmer didn't send you away because she was tired of your antics.'

'I was a perfect lady in Hanmer, mother. Ask Ina if you don't believe me.'

'I will.'

'Llew didn't want to keep the girls at Caeo?' Owain asked.

'As they were intent on visiting you and Margaret, he didn't want to disappoint them, and you know these three. What is it your uncle Gruffydd Hanmer calls you, Catrin?'

'The unholy trinity,' Catrin laughed.

'I don't think you quite caught the inflection he uses when you said that, niece,' Tudor said.

'My lord, my lady.' Poulson entered and bowed.

'Thank you for bringing my daughter, godchild and niece safely here, Poulson.'

'It was a pleasure, my lord.'

'Is that a smile on your face, Poulson?' Tudor asked. 'The memory of witnessing their tutors celebrating the departure of their charges perhaps?'

'We've had enough deportment, music and dancing lessons, this winter to last us a lifetime.' Catrin made a face that set her brothers sniggering, 'so it's only fair our tutors have had enough of us.'

'It was good of Aunt Hanmer to oversee your education,' Margaret rebuked her daughter.

'I presume Aunt Hanmer didn't set aside enough time for riding, hunting, archery and chasing squires to suit your ladyships?' Tudor's teasing earned him a scowl from Margaret as well as Catrin.

Hoping to change the subject, Owain asked Poulson, 'How is Llew?'

'Disgruntled. Complaining that his wife and daughters treat him like an old man in his dotage by smothering him with unwanted attention.'

'Then I take it he's well?'

'He appeared to be, my lord. He and his entire family, send you, Lord Tudor and your lady their respects and wishes for good health,' Poulson answered.

'The steward has prepared chambers for us and he was about to show me the house, which is as new to me as it is to you,' Margaret said to the girls. 'Would you care to come with us, and choose your own quarters?'

'Yes please, Aunt Margaret.' Elwy glanced shyly at Maredydd. He gave her a broad wink and she flushed crimson before following Margaret and Gwilym out of the door.

Gruffydd gave Jonnet a small smile as she and Catrin left. Owain and Tudor saw it as they did Maredydd's wink but they allowed both to pass without comment.

'Why did Hanmer choose to send Catrin and Elwy to us now, with the country poised to rise and the battle season about to open?' Owain asked as soon as the door closed behind Margaret and the girls. 'And Llew - I thought he would have known better than to send Jonnet.'

'They know the situation, my lord. Lord Gruffydd spoke to me at length in confidence.' Poulson was married to Owain's sister, Lowri, and was his brother-in-law as well as captain. 'He wanted the girls away from Hanmer because he received word from Bolingbroke's court the day before Rhys Ddu and I arrived. The king is expected in Wales any day and as all three ladies are of marriageable age - '

'And two betrothed to my sons and the third is my daughter Catrin, he wanted them out of Bolingbroke's reach. I hope God will allow us to keep them safe.'

'Why shouldn't he?' Tudor asked.

'You're not the only one with news,' Owain said. 'We'll talk later.'

'Lord Llewelyn suggested Elwy, Jonnet and Catrin should be sent to the convent at Llanllyr as even Henry would balk at searching a nunnery. He told me he received word from a friend at court, that Bolingbroke intends to visit as many Welsh lords as he can, before he meets you on the battlefield, my prince, so he can judge for himself who is loyal to him and who is not,' Poulson said.

'The girls seemed to assume they were staying here,' Owain said.

'I would play the coward if I found myself in Llew's and Gruffydd's place. Can you imagine the girls' reaction if they suspected they were being taken to a convent? Besides you won't be able to keep this one from our brother's daughter forever, Owain.' Tudor clamped his hand on Maredydd's shoulder. 'For all that they're cousins I've never seen two young people more in love.'

'They may be in love but they still need a dispensation from the pope to marry,' Owain warned.

'You did write to him, father?' Maredydd checked.

'I did and I'm awaiting a reply. You're both very young . . . '

'And growing older every day,' Tudor broke in. 'Have you forgotten what it is to be young and in love, brother?'

'If you're sure you want to take Elwy as your wife . . . '

'I've never been more certain of anything in my life, father,' Maredydd broke in.

'I'd rather leave this conversation for a year or two, but as you're determined,' Owain eyed his younger son before capitulating. 'If the pope should issue you with a dispensation granting you the right to marry Elwy, I'll give you my permission and blessing to wed. But I'm with Llew and your uncle. The safest place for the girls at the moment is the convent.'

'Not before we've secured the area to ensure the roads are safe,' Poulson warned.

'As soon as that's done they'll be on their way.' Owain turned to his eldest son. 'Are you of a mind to marry Jonnet soon, Gruffydd?'

'I'd prefer to get to know her before we exchange vows, father,' Gruffydd replied.

'That's a cold blooded answer for a Glyndŵr,' Tudor mocked.

'I'd rather be called cold blooded than risk a wife I can't get on with like . . . '

'No need to say more. I can see you've been talking to David. I doubt conversation with Jonnet will warm your blood or attitude. I'd try something else if I were you,' Tudor examined the goblets set out on a side table.

'You're not me, Uncle Tudor . . . '

'As for you, Maredydd,' Owain interrupted before the conversation between Tudor and Gruffydd grew any sharper, 'it's as well you bear in mind that applying for a dispensation is no guarantee the pope will give you one.' Owain pulled a chair close to one of the fires.

Tudor took a small barrel from a footman and set it beside the goblets. 'A gift, Owain, from the abbot of Strata Florida with his compliments after Gruffydd and I enjoyed his hospitality. He suggested you share this barrel with your captains to toast your new quarters and the success of your summer campaign.'

'No doubt you can vouch for its quality.'

'You know me brother, and this wine is as good as the news Gruffydd and I carry.' Tudor removed the cork from the barrel.

***

'It's little wonder Bolingbroke is heading into Wales. The whole of Ceredigion and Powys have declared themselves for the Prince. The cry of "Glyndŵr, our rightful prince," rings out in the most isolated farms and villages. And . . . ' Tudor glanced at Poulson, 'we heard first-hand how Glyndŵr, the Prince of Wales in the guise of Rhys Coch and Poulson made your presence felt in the North.'

'As Poulson has just arrived, who told you about the events in the North and how do you know about Ceredigion and Powys?' Owain asked his brother.

Tudor grinned at Gruffydd who answered his father.

'We captured a king's messenger.'

'Tudor!' Owain growled.

Tudor beamed at Owain. 'We didn't hurt a hair on his head.'

'What about the rest of him?' Owain demanded.

'You can see for yourself. I ordered him tied hand and foot but that's no more than a sensible precaution. I also ordered the straw be changed on the floor of his cage twice a day, which was generous of me considering the speed we travelled. It's not always easy to find clean straw. The cage is in the stables if you want to check the man's condition. Mind you, the roof in there is leaking so he'll be wet. From what he told us he was on his way from Charleton, Lord of Powys - damn the traitorous bastard for putting England before Wales - to Henry - but he'd also picked up other letters for Henry en route.'

'Where is Henry?' Owain asked.

'The messenger had orders to travel to Worcester but was told to head for Westminster if the king wasn't there. His pouch.' Tudor took a leather satchel from Gruffydd and gave it to Owain who opened it and pulled out six packets.

The seals had been expertly lifted on all of them. Owain didn't have to ask Tudor who'd done it. He'd taught his brother how to open packages and letters when they'd been children. A few seconds over a candle to soften the wax would disguise the fact they'd been tampered with - or read. Owain unfolded the thickest and began to read

'*My most honoured most noble and powerful lord* . . . '

'Etc etc etc etc,' Tudor chanted as he filled the tray of goblets from the wine barrel. 'Why do official letters always begin so tediously?'

Owain ignored Tudor and continued to read aloud. '*The Welsh rebels are challenging your civilian administration, my king, and refusing to pay their fines, debts and rents. They have defected to the rebel prince Owain Lord of Glyndyfrdwy and have risen up with him in armed rebellion seizing numerous castles . . .* '

'Castles?' Maredydd repeated in amusement. He turned to Gruffydd. 'You and Uncle Tudor have taken castles?'

115

'As Uncle Tudor says, there's nothing like a bit of exaggeration in love and war,' Gruffydd answered.

'Charleton must have felt threatened to have sent this to Henry.' Owain continued to read.

'He probably hoped Henry would rush to his side with an army to keep us evil "castle grabbing" Welsh swine at bay.' Tudor cradled his goblet.

' . . . *and Owain Glyndŵr was everywhere plundering and burning the towns inhabited by the English and forcing them to flee. Defections to the rebel leader Glyndŵr are spreading throughout Carmarthenshire* . . . '

'The English are not very bright are they,' Tudor said. '"*And was everywhere*". They still haven't worked out we're putting more than one Glyndŵr in the field at any given time. Do you want me to kill the messenger?'

'No,' Owain answered. 'Dafydd?' he called his squire.

'My lord?'

'See the messenger is washed and given decent clothes and fed, but keep him under lock and key. Is there a high tower?'

'In the gatehouse, my prince,' a footman answered. 'There are secure rooms at the top Gwilym has marked for use as strong rooms.'

'Incarcerate the messenger there, Dafydd, and give the key to Gwilym. Tell him to keep it on his person. No one is to be given access to the man unless Gwilym, you or I are with them.'

'Yes, my prince.' Dafydd bowed and left the hall.

'What do you intend to do with the prisoner?' Tudor asked.

'Nothing for the moment,' Owain answered. 'But he may prove useful should we send a missive to Henry.'

'He was carrying other letters,' Tudor reminded.

Owain unfolded the second one and frowned. 'This is from Hotspur to the king.'

'Isn't Hotspur in Conwy?' Tudor asked.

'Where did you pick up the messenger?'

'On the Hereford road, but you can't read anything into that. We know letters to Henry are channelled through a central collecting point somewhere on the border. We need to find out exactly where.'

'I agree,' Owain concurred. 'A raid there might save us days of reconnoitring.'

'As you'll see from that letter, father, Hotspur claims to have been ambushed by you at Cader Idris on the same day Charleton fought you - or rather Rhys Fierce in the guise of you - at Dinas Mawddwy,' Gruffydd commented.

'I congratulate you on your speed, brother, I thought you were in Carmarthen on that date.'

Owain scanned the letter. 'The fewer people who know my movements, the safer our cause.'

'Agreed. I also know why Hotspur would claim you ambushed him at Cader Idris,' Tudor said. 'I hope Henry never finds out the double game you two are playing. If he should, neither you nor Hotspur will keep your heads.' Tudor leaned over Owain's shoulder and read Hotspur's missive to the king.

'*I see much pillage and mischief in the country . . . All the country is without doubt in great peril of being destroyed by the rebels, if I should leave Conwy before the arrival of my successor, it will be from necessity for I cannot bear the cost I am put to without recompense from you . . .* '

Owain refolded the letter. 'Henry is a fool. How can he expect Hotspur to defend his interests in Wales for no payment other than the glory of having the task entrusted to him?'

'Because he's English, and arrogant and stupid to boot.' Tudor stretched his legs out towards the fire. 'You might find the letter from Charleton to the king's son Prince Hal more amusing.'

Owain eyed Tudor suspiciously before glancing at the remaining letters. Reading the address on the outside, he opened it out on the table.

'*My most honoured, most noble, and powerful lord. I commend myself to your nobility as humbly as I know how or can do honourably with all manner of reverences. And may it please your nobility to know how this past Monday during a chevauchee with my men over the mountains of my country of Powys . . .* '

'Chevauchee?' Owain asked Tudor.

'Charleton burned and destroyed everything he couldn't carry and slaughtered or enslaved every living being he found.' Tudor set his mouth into a thin, hard line. 'Gruffydd and I found a few survivors in hiding and escorted them to Tintern Abbey, but read on, brother.'

'*I divided my good men into many parts with 400 archers and shortly after this we caught sight of Owain and his men on the mountains . . .* '

'You have to commend them on their sight considering they were in Powys and you miles away in the west,' Tudor observed.

Owain scanned the next few lines before continuing to read. '*We chased the said Owain and his men forcibly until the night . . . I do not know his whereabouts for certain at present, but my scouts said that he headed towards K . . .* ' Owain looked Tudor. 'Knighton?' he suggested.

'Who knows,' Tudor answered carelessly. 'You've reached the interesting bit.'

'*In this chase were taken certain prizes of the armour of the said Owain, certain horses and lances and a long drape of painted cloth, as well as his henchmen. These things I intend to send to our lord the king your father. And that night I lodged myself with my other men at M . . .*'

'M?'

Tudor shrugged. 'Your guess is as good as mine.'

' *. . . in order to guard those parts . . . Of this painted cloth I send you a portion through the bearer of this letter.*

'*The remainder has been sent to our lord the king your said father. I have suggested that my lord, the king, your father take his part of this banner the Welsh hold in such esteem and make a nightshirt from it and may I humbly suggest you do the same.*

'And if this thing pleases you coming from me, that it should honour and please you, then I would be pleased to have of your nobility, your most noble orders, as you forever command me in all matters. Most honoured etc. John Charleton to the Prince.'

'How many grovelling "pleases and pleased" can one man put into one sentence?'

'Never enough or it so it seems for John Charleton,' Owain declared.

'You can take it from me brother, when Charleton refers to "the Prince" he is not referring to you,' Tudor said drily, 'although you are reading his missive.'

'That much I gathered. Was the messenger carrying any armour? Not that it would have been mine even if he was.'

'No. If the king asks Charleton what he did with it, I suspect he will say it was too bulky to send with the messenger and too heavy for him to haul any distance so he left it where he captured it.'

Owain frowned. 'What of this cloth?'

Tudor reached for two parcels wrapped in lengths of waxed linen. He unfolded them to reveal two banners, that judging by the rough cut on the edges had once been a single length of cloth.

'A row of maidens with red hands,' Owain stared at the beautifully worked tapestry.

'As Charleton wrote, the two halves were in separate parcels in the mail destined for Bolingbroke and Prince Hal. I haven't heard of Charleton skirmishing with any of our Glyndŵrs or capturing any "esteemed" Welsh treasures. Have you?' Tudor questioned.

'No,' Owain examined the tapestries.

'I talked to "walking women" who carried words from two Rhys', two Philips and John. They all left the captains after the date on this letter of Charleton's. If any group had been attacked the women would have mentioned it. I think

Charleton made up this story of heroics to impress Prince Hal and king,' Tudor declared.

'Probably, but that doesn't explain the origin of this cloth.' Owain called to a footman. 'Find Brother Mark.'

'Yes, my prince.'

'If this banner has any religious significance, the monk may know of it.'

'Could it be connected to Owain Lawgoch, father?' Gruffydd asked.

Owain considered Gruffydd's question. The Welsh still burned at the fate meted out to Owain Lawgoch or "Owain of the Red Hands" as the English called him. The last Welshman before him to lay claim to the title of Prince of Wales, had been murdered twenty two years ago in France, on the orders of the English court.

Richard II's guardians were determined to eradicate the Welsh royal lines. Llewelyn the Great's grandson and heir, Llewelyn the Last had been beheaded. His only legitimate child, his two year old daughter Gwenllian imprisoned in a nunnery to ensure she would die unaware of her heritage - and more importantly childless. Llewelyn's heir, his brother Dafydd, had been hung drawn and quartered in Shrewsbury, and Dafydd's two sons incarcerated in open cages in the grounds of Bristol castle until their deaths to prevent them from procreating, Dafydd's daughter, like her cousin Gwenllian, was cast into a convent.

Owain Lawgoch was the grandson of Llewelyn's brother, Rhodri, who'd been allowed to live after renouncing his inheritance. Owain was a soldier who'd fought for the French. When his father died, he reclaimed his patrimony, only to be killed by the English like his grandfather and uncles.

Some believed Owain Lawgoch's death marked the end of Welsh Royalty. But Llewelyn the Last's bloodline had survived. His mother's paternal grandmother had been Eleanor of England, the legitimate daughter of Edward I, her maternal grandmother was Catherine ferch Llewelyn, the illegitimate daughter of Llewelyn the Last. Unlike the

English the Welsh didn't differentiate between illegitimate and legitimate bloodlines, not even in royalty. Which made him and his sons Owain Lawgoch's heirs and successors.

***

Brother Mark entered the chamber. After bowing to Owain and greeting everyone, he read Charleton's letter to Prince Hal.

'The cloth is very fine wool,' Tudor observed.

'It is, Lord Tudor,' Brother Mark fingered the fabric. 'I have never seen such delicately spun yarn in a tapestry before.'

'Has it any sacred significance?' Owain questioned.

'In ecclesiastical terms, red hands can signify the bearer has fulfilled a great valiant deed, or . . . ' he hesitated.

'Or,' Tudor prompted impatiently.

'Or broken the Lord's commandment, "Thou shalt not kill."'

'Those particular ladies look too young and frail to perform great valiant deeds and too pretty to murder.'

'You think pretty girls can't murder?' Maredydd asked Tudor in amusement.

'Not so they'd get blood on their hands, although they might resort to poison. Can you tell us anything else about it, Brother Mark?'

'Only that I've never heard mention of it. I believe I would have if it held any value as a holy relic.'

'It looks old,' Tudor examined it closely.

'That doesn't mean it is, my lord,' Brother Mark cautioned. 'Or that the banner has no merit. The fact that I'm not aware of its significance could be attributed to my ignorance.'

'So, do we send what might be a great Welsh treasure to Bolingbroke and young Hal, or keep the banner in the hope of discovering more about its origins? Or keep it anyway and risk the English finding out that we're waylaying their mail?' Tudor asked Owain.

'If my lords will permit me to speak?' Brother Mark took a small stone pot from the sleeve of his robe and opened the lid. He sniffed the contents before offering it to Owain. 'The sap of the Hogweed plant is soon absorbed by wool, even fine wool like this. It is also hard to detect. When placed on cloth it possesses . . . certain qualities that curse the skin of whoever wears the garment. Left untreated the damage may be long lasting, possibly even permanent. If the king and his son follow Charleton's suggestions and have this banner made into nightshirts . . .'

Tudor burst out laughing and slapped Brother Mark across his shoulders. 'When it comes to revenge there's no gainsaying the imagination of the pious. Brother, you were right to care for that messenger. It's time to send him back on his interrupted journey with his packages.'

CHAPTER EIGHT

Glyndŵr's Headquarters Glyncoch Valley Berwyn Mountains, Wales June 1401

'The servants' beds are in the attics, my lady.' Gwilym led the way up the narrow staircase to the top floor of the house, ahead of her because no gentleman of high or low rank would dare walk behind a lady on a staircase lest he inadvertently see up her skirts.

A square landing housed four doors, two facing them side by side in a recess. Gwilym opened them to reveal planks suspended over raised open ended wooden boxes. 'The garde-robes, my lady. One for ladies another for men. They open into a dry pit at the side of the house. I've ordered the stable boys to cover the waste with fresh earth every morning.'

He opened side doors to the left and right. They led into cubicles each identically furnished with a single narrow cot, a peg on which to hang clothes and a metal jug and basin set on a stool. Doors opened from both into communal dormitories, furnished with eighteen pallets set opposite one another. Small windows were framed in gables at the far ends of the attics. Fires burned in the hearths set in the outside walls below chimneys large enough to draw up most of the heat. Piles of logs were stacked beside each one.

'The first thing I did when I arrived, my lady, was order fires to be lit in every room to drive out the damp.'

'Even if we're fortunate enough to have a fine summer, Gwilym, it will take months to dry these walls. My brother has neglected this house for years.'

'I haven't succeeded in making much headway yet, my lady,' Gwilym confessed, 'but I'm determined to do better.'

'I don't doubt you will, Gwilym. You've accomplished wonders in a short time.'

'I thought the chaperons could sleep in the outer cubicles to ensure everyone remains in their own beds. Mrs Evans volunteered to look after the women and I asked the senior clerk, Gwynfo, to supervise the men.'

'Gwynfo didn't volunteer?' Margaret asked.

'He did when I reminded him the path to promotion was open to those prepared to shoulder extra responsibility, my lady.'

'I bow to the powers of your persuasion, Gwilym.'

'Thank you, my lady. I've housed the squires in the dormitory on the floor below. Knowing how boisterous they are, I thought it as well to keep them at a distance from the maids.'

Margaret walked into a dormitory and inspected a sleeping pallet. They were thick enough to cushion the wooden floor and absorb any splinters and there was an abundance of pillows and blankets.

'Mair,' Margaret greeted the girl as she entered the attic. 'I trust you're finding your way around.'

'I'm trying, my lady. This house is a palace. I've never seen so many rooms.'

'It's large but hardly a palace.'

'Sorry, my lady,' remembering her manners Mair dropped a curtsey. 'A page said there were beds up here for the maids . . . ' embarrassed at her presumption, she lowered her head in the face of Gwilym's stern look.

Gwilym continued to stare at Mair. 'Mrs Evans will be in charge of allocating the beds.'

'Yes, sir, thank you, sir.'

'You may call me steward.'

'Yes, steward, sir.'

'You will find Mrs Evans in the still room off the kitchen next to the pantries.'

'Yes, sir. Thank you, steward sir, my lady. If I may speak, my lady?' Mair murmured diffidently.

'Of course, Mair.'

'Enyd took me to see the blacksmith, my lady. I spoke to him . . . '

'Hunith or Dewi?' Margaret checked

'I didn't hear his name, my lady, but I asked if I could help polish the weapons and armour. He said if it was all right with you, it was all right with him, my lady. He said he'd try me for a day or two to see if I was up to the work. If I proved useful, he'd allow me to remain in the forge and work alongside his apprentices.'

'Are you sure you want to do heavy work, Mair?' Margaret asked. 'The seamstress can never find enough girls to assist her and the cooks are always looking for help in the kitchens.'

'I'd prefer to work in the forge, my lady. My father was a blacksmith. He showed me how to shoe horses, and polish metal hoes, spades and ploughs so they don't rust. Weapons can't be that different. Besides I . . . I like the work,' she stammered, realising she'd been speaking too forcefully and quickly.

'In which case I'm sure you'll be a great help to our blacksmiths. If you need anything, Mair, find me, or Enyd. She usually knows my whereabouts.'

'Yes, my lady, thank you, my lady.'

'It would be as well if you go to Mrs Evans next time you need to ask questions, before bothering my lady, who is very busy,' Gwilym warned.

'Yes, sir. I will, steward sir. I'm sorry, I didn't mean to interrupt or be a bother.' Mair curtseyed and fled down the stairs.

'Don't be hard on the girl, Gwilym,' Margaret said. 'She was ill used by the English constables after they took her from her husband.'

'Even so, my lady, we have set procedures and precedence among the servants. If we didn't, the maids would be running to you every time they have a sniffle or a hole in their hose.'

'I understand, Gwilym, and I'm grateful for your advice. It's just that I saw Mair after she was rescued. She was badly treated by her husband as well as the constables.'

'I will ask Mrs Evans to bear that in mind when she has dealings with the girl.'

'Thank you, Gwilym. I don't want to interfere with your running of our household, when you do it so well.'

Gwilym followed Margaret down the stairs. 'This is the floor where I've housed the squires.' He opened a door. 'The bed pallets are the same as those in the attics.'

Margaret looked in. The dormitory was clean and as Spartan, cheerless and damp as the two in the attics. She continued down the second flight of stairs.

'There are three large chambers on this floor besides the one the ladies, Catrin, Jonnet and Elwy chose, my lady. They are much of a size and ready to receive guests or family. I prepared the front bedchamber that overlooks the drive for you and the prince and a smaller chamber for Lord Xian and Mistress Gweni when they arrive.'

Margaret looked into the chamber Gwilym had set aside for her and Owain. Enyd was already at work, folding her gowns into a press.

'Thank you, Gwilym, this looks perfect. Will my sons be sleeping in the house?'

'I have set aside accommodation for the lords Tudor, Poulson, Hanmers, Scudamore, Rhys, Gruffydd, Maredydd, David and Ieuan in the cottages, my lady.'

Margaret smiled. 'You know us so well, Gwilym.'

'I have tried to make everything as comfortable as resources allow.'

'The young men will have what they crave most in the cottages.'

'My lady?' Gwilym turned to her in confusion.

'Privacy, Gwilym. I hope they appreciate your thoughtfulness.' Margaret had seen the cottages when they'd ridden in. She'd also seen the expression on Owain's face.

If English men at arms found their way to the stone built house, Owain would order the doors and shutters barred and bolted, and hold out, hopefully for as long as it would take a relief force to arrive to break the siege. But the doors on the cottages didn't looked strong enough to withstand a determined kick from an enemy boot.

She pushed the thought from her mind. Security and safety were Owain's concerns, not hers. She'd learned early in marriage that if she voiced her fears all she'd accomplish was an argument that wouldn't help Owain – or her. Because the one thing she could least bear was discord between them.

***

Owain studied the map Maredydd had rolled out on the table. 'We need to establish ourselves in this and the surrounding area. Note every garrison and outpost and the number of men we need to man them, before making and distributing copies of the updated map.'

'I'll help with copying it,' Brother Mark volunteered.

'Thank you. I'll give you a list of the men we'll need as soon as I've made it.' Tudor ran his hands through his hair brushing it back from his forehead. 'I'll take a group out tomorrow and scout north. You'll ride with me?' he asked Gruffydd, 'or would you prefer to idle your time in "acquainting conversation" with your lady?'

'I'll ride with you, uncle. We could take Elwy and Jonnet with us,' Maredydd suggested eagerly. 'It's beautiful country up there.'

'That's my boy. Don't allow war to interfere with your courting,' Tudor mocked. 'One lovesick couple would be a liability in a scouting party. Two and I may as well look for English soldiers to offer my surrender.'

'There are no English soldiers in the Berwyn Mountains, Uncle Tudor,' Gruffydd retorted.

'Yet,' Tudor qualified. 'But they'll swarm in when they've heard I'm leading a picnic party, boy.'

'There's no way Margaret will allow the girls to ride out more than a mile from here,' Owain put an end to the argument. 'And even for that mile she'd insist that the girls are chaperoned.'

'Elwy's nursemaid travelled with us. She's so unaccustomed to riding, her muscles seized in the saddle.

Uncle Tudor had to hoist her bodily from her mount when we reached here,' Gruffydd grinned. 'I doubt she'll be up to riding again for a month or more.'

'All the more reason for the girls to stay close to this house.' Owain turned to the door as it opened.

Gwilym bowed. 'Two messengers just rode in, my prince.'

'Send them in.'

'You will want to talk to these alone, my prince. And a party from Glyndyfrdwy is close behind them.'

'Will you be able to accommodate them, Gwilym?'

'We're pressed for space my lord, but with my lady's help we'll manage,' Gwilym replied philosophically.

Xian and Gweni's chamber, Owain Glyndŵr's Headquarters the Berwyn Mountains June 1401
'There are more holes than cloth in some of these old tunics of Lord Xian's.' Gweni's maid Betsi tossed the garment she'd been examining on to the pile Gweni had earmarked for "rags".

'The moths didn't even leave enough cloth to make a rag in this one of Konrad's.' Gweni pulled the tunic apart. It disintegrated into dust. 'It's as well I bought three bales of linen from the pedlar last autumn to make new ones.'

She was folding the last of the wearable garments into the clothes press when Xian opened the door.

'Take the clothes that need shredding to make fuses to the seamstress, please, Betsi.'

Betsi bobbed a curtsy. 'Yes, Mistress Gweni.' She gathered the bundle and left. Xian closed the door behind her and turned the key.

'You're locking us in?' Gweni returned Xian's smile.

'After spending the last few nights with only a thin strip of cloth between our bed and a bunch of uncouth men who ogled my wife at every opportunity, yes.' He strode across the room, and with three flicks of his fingers unfastened her belt and the shoulder clips on her gown.

The blue wool fell in folds around her lambskin slippers leaving her shivering in her linen shift.

'You're cold.' He folded his arms around her.

'You're colder, and embracing you in your leather jerkin is like hugging a dead cow.'

'How many dead cows have you hugged?' He cupped her face in his hands and kissed her lips.

'You're my first.' She returned his kiss with interest.

He unfastened his jerkin, tossed it on the table, reached behind his back and pulled his tunic over his head. He stood in his shirt and hose, but not for long. He peeled them off and flung them on top of his jerkin and tunic.

'Would, my lady, care to test the bed?' He untied the ribbon at the neck of her shift.

She shrugged and the linen garment joined the woollen gown on the floor. She wrapped her arms around Xian's neck.

'Bed before you freeze me, wife.'

'Bed while the sun shines? True decadence.'

'Why decadence?' He stroked his hand down the length of her body, before caressing the soft flesh on her thighs.

'Because there's much to be done.' She glanced around the chamber. Packets and parcels were strewn around her open trunk and Xian's satchels.

'Betsi will see to it. I need tenderness after days spent riding from dawn 'til dusk, sleeping on hard ground, and parrying practice swords with beefy Welshmen.' He pulled her so close their bodies meshed. He turned back the covers and flung himself backwards on the bed, pulling her down on top of him.

'After tenderness – a long while afterwards because I'm in need of a great deal - I intend to catch up on my sleep.' He pulled a linen sheet over both of them. 'You even smell soft.'

'What does "soft" smell like?'

'Lavender, chamomile and roses.'

'That's the dried flower petals Betsi layers in our clothes to keep moths at bay.'

His dark eyes shone, reflecting her image. She gasped as his hands closed over her breasts. He teased her nipples with his fingertips and closed his mouth over hers. His tongue probed her mouth as his body moved slowly, surely beneath hers.

The sounds of a full and busy household, footsteps running up and down stairs and over wooden floorboards, people calling to one another, the thud of furniture being moved between rooms, faded in the intimacy of the moment.

Gweni was only conscious of Xian, his face below hers, the intense loving expression in his eyes She drew in her breath sharply as he entered her.

'You can breathe again, sweetheart,' he murmured when they fell back, exhausted on to the pillows some time later.

'I wanted the moment to last forever.'

'We can recreate it – but you'll have to give me a little time.' He pulled her against him, curving his body around hers, nuzzling the back of her neck while his hands continued to explore her body.

She faced the window. The sun shone brightly but the room was cold.

'You hungry?' he asked.

'Only for you.'

'You can't live on love,' he stroked the sensitive skin below her ear.

'It would be fun to try but you obviously want more than the food of love.'

'Not yet but I soon will.'

'I'll forage and bring something back.'

'No, I will,' he insisted, 'provided you promise not to move from there while I hunt for provisions.'

'The entire household will be talking about us?' She turned her head and looked at him through half closed eyes. 'They probably guessed why you locked the door.'

'I hope so, I also hope they'll have enough tact to leave us alone to your debauchery.'

'My debauchery?' she laughed.

'I came here to change out of my travelling clothes. But you seduced me.'

She writhed as he tickled her.

'Ow, that was my shin you kicked . . . '

Xian's laughter joined hers as they rolled in a tangle of linen sheet and woollen coverlet off the bed and on to the floor.

Kitchen yard Owain Glyndŵr's Headquarters the Berwyn Mountains Wales late afternoon June 1401
Ieuan heard Xian's heavily accented voice and Gweni's laughter as he sat two stories below on a stone bench outside the kitchen door.

David left the stables, saw him, and disappeared into the brewing cellar. He emerged carrying two tankards of small beer.

'That sounds like Gweni,' he commented sitting beside his brother.

'She and Xian just came in with a party from Glyndyfrdwy.' Ieuan took one of the tankards from his brother. 'Thank you.'

'Here's to a warm summer.' David shivered,

'We need one after last year's gales and freezing rains and this month doesn't feel like June.'

'It wouldn't in these hills,' David said. 'Gweni sounds happy.'

'She was smiling when I greeted her, but not as broadly at Xian.' Ieuan lifted the tankard, drank and wiped the froth from his lips with the back of his sleeve.

'Ieuan . . . '

Ieuan held up his hand to silence his brother. 'Not another word. It's enough for me that Gweni is happy, Robert safe in Glyndyfrdwy and you . . . '

'Me?' David looked questioningly at his brother.

'You appear to be content with your many lady friends.'

'Content with them? I'm positively happy - as the devil must be - otherwise he would have struck me by lightening by now for my sins. But it's not easy to remain cheerful watching you wallow in misery.'

'Abertha is beckoning to you from the door of the still room. Looks like she needs your help and I doubt it's with counting the cook's preserves, cordials and cakes.'

'I hope not.' Glad of an excuse to leave his brother to his mood, David drained his tankard, set the empty pot on the bench and walked across the yard.

Ieuan wasn't alone for long. He glanced up as a shadow blotted out the light. Mair was looking down at him. She was wearing a leather apron and armguards.

'You persuaded one of the blacksmiths to give you a place in his workshop?'

'Yes. Then I did as you suggested and begged my lady's permission to be allowed to take it.' She moved David's tankard and perched on the bench beside him. 'When I told Hunith the blacksmith I had my lady's blessing, he gave me a room of my own off the storeroom so I can light the forges first thing in the morning. It's not much, but at least I'll be able to sleep alone and not in a line of maids in the attic.' She looked him in the eye. 'I told you I'm not looking for a man.'

'I didn't think you were.'

'Men only want women for one thing . . . '

'I offered you friendship, nothing more.'

'But women have the same needs as men. Should I invite you to visit my room alone and discreetly, would you be inclined to do so?'

Ieuan thought of David and Abertha and Morfel and how casually and happily his brother went from one woman to another. David was right, Lizzie wasn't with him and in his blackest moments he sensed she never would be again. He felt guilty every time he touched Efa. It was hardly her fault. She couldn't help being Efa's sister, no more than he could help feeling guilty for lying with her. And Mair was smiling, and willing.

He rose from the bench. 'Like now for instance?'

***

The room behind the forge had no window. The air hung warm and heavy, and smelled of wild mint.

'Mair . . . '

She held her finger to his mouth. 'We don't need to talk.'

To his surprise he discovered they didn't. They undressed, fulfilled their need for one another and when they finished, he dressed. She blew him a kiss as he went to the door.

'That was nice, Ieuan, I'd like to repeat it, but I'd rather not be the subject of gossip, so never visit here without an invitation.'

'I won't.' He hesitated. It sounded strange to thank a woman for what they'd just done but he did anyway. 'Thank you, Mair.'

He opened the door and an image of Lizzie standing before him in her blue dress blocked his path. It was so vivid, so real he reached out to take the hand she extended towards him. It faded before he touched it.

Hearing movement behind him, he turned half expecting to see Lizzie again. Mair was sitting on the edge of her sleeping pallet, dressing. She looked up at him.

'This woman you keep thinking about must be very special.'

'She's not a woman a man can easily forget.' Ieuan closed the door behind him, left the forge and returned to the kitchen yard.

Efa was hovering in the corridor that led to the storerooms. He nodded and went to walk past her. Efa followed him.

'Ieuan?'

Lost in thoughts of Lizzie he snapped at her for wrenching him away from them. 'What do you want?'

She flinched as though he'd slapped her.

Ashamed, he muttered, 'I'm sorry. I didn't mean to shout.'

It wasn't much of an apology but it gave her the courage she needed, to ask him a question. 'Why did you visit that woman in the forge?'

'Mair? Because she invited me.'

'Who is she?'

'Someone who's been badly used and needed help.' He could resist adding. 'As you did. Why do you want to know?'

'Because I'm carrying your child.'

'Are you certain it's mine?'

She chocked back a sob, turned on her heel and fled into the kitchen.

***

'Are you certain the men you saw were Fleming mercenaries?' Owain asked Joshua and Peter.

'They were Flemish, my prince. We'd recognise their armour anywhere. They were at least five hundred strong,' Joshua ap Gwilym answered.

'We counted them twice using the maths our tutor taught us in Oxford. Counting the number in one area and multiplying that by the number of areas they filled.' Peter ap Geraint explained.

'Where are they exactly?' Owain cut Peter short and produced a map on which the principal rivers, streams and peaks had been marked.

'This is where we saw them, my prince,' Peter placed his forefinger on a hilltop. 'Jeremiah, who's in charge of the lookout post there was about to ride here to warn you he'd seen them but we told him we'd do it . . . '

'But we did take him up on his offer of fresh horses, my prince,' Peter interrupted Joshua.

'Well done, men.' Owain looked at Tudor, the two Rhys's and Poulson. 'We'll take it from here.'

'You will take us with you, my prince,' Peter pleaded,

'Where?' Tudor asked.

'You're going to fight the Flemings?' Joshua said.

'Are we?' Owain questioned.

'Aren't you?' Peter pressed.

'Go and see Gwilym. He'll tell you where you're sleeping, dinner will be served in the great hall shortly.'

'And the Flemings,' Peter persisted. 'We want to kill them ... '

'First you wash, eat and sleep. Then you wait and see what tomorrow will bring,' Tudor advised.

Owain watched Gwilym close the door behind the boys before turning to John Hanmer who'd just returned from patrol. 'You said you'd seen a party of fifteen hundred or more.'

'I did, my lord,' John confirmed. He checked the map. 'From the report we just heard, it appears they split into two groups before the students saw the smaller band. And from the direction both groups were travelling, I'd say we haven't more than a day and a half before they hit us.'

'Call a conference after we've eaten and warn everyone not to linger at the table, no matter how appetising the meats, or seductive Crab's singing.'

CHAPTER NINE

Owain Glyndŵr's Headquarters Glyncoch June 1401
Owain looked around the table at his senior captains. The conference he'd called had lasted deep into the night, principally because they were trying to cover all eventualities in the advent of an attack. It made no difference that experience had taught them it wasn't possible to plan for every situation that might arise.

'We're agreed, gentlemen. Tudor will leave for Hyddgen at sunrise with four men at arms and their retinues to build a watch tower. The first thing you'll do?' Owain looked at Tudor.

'Raise Y Ddriag Aur on top of the tower in the hope the Flemings will see the Golden Dragon and assume that's where you've set up your headquarters. It's a plan,' Tudor acknowledged. 'But I'd be grateful for advice as to how I and my band of thirty can beat back an attack by 500 - a 1000, or if the reports are to be believed an army of 1500 Flemish mercenaries if you don't arrive in time to help us.'

'My party of thirty men at arms and their attendant retinues will be in receipt of regular reports on the progress of the Flemish army from the manned watchtowers. We'll join you before any Fleming comes within arrow shot of Hyddgen.'

'We could spare more men for your and Lord Tudor's parties, my lord,' Rhys Coch interceded.

'The safety of our families is paramount, Rhys. The whole point of this exercise is for Tudor to draw the Flemings away from Glyncoch, leaving you to protect our loved ones. I trust you, Poulson and the men we leave here to do that. I will leave Rhys Ddu and Fierce written orders against their return, commanding them and their men to remain with you and assist you by watching over everyone here. You know what to do?'

'Lie low, keep out of sight and deal with any enemy who crawl too close for comfort,' Poulson answered.

'Don't forget to check the pedigree of any captives in case they're worth ransoming,' Tudor added.

'But your main objective is to keep this valley safe and secure,' Owain emphasised.

'I second that as I was the one to set up here with Gwilym, and the help of a few others.' Tudor nodded to the steward.

Owain left his chair and went to the shutters. He opened them and a roll of thunder accompanied by the drumming of a cloudburst filled the room. He looked up at the sky.

'Instinct tells me we have about two hours to dawn, gentlemen, I suggest we sleep them away.'

***

Maredydd shook his head at Gruffydd who held up a flagon. 'I can't keep my eyes open after listening to Uncle Tudor drone on. I wish I was already in bed.'

'You're a weakling with no staying powers,' Gruffydd mocked.

'That's me.' Maredydd was too tired to rise to Gruffydd's bait. He left his brothers, stumbled up the ladder that led to their sleeping quarters and fell over his squire Ioric who was sleeping on the floor in front of his door.

'What the ... '

Ioric woke, clamped his hand over Maredydd's mouth and whispered in his ear. 'You have a visitor in your bed, my lord.'

Maredydd nodded and Ioric removed his hand.

'I thought it best to sleep here to ensure your lady wouldn't be disturbed, my lord.'

'Thank you, Ioric. Return to your own bed.'

'I'd rather stay, my lord. You or your lady may have need of me at daybreak when you need to smuggle her out.'

'Everything all right up there?' Gruffydd shouted.

'Fine,' Maredydd called back. 'I just fell over Ioric.'

'He's a coward to be driven out of his quarters by bats. Weakling master, weakling squire,' Gruffydd chanted.

'Bats?' Maredydd mouthed at Ioric.

'I had to give him an excuse for wanting to sleep here, lord, after I smuggled the lady in.'

Maredydd didn't hear him. He'd already slipped into his attic. Elwy was sitting up in his bed reading her psalter by candlelight. She set it aside and opened her arms.

He closed the door.

***

Margaret slid over the linen sheet, gravitating towards Owain's warmth. She wrapped her arm around his waist, tucked her head beneath his chin and rested her cheek on his shoulder.

'You were late to bed,' she said. 'I doubt you slept more than an hour.'

'I tried not to disturb you.'

'Really?' She opened a sceptical eye.

'You didn't seem to mind my presence in your bed.'

'I would have minded less if you'd joined me at a more civilised hour.' She snuggled closer to him.

'There were plans to be made.'

'Plans for what in this storm?'

'To manufacture and cast weather controlling spells to sell to the English,' he joked.

'Given Crach's stories about the English believing you're a magician who can materialise in a dozen places at once, while conjuring hail, snow and blizzards at will, they just might buy them.'

They both lay quiet for a moment, listening to the wind blast hailstones and spray rain against the walls of the ancient stone house. It rattled the shutters and sent gusts of water down the chimney that hissed into steam when they met the glowing embers in the hearth.

'Do you think dawn's broken?' Margaret asked. No natural light entered the chamber because Gwilym had hung thick drapes over the shuttered windows. The only illumination came from the hearth and a small oil lamp.

'No. The house is too quiet,' Owain answered.

'Crach warned storms would blow in overnight and remain for a week or more.' She combed her fingers through the thick curls on Owain's chest. 'It's luxury to lie here safe and warm in your arms when it's wild outside.'

'It's luxury to hold you naked in our bed.' He kissed the top of her head.

She entwined her limbs in his. 'I can't recall ever being this happy.'

'Here, in this crumbling barn of Hanmer's?' he laughed. 'Don't you miss the comfort of Sycharth and Glyndyfrdwy?'

'Sycharth perhaps, just a little,' she allowed, 'but not Glyndyfrdwy. I never liked that house. Inside and out it's grey, forbidding and freezing, and that's at the height of summer. Not that we've had much of one the last few years.'

'And this house isn't grey forbidding and freezing?' He closed his hand over hers and lifted it to his lips.

'It's all of those things,' she conceded. 'It's also leaking and not just from the roof. Draughts seem to blast up from beneath the floors as well as through the walls. It has more damp and offers less protection than a tent against the elements. But I can forget its shortcomings by cwtching you. I also take consolation that the house is borrowed. If it falls down around our ears it's brother Hanmer's problem, not ours.'

'I should think he'd be grateful to us for sparing him the expense of demolition. But whatever else, it's warmer than a cave.'

'Which, you of course would know.'

'You wouldn't believe the frost that seeps through the walls of a hole in a hillside, or how it can freeze flesh and blood until it's colder than marble.' Owain shuddered at the memory.

'I have an imagination.'

'It won't touch reality, and I hope you never find out.'

She poked her nose out the blankets and sniffed the air. 'The air in here even smells of a decaying past. Gwilym told me the locals believe the place was built by the Romans and they still haunt it.'

'They aren't the only ones to believe in Roman ghosts. It's why so many villas were abandoned when the legions marched back to Rome. But I doubt they built this place. You only have to look at the wall they built on the Scottish border. They built solidly for posterity and this looks as though it was falling apart before the builders set the mortar between the stones.'

'Gwilym told me there's a legend that Vortigern used it as his headquarters when the Saxons invaded.'

'The Saxons didn't reach Wales, just pushed our belligerent forefathers back beyond the mountains before deciding our country wasn't worth the effort of following them,' Owain said. 'But it's possible Vortigern hid here between fighting the Saxons further east.'

'The only wonder is Hanmer didn't pull it down when he inherited it to save himself the expense of a caretaker.' Margaret smiled when she saw Owain watching her. She knew he was imprinting her image in his mind, so he could refer to it later because she did the same during their private moments.

'Hanmer was probably concerned for the colonies of rats and cockroaches that reside here. It would be brutal to evict them, but as long as the vermin leave us alone in our bed I don't mind sharing our chamber with them.' Owain stared at the patches of damp and mould that marred the oak beams and lime plaster on the ceiling. 'I pity poor Vortigern and his captains if they've been sentenced to ghostly eternity in this grim unforgiving place.'

'Have you thought where you'd like to spend the hereafter?' she asked.

Owain didn't hesitate. 'Sycharth, just after harvest, when the store pits and cupboards are full, the cooks busy baking, broiling and roasting in preparation for feasts and every room occupied by visiting bards, friends and family.'

The front door banged open and masculine shouts and conversation drifted up the stairs, followed by boots pounding the wooden staircase.'

'It's morning. I recognise Konrad's dancing step on his way to his master's chamber.' Owain sat up and flung back the bedcovers. 'I've cause to be grateful to Xian for pledging me his service and the secret of flying fire, but it's also heartening to see Gweni happy in her choice of husband.'

'It is.' Margaret curled her body around his naked back. 'Must you go now? Right this minute?'

'I must.'

'It sounds foul out there. You'll be drenched to the skin the moment you ride out.'

'How do you know I'm riding out?'

'Because I hear more squires' boots than Konrad's on the stairs.'

Owain wrenched himself reluctantly from her grasp, left the bed and went to the window. He opened the drapes, flung the shutters wide and stared at the hail sheeting down on the yard and pooling in the cracks in the cobblestones. 'You're right. It's wet even for wild ducks. If I were you I'd pull the blankets over my head and spend the rest of the day in bed.'

'I will, if you will.'

He turned and smiled at her.

'My heart stops beating every you do that.'

'What?'

'Look at me as if you loved me.'

'I do love you.' He leaned over and kissed her.

She reached up and pulled him down for a second kiss.

'No, you don't. If I get back in that bed I won't be going anywhere today.'

'Would that be so terrible?' When he didn't reply, she pleaded. 'Take me with you?'

'Absolutely not. It's incumbent on a lord to keep his lady safe and dry. And, as I won't be able to keep you dry if you go out in this, you'll have to settle for safe while I check our outposts and defences.' He bowed to her.

'A man dressed only in his skin should not bow to his lady. It's difficult to see romance in a backside.'

He laughed. 'You've complimented that view of my anatomy before.'

'When it was firmer and younger.'

'Ouch, that hurt.'

They were disturbed by a knock at the door. Enyd entered with a board of bread and cheese and a pitcher of small ale. Two maids followed, one with knives, cups and napkins the other a pitcher of warm water for washing.

'Thank you, Enyd, please hand me my robe.'

Enyd did as Margaret asked. 'Would you like me to stay, my lady?'

'No, thank you, Enyd, but please return after my lord leaves.'

'My lady.' Enyd waved the girls out ahead of her dropped a curtsy and closed the door behind them.

Owain poured warm water into the bowl and washed his hands and face.

'Did the messengers bring news yesterday?' Margaret asked.

'They did,' Owain confirmed. He picked up the tallow soap from its dish and rubbed it over a linen rag.

'Is Bolingbroke about to invade Wales again as he did last autumn?'

'He's probably already here. It's battle season, and he generally arrives before the birds. Knowing him, he'll travel in the middle of his flock so his soldiers can watch his front as well as his back, which will make it impossible for me to challenge him to single combat.' Owain finished washing, dried himself and reached for his clothes.

'Will he wait for the rains to stop?'

'If he has sense, but experience and my spies tell me he lacks both foresight and logic. And he and his army are not the only predators seeking Welsh hides.'

'The South Pembrokeshire Flemings,' she said softly.

He sat on the bed to pull on his braise and hose. 'Where did you hear that?'

'Crach Ffinant.'

'I'll send that man to the archers to be used for target practice.'

'I overheard him talking to Crab at dinner. She was complaining you'd asked Crach to ride with you but not her. Did the messengers warn of an impending attack?'

He avoided lying by not answering her question. 'They travelled on secluded roads to stay out of sight. I decided to send out scouts today to check the outposts to see if anyone has spotted movement. Tudor is going to set up a lookout post on top of Hyddgen. You can see for miles from its summit.' He reached for his tunic.

'Owain . . . '

'Order the cooks to prepare a feast for our return and I'll ask Crach and Crab to entertain us. We'll make it a celebration to welcome Catrin, Jonnet and Elwy.'

'How long will you be away?'

'A week or so. I'll send a messenger to give you a day or two's notice.'

'I won't be able to order a lavish dinner if you return on a meatless day.'

'If I plead with Yonge, he'll give us a dispensation.' Owain picked up his boots, gave her a last kiss and headed out of the door.

He was aware that Margaret knew exactly why he and Tudor were taking parties of men out on to the hills. He was also grateful to her for not starting an argument by insisting he remain with her.

***

The benches in the Great Hall were packed with men eating as much as they could stomach in one sitting, because they weren't sure when they'd next see food. The tables were set with bread, biscuits, and bowls of pea and oat pottage the cooks had baked overnight. Baskets of cheese, wrinkled winter apples and twice baked bread imported from the storerooms of Sycharth and Glyndyfrdwy were set among the trenchers and goblets for the men to pack into their satchels and saddlebags.

Maredydd and Elwy were sharing a bench with Catrin and Jonnet. Joshua, Peter, Ieuan and half a dozen squires and students had gathered around them, but there was no sign of Gruffydd. The girls were giggling, the young men preening and rattling off jokes to entertain them. Owain was relieved to see Catrin's maid and chaperon sitting between her and Joshua. He recalled his promise to Margaret. She was right, it was time to find Catrin a husband.

He looked around for his brother. The door that led into the ante room opened, a page emerged and he saw Tudor and Gruffydd crowded around the small table with Crach Ffinant, Crab, Poulson, Rhys and Philip Hanmer. He picked up a goblet and carried it into the room, closing the door behind him.

'Your messengers appear to be enjoying themselves, Owain.' Tudor moved from the only chair to a bench to make room.

'They do.' Owain helped himself to white cheese. Gwilym handed him a bread trencher and filled his goblet.

'What news did they bring, father?' Gruffydd asked.

'A letter sent via Talley Abbey from your uncle Gruffydd.'

'Who is under the thumb of his wife who sees thieves and wolves' heads behind every tree. You'd think our brother would show more backbone considering the blood that flows through his veins is the same as ours.' Tudor spiked an apple with his dagger and proceeded to slice it. 'Not that outlaws and the enemy soldiers aren't hiding behind every tree, just not in the quantities she sees,' he added.

'What makes you say that?' Owain asked.

'No reason in particular.'

Owain glanced at his brother then at Crab. 'You wouldn't have mentioned soldiers if you had no reason.'

Crab concentrated on cutting the rind from a cheese. She knew Owain was watching her but she didn't look up. 'Given the weather, I advise you to delay your scouting trip.'

'You've had one of your premonitions?' Owain challenged.

'No premonition. Only a dream.'

Owain pushed his chair back from the table. 'Do I have to drag it out of you?'

'I saw you mounted on Ariston in full armour on a rise in a desolate landscape. A storm raged, thunder rolled, lightning flashed, illuminating hundreds of English men at arms and archers at the base of the hill. Pembroke, Flemish and Bolingbroke's battle banners and flags flew above them, buffeted by wind and drenched by rain. Every archer's bow was angled upwards, all their arrows and quarrels aimed at your heart. Tudor and Gruffydd were on horseback either side of you, David, Ieuan and Maredydd behind you . . . '

Owain interrupted. 'You're right, it was a dream, Crab, not a premonition. Gruffydd fights alongside Tudor, Maredydd with me, and David is Philip Hanmer's captain. We're never together in one place long enough to be cornered.'

'I could smell the wind, feel the rain on my face . . . '

'Hardly surprising given the inadequacies of this house.'

'Don't joke about my sight, my lord.'

'I've had cause to be grateful to your powers too often to make light of them, Crab. But you have little faith in me if you think I'd allow my men to be trapped on a hilltop.'

'The Flemings have hired a formidable army of mercenaries,' Crach murmured.

'And where did you hear that?' Owain asked.

'Round and about.'

'From the birds?' Tudor suggested.

'They fly into many abbeys,' Crach grinned.

'They do,' Tudor agreed. 'But a great deal can happen between hiring an army and ordering them to attack. Especially if the other side have coin enough to offer a bribe to sheath their blades.'

'I can't understand the Flemings wanting to meet us on a battlefield,' Gruffydd said. 'The king taxes them as severely as he does us and treats them no better.'

'The Flemings are sheep who follow their shepherd,' Tudor said. 'They've seen the king slit the throats of their ilk after he's sheared them but they still hope he'll treat them with more compassion when the time comes for them to be fleeced.'

'They traipsed to Britain behind William the Conqueror and their descendants continue to follow his with the tenacity of fleas who cling to a dog's carcass long after the animal is dead.' Rhys chopped a wrinkled winter apple as if he were punishing a Flemish mercenary.

'Because their grandsires swore allegiance to the Normans, they pledge support to whichever arse occupies the throne, even Bolingbroke who wrested the throne from the rightful heir.' Philip pushed his empty bowl aside. 'Not that William had a claim worth a groat being born a bastard.'

'Did your birds estimate the size of this Flemish army?' Owain asked Crach.

Crach shrugged his muscled shoulders. 'Not in numbers but they did say defectors from Hotspur's mercenaries in Conwy were flocking to join them.'

'You can't blame them for walking away from the siege in search of coin,' Tudor defended them. 'Hotspur's been paying Henry's army for years. When he left, he took his treasure chests with him. You know how reluctant Bolingbroke is to open his purse.'

'I've heard Hotspur complain,' Owain said drily.

'With good reason, he and his father have bankrupted themselves fighting Henry's battles,' Crach declared.

'Are you certain the birds didn't fix a number on the army?' Owain asked Crach again.

'Other than it was large enough to sate even Tudor's lust for blood, no. But we'll put a size to it when we sight them.'

'If we sight them.' Gruffydd rose from the table. 'They could seek shelter in this weather.'

'Which gives us time to set up a command post on Hyddgen and from there we'll be able to spot them even if they haven't left Pembrokeshire,' Tudor joked.

'Not in these mists you won't.' Crab pointed out.

'Mists work both ways. We won't be able to see them, they won't be able to see us - but when they clear . . . '

'You'll kill one another?' Crab said grimly.

'In time. It will take them weeks to reach here,' Tudor predicted.

'Unless they're already halfway here.'

'If you're not expecting an imminent attack, my lords, why in the name of all the saints are you riding out in this?' Philip Scudamore demanded.

'To toughen the men,' Tudor retorted.

'I would have thought living in this house would toughen them enough, even for you.'

Tudor indicated the table. 'They're growing fat and idle living off the cream of the crops, listening to Crab's songs and Crach's tales, and making love to their women.'

'For which I trust the women are duly grateful,' Crach grinned.

'That depends on how well the man serves them.' It was Tudor's turn to raise his eyebrows.

'And whether the woman is easily gratified,' Crab added.

'To return to business, gentlemen, before I leave to check our watchtowers, and probe for weaknesses in our defences, is there anything anyone wishes to say?'

'How long will you be gone, my prince?' Philip asked.

'A week maybe ten days,' Owain answered.

'Tudor?' Philip questioned.

'I won't leave Hyddgen until the watchtower is finished, but if this weather continues we can't expect any of the men to stay in the outposts for more than a few days. We need to set up a relief rota.'

'Draw up a schedule, Rhys, and have it ready on our return,' Owain drew on his leather gloves.

'I will, my lord.'

'David you can stay with your uncle or ride with us whichever you chose.'

'I'll ride with you, father.'

Owain nodded. 'Time we were on our way, gentlemen.'

***

After dressing and breakfasting with Gweni, Xian picked up the weapons Konrad had cleaned and brought up that morning, and went downstairs to look for him. He found his squire breakfasting with Ulrich in the Great Hall.

'Are the horses ready?' he asked Konrad.

'Saddled and in the stable, my lord. Rhodri said he'd send his stable boys to the front of the house with them as soon as we're ready to leave.'

'The pottery . . . '

'Is well packed in oiled cloth, my lord. My lady . . . '

'Is not riding with us,' Xian said abruptly.

'I thought my sister had you tied to her wrist along with her pet hawk Olwen,' Maredydd said as he passed them. 'Does she know you're leaving her behind?'

'We discussed it,' Xian replied.

'I doubt she was best pleased.;

'Second best pleased,' Xian quipped.

Maredydd laughed. 'Sometimes you sound as though you were born and bred in Wales.'

'One day you may wander far enough to realise people have the same needs, wants and hopes whatever their birth country.' Xian turned to Konrad. 'Tell the stable boy to bring our mounts to the door. Men and beasts will all be drenched the moment we go outside so it makes no difference when we leave.'

Maredydd stood still as his squire fastened on his leather and metal plated jerkin. Ieuan joined them and took the sword and scabbard Elias handed him. The student had managed to gain acceptance among the other squires despite his lack of training in swordplay and jousting.

'You're determined to ride out with us?' Ieuan asked Elias.

'Of course, my lord.'

Dafydd pushed past them and opened the front door. He stared out into the yard before shouting, 'Archers, move out!'

The hubbub quietened in the Great Hall as the archers shuffled off the benches and grabbed their saddlebags.

'Don't forget to tuck your bowstrings somewhere safe and dry,' Dafydd advised as they filed past him.

'Where the rain can't fall and the sun doesn't shine,' a wag shouted.

Owain beckoned to Xian from the doorway of the ante room. 'Is your flying fire to hand?' Owain asked.

'It's carefully packed, but useless in this downpour, lord.'

'As I thought,' Owain murmured. 'I think your talents would be better employed here.'

'Last night ... '

Owain led him back into the deserted ante room. 'I've had time to reflect on what was decided last night. I need reliable battle hardened fighters here.'

'You have them. Rhys Coch and Philip Hanmer ... '

'Are but two men, and there are more inexperienced men for them to lead than experienced. You've fought many battles, you know the best uses of flying fire ... ' Owain broke in.

'Should everything go to your plan nothing will happen here. I will be left sitting polishing my sword instead of striking a blow where it's needed.' Xian dared to interrupt.

Owain dropped his voice to a whisper. 'You and I both know how often plans go awry. My mind would be easier if you were with our ladies ... '

'Are you ordering me to remain here, my lord?' Xian interrupted again.

'You are your own man. I request not order, but should you remain here I would worry less.'

Xian eyed him for a moment.

'You will stay?' Owain pressed.

'If the rain stops . . . '

'You and your retinue could ride to Hyddgen with your flying fire if it's not needed here. Or if you've received fresh news.'

Xian finally understood Owain. 'I'll stay, my lord.'

Owain gripped his shoulder. 'Thank you.' He strode back to the door.

'You waiting for the rain to stop, Dafydd?'

'If I were, my lord, I would likely still be waiting at Michaelmas.' Dafydd hooked two fingers into his mouth and whistled. Two of the stable lads appeared leading Owain and Dafydd's destriers.

Owain hooked the hood of his cloak over his head, pulled it low and left the house. He climbed into Ariston 's saddle and glanced back as he rode to the gate while his men mounted their horses behind him.

Margaret leaned out of the window of their chamber. She blew him a kiss as Crach Ffinant spurred his pony and rode down the column to join Owain.

Owain lifted his hand in farewell to Margaret, turned back and led the way out of the yard on to the valley floor.

'My lady is reluctant to see you leave, my lord.'

'You spoke to her, Crach?' Owain asked.

'I did not need to. Not after I saw her face.'

'And the fate of this scouting party?'

'The rains will safeguard us from attack for the next few days, my lord, but it remains to be seen if the chills and fevers they carry, send us to early graves.'

'This is a fine Welsh summer, Crach.'

'It is, my lord, and experience as well as the sight has taught me there is nothing worse or more fearsome than a fine Welsh summer.'

***

'Do you want me to return our mounts to the stables, my lord?' Konrad asked Xian as they watched the rear guard ride off.

'Not yours or Ulrich's, Konrad. I want you to ride to Glyndyfrdwy.'

'But we only left there three days ago.'

'You did. But I need to get a message to John the Potter urgently, and I need you to explain what I want.'

CHAPTER TEN

Ruthyn Castle June 1401
'A fine boy for the master, Lizzie.' The midwife severed the umbilical cord and handed the child to Steward Alwyn's housekeeper, Mistress Evans.

Lizzie lay back on the pillows and watched Mistress Evans wash him in a bowl of warm water and wrap him in linen.

'Here, Lizzie, you can take a quick look at him before I show him to his father.' Mistress Evans held out the child.

Lizzie closed her eyes and shook her head. Every part of her body ached as though she'd been trampled on by a destrier. She felt as though she'd been torn apart. Too tired to think or move, she lacked the energy to even pretend she felt anything for the child.

Mistress Evans tucked the bundle of cloth and baby in the crook of her elbow. 'I'll bring him back when he needs feeding, Lizzie. That will give the midwife time to tidy you up, make you comfortable and settle you down.'

The midwife filled a basin with water and dropped in a linen rag. 'You had a nice easy time of it, Lizzie. '

'That was easy?' Lizzie opened her eyes and found enough energy to glare at the midwife.

'I've seen hundreds born in my time. That was a quick and almost painless birth. Why your labour only lasted half a day. You're made for childbearing and I'll tell your master so. His wife wasn't, poor girl.' The midwife's eyes clouded with the memory. 'She lost four, all before time after she gave birth to her daughter and her last labour lasted three days before the pains killed her and the baby.'

'I'll leave you to it, midwife, and show the master his son and Miss Mary her brother. She's been that excited at the thought of another child in the family.' Mistress Evans wiped the baby's head with a corner of the cloth. 'I've no doubt the master will be in here to see you, Lizzie, when the midwife's finished.' Mistress Evans opened the door with her free hand,

'You can tell your master if he wants more children, Lizzie's the one to bear them.' The midwife bustled around the bed. 'He's found himself a good breeder. I wouldn't be surprised to find myself delivering a second healthy boy a year from now.'

Lizzie retreated into her grief stricken thoughts and ignored what the midwife was doing to her. The last time she'd felt so bereft was when her grandmother had died. She was desolate, wretched at the loss of the man she would never marry and the child she would never bear. Ieuan's son, the boy they would have loved, cared for and nurtured, had died that day. In his place was a usurper she couldn't bear to look at.

She closed her eyes, and allowed her mind to drift to the last time she'd been happy. Pont Gweni, before Reginald de Grey's men had struck.

She was kissing Ieuan outside his mother's kitchen door, a bard was singing inside the house, her sisters were dancing, and Ieuan. . . .

'Lizzie . . . Lizzie . . . the master is here to see you.' She woke to the sound of a baby crying and the midwife shaking her. Resenting leaving her dream - and Ieuan - she opened her eyes to see the steward leaning over her. He laid the child in her arms.

'My son needs feeding. You know what to do?'

Too sick and tired to speak, she nodded.

'Leave us,' Alwyn ordered.

Mistress Evans ducked in from outside and gathered a bundle of soiled linen from the corner of the chamber before ushering the midwife out.

The steward pulled a stool up to the bed. He sat and watched Lizzie untie the ribbon at the neck of her shift pull it wide and lift the child to her breast. She winced as the baby closed his mouth over her nipple.

'Does that hurt?' he asked.

She nodded and stared down at the baby because it gave her an excuse not to meet the steward's eye.

'We'll name him Reginald.'

'No!'

'It's the Baron's name. He's my lord, I serve him, and you in turn serve me. It's fitting.'

She raised her head and glared at him.

'You think he should be named for me?' He pressed his fingertips together and considered for a moment. 'I could make Reginald his second name and give him mine, Alwyn, as a Christian name. Would you prefer that?'

'Call him what you will. I can't stop you.' She moved restlessly and the baby cried as her breast slipped from his mouth.

'You want no say in naming the boy?'

She shifted the baby in her arms without looking at him. 'If I had a say I wouldn't want him named for the man who gave the order to burn my village, enslave me, and murder my sister, mother, friends and neighbours.'

'Murder! The only people who died in your village were those who tried to kill the Baron's soldiers. You can't blame men for defending themselves against butchery.'

'And my sister?' she challenged. 'Grug never threatened anyone, yet the Baron had her hung from the ramparts.'

'Who told you Grug was hung from the ramparts?' he demanded.

When she refused to reply he repeated the question, followed by, 'it was Mistress Evans wasn't it?'

'Given that I've been locked up here with only Mistress Evans, you and Mary for company since the day after I arrived, it had to be her. You haven't allowed me to see or speak to anyone else.' She saw anger in his face, it roused her own and without a thought or care as to the consequences she raised her voice. 'Don't blame Mistress Evans. I wouldn't give her a minute's peace until she confirmed what I already knew.'

'She had no right . . . '

'I told you, I already knew.'

'How?'

She met his searching look head on. 'You said the Baron intended to hang all the Welsh servants in the castle when you pushed me into the hiding place below the window seat in your chamber.'

'Those closest to the Baron say his lordship regrets ordering his guard to hang those people that day,' he acknowledged.

'That's little comfort to the children he hung, or Grug and the others who are lying in their graves.'

'Baron de Grey had just cause, Lizzie. Everyone knows the Welsh are traitorous rebels intent on killing every English man woman and child, peasants as well as lords.'

'And the fear that the Welsh – even children – might harm the English is reason enough for the Baron to hang them unheard?'

'A woman can't be expected to understand the complexity of English law or the system that ensures the country is run smoothly, Lizzie. Government is too complicated a concept for any female to understand, but you must realise it's the Welsh who have declared war on the English.'

'How can an Englishman as rich and powerful as the Baron with his castle, gold and hundreds of soldiers at his disposal, feel threatened by a village of tenant Welsh farmers who weren't even on his land?' The pain in her breast intensified and she lifted the baby from one side to the other.

'The men in your village weren't the Baron's tenants. They were occupying his land illegally. There is nothing worse than theft by stealth. One day a lord looks out from his castle and sees his lands. The next, instead of woodland cared for by his gamekeepers, he sees villages of criminal usurpers tending crops they planted without paying him rent or heed.'

'Every family in our village had lived in Pont Gweni for generations ... '

'Illegally, Lizzie.' He paced to the window. 'Are you really so ignorant of the envy people nurture for the Baron? Or how difficult it is for men like him to protect their God-given divine right to nobility with all the advantages that entails?'

'The land the village stood on belonged to the manor of Sycharth - '

'It was part of Baron Ruthyn's holdings,' he cut in brusquely, 'and whoever encouraged your father and the other men in your village to move on to the Baron's land is culpable for killing your friends and neighbours, not Baron de Grey. He wasn't even present when your village was attacked.'

'It was never part of the Baron's holdings but the lordship of Glyndyfrdwy and Sycharth and we didn't "move on to the land"' she protested. 'We were born on it. Lord Glyndŵr owned it and leased it to Gwyneth for her lifetime, rent free ... '

He grabbed his wrist and gripped it. 'You will never speak that man's name in my presence again.'

Wanting to hurt him she repeated it. 'Lord Glyndŵr would never allow his men to invade a village, burn homes or kill and rape innocent people.'

He tightened his hold on her arm, she struggled to free herself and dropped the baby who promptly screamed. The sound of his son crying restored the steward to his senses.

'You're upset, which isn't good for you or the baby. Calm down, or you'll risk curdling your milk.'

'I don't care. I wish the bastard had never been born.' She grabbed the child and thrust him at the steward.

The child squalled even louder. Terrified of what Lizzie might do next, the steward snatched him from her. 'There's no point in arguing over what's done.' He forced himself to speak calmly in the hope of quietening her. 'As for who owned your village, it was for the king and parliament to decide, not the likes of you and me. And the king decided the land belongs to Baron de Grey. If villagers were killed when the Baron's men moved in to reclaim his property, it's their fault for provoking the soldiers. Men at arms can get carried away . . . '

'You call murdering men, women and children and raping women "getting carried away."'

'You've just given birth, Lizzie, you're emotional . . . '

The anger she'd kept in check since she'd been wrenched from her family finally erupted. 'I was happy in my village. I was in love . . . about to marry . . . '

'This man you were to marry?' he interrupted. 'He was a farmer?' There was ice in the steward's voice.

'And if he was?' she challenged.

'He farmed Baron de Grey's land?'

'He farmed his mother's land, leased to her by his father.'

'"Leased to her by his father,"' he repeated. 'We both know who stole that land from Baron de Grey. Glyndŵr was the father of your betrothed?'

'And if he was?' she challenged.

'Glyndŵr . . . '

'Now who'd speaking his name,' she taunted.

'He has been condemned by the king as a traitor, murderer, liar, thief and outlaw. If he "gave" anyone land, he gave them property stolen from Baron de Grey. You lived there illegally. If anyone is to blame for the loss of your village and the deaths of your neighbours it is Glyndŵr. It's also as well you remember if you'd married into his family of thieving Welsh paupers you'd have lived a life of drudgery and penury that would have ended on the scaffold. Whereas you and your child will be well looked after here?' He stared at her daring her to say otherwise. When she didn't answer, he said, 'what more could you want?'

'My freedom,' she whispered. 'To go where I want and feel the sun and wind on my face.'

'You want to go outside, go outside. If the guards see you, they'll hang you, but go ahead. I'll find a wet nurse for the child.'

She bent her head. To her shame a tear rolled down her cheek and fell on the bed linen.

He reached out awkwardly with his free hand and patted her arm. 'You're upset after giving birth. That's natural. But the way you are carrying on is not.' He coughed to hide his embarrassment at what he felt she might interpret as weakness. 'Baron de Grey is a busy man but if he grants me an audience I'll tell him about the child and plead the child's - and your - case.'

'To what end.' Her voice was thick with tears.

'My recognising and adopting the boy as my son. I'll also ask his permission to keep you as my servant together with an assurance that he'll allow me to protect you and the child.'

'Why would you need the Baron's permission to protect the child?'

'The child,' the steward snapped in exasperation, 'is half Welsh. Given that your countrymen have risen up against the king and are raiding and killing the English, no English lord, including the Baron, feels well-disposed to your race at present.'

'So if the Baron wants to hang me and the child … '

'The Baron's not a monster,' he broke in with a vehemence that suggested he was aware of what the Baron was capable of. 'He wouldn't hang a new born baby.'

'But he would hang the baby's mother?'

'I'm trying to safeguard you as well as the child. You're better off here than you would be if you'd stayed in your village, yet you have never thanked me … '

'You think I prefer living as a prisoner here than free in my village?' she asked incredulously.

Not trusting his temper he changed the subject. 'Regarding the child's name.' He looked down at him. 'If you have a family name, not a Welsh one, but a simple one like John perhaps … '

'Who told you my father's name was John?'

'No one. Was it? Would you like me to name the child Alwyn Reginald John?'

'No!'

If the steward heard the note of hysteria in her voice he ignored it.

'I told you I don't care what you name the bastard and I meant it.'

'Bastard he may be, but the midwife is right. He's a fine boy, Lizzie. I was beginning to think I'd never have a son and I thank you for him. If you don't want to feed him I will ask the midwife to find a wet nurse. It might be as well. Breast feeding can interfere with fertility or so the midwife told me. Children are blessings from God. I would like another as soon as possible, so you will return to my chamber and my bed as soon as the priest has baptised the child and churched and blessed you.'

'You expect me to continue living here as your mistress?'

'As my servant and acknowledged mother of my son. As a Welsh woman you cannot expect more.'

'I expect and want nothing from you.'

'Nevertheless, I will recognise this boy and even should I marry a woman of my class I give you my word I will never set this child or any future children you bear me aside. I will recognise them as mine.'

'And me, steward?' She found the courage to ask but her blood ran suddenly cold in her veins.

'Provided his lordship agrees that I may keep you as my servant, you will have a home and work here as long as I am steward, Lizzie. I'll send the midwife back in. If she knows of a wet nurse she may have suggestions on how to dry your milk. But you will have to feed the boy until we can find one.' He went to the door.

'You really expect me to bear another child for you after this?'

'You have proved yourself fertile and a good clerk. I want sons and someone to help me with my work. I'm not entirely unsympathetic to your situation. I've seen the way you look to the door that leads to the battlements whenever Mistress Evans steps outside. I trust in time you will realise I keep you secluded for the sake of your safety, not for fear of you running away. Indeed where would you run to, when the castle gates are manned by guards and the town gates garrisoned? I will let you know the outcome should I be fortunate enough to gain an audience with the Baron.' He opened the door and called to his housekeeper.

She entered and shook her head at the tears on Lizzie's cheek. 'Here, I'll take the child, master.'

He lowered his voice, 'don't leave him alone with Lizzie, not even when she feeds him.'

'I won't, master, but we'll need another servant to stay with Lizzie whenever she feeds or sees to the child.'

'Hire one and a wet nurse.'

'Yes, master. The captain of the guard is at the door.'

'What does he want?'

'To see you, master.'

Great Hall Ruthyn Castle June 1401
Steward Alwyn waited nervously outside the door of the great hall. He could hear the murmur of voices, but no matter how hard he strained, he couldn't decipher what was being said or who was speaking. Doors banged open and shut in the private apartments behind the hall, a footman emerged, beckoned him forward and opened the door.

Reginald de Grey and his wife, were sitting on the dais at the far end of the Hall with two of their daughters perched on stools at their side.

Alwyn waited to be announced before stepping forward. Margaret nodded to him, gathered her children and left the hall.

Alwyn bowed to her before approaching the Baron.

'Step up on the dais, Alwyn, or I'll crick my neck looking at you.'

'My lord.' Alwyn did as he was bid and stood ramrod straight before the Baron's chair.

'I've been expecting you to request an audience with me for some months, steward?' Reginald de Grey looked up from the letter he was reading and reached for his goblet.

'You have, my lord?' Unable to meet the Baron's eye Alwyn looked down at his boots. 'If there was problem with the accounts I would have come at once . . . '

'It's not the accounts that concern me. You are concealing a Welsh woman in your house?'

Alwyn swallowed hard. The castle was a busy place and too many people in the castle knew about Lizzie for him to even think of a denial. - The soldiers who had brought her to his apartment - the merchants who came his office for payment - the women who visited his housekeeper to gossip . . .

'I have a Welsh clerk to help with the accounts, my lord.'

The Baron smiled. Alwyn wasn't reassured. He'd seen his master laugh just before he issued an execution order.

'I've also heard that you've fathered a bastard on the slut, you rogue.'

Alwyn's heart pounded in his chest as his worse fears were realised. In keeping Lizzie he had disobeyed the Baron's direct order that all Welsh servants were to be handed over to the master of the wardrobe. The Baron was not one to disregard a flouted command.

'News travels fast, my lord,' he stammered. 'The child was born but an hour ago.'

'Healthy?'

'A healthy boy, my lord.'

'And the mother?'

'Also healthy, my lord. The labour was barely half a day. The midwife told me she's a good breeder.'

'You have one child, already, don't you?'

'A girl, my lord, Mary.'

'And this Welsh servant has given you a boy?'

'Yes, my lord.'

'I trust you'll teach him his letters and numbers so he can help with the castle accounts when he's older.'

'Of course, my lord. The boy will be brought up to serve you.'

'And learn to be more obedient than his sire, I trust.'

'I will teach him, my lord,' Alwyn said hastily. 'His mother has also been educated. She writes a fair hand and is excellent at accounting.'

'What plans do you have for the child's mother?'

'Plans, my lord?' Alwyn repeated, still staring at his boots.

'I ordered all Welsh servants in the castle executed when Glyndŵr, devil take the bastard, burned the town. Is the girl not Welsh?'

'She came from a Welsh village, my lord, but she speaks English, I find her an invaluable help ... '

'Are you suggesting she's English?'

'I have never enquired after her family, my lord.'

'You hid her?'

Alwyn squirmed. 'I thought if I confined the girl to my chambers she would pose no threat to you or anyone in the castle, my lord.'

'You admit deliberately disobeying my orders?'

The steward fell to his knees. 'I beg your forgiveness, my lord.'

'Did the girl bewitch you into bedding her?'

Aware of the fate that would befall any woman convicted of witchcraft, Alwyn was quick to deny the inference. 'She is no witch, my lord. She was a healthy girl, I longed for a healthy son ... '

'At the cost of disobeying your lord.'

'My only excuse is I craved a son to enter your service, my lord.'

'And you have been rewarded for your disobedience. Did you intend to keep the Welsh girl locked up in the hope that no one in the castle would discover her existence?'

'I hoped you would forgive me if I pleaded her case, my lord. She works very hard on the accounts.'

'I now know why you stopped pestering me to find you an assistant. I ask again, what do you intend to do with her?'

'With your lordship's permission, keep her in my service so she can continue to assist me with the accounts.'

'And breed from her again?'

'Yes, my lord. The midwife told me that breastfeeding can affect further breeding, so I asked my housekeeper to find a wet nurse for the child. As soon as he is baptised – with your permission I'd like to name him Reginald.'

'Permission refused. I want no bastard named for me.'

'Of course, my lord. Do I have your permission to name him Alwyn John, my lord?'

'Those are names befitting a bastard. This Welsh girl, is she comely?'

The blood began to cool in Alwyn's veins. 'Some might think so, my lord.'

'I will visit you and see her for myself.'

'You are welcome to visit my chambers whenever you see fit, my lord.'

'Order Mistress Evans to bake me one of her pies.'

'I will, my lord.'

'A woman who bears sons, even bastard sons, is heaven sent. Too many wives present their husbands with daughters.'

Alwyn remained silent. Baron de Grey's wife had presented him with only two sons to offset against his three daughters.

'If this Welsh slut is as pleasing as your description would suggest, I will reconsider her position. But a man who disregards a direct order from his lord should never be rewarded.'

'My lord.'

Reginald rose to his feet. 'I will consider her fate. A half Welsh bastard could prove useful in years to come especially if he is accepted by his mother's people. This woman of yours, does she have living relatives?'

'The master of arms told me that survivors from her village were taken in by the Abbot of Valle Crucis, my lord.'

'Did he name these survivors?'

'Not to me, my lord.'

'I will call on the Abbot the next time I am near the abbey. You may rise and leave us, Alwyn. Remember to remind Mrs Evans about the pie, let me know when it is ready for eating.'

'Yes, my lord.'

Alwyn walked backwards out of the Great Hall. He took little comfort from the fact that Lizzie was in no immediate danger.

If the Baron took a liking to her when he saw her, he knew he'd lose her. And for a reason he couldn't quite fathom given the number of available women within the castle, he found the idea of her absence from his bed upsetting.

CHAPTER ELEVEN

The summit of Hyddgen Mountain in the Plynlimmon, Range last week of June 1401

Tudor walked to the rock that crowned the hilltop. Beneath it was a natural depression he'd ordered the squires to excavate. He peered under the Welsh wool cloak they'd rigged up to protect them from the rain. It was so saturated, there was as much water dripping from the underside as landing on top of the thick well-oiled weave.

'That's supposed to be a shelter not a well, boys,' he criticised.

Only his squire Alun dared answer. 'The water pours in faster than we can bail it out with our helmets, my lord.'

'Then you'll have to scoop quicker. Don't dig out too far beneath that boulder or it will come crashing down, pounding everyone beneath it to pottage. And that space has to be larger. It has to take at least four men. Eight will be stationed up here to keep watch in shifts and this will be rest and sleeping quarters for those off duty.'

'It's only a ten minute ride downhill to the hideout in the copse of trees, my lord . . . '

'True,' Tudor interrupted Alun. 'But those minutes could become eternity for any man caught in the sights of an English archer.' He pulled the hood of his cloak further over his head so the rain dripped in front of his eyes instead of into them. The woollen cloth was sodden, but it held some of the residual warmth from his body.

He walked to the edge of the hill. It was just as well he was familiar with the view. The vista of river floored valley, softly rolling hills and ancient sarsens was shrouded in rain so cold it had generated a smoking mist that obscured it completely.

'See anything?' Gruffydd, swathed heel to nose in his cloak, joined him.

'Henry could be sitting fifty yards away with ten thousand mercenaries and we wouldn't know it. This downpour would mask even their stench.'

Gruffydd laughed.

'It's no laughing matter, nephew. Breathe while you can. Flemish mercenaries stink worse than rotting dung in a tanner's yard. It's down to the maggoty cheese they eat. As you'll soon discover for yourself.'

'That time can't come quick enough for me, uncle.'

'Anything's better than this damned waiting in the wet. Five days up here and all we've seen . . . ' Tudor stopped talking and held up his hand for silence.

Rain continued to hammer down. The wind whistled, gusting sharp needles of iced water that stung on contact. Then Gruffydd felt it. A definite tremor. He froze and strained his ears.

He continued to sense vibration but heard nothing. Something or someone was pounding the waterlogged soil on the slope below them. His uncle drew his sword, flicked his cloak over his shoulder to free his right arm and stood erect, legs apart, in readiness to do battle.

Gruffydd swept his hand downwards in the direction of the squires indicating they should lie low, before opening his cloak and reaching for his own broad sword.

'Hear it?' Tudor whispered.

Gruffydd shook his head.

'You will.'

A long minute dragged past before a gigantic monstrous shape emerged from the low lying clouds that blanketed the crest of the hill. It loomed above them. Startled, overwhelmed by the size Gruffydd jumped back before realising it was a horse.

'Ariston scare you, Gruffydd?' His father dismounted, stepped out of a shroud of rain and embraced him. Dafydd walked his own and Owain's horse to the centre of the summit where Tudor had ordered the destriers tethered around a shallow pool of rainwater.

'Alerted, not frightened us, father.' Gruffydd glanced sheepishly at Tudor.

'I see you're keeping your men busy, brother.' Owain indicated the squires excavating beneath the rock.

'Remind me to pack a horse whip next time you order me to supervise fledglings. The only skill these specimens can boast is idleness and they practise it every chance they get.' Tudor led Owain out of earshot of the men. 'The Flemings?'

'The main party 1000 strong is two miles south west, heading here,' Owain murmured. 'We laid a trail even English scouts can't miss.'

'The second party?'

'Also headed here, half the size of the other and travelling from the north. They're a good hour behind the main one.'

Tudor dropped his voice to a whisper. 'So, they intend to attack us from two sides.'

'I doubt they've reckoned with the incline. They'll skid to the bottom if they try climbing the slopes in this.'

'Pity our archers don't have waterproof bow strings,' Tudor mused.

'They don't. But neither do the Fleming bowmen,' Owain reminded.

Tudor raised his voice. 'We've been expecting company since we fed a courier a basin of watery stew yesterday ... '

Owain interrupted. 'Would that be the courier who was carrying Hanmer's letter addressed to me?'

Tudor grinned. 'I liked the postscript about peace returning to Hanmer after Catrin left.'

'You didn't notice Hanmer's letter was marked private, and addressed to me?'

'Difficult to see who it was addressed to,' Tudor shrugged. 'The directions were soaked and illegible.'

'So you couldn't read the address but you could read the letter?'

'Only the outer page was soaked, the script inside decipherable. I took care to read it in my tent so it would be delivered to you in good condition.' Tudor lowered his voice again. 'Clever of Hanmer to suggest you prepare a feast to celebrate the arrival of the Flemings. Your brother-in-law is a consummate politician. Should it have fallen into the wrong hands a trusting man might even have believed the sentiments he expressed.'

'Really?' Owain folded his arms across his chest beneath his cloak.

'Don't blame the messenger ... '

'He thought you were me?' Owain enquired sceptically.

'I told him as brothers we share everything.'

'I should have realised that the seal had been tampered with.'

'It was you who taught me how to peel back a wax seal without damaging it.'

'I remember,' Owain said, 'but I don't recall giving you leave to use the skill on my missives.'

'If you didn't want me to practise on your correspondence, you shouldn't have given me lessons.'

'So it's my fault you open my private letters?'

'Why teach me a skill if you don't want me to use it?' Tudor glanced back at the squires huddled around the stone. 'I've hidden a second camp in a copse of woodland.'

'It wasn't that well-hidden. I ordered the men there to pack up and join us.'

'Just as well. There's work to be done up here but I suspect it will be a wasted effort. Our time would be best spent building an Ark like Noah because I can't see the damned Flemings making a move while the heavens remain open, can you?'

'I think only a fool would try to predict an enemy's move before he makes it.' Owain watched Maredydd climb over the northern crest of the hill at the head of his men. They were leading their horses by the reins. Unlike him and Dafydd, none had persuaded their mounts to carry them the last fifty yards up the steep slippery slope.

'If Henry was stuck on this hill would you attack?' Tudor asked.

'Not in this maelstrom. Men at arms would soon get bogged down in the waterlogged ground.'

'You and I have fought over worse ground on the peat moors in Scotland . . . ' The remainder of Tudor's sentence was lost in a thunder of hooves.

Horses foaming at the mouth, Philip Hanmer and David who'd been sent out to scout the area, raced on to the summit. Both were dressed in the uniforms of kings' constables Maredydd had ordered stripped from the English bodies after the Cydweli skirmish.

Philip flung himself from his mount and ran to Owain. 'There are two parties of Flemings. The second are coming down from the north. They are less than an hour behind us,' he gasped.

'Bloody thousands, spread over a mile with outriders,' David added, as he raced to join Philip.

'We saw single riders travelling between the two groups.' Philip divulged between breaths.

'We spoke to your men, Uncle Tudor. They're abandoning their camp and packing to join you here.' David hit the back of his horse and sent it careering to join the herd around the pond of rainwater.

'Thank you for visiting us, David. As your news suggests we're doomed it will be comforting to have company.' Tudor sheathed his sword and looked to Owain. He smiled but his eyes were dark. 'Our men realise that we've been caught between the claws of a bloody big crab, brother.'

'At least the crab is snapping its claws at us here, not Glyncoch. Did you see any soldiers heading there?'

'Only our own, father,' David replied.

'Everything was quiet in the hills around the house?' Owain checked.

'So the men in the watchtowers confirmed,' David answered.

'Rhys Coch and Xian have stationed enough sentries to alert them to any movement?'

'More than enough. Rhys has placed them where they're well hidden.'

'Xian?' Owain's face darkened when he realised David hadn't mentioned him.

'He and Gweni have shut themselves in their chamber. I heard Gwilym complain that Xian's page had commandeered all the clay drinking vessels in the house.'

'Perhaps they've decided to drink their way through the cellars,' Tudor suggested.

'Who knows what they're doing with them. Gwilym offered Xian some of the chipped and cracked wooden goblets and drinking cups but he wouldn't take them. Xian also sent Konrad and Ulrich to Glyndyfrdwy.'

'Why?' Owain asked.

'They and Xian wouldn't say.'

'Xian must be up to something,' Tudor said.

'He's his own man.' Owain turned back to David and Philip. 'Were you followed?'

'No, but we garnered a couple of friendly waves from the Flemings.'

'We waved back,' David grinned.

'You planned this, didn't you, father?' Gruffydd dared to say what every man hoped because the alternative - that his father had led them all into a trap - was unthinkable.

'I hoped to draw the Flemings away from Glyncoch and our valley so Rhys Coch could keep our families safe,' Owain admitted.

Tudor looked at the men standing around them. Every one of them had a wife, child or parents at their headquarters. 'They're safer there than we are here,' he assured them.

'You think the mercenaries won't find Glyncoch after they've decimated us?' Philip asked.

'They don't stand a chance of beating us,' Tudor scorned. 'The choice is ours, not theirs. We can either move out and fight our way through David's "bloody thousands of Flemings" and hit them harder and more painfully than they hit us, or retreat further into the hills and induce them to follow us so our rear guard can drown them in the bogs.'

Owain pushed his hood back and combed the water from his hair with his fingers. 'Before we make any decisions, we do what all beleaguered soldiers do before a siege.'

'A siege, my lord?' Philip looked confused.

'This hill might not be a castle, but make no mistake, we are besieged, gentlemen. It's time to rest, take stock, protect our rear guard to ensure the enemy doesn't pick them off, pray to God and the saints, and wait for the Flemings to make the first move. And, if fortune smiles on us, their first mistake.'

The summit of Hyddgen Mountain late June 1401 night
Darkness fell shortly after the last of Tudor's men hauled themselves on to the crown of Hyddgen. With the moon and stars blotted out by rain clouds, grey twilight was transformed into impenetrable darkness.

The beleaguered men congregated together, seeking warmth and shelter, but there was none to be had beyond what they could offer one another. A few of the younger, less experienced men, tried to light fires but when they were doused by the relentless downpour they conceded defeat.

They crouched in wet, miserable, silent groups alongside their mounts, the blood in their veins growing sluggish as wintry rain continued to teem earthwards and the temperature dropped.

Owain, his sons, Tudor, Dafydd, and Philip lay side by side, face down in a line close to the summit. Occasionally one of them leaned over and peered down but it was no more than a futile gesture, as nothing could be seen beyond water filled darkness.

'I thought I heard the clink of harness,' David said.

'No thought about it, boy,' I heard it too,' Tudor said. 'Sounds like mercenaries are still riding in below.'

'Do you think it's the thousands Uncle Philip and I saw, or stragglers from the first party?'

'Could be both.' Tudor was laconic.

'They're probably preparing to attack at first light. And we're caught up here like newly hatched chicks in a nest waiting to become fodder for eagles.' Philip was prone to see the worst in any given situation.

'As Flemings can't fly, I'd say we're more like hares encircled by hounds, and hares can go to ground,' Tudor said.

'There isn't even a dandelion to offer shelter up here,' Philip grumbled.

'There are one or two places where the ground is soft enough to dig. The boys left the spades under that boulder.'

'I can't even see a boulder,' Philip snapped.

'The Flemings won't be able to use arrows in this. It will be swords, flails, axes and spears at close quarters,' Dafydd predicted.

'What good are close quarters when no one will be able to see further than their nose?' Philip mocked.

'The Bible tells that the sun rises every day. It can't rain forever,' Tudor said.

'Experience of Wales tells me otherwise. Can you remember the last fine day?' Philip demanded.

'Tudor,' Owain's disembodied voice echoed low. 'Check the food supplies at first light.'

'They'll be scant . . . '

'All the more reason to account for and conserve what we have. Philip, monitor the water situation, the pool level will soon drop despite the rain, given the number of men and beasts drinking from it. Did you order all the helmets to be put out to catch rainwater.'

172

'I did and they were, my lord.'

'And when I've checked the supplies?' Tudor asked.

'If the rain and mist clear by dawn, we'll be able to see what we're up against. Before then everyone should get as much rest as they can.'

'And when we open our eyes to see a Flemish army of thousands surrounding us in the morning?' Philip pitched his voice too low for the men to hear.

'We'll be able to draw up battle plans based on what's in front of us not our imagination,' Owain replied.

***

Tired of trying to decipher shapes in the darkness, David, Maredydd, Gruffydd and Ieuan moved away from the edge of the mountain and followed Tudor's suggestion that they try to stiffen the backbones of some of the younger volunteers. When Ieuan heard his father and uncles whispering after they'd left, it occurred to him that they wanted a private conversation, but too tired to think straight he was glad to leave the tactical planning to them.

'Will the enemy attack in the dark?' Elias asked Ieuan as he watched him lower himself on to a cushion of moss that leaked water.

'Your first battle?' David lay on his saddle next to them and covered his body and most of his head with his cloak.

'How do you know?' Elias feigned a cough in the forlorn hope of concealing the tremble in his voice.

'The question gave you away.'

'Is it *that* obvious I'm green when it comes to battle?' Elias demanded.

'Wanting to know if the enemy will attack when it's too dark to see anything, gave it away.' David spread his horse's felt blanket over his cloak and stretched out his limbs.

'I have little experience of soldiering but I'm willing to learn.' Elias protested.

'*Little* experience?' David repeated sceptically.

'I've taken Elias on as my squire,' Ieuan told his brother.

'You haven't taught him the first rule of soldiering. It applies to all who bear arms but particularly squires. "Leave the thinking and decisions to the officers."' David rummaged in his saddlebag and took out a handful of dried apple slices.

'You're an officer,' Ieuan pointed out.

'A lowly one, who obeys orders as they come down from above, or in my case, my uncle Philip Hanmer.' Despite the darkness, David glanced in the direction of the southern edge of the hilltop. He could hear his father's and Tudor's voices but they were speaking too low for him to decipher their words.

'Have you been in battle?' Joshua asked David.

'I have.'

'More than once?'

'If you count skirmishes.'

'Attacking or attacked.'

David recognised fear in Joshua's question.

'There's no difference once "Havoc" is cried and blades clash. It's every man for the man battling alongside him - and himself - against the enemy. And when the fighting starts there's no time for anything beyond your next move. Has Ieuan been teaching you sword play?'

'He has. I tried archery . . . '

David laughed. 'The time to start learning to shoot a longbow is when you start walking, and some start before that. It's the only way to build and develop the muscles needed to draw and loose a bowstring. Crossbow archers can begin training later, when they're seven or eight, but all archers need more strength in their arms than the common man. And, no matter what an Oxford tutor versed in the military tactics employed by Alexander the Great and Julius Caesar says about the battles of the ancients, it's generally the archers who win – or lose the day. Victory is usually decided when the first hail of arrows homes in on, or misses their targets.'

'The archers say they can't fire in this downpour. Not even downhill,' Elias added.

'They can't, more's the pity,' David agreed cheerfully. 'But the archers at the foot of the hill won't be able to fire up either.' He bit into a slice of apple.

'What do you think father will do?' Ieuan conjured an eagle eye image of their predicament. A clump of bedraggled, rain-soaked men, marooned on a high plateau surrounded by a sea of mercenaries. He visualised the grids on the enemy helmets. The murderous expression in the eyes behind them. Heard the snarls from behind barred teeth as they wielded their blades . . .

'Father will do what he always does.' David made himself as comfortable as he could, given that he was lying on wet ground in the rain.

'Which is?' Elias's voice was as unsteady as Ieuan knew his would be if he'd dared speak.

'Whatever is necessary to gain victory.'

'Which will be?' Ieuan wondered if their father had confided more to David than he had to him.

'As much of a surprise to us, as it will be to the enemy. Excuse me, gentlemen, I have to shut my eyes. If I don't, I won't be capable of striking a blow tomorrow.'

It was too dark to see whether David did close his eyes but given the snores that emanated from his direction seconds later, despite the rain, he slept.

'Do you think we'll attack . . . '

'I think we should take my brother's advice and not think on things that can't be influenced by us, Elias.' Ieuan followed David's example, and rested his head on his brother's soaked and blanketed arm. He would have given a great deal to be back sharing his bed with David in the attic of their mother's farmhouse in Pont Gweni, listening to the hum of conversation drifting up through the floorboards as his mother and their cook discussed the contents of the pantry.

An image of Lizzie flooded his mind. If he and David were in their bed in Pont Gweni, Lizzie would be safe in her bed with her sisters in the potter's house. He indulged in day-dreams of her so frequently, he could no longer be certain what he recalled and what he'd imagined.

Had her hair really shone the colour of ripe chestnuts and her eyes gleamed like polished pewter? Had her head reached his shoulder? He recalled resting his chin on the crown of her head when he'd embraced her. Had he done that? Or wished it so often he'd believed he'd done so?

He was cold. His wet clothes chafed his skin, yet despite his discomfort he must have slept because a dream was the only explanation for what followed.

He could hear Lizzie calling his name. She was the other side of an oak door, but the planks were uneven and there were splits and knotholes that enabled him to catch glimpses of her. She was dressed in her best blue woollen gown but it was grubby, worn, and so thin in places he could see the outline of her arms and legs through the cloth.

He wondered why she hadn't washed and repaired it, then realised it was what she'd been wearing when he'd last seen her, and she might not have another gown to change into. She realised he was watching her, ran to the door, pressed her face against the largest crack and stared at him, before stepping back and raising her arms, holding them out to him.

They seemed to be indoors yet Lizzie's hair was blowing away from her face as if she was facing the wind. Her eyes looked into his. They shone with love, but she was pale and sickly.

He went to the door placed his hands on the rough-hewn planks and pushed with all his strength. When he failed to open it, he raised his fists in preparation to smash it.

Lizzie shook her head and retreated. She spoke. Her voice was low, her words heartfelt.

'I'm no longer worthy of you, Ieuan. Please, go, forget me.'

He continued to watch her through the cracks. She rose from the ground, and began gliding - floating away from him.

Glyndŵr's headquarters Glyncoch mountains June 1401 dawn

Crab shivered as she left the small cubicle she'd claimed behind the kitchens. She clutched the edges of her cloak and walked down the stone passageway that led to the pantries and store rooms.

She'd seen Gwilym carry the triptych, silver paten, altar candlesticks and chalice, he'd taken from the chapel in Glyndyfrdwy into the chamber nearest the outside door last evening and assumed he'd set up a chapel there.

She opened the door and was surprised to find the small chamber was already furnished for worship, and given the faded paintings on the stone walls, had been for years.

The side and back walls were decorated with Biblical pictures in the late Roman style, depicting old testament stories. She recognised scenes from the life of Moses. Of him leading his people out of Egypt, parting the Red Sea, and speaking to the burning bush in the desert.

Adam, Eve the serpent and the apple were depicted in a frieze around the window. David and Goliath fought their battle on the opposite wall, but the most beautiful paintings had been reserved for the eastern wall. Jesus and his twelve apostles looked down on an altar draped with a white linen cloth. Above them Madonna robed in blue cradled an infant Jesus. And kneeling below the altar that held the chapel silver and family Bible was Margaret.

Crab murmured an apology and stepped back.

Margaret turned her head. 'Your sight?' she asked. 'You've seen something?'

Crab remained silent.

'Tell me?'

Crab shook her head.

'Please. I know that he - the boys - Tudor - all of them are in terrible danger. I feel it.'

'They are in danger,' Crab admitted. 'But they are not lost. Not yet and maybe not at all.'

'They left to draw the Flemings away from here, didn't they?'

'My lord confided his plans to you?'

Margaret shook her head. 'Did he consult you?'

'Not I, my lady, but I know he spoke to Crach.'

'I saw he was troubled. There were whispers of Flemish mercenaries . . . '

'Whispers only, my lady. You didn't ask his intentions?'

'I didn't want to add to concerns. But now . . . ' Margaret knotted her fingers so tightly Crab believed her fingers would break under the strain. 'I need to do something!'

Crab fought emotion. 'So do I, my lady. We could pray together?'

'I would welcome your companionship, Crab.'

Crab kneeled beside her, and Margaret bowed her head, but even as she did so she wondered if their prayers would be enough.

Lost in their devotions they didn't see Mair and Efa enter the room arm in arm, or see them kneel together behind the font in the darkest corner of the chapel.

CHAPTER TWELVE

The summit of Hyddgen Mountain in the Plynlimmon, Range midday June 1401

'What are they waiting for?' Nervous, Elias's voice pitched unusually high.

'The rain to stop.' David shook out his cloak and it shed a sheet of rainwater.

'We can fight in the rain . . . '

'We could. But as it appears the Flemings are reluctant to climb up here it means we'd have to run down the hill, and that would be tiring.' Maredydd adjusted his leather cloak so it covered most of his woollen cloak beneath it.

'We'd be lucky to get halfway down before losing our footing, sliding down to the bottom and landing on our arses,' Gruffydd said, 'and that would make us soft targets for Flemish spears. They'd slit our throats before we could prise ourselves out of the mud. It's as thick as pottage down there . . . '

'And twice as sticky as the sludge in the bottom of shit creek. We'd be glued in fast.' David said cheerfully.

'Are you saying the Flemings won't climb up and attack us in the rain?' Joshua brightened at the thought.

'We're saying it would be foolish of them, and despite appearances not all Flemings are fools ' Maredydd looked for somewhere drier than the rain soaked grass to put his saddle, decided there was nowhere, and left it where it was. 'Their archers can't fire, neither can ours, so the only way to break this deadlock is for one side or the other to run up or down the hill and clash blades.'

'In the meantime,' Gruffydd handed Elias a waxed bag. 'There might be a crumb or two of twice baked bread in there worth eating.'

Elias refused to take the bag. 'I'm not hungry.'

'If you don't eat it, boy, someone else will, and when you're starving you'll regret refusing it. There's nothing like a bellyful of solid twice baked bread to give a man the energy he needs to kick an enemy back to his maker.' Tudor strode into sight and checked his destrier.

A cry went up from the men on watch. 'They're moving!'

'If mountains could tip over, this one would be staggering like a cripple without a crutch.' Tudor watched every man who wasn't on sentry duty rush to the edge. He strolled over to join Owain, Dafydd and Philip Hanmer on a tump that overlooked the Flemish camp.

A bugle sounded, its single note muted by distance and the incessant beat of falling rain. Before it died, the Flemish archers stepped forward in a double line and stood facing the summit.

'The idiots are going to try picking us off. This is going to be interesting.' Tudor pulled a bag of dried beef strips from inside his cotte and handed them out to Owain, Philip and Dafydd as they watched the archers fasten their bowstrings.

'Do you think they've found the secret to keeping bowstrings dry in a rainstorm?' Philip asked.

'If they have, we're in trouble.' Tudor's comment was drowned by a sudden burst of hail.

When it ended a sergeant in the Flemish camp shouted, 'Knock!' The cry was taken up and shouted down the line loud enough for them to hear.

The archers reached into their quivers and fixed their arrows to their bows.

'Draw.'

They drew back their bowstrings to their chins.

'Now comes the test,' Tudor muttered.

'Loose!'

The strings twanged. Instead of flying upwards the arrows fell horizontally. One or two managed to fall in front of the feet of the archers but most hit their boots.

The roar from Owain's men on the hill was derisive and deafening.

'Well I guess that's the Flemish attack done for the day.' Tudor handed around his bag of dried beef again before stowing it back in his cotte.

'Not quite.' Dafydd pointed down to where a score or more Fleming squires were running up the hill. The foremost one slid and tumbled into the man behind him, who in turn fell and knocked over three behind him.

'Novel way to play ninepins.' Tudor laughed as the archers tumbled into a heap. 'As we've nothing better to do than watch them we may as well make ourselves comfortable.' He settled back on his haunches and continued to monitor the "attack".

Dafydd looked around. 'We've a fair number of stones up here.'

'We have,' Gruffydd knew exactly what Dafydd had in mind. 'Do you want me to order the men to pile them up at intervals along the summit?'

'They could prove useful,' Dafydd said. 'Enjoy the show, gentlemen.'

'You're not watching, Dafydd?' Gruffydd asked.

'Later, when I've done all I can to prepare a warm welcome against their arrival.'

***

'You really want to marry Elwy, don't you?'

'Yesterday couldn't have come quick enough for me but I'll settle for the next time I see her and a priest who can spare an hour to conduct the ceremony. What prompted you to ask that now?' Maredydd asked Gruffydd.

They'd slung their leather cloaks end to end over a couple of spears and hooked flails to provide shelter while they ate the last of their rations. Their thigh muscles ached from crouching, their bread dripped rainwater, and the best that could be said about their make-shift shelter was it prevented the worst of the rain from soaking their backs.

'Father asking if I wanted to marry Jonnet,' Gruffydd answered.

'Do you?'

'I don't know.'
'Does Jonnet want to marry you?'
'I don't know.'
'Have you asked her?'
'No.'
'Have you talked to her about it?' Maredydd pressed in amusement.

'There hasn't been time.' As soon as Gruffydd made the excuse he realised it sounded lame.

'Elwy and I found some.' Maredydd grinned knowingly at his brother.

'Some what?' Gruffydd demanded irritably.

'Time.' Maredydd's smile broadened.

'I wondered why your squire slept on the floor outside your door that last night in Glyncoch. "Bats indeed!" One day you and Elwy are going to go too far,' Gruffydd warned.

'Too far like you with your paramour? I've seen you sloping off with her, not to mention the nights she slept on your mattress in our tent in Carmarthen.'

'I know exactly where I am with my lady and ... '

'And should she have your child?' Maredydd interrupted.

'She won't. She's an experienced woman, not a girl like Elwy.'

'An experienced woman old enough to be our mother.'

'Which makes her unlikely to bear a child. And given this conversation, what would you and Elwy say to father and Uncle Gruffydd if she finds herself carrying your baby before you stand in front of the altar?'

'Dear fathers, we've been begging you to organise our wedding for some time, now you need to make haste.' Maredydd shook the last few crumbs from his bag on to the palm of his hand and licked them up. 'Don't you want a wife you can talk to?'

'I talk to women.'

'About what?'

'Life - poetry - '

Maredydd burst out laughing. 'I remember the women you chose to spend time with before you settled on your paramour. I find it difficult to believe you discussed life and poetry with Morfel and Abertha.'

'Not them,' Gruffydd snapped irritably. 'My conversation with those two was limited to what I wanted them to do and how much it would cost me.'

'You've been spending too much time with Uncle Tudor.'

'As we fight together it's difficult not to.'

'Have you thought of actually spending time with your betrothed?'

'I've considered it.'

'Then why don't you?' Maredydd asked in exasperation.

'Because I don't know Jonnet.'

'You won't get to know her if you don't talk to her.'

'It's all right for you . . . ' Gruffydd faltered.

'Why is it all right for me?' Maredydd demanded.

'Because you knew Elwy was the one you wanted the moment you set eyes on her. Whereas Jonnet is years and years older than me . . . '

'Years!' Maredydd exclaimed. 'I thought she was twenty three which makes her considerably younger than your paramour.'

'Jonnet is twenty four which makes her almost six years older than me.'

'Hardly a lifetime, and she is pretty.'

'You think so?'

'In a statuesque, exotic, dark eyed way.'

'That means you find her huge, clumsy and unattractive.'

'It means I prefer small, green eyed girls with auburn hair,' Maredydd said. 'If you're not attracted to Jonnet wouldn't it be better to tell her, so she can find herself another husband.'

'I've considered it.'

'Two considers in one conversation. Something tells me you need to learn to be decisive. You've been betrothed now for how many years?'

'I don't need reminding. Or advice from a younger brother.'

'I overheard father and Uncle Tudor talking. Uncle Llew asked them to take the girls to Llanllyr convent. He thought they'd be safer locked up with the nuns while the king heads into Wales with his army.'

'Uncle Llew thinks Bolingbroke will win against us?' Gruffydd was shocked.

'No, but he thought the girls would be safer away from the king and his lords, particularly if the king has heard that Elwy and Jonnet are betrothed to us. Bolingbroke is always testing the Welsh lords' loyalty. I imagine uncle Gruffydd is high on that list. He might be father and Uncle Tudor's younger brother but to quote uncle Tudor "Gruffydd Glyndŵr has always tried to run with the hare and the hounds". And Elwy and Jonnet's dowries would attract the interest of English lords in Bolingbroke's retinue.'

'You think Bolingbroke would prefer to see the girls and their dowries with his lords rather than us.'

'As he's branded father a traitor, it stands to reason doesn't it?' Maredydd closed his bag of bread and replaced it in his tunic.

'Do you really consider Jonnet pretty?' Gruffydd changed the subject abruptly.

'I don't think she's pretty. I think she's beautiful,' Maredydd answered tactfully.

'It has to be different.'

'What does?' Maredydd was bemused.

'Making love to a high born lady as opposed to a . . . ' his voice tailed.

'Paramour?' Maredydd suggested. 'I doubt it.'

'You don't know?'

Maredydd shrugged. 'I've never lain with a whore.'

'Never!' Gruffydd's voice rose in disbelief.

'Why would I, when I've lain with Elwy since we were fourteen?' Maredydd couldn't resist a sly dig at his older brother, 'a year younger than you were when you first visited the still room with Morfel.'

'How did you . . . ' Gruffydd fell silent when he realised Maredydd must have been watching him.

'According to Elwy, girls dwell as much on lying with men as we do of getting naked with women, if not more.'

'Now I know you're lying.'

'I'm not. Elwy and I talked at length about it before we made love for the first time.'

'But you don't talk about it now?'

'Now, we're too busy practising to waste time talking.' Maredydd hesitated. 'I hope she's safe.'

'Given the number of men Father left in Glyncoch, I'd say she's safer than us,' Gruffydd answered.

Owain Glyndŵr's headquarters at Glyncoch June 1401
Xian and Gweni stood in the shelter of the barn's open door and watched Konrad ride to the edge of the meadow.

'Make sure the grease and straw cap is angled down and protected by the leather flap,' Xian called out.

Konrad's exasperated reply was carried away by the wind and drowned out by the rain, which was probably as well for Xian's temper.

Not wanting to shout himself hoarse, Xian lifted his arm high and brought it down suddenly. Konrad opened the door of a small lantern that held a flame, lit the wick that trailed from a clay pot in his hand, spurred his mount, raced forward and tossed the pot into a copse of ragged willow. It exploded within seconds, flinging sharp shards of baked clay high in the air, fortunately away from him and his mount.

Konrad turned in his saddle and shouted to Xian. 'We have to move quickly after we throw them.'

'Faster than a jumping frog,' Xian qualified. 'But now we know they work, we'll start producing them.'

Konrad saluted him, waved to Fritz and Ulrich in the stables and cantered towards them.

Gweni turned and went into the "dry" section of the slate barn that Xian had lined with bales of straw and hay.

'How many do you think we can fill by morning?' she asked Xian.

'If all five of us work through the night . . . '

'Six with Betsi,' Gweni corrected.

'You're right, six, she'll want to help, Konrad.' Xian followed her, sat on a bale of straw and stared at the pile of baked clay cups he'd set to one side.

'How long will it take?' she repeated.

'You're thinking of what the shepherd told us about your father and brothers being trapped on the mountain?'

'They need help. We must go . . . '

'*We* are not going anywhere. Poulson and Rhys Coch are under strict orders to remain here and protect the women and children. You promised to obey me . . . '

'Not in your absence I didn't. You're going to take these to my father?'

'When they're filled.'

'I'm going with you.' She gave him one of her looks which he'd christened her "we'll see about that" look, but instead of persisting she said, 'Which brings me back to the question, how long will it take us to fill them?'

'A ridiculously long time if we don't set to work right now.' Xian rolled up the sleeves of his tunic, picked up a cup and started filling it.

Gweni sat alongside him. 'Grain husks and dried grass,' she murmured, dropping them into her container, 'a fair dose of flying fire, push the mixture down with the flattened end of a horn . . . '

'Don't forget to leave room for the wick,' Xian warned.

'Sealed with mutton or pork fat,' Gweni sniffed. 'I'm not sure which this is, but it's definitely off.'

'For once I wish I possessed a less acute sense of smell.' Xian looked up as his Franz and Ulrich joined them. He set down the cup he was filling and tossed them two bales of straw to serve as seats.

Konrad joined them after he'd bedded down his horse, as Gweni had prophesied with Betsi following in his wake. They sat in silence and worked solidly until the light began to fail.

Konrad lit lanterns and hooked them high on the ceiling away from the barrels of flying fire powder.

Grey dusk darkened to unrelieved black and still the rain beat down relentlessly.

When Konrad and Ulrich's stomachs started rumbling, they sent Fritz to the kitchens. He returned with a tray of meat and apple pies and a cask of small beer.

They took a few minutes out to eat and drink before continuing to work through the night, until they reached a point where every movement they made was as mechanical as the turn of a mill wheel in a stream.

Xian called a halt when a strip of pearl light showed through a crack in the wooden shutters. He placed the last pot he'd filled into one of the fleece lined, tarpaulin covered baskets they'd packed, rose from his makeshift seat and stepped outside.

Sometime during the small hours the rain had stopped. Dawn was breaking, enamelling the eastern clouds with streaks of bright crimson and gleaming gold. He was standing, absorbing the colours and breathing in the cool morning air when Konrad brought another basket to the door.

'A day of sun, my lord, will dry the ground and make it less treacherous.'

'But not firm enough for battle. That will need a week or two. Longer if the rains return.' Xian looked back into the barn. Gweni's fingers were busy packing the clay pots as nimbly as they had done all night, but her eyelids were heavy. 'Our ladies need rest.'

'That they do, my lord.' Konrad smiled at Betsi who was hunched over the pot she was working on.

Xian tested the ground with his foot. Konrad did the same and dropped his voice to a whisper. 'When do you want to leave?'

'You have the shepherd's fleeces and hill ponies ready?'

'Four for riding and four to act as pack horses, my lord.'

'As soon as my lady and yours are asleep and we've changed our clothes, we ride.' Xian returned to the barn, picked up Gweni who'd fallen asleep and carried her into the house.

The summit of Hyddgen Mountain in the Plynlimmon, Range midday June 1401 Daybreak the third day of the siege

'The Flemings are sending up wasp stings again but they're still not hitting any targets.' David joined his brothers and crouched alongside them beside the fire they'd lit and nurtured the moment the rain had ceased. The green wood smouldered, emitting more eye stinging smoke than warmth, which was hardly surprising given the soaking the pack horses had been subjected to on the climb up but it provided a focal point for the junior officers.

'Anyone wounded?' Maredydd delved in his pocket and took out a stick of dried beef Tudor had given him when he'd distributed the last of their supplies that morning.

'Their archers haven't managed to get an arrow further than halfway up the hill. I overheard some of the squires making plans to go down at dusk to collect them.'

'Are our archers so short of arrows they have to scavenge for casts off?' Maredydd questioned.

'I asked them that,' David said. 'The thinking appears to be "render unto Caesar that which is Caesar's". The squires find the idea of killing the Flemings with their own arrows poetic justice.'

'Want this?' Maredydd passed David half of his stick of dried beef.

'Because you've gorged yourself on the other half and your stomach is so full you can't eat another thing?' David joked. 'Uncle Tudor gave us all a fair share, although some of us ate their share quickly lest it spoil.' He scowled at Ieuan who returned to the campfire with a string of water bottles he'd filled at the drinking pool.

'I took Uncle Tudor's advice. Eat while the food's there because it might not be for long.' Ieuan protested. 'I didn't stop you from hoarding yours.'

'No, just suggested it would be companionable if I joined you in a meal.'

'I advise you to think twice before you act on our uncle's suggestions. They can lead you into trouble, and that's coming from someone who rides with him.' Gruffydd caught the water bottle Ieuan threw to him.

'If something doesn't change soon we'll be reduced to harvesting the grass the horses haven't trampled into the dirt and boiling it for dinner,' Maredydd said. 'Anyone know what it tastes like?'

'Not personally but I could ask a sheep,' Gruffydd quipped.

'If you're hungry you could let Bran fly?' Maredydd commented. David's hawk was a legendary hunter.

'I did twice after dawn this morning without luck. There's not a mouse or sparrow to be found on this mountain. Bran is as hungry as we are and I dared not allow him to fly long because whenever he flew low the Fleming archers used him for target practice. They didn't succeed with Bran but they did shoot down Uncle Philip Hanmer's, Mac. He's probably been plucked and is stewing in a pot in their camp right now. Of course, Ieuan could always try letting Math fly ... '

'Even on a good day he never brings anything worth eating,' Ieuan said gloomily.

'He doesn't,' Gruffydd agreed. 'Which is all the more reason to allow his carcass to grace our stew pot.'

'Don't you dare suggest eating my hawk! He may not be the best hunter but he is mine.' Ieuan threw a clod of mud at Gruffydd. It missed and landed on Maredydd's forehead.

'Do you know if father has a plan?' David asked Gruffydd under cover of the ensuing laughter.

'I'm sure he does,' Gruffydd answered, 'but whatever it is, he won't confide it to anyone until he's ready to share it.'

They both glanced over to where their father was holding counsel with Tudor, Dafydd and his captains.

***

'If the Flemings are still sitting down there, watching us, watching them from up here, when Bolingbroke marches into Wales, we'll have the English army as well as our Pembroke friends to contend with,' Tudor declared.

'How large an army do you think Bolingbroke has?' Philip Scudamore asked.

'Large.' Tudor answered evasively as he pulled out his gwisgi flask. 'Henry may baulk at paying Hotspur for the use of his mercenaries but he takes care to pay his own and ensure their numbers remain steady as they are all that stands between him and the sharp edge of our broadswords.'

'Do you think Bolingbroke is already in Wales, my lord?' Philip asked Owain,

'There were no reports that he'd crossed the border before we left Glyncoch, but it's anyone's guess what's happened since,' Owain answered.

Tudor leaned back against his saddle. 'So what are our orders, my prince?'

Owain held up his hand as a shadow blocked the sun.

'My lord.' Philip Hanmer and the sheep dog he'd adopted to assist his disguise ran to Owain. After bowing, Philip dropped his shepherd's hook and pulled the fleece he was wearing over his head.

'You've heard from our outposts?' Owain asked.

'The woman they sent, said the Flemings below us and our men in their concealed lookout posts are the only soldiers for miles.'

'Our food situation?' Owain looked to Tudor.

'I distributed the last of our stocks this morning. I doubt anyone has more than a few crumbs left. Every hare that values its life has legged it north to safety and Snowdon, so unless an archer shoots a bird there'll be no flesh worth eating for us.'

'I've seen a few sheep,' Philip said.

'None close,' Tudor qualified. 'I refused the men leave to go after any they see wandering uphill towards us lest the Flemings are using them as bait. Our besiegers might not know for certain that we're down to chewing grass and swallowing fresh air, but I've no doubt they suspect it.'

'So dinner tonight will be stewed waxed food bags?' Philip lifted a suggestive eyebrow.

'We could always add a slug or two for flavour.' Tudor poked at one with the toe of his boot.

Owain looked beyond his captains to the men congregated around the campfires. From his own hunger pangs he knew how just how starved they were, and it wasn't only lack of food that concerned him. The level had dropped to mud in the pool they'd been using for drinking water and the pool where they tethered their horses had been churned by the horses into a thick brown sludge.

'Time won't endow us with more strength than we possess now,' Owain murmured.

Tudor knew his brother was simply voicing his thoughts.

Owain continued to watch the young men laughing and joking around the fires.

'You want me to line the archers up on the perimeter, my lord?' Dafydd asked.

'No.' Owain was decisive. 'Order those on watch to report any untoward movement in the camp below, and the squires to saddle all the horses and prepare to help their masters don their armour. Tell the archers to check their stock of arrows and dress for combat and bring my sons to me.'

'We're going to fight?' Tudor asked.

Tudor waited but Owain didn't answer.

CHAPTER THIRTEEN

The summit of Hyddgen Mountain in the Plynlimmon, Range midday June 1401 Daybreak the third day of the siege

Maredydd and Gruffydd took the lead. David and Ieuan rode behind them. They slowly circled the perimeter of the summit of Hyddgen several times as their father had instructed, noting the placements of the Flemings' officers' tents and the crude defences that had been erected around the makeshift camp.

David was usually in high spirits before any fight, even if it was only weapons practice, and as Ieuan, along with the other captains had assumed their father was preparing for battle, he was unnerved by his brother's silence.

'You're not ill, are you?' he ventured.

'My clothes are damp and chafing, I'm starving, thirsty and uncomfortable, but otherwise perfectly fine,' David answered.

'Sorry I asked.'

'Sorry I growled.' David reverted to one of his favoured childhood apologies. 'Do me a favour?'

'If I can.'

'If anything happens to me . . . '

An icy snake of fear slivered down Ieuan's spine. 'You've had a premonition . . . '

'No, and I haven't suddenly developed the sight.' Despite his apology David snapped again. 'But I have been considering my sons' future. You know as well me, once swords are drawn anything can happen. We could be captured, and given our father, held for ransom for years, or we could be wounded . . . ' David held back from predicting the worst outcome and continued, 'I want you to promise me that if I'm unable to care for my sons, you will.'

'Of course I'll promise, but Enfys . . . '

'It's been agreed between us. If I can't oversee the boys into manhood she will keep them only until their fourth birthday. Then she will hand them over to you.'

'Enfys would never allow me to take your sons from her.'

'I settled it with her. She knows I believe you to be the best person to guide them into manhood.'

'But I'm not married ... '

'Which makes you the perfect father figure because you'll never fall prey to the wiles of a conniving, unfaithful woman.'

'You've had other women ... ' Ieuan began.

'Not before Enfys strayed from our marriage bed,' David interrupted. 'But Enfys's sins are between her and God.'

'I'm sorry ... '

'I don't want your pity,' David said angrily. 'I've chosen you to oversee my sons to manhood because you're mourning the loss of an unattainable woman. No one will ever rival Lizzie in your affections. You'll remember her as flawless, something no living woman can ever be. Efa worships you and will do whatever you ask and that includes looking after young Owain, Gruffydd and Maredydd. She'll keep them and their clothes clean and see they're well fed, leaving you to supervise their training for life and in the use of weapons. Should you decide to replace Efa, you'd have to physically drive her from whatever door you're living behind. Even then, she'd probably beg to be allowed to stay on as your servant to serve your new lady.'

'I thought you disapproved of me and Efa.'

David gave a grim laugh. 'Jealous more like. You've an expertly trained whore warming your bed if half of what I've heard of Efa's prowess is true. And, as if saving a fortune in brothel fees is not enough, Efa will be eternally grateful to you for rescuing her from her sister. Llibio had her servicing men morning noon and night, and catering to one man's needs has to be less onerous than that of an entire brothel.'

'David, Efa . . . I . . . '

His brother spurred his horse. 'Later. Father's about to speak. You won't forget your promise?'

Ieuan shook his head, but confident of his brother's answer David was already riding ahead.

***

'Apart from a few Flemish archers who are using the lower slopes for target practice the enemy appear to be taking their ease, my lords,' Maredydd reported.

'How is their archers' aim?' Tudor asked.

'They hit the side of the hill. But that was more down to luck and the direction of the wind than their skill.'

'So we're up against superior bowmen,' Tudor declared.

'It appears so,' Maredydd kept a straight face.

'There are cauldrons on their fires. They're emptying sacks of peas and beans into them and their butchers are chopping sheep carcasses into stewing joints,' Gruffydd added.

'So, by the time we've flattened and disarmed them, the stew should be ready for us,' Tudor beamed at the prospect.

Owain made a final adjustment to his breastplate, and climbed on his destrier so he could be seen by all his men.

With the exception of the sentries who'd stationed themselves out of arrow range of the Flemings, Owain's captains and soldiers gathered around him. Owain reined in Ariston and waited for silence. He didn't have to wait long.

'In our eagerness to lead the Flemings away from our headquarters, we appear to have walked into a trap, boys.'

When the laughter that greeted his observation died, Owain continued.

'Whichever way we turn we can see the enemy looking up at us. But the Bible tells us that everyone has to lift their head to those above them.

'These mercenaries deserve our pity. Their destiny is to crouch in the mud, ignorant and blind to beauty like toads, while watching us, the hawks, soar overhead. They do not fight for the love of a land, a family, their friends or freedom.

'Driven by greed they crave coin and kill honest men to sate the bloodlust of tyrants who enslave them with silver. They are incapable of feeling the emotion our country evokes and for that we should pity them.

'We know what we fight for. Our wives, our children, our people and Hiraeth - the sense of home and belonging Wales endows on every child at birth.

'I love and respect you too much to lie. We are trapped. But God has given us a choice.

'We can remain here cowed, trembling, waiting for death from starvation or a Fleming arrow to find its mark. Or, we can face whatever fate God sends us like men of Cymru.

'Blade in hand we can charge down this hill and attack those who would steal our lives and birth right, giving them a taste of Welsh justice delivered by Welsh courage.

'I do not command but beg every one of you. Sell your lives dearly, and if God gives fate leave to deliver our death this day, let us meet it like Welshmen. Sword in hand, stout in heart ready to deliver to the enemy what he would deliver to us if we allowed him the chance. No quarter.'

***

When Owain finished speaking the only sound that could be heard was the eerie childlike cry of a kite circling overhead.

Every man on the hilltop looked upwards. Tudor was the first to cheer and when other voices joined his, it felt as though the entire mountain was reverberating.

Owain's thirty men at arms and Tudor's five called to their squires for their armour, gauntlets and helmets. Pages ran to saddle their own and the archers' mounts. Archers retrieved their bowstrings from the greased cloth wrappings they'd used to secrete them on their body. Every man knew his task and worked swiftly and in silence.

Owain took the tabard embroidered with images from his banner and dropped it over his armour. Dafydd tied it on before checking the single red flamingo feather on the pinnacle of Owain's helmet. When he was satisfied it was secure, he handed it to Owain who placed it on his head. Owain drew his sword and used it to slam down his visor. He rode to the perimeter of the mountain conscious of his men moving en masse behind him.

As Maredydd had said, apart from a few of the Flemish archers the enemy appeared to be taking their ease.

Tudor, Gruffydd, Maredydd, David and Ieuan drew alongside him with Dafydd who carried his battle banner.

Owain urged Ariston over the precipice. The horse forged ahead, treading carefully at first, then as the hooves of the horses behind began to thunder, the destrier picked up speed.

Owain urged him on as battle cries resounded behind them.

'Y Mab Daragon!'
'Glyndŵr, the Foretold Son!'
'Glyndŵr, the true Prince of Wales!'
'Glyndŵr, Tywasog Cymru!'

CHAPTER FOURTEEN

The foot of Hyddgen Mountain in the Plynlimmon, Range, midday June 1401 the third day of the siege
Owain had lost count of the number of skirmishes and battles he'd fought. After decades spent waging war in the service of the Earl of Arundel and King Richard in Scotland, Ireland, France and the English Channel, his recollections of engagements had blurred into a single chaotic memory. One of fighting for his life in a melee of panicked sweating men clashing blades and axes beneath an arrow storm

For him, smells delineated war more than fractured images. Human sweat, acrid with fear. The iron taint of fresh flowing blood. The stench of piss and faeces as wounds and death, relaxed bowels and bladders. He breathed in the unique reek, and experienced the single recollection that remained with him. The peculiar way time froze at the first cry of "Havoc".

Ariston galloped off Hyddgen on to the flat of the valley floor, raised his hooves to enter the Flemish camp and there he and his mount remained. Static, like a Roman general and his horse carved in marble.

Missiles flew above his head from the bows of his Welsh archers. He trusted their skill to aim true on the targets ahead, but trust didn't prevent him from ducking when he heard whistling slice through the air. Quarrels and arrows scudded into enemy bodies, eliciting screams of pain and more screeches of "Havoc".

Raw panic broke out among the Flemings. The mercenaries' eyes rounded in blind shock. They charged aimlessly and clumsily in every direction, falling into and over one another in desperate attempts to evade the onslaught.

Dafydd's and his captains' commands of, "Knock! - Draw! - Loose!" were shouted, repeated and repeated.

He dropped Ariston's reins. Long sword in right hand, short sword in left, he clung to his saddle with his thighs. Time jerked forward, Ariston's hooves hit the ground and the stallion thundered through a make-shift barrier of thorn and stones.

A Flemish sergeant in a studded leather cap and jerkin blocked Owain's path. He held a battle banner in one hand a sword in the other and faced the onslaught of Welsh cavalry, stolidly and unflinchingly.

Owain admired the man's courage, but admiration didn't prevent him from riding him down.

He heard the sergeant's bones crunch beneath Ariston's hooves as he charged towards the tents. Inside one of them he'd find the commander who'd led the mercenary army into his Welsh mountains.

He wanted to meet him.

Within sight of the battle. The foot of Hyddgen Mountain in the Plynlimmon, Range, midday June 1401
'We're too late.'

Xian heard Konrad but a single glance at the battle raging beneath the Flemish banners had told him that much. He reined in his rough bred mountain pony.

Even if they'd been able to unpack their vessels of flying fire without attracting attention, the fighting was too close quartered to risk using them. The din of clashing blades was deafening, the high pitched screams and cries of the wounded and dying, excruciating.

'Stay here with Fritz, Ulrich and the pack ponies,' Xian ordered Konrad. 'Keep out of the fighting. If you can throw flying fire without risk to yourselves, the Prince or his men, do so.'

Konrad studied movement on the fringe of the camp. 'Enemy soldiers are breaking away and retreating westwards on foot, my lord.'

'If the prince's men don't follow, light a few fuses to hasten them on their way.'

'And you, my lord?'

'One more man at arms never goes amiss in a battle.'
Xian pulled off the hooded shepherd's fleece that partially covered his face to reveal a chain mail tunic and head coif. He retrieved the sword he'd hidden beneath his saddlebag, and spurred his pony.

He'd seen Glyndŵr's flamingo feather flying above the thickest fighting. He rode as fast as his pony could take him towards it.

The foot of Hyddgen Mountain in the Plynlimmon, Range, midday June 1401.

Ieuan cut and thrust through the Flemish swordsmen who were trampling over the bodies of their fallen in their eagerness to escape the field. He was conscious of his father fighting ahead of him, Maredydd wielding blades on his left, and David on his right. He ducked to avoid a lance and caught a glimpse of Tudor's black stallion and Gruffydd's grey on the edge of the camp where the Flemings had "stabled" their mounts.

The blade of Tudor's broadsword flashed, catching the light as he brought it down on the rope that tethered a string of enemy horses.

A sharp stabbing pain tore upwards from his leg. He cried out and turned in his saddle. A mercenary tugged at the pick he'd thrust beneath the poleyn that covered his right knee and ripped it upwards. Blood spurted out from beneath the armoured plates, soaking the man's face.

He failed to turn his mount in time to loosen the mercenary's grasp on the pick, or prevent him from wrenching it free and aiming it in readiness to inflict a second blow.

A blade flashed. The pick wavered in the air. Ieuan blinked, and opened his eyes to see both pick and the mercenary's arm hover unsupported, before crashing to the ground.

David smiled briefly before swaying in his saddle and falling sideways from his mount. It was then Ieuan saw the inner blade of a hooked flail caught between his brother's breast plate and helmet.

***

Maredydd rode behind his father, lashing out right and left, at the blades that surrounded them. He'd hoped to protect his father's back, but found it impossible to determine whether the blows that were raining from all sides came from friend or foe.

He slashed down hard with the intention of deflecting a sword aimed at the neck of his mount, and shuddered when it remained firm. His blade bounced back. He lifted it again, crashing it down on the crown of a helmet he trusted was an enemy's.

He looked down as his assailant fell and saw Ieuan crouched on the ground protecting David's body with his own.

Obeying every instinct to help his brother, he kicked his feet free from his stirrups.

'No!' Dafydd shouted. 'Stay mounted! Fight! It's the only way to help them!'

***

Reeling at a blow from Tudor's sword to his shoulder gard-brace the sergeant dropped his broad sword, and fell to his knees.

'Mercy!'

'Order your men to surrender!' Tudor demanded.

The sergeant turned his head. 'Yield! The day is lost!'

'On your knees.' Tudor shouted at the mercenaries. He waved the Welsh forward behind him. 'Keep them in the dirt, and take their weapons.'

While his men carried out his orders, Tudor leaned forward in his saddle and pushed the tip of his broad sword beneath the sergeant's chin.

Terrified the man croaked, 'I surrender unconditionally, Lord Glyndŵr.'

Only one man on the field was wearing Glyndŵr's armour, tabard and distinctive red flamingo feather but Tudor didn't correct the officer.

'Your name?'

'Watkins of Hundleton, my lord.'

'Is Hundleton a wealthy manor?' Tudor asked.

'A poor threadbare holding, my lord. My hovel has only one room, a roof that leaks, a well run dry, and four fields too barren to keep a goat. Our neighbours fare no better. Between the ravages of plague and crop blight, the village has nothing to recommend it.'

'Yet this broken place has produced sufficient to outfit you in style. It's a long time since I've seen a blade or armour so well made and polished.' Tudor lifted his sword from the man's throat, and flicked open the visor of his helmet before dismounting.

'The armour was my father's, my lord. He fought for King Richard in Scotland and won it on the field in return for sparing the life of its owner. He did not live to wear it long. He died from wounds shortly after his return home.'

'Which makes it at least three years old yet it looks newly wrought.' Tudor commented.

'Hundleton's blacksmith is poor but skilled, my lord. He repaired and polished the armour for me.'

'And now he'll be able to earn more by making a replacement suit and weapons for you.' Tudor motioned to his squire. 'Relieve the man of his accoutrements.'

'But how will I pay the blacksmith to manufacture new, my lord? I can't earn a living without blade or armour. I need them to sell my services ... '

'Given the company you keep, I advise you to give up soldiering and return to farming. Maybe even improve that threadbare holding you spoke about,' Tudor reached out to one of the horses he'd freed and grabbed its bridle. He looked from the stallion to his captive. There was a proprietary look in Watkin's eye. 'Yours?' he asked.

'My captain's. He allowed me to ride it.'

'Generous captain. But this is no farm horse. From what you said it would starve for pasture in your fields.'

'It would, my lord.'

'I know Pembroke well, as does my squire. Do you recollect seeing any poor hill farms there, Alun?'

Tudor's squire was accustomed to his master's odd humour. He shook his head. 'Only rich ones with lush pasture, my lord.'

'Perhaps we should ride down there, take a look at Hundleton and see what it has to offer as ransom payment besides armour and weapons.' Tudor reached down and hauled the sergeant upright. 'On your feet, Watkins.'

'No one will pay anything to ransom me, my lord.'

'Your wife won't give what little you possess to secure your return?'

'I have no wife, my lord.'

'Your mother then?'

'She died a week after my father, there's only my brother, Lord Prince Glyndŵr ... '

'I'm not the Prince of Wales. He's over there.' Tudor nodded to Owain who was dismounting in front of the largest tent in the field. He pushed Watkins towards Alun. 'See if he can scrape up anything else besides his armour and blades to pay for his freedom.'

'And if he can't my lord?'

Tudor winked, 'sell him into servitude. The abbeys are always looking for strong young men to do the rough work.'

'I pray you, my lord. Please don't sell me to a religious order ... '

Tudor turned his back as his squire pushed the man towards the strings of captives they'd taken.

***

'That was easier than I anticipated, and quick too, my prince,' John Hanmer strode across the field, tore a Fleming battle banner from a pole and used it to wipe the blood from his blade.

'They ran squawking like chickens from a fox,' Philip declared as he joined Owain and John.

'Do you want me to pick out a few of our men and follow them, my lord?' John asked.

'Yes, but stay out of sight and don't engage them unless you have to. Once you're certain they won't return, ride back here. Aside from a few watchers to man the lookout posts we'll be leaving in the morning. If we're already gone when you return, head for Glyncoch.'

'Yes, my lord.'

'Eat before you leave and be sure to carry enough provisions with you. It appears the Flemings have left plenty.'

'That I can promise you, my lord.' John called to his squire and sergeant.

***

Tudor eyed the field with a practised eye. The squires were checking the wounded, the sergeants evaluating injuries and directing the apothecary to treat those who had a chance, albeit slim in some cases, of survival. Pages were supervising captured enemy soldiers who'd been ordered to carry the dead off the field and place them in one of two very separate piles, Fleming and Welsh.

'Who decided those who fight one another can't be buried together?' Tudor only realised he'd spoken aloud when Philip Scudamore answered from behind him.

'Probably the church, afraid that the spirits of the fallen will return from the other world and carry on battling.'

'"Other world?"' Tudor fell into step besides Philip. 'Doesn't every soldier who dies fighting for God might and right, go through a one way door to heaven?'

'I've no idea. I've never spoken to anyone who's stepped through it either way. Have you?' Philip asked,

'Several times,' Tudor reached for his flask. 'But never without a good few belts of good Welsh gwisgi inside me. The golden river that carries all soldiers to heaven.' He drank before handing the flask to Philip who in turn gave it to Gruffydd when he emerged from a Fleming supply tent.

Gruffydd tossed two sacks of bread to his squire. 'Take these to the cooks so they can hand it out with the stew.' He uncorked the flask and drank before returning it to Tudor.

'Someone isn't pleased at being captured,' Tudor frowned as the protest became an agonised cry.

'That's Ieuan's voice.' Gruffydd started running.

***

Dry eyed, face the colour of bleached parchment, Ieuan lay on the ground. Oblivious to the blood pumping from his knee he cradled David's body against his own as sobs tore from his throat.

Gruffydd couldn't see a mark on David but his brother's eyes were open, staring sightlessly. He looked to Maredydd who was kneeling next to Ieuan and David. Maredydd saw him and shook his head. He had seen enough death on the battlefield to recognise David had taken his last breath, but his mind refused to believe his eyes. David couldn't be dead. He loved his oldest brother too much to lose him.

Gruffydd laid a hand on Ieuan's arm. Ieuan turned to him but his eyes remained dark, focused inwards.

'Tell them, Gruffydd. Tell them they can't take David. That he has to go back to Pont Gweni. He belongs in the village with our mother.'

Ieuan closed his eyes, and Gruffydd sensed him concentrating with every fibre of his being, conjuring an image of David as he had been in life

'If you want to take David back to Pont Gweni, Ieuan, that's what we'll do.' Owain appeared and laid a hand on Ieuan's shoulder. He crouched beside him and handed him his gwisgi flask.

When Ieuan returned the flask, Owain picked up David. Unsupported by Ieuan, David's head fell backwards, revealing the fatal gash inflicted by the flail. It had sliced David's throat from ear to ear above his breast plate.

Gruffydd spread out his cloak and Owain laid David on it. Together Maredydd and Gruffydd lifted his body.

Walking slowly behind their father and brother they carried David through the avenue of men who were already hanging their heads in respect to the fallen.

The foot of Hyddgen Mountain early hours of the morning after the battle.

The moon hung low, illuminating a field draped in purple shadows, littered with shattered arrows and splintered quarrels. Moonlight flashed silver on broken spears, flails and axe heads that had been trampled into the mud. The scent of grass was overwhelmed by the stench of putrefying flesh, horse and human manure.

Tudor had ordered a hollow in the base of a neighbouring hill dug out and extended. When his men had widened and deepened it, he oversaw the removal of the Welsh dead into the pit. The men laid out the bodies of their twenty-six fallen comrades in a row, linking their arms before covering each individual with his cloak. When they finished, Tudor distributed flasks of gwisgi to the gravediggers and left them and the dead to the prayers of those who'd known them best in life.

He turned back to the battlefield. Owain, Xian and Gruffydd were crouched before a campfire in front of the largest pavilion. As he negotiated a path towards them, the wind shifted and he caught a foul whiff of roasting flesh from the heap of burning enemy corpses on the far edge of the field. They'd been covered with brushwood laced with mutton fat but there hadn't been enough fat to feed the fire and it didn't burn as fiercely as he'd have wished.

When he drew near he saw Ieuan lying on a palette behind the others. The boy's face burned bright in the firelight as he tossed and turned feverishly, mumbling to himself and fighting Maredydd who was trying to force water between his swollen lips.

'Dafydd and the apothecary have doctored him,' Owain informed Tudor. 'His fever is lessoning. They expect it to abate by morning.'

'And the wound in his knee?'

'Is clean. Provided it remains so, Dafydd says it will heal, but you know how painful joint injuries can be.'

'Unfortunately.' Tudor laid his hand on Ieuan's forehead.

'Do you think Dafydd is right about Ieuan's knee healing?' Maredydd asked.

'I wouldn't argue with Dafydd, given his experience of wounds and Ieuan's fever has to be partly down to the shock of losing David. They are - were - very close.' Tudor lowered himself on the ground next to Owain and Xian.

'His loss is unbearable,' Gruffydd said bitterly.

Tudor laid his arm across Gruffydd's shoulders. 'But we will bear it. And do so together because we've no choice but to face it.'

'He did so much for all of us younger boys . . . ' Maredydd laid his hand on Ieuan's cheek to reassure himself that his temperature really was falling.

'David gave you your first taste of gwisgi at four years old after stealing a flask from my saddlebag,' Tudor smiled at the memory. 'I don't think it occurred to him that I had an older brother who did the same for me when I was a boy. And, after introducing you to gwisgi, he introduced you to women who wanted to make men of you years before you were ready for the experience. He also taught you the exact moment when to forgo the rules of chivalry and fight dirty.'

'He showed me how to tell when a spavined mount has been doctored to look better than it is,' Maredydd added.

'And yesterday he taught me how to keep your dignity when you find yourself married to a whore.'

They all turned to Ieuan.

Tudor was the first to recover from seeing Ieuan awake and what he'd said. 'That too,' he agreed.

'What did Dafydd give me?' Ieuan asked.

Owain crouched beside his son. 'Something to lessen your pain.'

'It lessened all of me,' Ieuan's voice grew faint as he struggled to sit up.

'All the more reason for you to rest,' Owain advised.

Ieuan didn't need any more persuading. Maredydd slipped his arm behind his back and lowered him gently to the ground.

'David visited me in my dreams.' Ieuan's voice wavered from the effects of Dafydd's draught. 'He told me he wants to stay here with the others.'

'You wanted to bury him in Pont Gweni,' Owain reminded.

'He said that soon there won't be anyone left in Pont Gweni to remember our family once lived there. Here, he will lie with friends.'

'Are you sure you want to leave David here, Ieuan?' Owain reiterated.

'Quite sure. It's what he wants.' Exhausted by the effort of speaking, Ieuan closed his eyes and slipped effortlessly back into unconsciousness.

Owain entered the tent and crouched beside David's shrouded body. He uncovered his face and looked at it for a long time - remembering.

How proud he'd been when Gwyneth had introduced him to his first born son. David had opened his eyes when he'd taken him into his arms and Gwyneth had said it was impossible to tell which pair of eyes held the most wonder, his or David's.

David training as a knight shortly after his seventh birthday, insisting on practising and exercising even when exhaustion had set in and he no longer had the strength to lift a blade.

David marrying Enfys. The pride in David's face when he had shown his father his first born grandson, young Owain . . .

'I know what you're thinking, Owain.'

Owain turned to see his brother Tudor standing behind him.'

'If I'd known the price was David's life . . . '

'You'd what?' Tudor cut in ruthlessly. 'Allowed the Flemings to win a victory without meeting any resistance? Given Bolingbroke leave to continue to ride roughshod over us and steal our lands and birth-right? To evict us from our houses and towns, disarm us, enslave us in our own country?'

Tudor continued to watch his brother. He'd never seen Owain look so desolate or broken. But there were too many men looking to the Prince of Wales to lead and guide them for him to offer sympathy.

'David was a man not a boy, Owain. Like you, and like all of us, he knew the risks of battle. He made his choice.'

'It was too high . . . '

'For Owain Glyndŵr the father, it was,' Tudor agreed, 'but not for a Prince, who has sworn to free his country from the yoke of an oppressor.'

Tudor turned aside to give Owain the only thing he could, and the one thing he sensed Owain needed. Privacy.

He knelt beside David and kissed his forehead.

'Sleep well, my nephew.' He reached out to Owain. 'When you're ready I'll help you carry David to his grave.'

***

'I'm perfectly capable of riding without being trussed like a parcel, uncle,' Ieuan snapped.

'Of course, you are, nephew,' Tudor retorted. 'We won't get in your way if you'd like to vault on to your mount.'

'I may need some help to get up.' Ieuan glared at Tudor, but relented enough to take his extended hand.

'Gruffydd, assist me here with your brother?' Tudor asked.

'Only if you promise he won't bite.'

That I can't do.' Tudor checked that the improvised splint he'd fashioned from an enemy flagpole was holding Ieuan's knee straight before nodding to Gruffydd. Together they hoisted Ieuan, still protesting he didn't need manhandling, up and into his saddle. Once he was there Tudor roped Ieuan securely to his destrier so if he did fall he wouldn't hit the ground, and while he worked, Gruffydd handed Ieuan David's hawk, Bran.

'If you want him . . . ' Ieuan began.

'The bird knows his new master, it's fitting you inherit him,' Gruffydd gave a sad smiled as the hawk nestled close to Ieuan's neck.

When the men saw Owain mount Ariston, they ran from their last minute excursions to ensure they'd picked the Flemish camp clean, and followed suit

'I'll ride alongside you, Ieuan.' Tudor walked his horse beside Ieuan's.

'If you try to fasten a leading rein to my mount's bridle I'll . . . '

'You'll what?' Tudor waited for Ieuan to finish his sentence.

'I'll order Bran to peck you,' Ieuan threatened, pain making him irritable.

'No leading rein,' Tudor agreed, 'provided you ride quietly alongside me.'

'For the moment,' Ieuan qualified.

Owain walked Ariston to the mound of freshly turned soil at the foot of Hyddgen. His men rode behind him out of the camp and gathered in front of the grave. It had been filled in shortly after dawn, the thud of water logged clumps of earth accompanying the prayers of Friar Brown reciting masses for the souls of the dead.

Three archers stood at the foot of the mound. When the men halted, the only sounds in the valley were the clink of their harnesses and the cries of the kites and hawks circling overhead. The archers lit their arrows and fired at the head of the mound. The arrows flared and Friar Brown said a short and final prayer.

Owain turned to face his army. His voice, loud, clear echoed through the valley and up to the lookouts stationed on the hilltops.

'We leave our heroes safe in the heart of this mountain that stands deep in the heart of Wales. We hope God in his mercy will allow them to lie in peace for all eternity. They gave their most precious gift, their lives, fighting for the holiest of causes. Freedom for this land and its people.

'We are grateful for their sacrifice, their courage, their patriotism and we will remember them for this hard won victory. Any sane commander would have considered odds of more than seven to one, an impossible gamble. But yesterday you proved that one Welshman fighting to free his land from injustice, is more than equal to seven paid mercenaries.

'Thank you, gentlemen. Both the dead,' Owain turned to the grave and bowed before it, before turning back to his men. 'And the living.'

He bowed to his men.

'For those we leave, the war is over. For the rest of us, it begins in earnest.'

Owain turned Ariston to take a last look at the grave.

Tudor waved John Hanmer on. He led the men south east out of the valley, past Owain, Tudor, Ieuan and Gruffydd. As Xian passed Tudor he handed him the leading rein of one of the packhorses he'd brought from Glyncoch. Tudor took it and nodded his thanks.

Dafydd and Maredydd were the last of Owain's men to join the column.

***

When the first riders in the column reached the bank of the Afon Rheidol river, Tudor approached Owain.

'You don't need Crab, Crach, or the sight to know that this victory will send the name of Glyndŵr, Prince of Wales, resonating throughout the world. Soon your name will be shouted from every hilltop and mountain in England as well as Wales.'

When Owain didn't answer, Tudor continued. 'I feel your pain but it's time for all of us to say goodbye to David and the others.'

Owain took a last look at the grave and turned his mount. He didn't glance back at Tudor and his sons as he headed south, while they turned their horses towards the northern pass out of the valley.

CHAPTER FIFTEEN

Glyncoch Glyndŵr's HQ in the Berwyn mountains July 1401

'There has to be something wrong with me.'

Margaret saw tears start in Gweni's eyes. She sat on the bed, wrapped her arms around her and held her close.

'There is nothing wrong with you, Gweni,' she reassured. 'Miscarrying a child is more common than most women realise. If it's not talked about, it's for the same reason we don't dwell on the pains of childbirth. Once a woman bears a living baby and holds the child in her arms, as I promise, you will one day, all this pain of a lost child who never lived to draw breath will be forgotten.'

'You don't think . . . '

Margaret waited but when Gweni didn't continue she prompted, 'what?'

'Some of the maids . . . '

'Not Enyd or Betsi?' Margaret interrupted.

'Abertha and the cook,' Gweni revealed reluctantly.

'The two worst gossips in the household. Whatever they said, ignore it.' Margaret took the towel Gweni had used to dry her hands and face, folded it and placed it on the side of the washbowl.

'I wish Xian was here,' Gweni murmured.

'Philip Scudamore told me Owain hopes to be here tomorrow or the day after at the latest.' The message Philip had given her was that Owain was aiming to reach Glyncoch by nightfall, but Margaret knew how easily a lame horse or flooded ford could delay a journey and she wanted to spare Gweni another disappointment. There was also one other piece of news Margaret had kept from Gweni. But she'd recognised Owain's insistence in the wording of his message. It was his place to give Gweni the tragic news of David's death, and Xian needed to be there to support Gweni when he did.

'You really think they'll be here tomorrow?' Gweni asked.

'We can hope,' Margaret hated lying. 'I can understand you missing Xian. The worst part of being a soldier's wife is the absences, but men are best away from situations they can't physically fight. I believe Owain would challenge the devil himself to save me one twinge of pain. But he's never been good at coping with situations he can't remedy.'

They were disturbed by a knock at the door. Margaret called out, "Enter," and Betsi walked in.

'My lord has returned with his soldiers, my lady.'

'Xian . . . ' Gweni broke in eagerly.

'I didn't see him, my lady, but Konrad said he was fine.'

'Stay here with your mistress, Betsi. I'll find Lord Xian and send him here.'

Betsi dropped a curtsy. 'My lady.'

Margaret left the room and ran down the stairs. The narrow hallway was teeming with men who were streaming into the great hall. She knew better than to look for Owain among them.

Her brother John saw her, pushed the men out of her path, and shouted, 'Make way for, my lady.' He opened the door to the ante room.

Owain, Maredydd, Dafydd and Xian were standing in front of the hearth. Owain was leaning on the shelf above it staring down into the flames. Margaret saw the lines of exhaustion and pain etched around his eyes and her heart went out to him.

He glanced up, saw her and smiled. 'Did my messenger arrive?' He wrapped his arm around her shoulders.

'Two hours ago. Gweni is in your chamber Xian.'

'Is she . . . '

'She's lost your child but she will recover. All the quicker now you're here,' she answered. 'I haven't told her about David.'

'You know Ieuan's wounded?' Owain asked.

'Yes. I asked Efa to get his room ready.'

'He's not with us.'

'He's . . . ' Margaret's voice faltered.

'He insisted on going to Pont Gweni with Tudor and Gruffydd to see Enfys.'

'But his wound . . . '

'A leg wound,' Owain explained. 'Dafydd tended it.'

'Robert is here.'

'The scamp was told to stay in Glyndyfrdwy,' Owain allowed his irritation to show.

'Hunith delivered a load of weapons he'd repaired. He said Robert hid among them in the back of the cart. Don't be too hard on him, Owain, he was missing his brothers and sister.'

'Maybe it's as well that Ieuan, Maredydd and Gruffydd are reminded they have a small brother who will also suffer the loss of David,' Owain conceded.

'Is Elwy still here?' Maredydd asked.

Margaret nodded. 'She and Jonnet were in the seamstress's room the last time I saw them.'

'Do you want me to tell Jonnet that Gruffydd's gone to Pont Gweni, mother?'

'And, incidentally see Elwy?' Margaret shook her head fondly at him. 'Go, Maredydd.'

Maredydd's hand was already on the latch of the door.

'I hope you told Tudor and Gruffydd to bring Enfys and the boys here,' Margaret said to Owain.

'This is a campaign headquarters not a children's nursery.'

'There's no reason why it can't be both.'

'I suppose it can as long as we're able to keep them safe,' Owain hugged her again. 'Dafydd, spread the word, captains' council here in one hour.'

Pont Gweni July 1401

The solidly built wooden bridge that had given "Pont" Gweni its name had been burned by Reginald de Grey's soldiers the previous autumn. The pillars on the banks that had supported it remained in place although the damage to the wooden brace around them had caused most of the stones to slip out of place.

Rough cut tree trunks now spanned the deep waters but they didn't look strong enough to hold a man's weight much less a horse and cart.

'I don't fancy leaving Satan here. There's no way of knowing how long we'll be in the village. Besides I don't want to risk putting my weight on those beams.'

'Neither do I, and I'm half your width.' Gruffydd joked, despite David's death gnawing at his mind like a sickness. Given Enfys's temper and fondness for creating scenes he was dreading seeing her. Almost as much as David would have been he reflected, finally understanding his brother's need to live apart from his wife.

'I'll explain the difference between fat and muscle to you later, boy.' Tudor looked up and down the river, swollen by the recent rains it gushed and boiled fiercely. 'I suppose there's nothing for it but to look for a crossing that offers firm ground underfoot. What do you say, Ieuan, this is your home territory, left or right?'

Ieuan frowned from more than the pain in his knee. It wasn't the quantity of water or even the speed it surged. The stream was thick with debris, small trees, large branches, bushes and plants, any one of which could hit a horse and knock it off its feet.

'You waiting for sunset?' Tudor asked after a full minute passed without an answer from Ieuan.

'I was going to say right, until I saw that pall of smoke rising above where the village should be.'

Tudor stared at the black plume. 'It's too thick to have come from a hearth. We'll investigate, but first we have to find a crossing point that isn't overlooked. You still say right?'

'Yes.'

'You sure?'

'No, but at least I've made a decision which is more than you appear to be capable of doing.'

'You insolent pup.'

'That's me, uncle.' Ieuan grimaced.

Tudor turned his mount right. 'I'll take your advice, but when we find a crossing, you go first.'

The spot they found was a mile and half upstream and far from perfect.

'Either the river is shallower here or the rocks are larger,' Tudor declared philosophically as he tried to gauge the size of the stones from what could be seen above the waterline. 'Care to find out?'

'I'll go first, unlike Ieuan I have two good knees.' Gruffydd volunteered. He walked his horse slowly off the bank and into the water. His destrier bent his head and gingerly moved forward. Gruffydd let the reins dangle, and his mount set the pace. The trust he put in his horse was rewarded, although it took him longer than he'd hoped to reach the opposite bank.

Once the horse saw firm ground within reach, he heaved his legs out of the cloying mud. Half an hour later Ieuan and Tudor joined him on the bank.

Dusk was falling, tinging the air with a hazy purple light. The smoke had thinned since they'd seen it on the opposite bank, but the stench of fire hung thick in the air.

Gruffydd sniffed. 'I smell roasting meat,' he whispered.

'Let's hope it is meat, boy.' Tudor held his finger to his lips.

'Given way my knee feels I'll stay mounted until you return,' Ieuan whispered.

Tudor nodded agreement before helping Gruffydd hobble and tie their mounts and the pack horse in a copse of trees. Nephew and uncle had lived and fought together so long there was no need for words between them. When they reached the thicket that bordered what had been the fields of Pont Gweni they crouched down and surveyed the remains of the village de Grey's men had destroyed.

Nettles, blackberry thorn, and willow seedlings sprouted where corn, oats, rye and pasture had grown. The vegetable beds had been overtaken by couch grass, and the paths between them slimed with moss after the rain.

The new timbers that had been erected on the church roof to replace those de Grey's men had burned had been torn down, piled up and set alight in the churchyard. Sparks had been carried by the breeze, and a few of the wooden grave markers left standing were also in flames.

The mill David had paid a carpenter to rebuild to provide a home and business for his wife and family was a heap of smouldering ashes, and all that remained of the village houses was an avenue of stone foundations.

Gruffydd's eye was drawn to the broken stones that outlined the plot where David, Ieuan, Gweni and Robert had lived with their mother. He recalled the warm welcomes extended to him, his brothers and sisters within its walls. The harvest suppers he'd eaten in Gwyneth's kitchen after he'd helped bring in the crops.

A sudden nudge from Tudor alerted him to movement inside the village barn. A soldier in de Grey's livery emerged leading a horse by the reins. He reached for a flask, opened it, drank, replaced it in his jerkin and mounted. Turning his horse's head he rode east.

Gruffydd moved. Tudor stretched out his arm to prevent him rising and shook his head. They both listened hard for a few minutes before rising to their feet and walking over to the barn. They could see that more than one horse had been stabled there from the heaps of manure. They checked around before heading for the mill that had been reduced to smouldering ashes.

Tudor tore a branch from an apple tree and poked around in the black cinders until he uncovered a charred ribcage.

'God help us. Is that . . . '

'There's no way of knowing who it was other than human.' Tudor interrupted Gruffydd. 'The least we can do is give the bones as much of a Christian burial as we're capable of.'

Glyncoch Glyndŵr's HQ in the Berwyn mountains July 1401

Xian charged up the stairs and burst into his chamber. He ran across the room and forgetting muddy boots, travel soiled clothing and everything except Gweni, gathered her into his arms.

Sensing her mistress no longer needed her, Betsi tiptoed out of the room and closed the door softly behind her.

It was a long while before Xian managed to kiss away Gweni's tears and even then, she clung to him, her entire body racked by sobs.

'You wanted to be a father, so much.'

'And I will be. Just not yet.' He pulled her even closer to him.

'Not ever,' she murmured.

'What do you say that, my heart?'

'You're different from me ... '

'I am,' he forced a smile. 'But I didn't hide my face from you when we married.'

'I'm not accusing you of anything just stating the truth,' she said. 'I lost our child because we're two different species. Like a sheep and a dog or a horse and a cow ... ' The bed started shaking she turned and looked at him You're laughing!' she exclaimed furiously.

He struggled to straighten his face. 'Dare I ask which of us is which? Or would you like to bring other animals into the equation. A chicken, or pig perhaps.'

She glared at him. His mouth was still twitching and she simply couldn't help herself. She started to laugh too.

'I'm a man, you're a woman and when you have recovered from losing our child, we'll make another and next time you'll succeed in carrying her, my heart.'

'Him,' she corrected, smiling through her tears.

'Him - her - whatever God sends, but now I have to give you some bad news, but we will bear it together.' He gazed into her eyes and told her as simply as he could that her beloved brother David had been killed in battle.

Afterwards they lay on the bed and clung to one another. When dusk fell they both surrendered to exhaustion, and finally slept. Only then, did Betsi who'd been listening at their door, tiptoe away and creep downstairs in search of Konrad.

Pont Gweni July 1401

After weeks of rain and hailstorms the sun was setting in a sky totally devoid of clouds. Ieuan leaned against the wall of the roofless church in Pont Gweni, watching the disc turn from gold to red as it sank slowly over the western hills.

Tudor was digging a grave a few feet away. The ground was wet, the earth he piled up saturated. They'd found four distinct sets of bones in the burned out ashes of the mill, one a skull small enough to have been a baby. Lacking a shroud to wrap the remains, Gruffydd had lined an old manger he found in the barn with grass before reverently placing all the charred bone fragments they'd found inside it.

He'd covered the contents with a "blanket" of turf. Ieuan cut a handful of reeds and used them to tie two sticks together. He laid the crude cross he'd fashioned on top of the turf.

Tudor finished digging, took the manger and placed it at the bottom of the grave.

He recited what he could remember of a prayer for the souls of the dead and Gruffydd filled in the grave with the spade they'd found in the barn.

'Shouldn't we leave a marker?' Ieuan asked when Gruffydd tamped down the earth with the back of the spade.

'We should,' Tudor answered, 'but what would you put on it?'

'Do you think . . . '

'I think we should ride from here to Valle Crucis,' Tudor suggested. 'If anyone knows what happened here, it will be Abbot David.'

A mixture of pain and exhaustion had smoothed Ieuan's rough edge of irritation. He accepted Tudor's offer to help him mount his horse graciously, and even submitted to being roped on to his saddle again.

'You're heading the wrong way for Valle Crucis,' Gruffydd pointed out, when Tudor took the northern road out of Pont Gweni.

'I am,' Tudor said flatly.

Gruffydd was accustomed to his uncle's idiosyncrasies, but he was also saddened by the fate of those who'd burned to death in the mill.

People he suspected had included his sister-in-law and one of his nephews, their remains left to be blown in the wind like so much rubbish, and he wasn't proud of the part he'd played in consigning their bones to an unmarked grave.

'Shouldn't we turn around?' he snapped.

'We will,' Tudor replied, 'just as soon as I've found and talked to the soldier who rode away from here before us.'

Glyncoch Glyndŵr's HQ in the Berwyn mountains July 1401

Owain had bathed and changed his clothes and was sitting at a table in front of the window studying a map of Wales when Margaret entered their chamber.

'How is Gweni?'

'How you'd expect someone to be after losing a brother and a baby and hearing another brother has had a pickaxe stuck in his knee. Robert and Xian are doing their best to cheer her.'

He pulled her down on to his knee. 'Ask her if I may visit her in her chamber.'

She slipped her arm around his neck to steady herself. 'You're going away again soon, aren't you?'

'Not for a few days - and perhaps longer -'

'Perhaps?' she questioned sceptically.

'Decisions need to be made. I have to talk to my captains.'

When she continued to stare at him, he said, 'when I've made firm plans you'll be the first to know them.'

'When you leave here, Owain, I will ride with you.'

'We'll discuss it.'

'Does that mean you've no desire to ride into a deliberate trap a second time to deflect the enemy's attention from Glyncoch?'

'You know me so well, my love.' He kissed her. 'I hope you've organised a good dinner. The men deserve one.'

'Don't change the subject.' She hugged him tight. 'I was afraid I'd never see you again.'

'That thought is too painful to dwell on. I can't imagine a world without you in it.'

'Do you think God will house us together in heaven?' she asked seriously.

'Given your temper he wouldn't dare do otherwise.' He glanced at the bed. 'How long until the meal?'

As if to answer his question, the clang of the gong resounded up the stairs.

'It wouldn't do to be late.' She was desperately trying to remain cheerful but he could hear unshed grief in her voice.

She climbed from his lap and walked to a table set with a glass and checked the veil covering her hair.

'We have toasts to make and drink to the dead and the brave,' he agreed. 'An emissary arrived as I came upstairs to warn us of John Trefor's imminent arrival.'

'Bishop Trefor will always be welcome in any house of ours.'

'He knows that, my love.'

'Then why did he send word?' Margaret asked.

'The messenger told me he carries permissions from your brother Hanmer and Llewelyn ap Gruffydd Fychan for Gruffydd to marry Jonnet and Maredydd to marry Elwy.'

'News travels fast,' Margaret mused,

'You think they'd heard about Hyddgen?' he asked.

'From what Gwilym told me after speaking to the messengers who've called the past few days, everyone regards it as a huge victory. The turning point of the war, Owain.'

'I'll grant you it was an unexpected success, and one that was entirely down to luck and surprise. We caught the Flemings when their only thoughts were of supper.' He shook his head. 'But a turning point in the war? It's too early to predict which way the banners will blow, or even whose arms will be on them'

'You know my brother Hanmer.'

'I do,' he said drily. 'It's an acquaintance I've not always delighted in.'

'I've no doubt he could say the same of you. He told me at Christmas that he wanted to wait for a papal dispensation before giving Elwy and Maredydd his blessing, but both he and I knew, what he was really waiting for was to see if victory in Wales would be yours or Bolingbroke's. One night, well into his fourth goblet, he said he believed you were being reckless in challenging the king's authority and no good could come from your intransigence.'

'Did he really think I should have handed my land and tenants over to Reginald de Grey, and thanked him for freeing me of the responsibility of caring for my inheritance?'

'Presumably just as presumably your triumph at Hyddgen has made him reconsider the situation. The fact that he now wants Elwy to marry Maredydd, must mean he's decided you're worth courting as well as Bolingbroke.'

'Either that or the splinters he's collected in his backside from sitting on the fence are giving him more trouble than usual,' Owain joked.

'It was a victory . . . ' Margaret contradicted.

'It was, but not momentous enough to shake Bolingbroke from the throne and before you imagine it as a portend of triumphs to come, the Abbot of Tintern also sent a walking woman with news from London. Bolingbroke is recruiting an even larger army of mercenaries than he brought into Wales last autumn. It's rumoured they'll soon be marching this way. I'm sorry, my love.' He closed both his hands around hers. 'This is not the end, or even midway. This is just the beginning of our battle. to regain what is rightfully ours.'

'In which case it's time to make a start. You have a supper table to preside over, a son and soldiers to mourn, toast and thank, a costly victory to announce and two marriages to arrange. And that's without planning the rest of this year's campaign.' She opened the door and held it open.

The countryside around Pont Gweni July 1401
Tudor, Gruffydd and Ieuan found the soldier two miles from Pont Gweni. They didn't have to search, only follow the bellow of gwisgi laced snores. He was lying in a stupor on a bed of green bracken. They dismounted and crept up on him quietly but he didn't even open his eyes when Tudor prodded his shoulder with the toe of his boot.

When he finally jerked awake it was to find Tudor's hand clamped over his mouth and Gruffydd trussing his hands behind his back. He screamed when Tudor released his hold, and Gruffydd took the opportunity to stuff a rag between his teeth and tie it in place.

After they silenced him, they threw him face down across his saddle, secured his wrists to one stirrup, and lashed his ankles to the other. Tudor fastened a leading rein to bridle of the soldier's mount and they took the road to Valle Crucis.

CHAPTER SIXTEEN

Glyncoch Glyndŵr's HQ in the Berwyn mountains July 1401

'Maredydd and Elwy can't stop looking at one another,' Owain observed to Margaret beneath the hubbub of conversation at their table.

'I spoke to them earlier, they're devastated by the loss of David, but it seems to have made them all the more determined to wring happiness from every moment while they can.'

The thought of what another battle might bring hung heavy and unspoken between them. Owain covered Margaret's hand with his own.

'Tudor talked to the men after the battle. He advised them to recall the best jokes of those who'd died, remember them angry, happy and thoughtful, and never whisper their names.'

'Your brother has a talent finding solace in even the most heart breaking of situations which your sons seem to have inherited.' Margaret watched as Elwy held out a dried plum in front of Maredydd's mouth. He snapped at it like a fish taking bait, to the amusement of Jonnet, Catrin and the squires.

'I have no doubt that Tudor is comforting Ieuan now, even in the throes of his own grief.' Owain frowned. 'I was surprised when Gruffydd volunteered to ride to Pont Gweni with them, rather than return to Jonnet. Is it my imagination, or does he treat her more coolly than a prospective bridegroom should?'

'Hopefully it's a chill that will disappear in time.'

'So it's not my imagination. He does keep her at arm's length?'

'For now,' she agreed,

'So Gruffydd won't be as delighted at being given Llew's permission to marry Jonnet, as Maredydd was when I told him your brother had given him and Elwy his blessing.'

'Gruffydd will learn to appreciate Jonnet when they have exchanged vows and he discovers a wife can replace a mistress.'

'Gruffydd has a mistress?'

Margaret smiled at the surprise etched on Owain's face. 'You didn't know?'

'I knew he and Maredydd were friendly with some of the maids ... '

'With Maredydd it is only friendship. I think he fell in love with Elwy before his twelfth birthday and hasn't looked at another girl since.'

Owain glanced down the row of tables to where Maredydd and Elwy were sitting and smiled.

'They are besotted with one another - and fortunate to have found one another so young,' Margaret commented.

'I found you when you were Elwy's age,' he reminded.

'I was fortunate to find myself wedded to an experienced worldly wise man, who knew everything there is to know about seducing women. Not that I'm complaining,' she added.

'So, which maid has Gruffydd made his mistress?' Owain deliberately moved the conversation on from his transgressions.

Margaret smiled at Bishop Trefor who was trying to attract Owain's attention. He'd arrived just as they were about to eat, in time to take a seat alongside Owain's right hand. 'Bishop Trefor would like to speak to you and this is not a suitable subject for the supper table.'

Valle Crucis Abbey July 1401
'My lord Tudor, my lord Gruffydd, my Lord Ieuan.' The novice manning the abbey gate, bowed after opening the wooden barriers. 'You have come from the great victory at Hyddgen?'

'We only just left the battlefield, did the birds carry the news ahead of us?' Tudor asked.

'A friar, my lord, who is visiting my lord abbot.'
'His name?'
'Friar Brown, my lord.'
'He left Hyddgen straight after the battle,' Gruffydd reminded Tudor.

'Not straight after. I saw him load a trencher from a Fleming camp kitchen after the fighting ceased. He stayed long enough to eat and fill a sack with twice baked bread and pies. There are trenchermen and then there are Friar trenchermen. I've never seen a man fill his mouth as full or often as Friar Brown.'

'What was it like at Hyddgen, my lords?' the boy broke in eagerly.

'It was an expensive victory. We left our own dead on the field as well as 200 Flemings.' Gruffydd's grief was too raw for him to speak David's name.

'Did you kill many of the enemy, my lord Gruffydd?'

'An account of battle and killing would sit ill within these hallowed walls,' Tudor cut the boy short. 'The affairs of the outside world are no longer your concern. You answered the call and you're looking well on it. The praying and contemplation must suit you, Stephen, isn't it?' Tudor remembered the boy as a scullion in Llewelyn's house in Caeo.

'Not Stephen. Not any longer, my lord. I hope to be a brother in time, but . . . ' he hesitated before mumbling, 'it's not easy.'

'To overcome the sins of the flesh?' Tudor raised a questioning eyebrow. 'I've never tried abstinence. The idea doesn't appeal to me. But those who have, tell me it's hard to resist temptation. However they also say success grants a sense of accomplishment.'

'I hope to experience such a sense soon, my lord. But as you said, it's not easy, especially coming from Lord Llewelyn's kitchens where there was always food on offer, even meat, except on meatless days, of course.'

'Of course.' Tudor knew how carelessly the church's dietary laws had been applied in the kitchens of Caeo when the cook's back was turned. 'Is it just the food you miss?'

'And sleep, my lord. We have to pray eight times in the span of a day and a night, and can never rest, not even during the darkness for more than three hours.'

'So, apart from starving and not being allowed to sleep, you're enjoying life here?' Before the boy had time to reply, Tudor continued. 'Do you have a secure empty cell where I can lock up this stray?' He dismounted but kept a hold on the leading rein of de Grey's soldier's horse.

'We have the lay brother's contemplation cell, my lord. It's only used when one of them has drunk more mead or beer than the rules allow. They're not allowed wine, or gwisgi, nor are we novices,' he added wistfully.

'How many keys are there to the cell?'

'Just the one, my lord.'

'Good we'll lock our charge in there and I'll keep the key. There's no need for you or any of the brothers or lay brothers to put yourselves out looking after him. I'll see to him myself.' Tudor lifted the man's head from the saddle. His eyes were closed. He was unconscious and mercifully quieter than when they'd found him.

Tudor slung the soldier over his shoulder and handed the reins of his horse to Gruffydd before following the novice to the contemplation cell. It was furnished with two buckets. One empty, one filled with clean water. He wrapped the man in his soldier's cloak and left him on the stone floor.

'Thank you for your help, Stephen. We'll see you at the evening meal?' Tudor locked the door.

'Please call me brother, not Stephen or the abbot will scold me for hankering after my old life again.'

'Again?' Gruffydd repeated.

'Are you hankering for it?' Tudor asked.

'As I've already said, my lord, I miss some things, and then we hear . . . '

'What?' Gruffydd asked.

'About the Prince's victories and how he's fighting to free Wales.'

'A soldier's life is hard. Armies are large so there's never enough food. Pickets are expected to stand on duty all night, so sleep can be scarcer than food. Defeats and wounds are cruel and the loss of friends bitter and painful,' Gruffydd warned.

'The prize of freedom is worth a little hardship and sacrifice, isn't it, my lord?'

'That depends entirely on who's paying the bill,' Tudor answered. 'If anyone asks about our stray tell them we'll be here to pick him up before we leave.'

Owain Glyndŵr's Headquarters the Berwyn Mountains July 1401
'I'll be outside your window an hour after you and Jonnet retire. We'll go to my room,' Maredydd whispered to Elwy, when Jonnet and Catrin obligingly diverted Ina's attention by discussing the relative merits of silk as opposed to velvet brocade.

'You're not expecting Gruffydd back tonight?' Elwy asked.

'Not for several days. Uncle Tudor said it would take that long to ensure David's sons have settled back into Pont Gweni.'

'Have many people returned to the village?'

'From what David told us, Enfys, his children, and her parents were the first.'

'Then they may bring Enfys and the boys here?'

'Ieuan said Enfys might not want to leave Pont Gweni.' Aware of the estrangement between David and his wife and not wanting to think about David, Maredydd returned to his plans. 'You'll be waiting for me at your window?'

'Aren't I always?'

'Bishop Trefor said he'll marry us whenever we're ready.'

'I always thought I'd marry in the church at Hanmer.'

'Does the place matter when God is everywhere? If it was up to me I'd ask Bishop Trefor to marry us at dawn tomorrow, but as your father's only just given us permission, he might think I'm being hasty.'

'And you're not?' she teased. 'Since I was old enough to understand the meaning behind the wedding mass I've dreamed of marrying in Hanmer Church in front of my parents.'

'Did you dream of marrying in Hanmer Church before you met me?'

'It's where my parents married ... '

'And mine,' Maredydd reminded her.

'My mother told me so many stories about her wedding. The red and blue silk gown her mother had made for her, the family jewels her father ordered placed in new settings, the feasting afterwards ... '

Maredydd was tempted to point out that she hadn't mentioned her father once, but he swallowed the impulse.

' ... after listening to her I never pictured myself marrying anywhere other than Hanmer Church,' she continued. 'But if you want to marry here ... '

'I do,' Maredydd broke in quickly. 'I wish we were standing before the altar in Hanmer this minute, but as it means journeying there, I'd settle for a quick service in the stables here.'

'Not the stables!'

'Then the chapel. Please, Elwy marry me tomorrow?' he begged.

'You know I can't deny you anything.'

Maredydd saw Ina watching them with her jackdaw eye. The look she sent his way, was enough for him to relinquish all thoughts of kissing Elwy.

'If you imagined yourself marrying in Hanmer Church, who did you picture as your bridegroom?' he whispered as he nodded to Ina and leaned away from Elwy.

'You're fishing for compliments, and I'm not biting.'

'Then it wasn't me?' he asked.

'I've said I'll marry you the in chapel here when Bishop Trefor is prepared to declare us man and wife. That's enough promises from me for one day, Maredydd Glyndŵr.'

Valle Crucis Abbey July 1401
'Lords Tudor, Gruffydd, and Ieuan, you are most welcome.' Abbot David rose from his chair and left the table and the book he'd been nodding over to greet them. 'Congratulations on your victory at Hyddgen and our deepest sympathy on the loss of your nephew and brother David. A Godly man. His soul will not be long in purgatory. I have no doubt that even now he is close to heaven.'

'That is a great comfort. Thank you, abbot,' Tudor grasped the old man's hand.

'Please tell the Prince of Wales and everyone who knew and loved David, that masses will be said for his soul within the walls of Valle Crucis for as long as I am abbot here.'

'I thank you for your messages for the Prince, Abbot David. Your kindness is much appreciated. Did Friar Brown bring you news of David's death in battle?' Tudor asked.

'He did, he also undertook to take word to his wife . . .'

'Enfys is alive?' Tudor questioned.

'She is,' the abbot looked at Tudor in surprise. 'Isn't that why you're here.'

'We went to Pont Gweni,' Gruffydd explained. 'The mill David had rebuilt for his family had burned to the ground.'

'We found bones in the ruins,' Ieuan added.

'They were too charred for us to identify any but friend or foe they deserved a Christian burial. We buried them in the churchyard with as much of the funeral mass as I could remember, but as you well know, I am no churchman, abbot,' Tudor said.

'That I can testify to. But you are a good kind Christian man, Tudor, and I'm certain that heaven will approve of your intentions to give the poor souls a Christian burial. I will send a brother there to conduct a full funeral mass.'

'I'd wait until the Flemish mercenaries have had time to disperse and the roads are safe if I were you, abbot,' Tudor advised.

'Please sit. You must be hungry.' Abbot David motioned them to a bench set before the hearth.

'Thank you, Abbot. We came here hoping to beg a night's lodging.'

'No one of the house of Glyndŵr begs here. This abbey is as much your home as it is ours, my lords.'

'Thank you, abbot. I think I can speak for Gruffydd and Ieuan as well as myself when I say we can wait for supper,' Tudor said. 'When did Enfys arrive? Are the children with her?'

'The two eldest, Owain and Gruffydd. The youngest died of plague along with Enfys's parents and the members of two other families who had also returned to Pont Gweni. The taverner Jeremiah brought Enfys here after he happened upon her on the road.'

'Plague in Pont Gweni! Did Enfys or the two boys ... '

'They escaped, thanks be to God,' the abbot said fervently.

'Who burned the mill?' Tudor asked.

'Reginald de Grey's men after Enfys and the boys left. Brother Cedric saw and spoke to them. He was making his way here from Strata Florida when he saw the smoke. He went to the village and asked the soldiers what they were doing.'

'Did they reply?' Gruffydd asked.

'They said they were clearing plague rats.'

Tudor rose from his stool. 'If you'll excuse us, abbot, I'd like to call on my niece and nephews before supper.'

The abbot was unable to conceal his unease but Tudor didn't press him as to the cause. 'We'll talk again this evening, Tudor Glyndŵr.'

'I will look forward to it, Abbot David.' Tudor kissed his ring.

Lay worker's cottages Valle Crucis Abbey July 1401
Brother Cedric accompanied Tudor, Ieuan and Gruffydd to the cottage Enfys had been allocated when she'd sought sanctuary in Valle Crucis after the first attack Reginald de Grey's soldiers had made on Pont Gweni.

Owain and Tudor's thrice great grandfather, Prince of Powys Fadog, Madog ap Gruffudd Maelor had founded Valle Crucis two hundred years ago. He'd given the brothers land and gold to build the abbey and added more coin to build cottages for the lay brothers and their families who worked on the order's farm and woodland.

The Cistercian Abbey had flourished for a hundred and fifty years until the Black Death had arrived in Wales fifty years ago, killing half the population. Lord, lady, cleric, labourer, monk or serf, the disease made no concession to rank, wealth or piety. The resulting devastation had emptied the abbey's humblest cottages along with the cloisters.

Since then the plague had revisited roughly every seven years, preventing the population of Wales from recovering from the effects of the first outbreak by claiming more lives, invariably the youngest and healthiest, but thankfully never with the same devasting severity.

Brother Cedric led the way through the woodland that encircled the abbey's fields, pausing frequently to allow Ieuan who was using a stick as a crutch to keep up with the rest of them.

If it hadn't been for his grief at the loss of David, Gruffydd reflected that he might have enjoyed the walk. The rains that had greyed the air and soaked the countryside for the past weeks had finally abated. The dying rays of the sun cast a warm golden light over the surrounding hills and danced on the bleached, carved stones of the Abbey buildings. Birdsong accompanied the melodic chanting that resounded from the chapel.

The ground was still waterlogged and the air was cool for summer, but it was preferable to the sodden conditions on Hyddgen. But then his brother had been alive on Hyddgen . . .

A sudden image of David, alive, smiling in mischief as he played the "knowing, teasing big brother" brought a rush of tears to Gruffydd's eyes. The agonising knowledge that he would never see his eldest brother again in this life, hit him anew with a paralyzing force, robbing him of breath.

Brother Cedric moved a wickerwork panel that protected the vegetable beds in front of the house from the chickens and pigs that ranged freely between the cottages, and knocked the door. Enfys opened it to reveal an unexpected domestic scene.

The taverner, Jeremiah was sitting on a stool at the head of the table with eighteen month old Gruffydd on his lap. Four year old Owain who'd been informally christened "Owain Bach" or "Owain Little" in English was crouched on a bench next to him, a bread trencher of peas pottage on the table in front of him. More trenchers and a wooden bowl of pottage were on the table. They'd obviously interrupted Enfys serving supper.

Brother Cedric stepped back into the garden and proceeded to study a row of beans, leaving Tudor, Ieuan and Gruffydd to stare into the cottage through the open doorway. When Enfys didn't speak, Tudor broke the silence.

'Abbot David told us that Friar Brown brought you news of David's death.'

'He did. Do you want to come in?' The invitation was perfunctory, with a strong hint that Enfys hoped they wouldn't accept, but Owain Bach had seen his uncles and jumped down from the table to meet them. He stretched his arms as wide as he could and hugged Tudor's legs. Tudor lifted him up. Owain nuzzled close and buried his head in Tudor's shoulder.

'I suppose you're here to take the boys. David told me he wanted them brought up in his father's house,' Enfys said.

'We went to Pont Gweni. After seeing the burned out mill we didn't expect to find you or the boys alive. When Abbot David told us you, Owain and Gruffydd had survived but Maredydd Bach had died from the plague we came to offer help,' Tudor said. 'But we won't interrupt your meal. We're staying the night in the abbey. We'll be leaving at first light. If you want to talk to us before then, send a message, and we'll return.'

'My father invited you and the boys to return to his headquarters with us,' Gruffydd said. 'My mother, Catrin and Gweni are there . . . '

'Your father didn't want me when David was alive. Why should he want me now? Or is he looking for my sons so they can follow their father to an early grave.' Enfys's face contorted in bitterness.

'My brother knew better than to step between husband and wife, Enfys. As do I,' Tudor said calmly. 'David is dead. He was my nephew. I loved him. Whatever trouble lay between you two was his and your business. We buried David with our fallen at Hyddgen. If you want to see his grave, I will take you there. You and the boys have an invitation to join his family. Whether you accept it or not is up to you.'

Owain Bach chose that moment to look up from Tudor's shoulder. 'Want to go with the uncles.'

'Go.' Enfys slammed the door shut leaving them in the garden.

'I guess you're going to finish your supper in the refectory with us, Owain Bach. Want to play horses?' Gruffydd smiled at the boy before taking him and placing him on his shoulders.

'Someone should talk to Enfys again before we leave.' Tudor looked at Brother Cedric.

'Someone?' Brother Cedric looked to the heavens as he repeated the word.

'A volunteer, someone like a kind benevolent man of God,' Tudor suggested.

Gruffydd winced as Owain Bach knotted his fingers in his hair and pulled at his curls as if they were a horse's reins. Gruffydd cried out in pain and Owain Bach giggled.

'Supper, then bed before you mangle your uncle Gruffydd, young man.' Tudor straightened Owain's fingers lifted him from Gruffydd's shoulders, and set him on the ground.

'Thank you.' Gruffydd winced as he ran his hands through his hair. 'Do you think we should try to persuade Enfys to ride with us tomorrow.'

'Her husband may not want to join you,' Brother Cedric warned. ' Friar Brown married her and Jeremiah in the church here this morning.'

Gruffydd finally understood why David had acted the way he had towards Enfys.

Small moments returned with a new startling clarity. Glances exchanged between Jeremiah and Enfys - and David and Enfys and any woman who smiled at David.

He thought of Jonnet - and then of his love. If he told his parents he loved another and could never love Jonnet, would they allow him to break his betrothal?

CHAPTER SEVENTEEN

Glyndŵr's Headquarters Glyncoch July 1401
Owain and his captains sat around the table in the ante room after supper from force of habit. All the plans that needed to be made, had been discussed earlier that day and the reality of their success at Hyddgen had finally begun to sink in after the euphoria of their homecoming celebrations two days ago.

Rhys Ddu and Rhys Fierce had arrived with their men before the tables had been cleared. More casks had been opened, and the ale coupled with gwisgi that remained in some of their flasks added to the general air of lassitude and inability of the men to think further than the pots and cups in front of them.

Crab's voice, low melodic drifted in through the open door to the Great Hall. Bishop Trefor caught himself nodding off, jerked awake and apologised to Owain.

'We'll talk again in the morning, Trefor, after the wedding.' Owain rose from the table and walked him into the hall.

He watched Trefor climb the stairs before returning to the ante room As he picked up his cup to finish his ale, the front door burst open and Tudor and Gruffydd strode in. Ieuan hobbled behind them leaning heavily on a staff. Gruffydd was carrying Owain Bach who had fallen asleep on his shoulder.

'We come bearing gifts as you see.' Tudor took Owain Bach from Gruffydd and handed him to Owain who lifted him into his arms.

The child opened his eyes saw his grandfather, smiled cuddled close to him and closed his eyes again.

'Take care to keep his hands away from your hair,' Gruffydd warned.

'Is Enfys with you?' Owain asked Tudor.

'She's staying in Valle Crucis with Gruffydd Bach.'

'Enfys left Pont Gweni after David paid for the rebuilding of the mill?' Maredydd asked in surprise.

'Pont Gweni left her,' Tudor answered. 'De Grey's men made another visit and burned down the new mill. They left a drunk behind. We brought him here as a gift for you, brother but given the state of him I asked Gwilym to lock him up in an empty stable. It will be easier to sluice him down there than the cell at the top of the house.'

'Are Enfys's parents with her?' Maredydd asked.

'Plague struck before de Grey's men arrived. It killed them and Maredydd Bach. Enfys, the two eldest boys and Jeremiah Taverner survived and sought sanctuary in the abbey. When news reached them of David's death, Jeremiah and Enfys married.'

Maredydd and Gruffydd found it impossible to read the expression on Owain's face at the news of Enfys's swift remarriage, but Tudor saw evidence of disapproval in the tense lines around Owain's mouth,

'Poor Maredydd Bach,' Ieuan murmured. 'But we can return to Pont Gweni when . . ?' he faltered when he considered what he was about to say.

'When the fighting ends we'll be able to make plans,' Owain said. 'But no matter what the outcome, Ieuan, I think too much will have changed for any of us to go back to where we were before Reginald de Grey attacked Pont Gweni.'

Tudor gave a wry smile. 'You, like the rest of us have to look forward not back, boy. Did I see John Trefor's horses in the stables?'

'You did,' Owain confirmed.

'Has he come to give us news or dispense God's blessings?'

'Neither, Llewelyn ap Gruffydd and our brother Gruffydd have given their blessing to Gruffydd's marriage to Jonnet and Maredydd's to Elwy.'

'It took some persuading because Elwy wanted us to be married in Hanmer church, but she agreed to become my wife tomorrow on condition we have our union blessed in

Hanmer as soon as it's safe for us to travel,' Maredydd smiled.

'If that grin gets any wider it will swallow your face, nephew,' Tudor teased. 'That's an accolade to you, brother. Llew has always been with you, but to win our younger brother over to our side, and seal his support with a wedding between his family and yours.' Tudor gave a derisive whistle. 'I bow to your diplomatic skills.'

Owain turned to Gruffydd. 'Would you like to join your betrothed at the altar tomorrow along with Maredydd and Elwy?'

'I'll let you know tomorrow, father, if you'll excuse me the only thing I want to see at the moment is my bed.'

***

Gruffydd was washing in the sluice room behind the kitchen when the door opened.

'So, it's true, you did manage to keep yourself in one piece.' Enyd pulled the bolt on the door behind her and went to him.

'Which is more than David did,' Gruffydd was hoarse with grief.

'I heard. I'm so sorry, Gruffydd.' Enyd buried her face in his naked back and wrapped her arms around his waist.

'You will get wet,' he warned, lifting her arms away. He turned to face her, bent his head and kissed her.

'Betsi married Konrad the day Lord Glyndŵr returned from Hyddgen.'

'He didn't waste any time.'

'They had nothing to wait for.'

He suddenly realised why she'd told him. 'So you sleep alone?'

'Not this night, I hope. I and my chamber will be waiting to receive you. You can stay all night.'

***

Gruffydd didn't bother to dress after he dried himself. He made a bundle of his clothes and boots, covered himself with his cloak and listened at the door. When he was certain it was silent in the passage outside he stepped out and opened the door that led to the servants' staircase. Enyd occupied a small cubicle accessed by a door halfway up the stairs. Gruffydd opened it, and dropped his bundle to the floor.

Enyd was sitting on her bed brushing out her hair. She smiled when she saw him enter.

'Pull the latch across, please. I'm not expecting anyone but I haven't seen Betsi since her marriage and since she's been married two whole days, she could have quarrelled with Konrad by now.'

'You think that's likely?' He did as she asked and shrugged off his cloak.

'Possible but not likely. We need to talk . . . but . . . ' her smile grew broader as he stepped towards her.

'We do need to talk, but not now, right this minute. We have more pressing things to do.' He untied the ribbons at the neck of her gown. It slid over her body to her waist, she rose, and it fell to her feet. She wore no shift and aside from stockings and garters she was naked beneath it. He lifted her and laid her on the bed.

'You are cold she complained as he stretched out on top of her.

'I'll lift the blankets over us, later,' he breathed headily as he entered her.

Glyndŵr's bedchamber, Headquarters Glyncoch July 1401

Owain entered his and Margaret's bedchamber and picked up his saddlebags.

'You're leaving?' Margaret asked.

'No. Not with at least one wedding taking place tomorrow.'

'I heard Tudor, Ieuan and Gruffydd coming in. Did you tell Gruffydd that Llew has given permission to marry Jonnet tomorrow?'

'I told him?'

'What did he say?' She wondered if Owain had heard her, until she looked at him and saw he was preoccupied, so she repeated the question.

'That he was tired and only fit for bed. He didn't mention Jonnet. As for my leaving, I have no intention of going anywhere for a few days possibly a week or more.'

'Then why were you and John Trefor locked in conversation all through supper this evening? And why are you checking the contents of that bag. There's no need to look. I've packed your war essentials.'

'I thought Dafydd saw to those.'

'He looks after your armour and weapons, Gwilym packs the supplies. I see to your change of clothes, soap, razor, towel, willow wands and salt.'

'So I have the necessities to ensure I ride nice and clean into battle. Heaven forbid that the enemy see me unshaven, with dirty teeth or grime on my face.' He set aside his thoughts to tease her.

'You told me when we married that a lord and his lady have to set the standard for their tenants.'

'And since then I have discovered a good wife's price is above rubies.'

'The quote is, "Who can find a woman of worth? For her price is far above rubies."'

'You always were a better Biblical scholar than me, but then,' he gave a wry smile, 'with nothing to do all day you had time to study.'

'You assume the estates ran themselves and the children brought themselves up?' She knew he was still teasing her but there was an edge to her voice.

'Of course, they were all born independent like me.'

Margaret picked up a pillow and threw it at Owain's head before unclipping the shoulder clasps on her dress.

He sat on the window seat and watched her undress. 'Enyd's late.'

'I gave her the evening off.'

'That was magnanimous of you.'

'Not entirely I was thinking of us more than her. I've scarcely seen you since your return. So what did Trefor tell you?' She went to the table that held the water jug and bowl, filled the basin, dropped in the soap and washed her hands and face.

'The Abbot of Cwmhir is causing problems.'

'What kind of problems?'

'It appears that after emptying the abbey's treasury into Bolingbroke's coffers he's been handing out Welsh valuables entrusted to the abbey for safekeeping, to Bolingbroke's supporters.'

'I thought Yonge brought all the Welsh crown jewels to Glyndyfrdwy before your coronation.'

'So did, Trefor and Yonge, but apparently the Welsh crown jewels weren't kept together when they were retrieved from Richard of Pudlicott after he stole them from Westminster.'

'And you think some of the Welsh valuables, like the tapestry of maidens with red hands were hidden in Cwmhir?'

'Exactly.'

'Did you send the tapestry you intercepted to Bolingbroke?'

'I heard it eventually reached him.'

'And?'

'No word as yet on whether he took Charleton's advice to use it as a nightshirt.' He stared at Margaret as she folded her gown and removed her garters and stockings. Anyone who didn't know Owain might assume he was admiring her, but she knew from the look in his eyes he'd returned to whatever problem he was mulling over.

'So we will see at least one son married tomorrow?' she attempted to return him to the present.

'Mmm?'

'Then we ride to Cwmhir Abbey?'

'Possibly but if "we" go, and the "we" is only if you agree to remain with the apothecary and rear guard . . . '

'How many times do I have to tell you I will?'

'I'm merely reminding you of your promise.' He smiled. 'If we travel there I'll leave Tudor and Rhys Fierce in charge here and take Rhys Coch with us. He was complaining about being left here to rust along with his armour.'

'And Maredydd and Elwy?'

'I'll order them to stay here until I return.'

'You know Elwy wants to visit her parents?'

'That's why I'll order Maredydd to remain here. It's better Bolingbroke remains ignorant of Elwy - and Maredydd's whereabouts.'

'Out of sight out of mind?' Margaret suggested.

'That's the intention. Your brother has hosted the king in the past and will no doubt do so again, but whichever road Bolingbroke takes, Tudor's pickets will give our people enough notice to retreat to safety in Snowdonia.' Owain frowned. 'I wish Gruffydd would make up his mind about marrying Jonnet.'

'He'll marry her tomorrow.' Margaret folded the blankets back on the bed and slid between the sheets.

'You're sure about that?'

'I am.'

'Does this have anything to do with the maid you mentioned earlier?'

'It has nothing to do with maids and everything to do with Gruffydd's happiness. He will marry Jonnet tomorrow.'

'Then we'll leave Gruffydd and Jonnet with Maredydd and Elwy and the boys can help Tudor and Rhys Fierce to pick out our next targets.'

'You are going to win this war. You do know that?'

'I hope you're right.'

'What are you plotting, Owain?'

'A great deal.' The look of preoccupation lifted as his entire expression changed. 'But first I have to get naked.' He stripped off his clothes. 'And join you in this bed.'

Enyd's chamber Glyndŵr's Headquarters Glyncoch July 1401

'This bed was made for skeletons with the flesh scraped off.' Gruffydd lifted Enyd from the bedcovers folded them back and lay beside her.

'That is a horrid idea. Both of us lying here with our flesh scraped off.'

'Sorry.' He lifted her hand in the air and looked at it in the candlelight. 'It's my poor way of saying that I love all your bones from your smallest finger.' He kissed her little finger. 'To your . . . ' he slid his hand downwards over the flat of her stomach.

'That tickles.' She grasped his hand and held it.

'I was going to ask you . . . '

'What?' she prompted as he turned on his side and looked down at her.

'Do you know your eyes glitter as if they're lined with gold in the light of an oil lamp.'

'You're the first one to tell me that.'

'Marry me.'

'Have you forgotten you're betrothed to Jonnet?'

'I love you . . . '

'No you don't, Gruffydd.' She sat up in the bed and stared at the wall so she wouldn't have to look at him.

'But I do,' he protested. 'I can't live without you . . . '

She finally turned to look at him, 'it's been fun, Gruffydd, but surely you knew from the outset this . . . '

'This what?' He demanded angrily when she hesitated.

'This sweet affair between us couldn't last.'

'It's lasted almost two years, and I can't - I won't give you up. '

'You've never owned me to give me up, Gruffydd.' She looked away unable to bring herself to look at him again.

'You love me,' he insisted fiercely. 'Almost as much as I love you. You know you do. Why deny it?'

'I'm the same age as your mother, Gruffydd. You're a boy . . . '

'You think of me as a boy . . . ' He seethed with hurt pride.

'The brightest, handsomest and best boy I've had the fortune to meet, but given the difference in our years a boy. What we had . . . '

'"Had,"' he repeated. 'So I was just a passing amusement to you?'

Enyd took a deep breath and hoped he wouldn't see the pain his anger was causing her.

'We both knew it would end, Gruffydd. You and Jonnet have been betrothed for years . . . '

'I don't need you to remind me. She's a . . . '

' . . . Betrothed woman who has every right to look forward to marriage.'

'I don't love her and I don't want her in my bed.'

She knew what she was about to say would hurt him. Knew it would drive him from her now, and probably for always, but she couldn't bear the thought of exchanging more angry words. She forced herself to meet his steady gaze.

'No more than I want a petulant boy in mine.'

Owain and Margaret's chamber Glyndŵr's Headquarters Glyncoch July 1401

'Are you all right, Enyd?' Owain asked as Enyd entered their chamber the next morning. The maid's face was pale, her eyes suspiciously bright.

'I have a summer cold, my lord.'

'Ask the cooks to make you a mint and lemon balm posset, Enyd. It will chase away the worst fever.'

'I will, my lord.'

Owain pulled on his boots, winked at Margaret and left the chamber.

Margaret waited until Owain had closed the door. When she heard his tread halfway down the stairs, she spoke.

'Will Gruffydd marry Jonnet?'

'I hope so, my lady. I've done all I can.'

'I know this has been hard on you . . . '

'I knew when it started that it couldn't last between us.' Enyd swallowed her tears. 'I pray he finds happiness.'

'And you?' Margaret asked.

'I'll be fine, my lady. Are you riding out with the prince when he leaves.'

'I am. Would it be a dreadful imposition if I asked you to ride with me.'

Enyd managed a small smile. 'Dreadful, my lady.'

'If Gruffydd and Jonnet marry as well as Maredydd and Elwy today there'll be feasting tonight but my lord will want to leave at daybreak tomorrow.'

'And if Lord Gruffydd doesn't marry today?'

Margaret opened the chest where she kept her gowns and removed her favourite burgundy wool embroidered with gold thread. 'He'll have to. This is my best gown and I've decided to wear it.'

Jonnet, Elwy and Catrin's chamber Glyndŵr's Headquarters July 1401

'There, perfect.' Catrin fastened the shoulder clips on Elwy's gown as Jonnet straightened Elwy's veil. 'Oil of lavender?' she handed her a small stone flask.

Elwy upended it and dabbed a few drops on her neck.

A knock at the door disturbed them. 'Good morning, Betsi.' Catrin opened the door to see Elwy outside on the landing. 'You're not Betsi.'

'I'm not. Unsure of the reception she'd receive,' Efa stepped back from the door.

'Please come in, join us, Efa.' Catrin pulled her into the room and closed the door behind her. 'Lest Maredydd comes nosing. He believes being betrothed to Elwy gives him the right to monopolise her.'

'Gruffydd asked me to convey a message to Jonnet,' Efa said.

Catrin turned her head. 'Jonnet, Efa has a message for you from Gruffydd. Do you want to hear it?'

'Yes, please, Efa.'

'I suppose you have to listen, Jonnet, as you're betrothed to the ... '

'Careful, almost sister-in-law,' Elwy warned.

'Most delightful brother I possess after Maredydd, Ieuan, Madoc and the little ones.' Catrin stuck her tongue firmly in her cheek. 'But you have to admit, like all men Gruffydd can be an idiot.'

'Everyone behaves foolishly at times,' Elwy ventured tactfully.

'Bless the saints, imminent marriage has only made you nicer, my almost sister in law.'

'Is that a compliment?' Like most of the Glyndŵr family Elwy was wary of Catrin's occasionally acerbic tongue.

'It was meant as one.'

'I'm happy,' Elwy admitted guardedly.

'You said you have a message for me?' Jonnet prompted.

'Am I allowed to hear it?' Catrin picked up a gown from a stool and folded it into her chest.

'As I haven't seen Gruffydd since his return last night, it can't be that personal,' Jonnet said.

'He suggested that ... ' Efa fell silent as she searched for the right words.

'Suggested!' Catrin set her hands on her hips and looked from Elwy to Jonnet and back.

Efa gave up trying to tactful. 'He asked me to ask Jonnet if she would like to marry him today.'

'"Would like to" how romantic. What were his exact words,' Catrin demanded.

'As far as I can recall, "Do me a favour, Efa, ask Jonnet if she wants to marry me today. If she does, tell her I'll ask my parents to speak to Bishop Trevor and arrange for us to sit at the top table for the wedding feast.'

'I suppose it's too much to expect poetry from Gruffydd, or hope that he would take it upon himself to organise the occasion,' Catrin declared. 'I like his comment about a wedding feast. He knows our mother is an expert at performing miracles at short notice, but it's the first time I've heard him acknowledge it.'

'No marriage arranged years ago between two children can possibly be romantic.' Jonnet sounded stoic, resigned to her fate.

'Love came before the ceremony for Maredydd and Elwy,' Catrin pointed out.

'Having to battle our fathers and the Pope for permission to be allowed to marry only served to strengthen our love, and our resolve,' Elwy said.

'You were nothing if not tenacious,' Catrin agreed. 'Considering you're first cousins I never thought father or Uncle Gruffydd would give in to you. But Maredydd was prepared to fight for you, Elwy. All Gruffydd can do is send Jonnet a message "suggesting" they marry today.'

'I'm sure Gruffydd didn't mean it to sound the way I delivered it,' Efa said. 'I phrased it clumsily.'

'You phrased it exactly the way Gruffydd did,' Catrin protested. 'Everyone knows that particular brother of mine has the romance of barnyard cock, and the tact of a marauding bull. If Jonnet hasn't discovered that much about her betrothed, she soon will.'

'Like all of us, Gruffydd's upset about David,' Efa spoke softly. 'He was very close to him.'

'You don't have to remind us how upset Gruffydd is, Efa, we all are,' Catrin said. 'Apart from David's habit of seeking out bored wives and leading them even further from their neglectful husbands he was a perfect big brother, but then you'd know that better than anyone having lived in Pont Gweni for most of your life.' Catrin slipped her arm around Efa's shoulders and hugged her.

'Even to me and he wasn't my brother,' Jonnet brushed aside a tear. 'But he always succeeded in persuading my brothers, Adam, Morgan and Hova, to include us girls in their archery competitions.'

'And he was kind enough to forgive us, even when we won,' Catrin added.

Silence fell and they all took a moment to remember David. As tall, handsome and solidly built as the man who'd sired him, with a smile, occasionally sardonic, that curved his mouth and lit his eyes.

Catrin felt his presence as though he were with them in the room, and she shivered despite the sunlight pouring through the open window.

She tried not to think about death or what came after life on earth, not even in church, because every time she did she ended up listing all the sins she'd committed that would prevent her from entering heaven.

What if David's sinful dalliances had the same effect? Had some celestial court sentenced him to walk the earth in perpetuity as a ghost . . .

'I need to talk to Gruffydd,' Jonnet said decisively.

'Why?' Catrin was glad of the interruption so she could abandon her imaginings and return to the mundane.

'I want to make sure no one has ordered him to marry me.'

Catrin laughed. 'Our parents and uncles have tried to persuade Gruffydd to do things he didn't want to, many times. His usual reaction is to stamp his foot and say no. Given his temper that's generally been the end of the matter.'

'Do you think he really wants to marry me today?' Jonnet asked seriously.

'I think he wouldn't have suggested the ceremony unless he wanted it to go ahead. If you see him, you'll need a chaperon. I'm not doing anything for the next hour or two,' Catrin volunteered mischievously.

'I'll manage fine without one, thank you,' Jonnet refused politely. 'Efa please ask Gruffydd to meet me . . .'

'It will have to be somewhere public so no one can accuse you two of doing something you shouldn't,' Elwy warned.

Catrin raised her eyebrows. 'Considering what you and Maredydd get up to, that's amusing. But Elwy's right,

Jonnet, it would be best to meet Gruffydd somewhere where you can be seen but not overheard.'

'How about the paddock?' Elwy suggested. 'The stable boys will be exercising the horses but it's large enough to keep a distance.'

'As Elwy well knows, if you slip behind the twin trunked old oak in the far corner you can get up to all sorts without being seen,' Catrin declared.

'Only because you told me,' Elwy protested.

'Perhaps I should have also told you that you have a perfect view of everything that goes on behind that oak, from the hay loft in the stables.'

Glyndŵr's Study, Headquarters Glyncoch July 1401
'You remember everything I said, Flur?' Owain asked the "walking woman".

'Syllable by syllable my prince,' she answered. Owain had given her his message in Latin. Despite carrying several of his messages in the tongue, especially to ecclesiastical establishments, she still didn't understand a word of it. But, by using her unique talents to memorise and recall sounds she had learned to replicate the words phonetically. 'You have no need to ask,' she added, taking his comment as criticism.

Forgive me for asking, but I need reassurance,' Owain answered.

'This man I am going to see. He's English?'

'He is,' Owain confirmed, 'he is also a friend.'

'You have English friends, my prince?' Flur looked sceptical.

'There are good and bad English men and women just as there are good and bad Welsh.'

'In my experience the bad English outweigh the Welsh by thousands.'

'Thousands?' Owain reiterated, supressing an impulse to smile.

'Thousands,' she repeated resolutely.

'You will leave today?'

'I will leave now, my prince.'

Owain reached into his cotte and removed a purse. 'Travel safely and do not stint on lodgings on your journey, Flur.'

'Thank you, my prince. If there is a reply, I will return right away.'

'Not before you've rested I trust.' Owain left his chair and opened the door for her.

She left and bobbed a curtsy to Bishop Trefor who was walking down the stone passageway.

'Good morning, Trefor, I trust you slept well.' Owain showed Bishop Trefor into the storeroom behind the kitchen. It was furnished with a table, two chairs a quill and inkpot, two buckets of maps and three books heaped on a stool. 'As you see, my new study, is not up to Sycharth or Glyndyfrdwy standards but it is private,' Owain apologised as he closed the door.

'And draughty and cold.'

'Which is why I spend more time in my bedchamber which boasts a hearth, but Margaret has commandeered it this morning.'

'Hardly surprising. The mother of the bridegrooms will need to attire herself in her finery. You mentioned Hugh Burnell last night. Are you aware that Bolingbroke has appointed him overseer of Radnorshire?'

'I am,' Owain confirmed.

'Everyone knows the office is only a sop to Burnell's vanity. The area is under the control of the Mortimers. And the Mortimers ... '

'Support Bolingbroke,' Owain broke in.

Trefor shook his head regretfully. 'I'm afraid you're right, Owain. I'm fond of all the Mortimers, especially Hotspur's wife, Elizabeth who was a Mortimer before her marriage. Were you expecting them to support you?'

'No.' Owain looked Trefor in the eye. Right or wrong he'd made his decision. 'But I have sent a walking woman who carries a private message from me to Edmund Mortimer.'

'Am I allowed to know what that message is?'

'Should Edmund Mortimer grant me the favour I've requested of him, you will know soon enough, Trefor. I promise you.'

CHAPTER EIGHTEEN

Glyndŵr's Headquarters Glyncoch July 1401
Jonnet remained in the shared chamber after Efa left for Ieuan's quarters and Elwy and Catrin went in search of Gruffydd. She brushed out her hair, left it loose, and stared disconsolately at her reflection in the glass. Compared to Catrin and Gweni who'd both inherited their respective mothers' blue eyed, golden haired beauty, and Elwy's fiery hair and green eyes, she was plain, dark and ugly.

If she tried desperately to please Gruffydd could he - would he - overlook her lack of looks? She was still considering his cryptic message and his decision to entrust it to Efa rather than seek her out, when Catrin returned.

'My brother's waiting in the paddock.'

'I'm sorry . . . '

'Don't apologise to me, or him when you get there. He's far too accepting of people's deference. And you'd better put some shoes on,' Catrin called after her. 'The grass is damp from dew.'

Jonnet dived back into the chamber grabbed her velvet slippers from the rug next to the bed and slid down the wooden stairs in her stockings. She raced to the kitchen door, before stopping to put on her shoes and take a breath.

'You're in a hurry, Mistress.' The scullion addressed her from the far side of the pig bin he was filling with kitchen scraps.

'I am, Iolo.' She returned his smile, smoothed her skirts and hair and crossed the yard to the paddock.

As Catrin had said, Gruffydd was there, leaning against the fence, watching the stable boys groom the horses.

Jonnet stepped up beside him but she was careful to keep an arm's length between them.

He turned to look at her but instinctively reverting to the conduct instilled in her since birth, she lowered her eyes.

'Good morning.'

'Good morning,' she echoed.

'It's a fine morning.'

'It is,' she agreed.

'My father has heard from yours.'

'Bishop Trefor's friar gave me letters from my family when he arrived yesterday. My father wrote that he has given us permission to marry.'

'My father agrees with him, it appears that both our families think it's time for us to marry.'

'What do you think?'

When he didn't answer she lifted her head. To her embarrassment she realised he was staring at her.

'I think we've been betrothed long enough.'

'Five years is a long time,' she murmured, allowing irritation to override her manners.

'Four since the papers were signed,' he corrected. 'You were twenty, I was fourteen. But four years are long enough to get to know someone.'

Irritated by his assumption she forgot her resolve to try to please him. 'They would be if you took the trouble to talk to them.'

'Are you complaining?'

There was an odd tone to his voice she couldn't quite decipher, because she didn't know him well enough to read his mood. Tired of fencing she braced herself and looked him the eye. 'Do you want to end our betrothal?'

He continued to watch her. 'Do you?'

'My father wouldn't allow me to end it, but if you informed him that you wished to, I doubt he'd argue.'

'Or blame you?' he said astutely.

'Or blame me,' she concurred.

'I wouldn't have sent Efa with a message asking if you wanted to marry me this afternoon, if I'd intended to end our betrothal.'

'Why the urgency to marry in haste?' she challenged.

'I don't think you can call it haste after the length of out betrothal. But the Bishop is here and willing to perform the ceremony. Can you be ready?'

'I could, but surely you don't want us to marry solely because the timing would be convenient for Bishop Trefor?'

He turned away from her and looked towards the sprinkling of trees that that fringed the paddock. 'My eldest brother who I thought was invincible, has just been killed. I could ride out with my father or uncle and die today or tomorrow . . . '

'And you'd like to leave a grieving widow to pay for masses to see your soul safely through purgatory?'

'Put like that it sounds rather selfish.' He gave her a wry smile.

'Possibly, because it is.' She didn't return his smile.

'David's death made me realise just how fragile life is. But he left a fine legacy. His sons . . . '

'Even if we marry within the next hour there's no guarantee you'll father one let alone three.'

There was no hint of a smile on her face and he realised she was right. He'd behaved selfishly and had never taken the trouble to get to know her the way he had Catrin, or his half-sister Gweni or even his brother's sweetheart Elwy.'

'It doesn't help that my younger brother is marrying today,' he added in an attempt to move the conversation on from David's death.

'Maredydd's besotted and in love. He can't wait to kneel before the altar with Elwy. But they were given the luxury of choice. Something denied to us.'

'You wanted to choose your own husband?'

'As much as you wanted to choose your own wife.' The expression on her face told him she knew about his affairs even if she didn't know the name of the woman or that he'd fallen in love. 'If you wish to end our betrothal to follow your heart, I will understand.' She smiled to prove her indifference.

'If I did release you, my father would never forgive me,' he said. 'Your father wrote to mine, suggesting an alliance through marriage between our families on the day

I was born. So, to please both our fathers and our families will you please marry me in the chapel this afternoon?'

'If you order me, I will be there because I have no choice.'

'Of course you have a choice ... '

'I am a woman. Your betrothed. If I meet you in the chapel this afternoon and we exchange vows, all responsibility for me and my actions will pass from my father to you.'

'You're forgetting I know your father. He'd never ask you to do anything you didn't want to, or use you cruelly.'

'He wouldn't,' she agreed.

'Neither will I.' He slipped his hand beneath her chin and lifted her head until her eyes were on a level with his.'

'Marry me this afternoon and I'll do everything within my power to make you happy.'

'Including forsaking your true love?'

'I ... '

'Don't answer that. I had no right to ask. We'll talk again. And if you're determined to marry me, I'll try to make you a good wife. I'll make a start by looking for a richer gown.' She turned on her heel and returned to the house.

***

Xian ran up the stairs and opened the door to his and Gweni's chamber. He stepped inside, fell over a pile of saddlebags and looked up at the bed. Gweni and Betsi were sitting side by side working on a gown of grey silk embroidered with silver thread.

'A new gown?' he brushed dust from his tunic as he climbed to his feet.

'New, but not mine. Maredydd and Elwy and Gruffydd and Jonnet are getting married in an hour. Betsi and I helped to lay out the bridal clothes. Some of the embroidery threads had worked loose on Jonnet's gown and since it's chaos in the girls' chamber we brought it in here to repair.'

'And the saddlebags?' He unbuckled his and poked around the spare hose and tunics it contained.

'I packed them because we'll be leaving with my father when he rides out. And knowing him, he'll give us hardly any notice.'

'*I'll* be leaving with your father,' he began heavily.

'We both will.'

'You'll stay here and rest.'

'I have rested enough for six lifetimes, thank you, and I'm perfectly well.' She knotted the thread she'd stitched back into place, and snipped it close to the cloth. 'As you see, I have packed for both of us ... '

'Gweni ... '

'Xian!' She crossed her arms and stared at him.

'Your father will set a swift pace. It will be hard riding.'

'I know.'

'You're not fully recovered ...'

'I am and I've never failed to keep up with father - or you as yet.'

Betsi finished stitching the last loose thread on the gown, shook it out, bobbed a curtsy, murmured, 'I'll take this to Mistress Jonnet, mistress,' before retreating.

Xian closed the door behind her.

'Gweni, you've only just lost our child ... '

'I haven't forgotten,' she snapped.

'If you should become ill on the journey ... '

'I won't.'

'But if you do,' he persisted.

'I'll beg hospitality at the nearest abbey or convent until you return.'

'Considering where we're going ... '

'Where are we going?' she questioned curiously.

'You know your father ... '

'He keeps his plans to himself for good reason, and we have more important things to attend to, like dressing for my brother's wedding. "Come in,"' she called out to a knock at the door. 'Betsi, I'll wear my blue velvet gown and gold slippers . . . '

Xian left for the ante room where he kept his clothes and weapons. A few months of marriage had taught him when to hold his tongue, and when to give ground.

***

Jonnet entered the chamber that had been occupied by Rhys Coch until that morning, but as it was one of the largest in the house he'd volunteered to move out and share Rhys Ddu's cottage, "in the interests of romance". Despite Jonnet's protestations, Gruffydd had accepted his offer.

Her maid, Non, had enlisted the help of Betsi and two others to move Jonnet's belongings into the chamber and every surface of the "bridal chamber" as Non insisted on referring to it, was cluttered with gowns, petticoats, under skirts, cottes, headdresses and jewel boxes.

'This mess needs to be tidied, Non,' Jonnet protested as the maid steered her on to a sheet she had laid out on the floor.

'I will put everything away, mistress as soon as the footmen bring in another chest.' Non kneeled on the cloth and straightened the skirt of Jonnet's linen chemise while Betsi gathered the folds of her blue under gown over her arm.

Catrin and Elwy were eyeing the proceedings critically when Gweni knocked and opened the door.

'Apologies, I didn't mean to barge into you, Catrin. Elwy you look beautiful.'

'Thank you, but I can't wait to be married so I can do something more than stand in the corner like a candle sconce.'

'You'll risk ruining the effect of my fine work if you do,' Catrin threatened,

Gweni held up a silver veil that matched Jonnet's gown. 'I remembered seeing one of the apprentices stitching this in the seamstress's room and I thought it might go well with your gown.'

'It does,' Jonnet took it from her. 'It's been made from the same cloth.'

'It's one of the bales we bought from the pedlar who visited my father's house.' Elwy took the veil from Jonnet, held it up and frowned. 'What do you think? Pinned to the back or front of Jonnet's hair?'

'Definitely the back,' Catrin declared, 'so it doesn't hide Jonnet's face, especially her eyes. They are her best feature.'

'I can hear you, Catrin, although you're talking about me as if I've turned deaf. Thank you for the compliment.'

'That's my Jonnet always polite. You do know my brother will take advantage of your generous nature to dominate you.' Catrin handed the veil to Non when she rose from the floor.

'Gruffydd wouldn't do that,' Gweni protested.

'I've lived with him longer than you, Gweni, and yes he would,' Catrin contradicted. She raised a finely arched eyebrow in Jonnet's direction. 'Are you looking forward to tonight?'

'The feast?' Jonnet murmured absently bending her knees and ducking before the glass in an attempt to see the veil her maid had pinned to her hair.

'Not the feast you naive soul. After the feast when you and Gruffydd will be bedded naked between these sheets and he has his way with you,' Catrin continued. 'If you want advice . . . '

'Don't ask a spinster. Ask a married woman,' Gweni interrupted.

'The way you - and you, Elwy, although you're not married - walk around with enormous smirks on your faces, anyone would think being bedded by a man is the ultimate, most pleasurable experience in life.' Catrin tweaked the edge of Jonnet's veil.

'It's the most pleasurable I've had,' Elwy countered.

'What about you, Gweni?' Catrin questioned when the same faraway expression Elwy was wearing, appeared on her sister's face.

'Most definitely.'

'And Xian? What does he think?' Catrin was curious.

'He says his pleasure stems from mine.'

'A considerate husband.' Catrin reached into the bag she wore on her belt and lifted out a small leather folder. She unrolled it to reveal a wad of ink and charcoal sketches on fragments of parchment and scraps of linen.

'What are those?' Jonnet asked.

'Sketches I stole from Friar Brown. I didn't mean to,' Catrin protested in response to the horrified look on their faces. 'He spent so much time studying the folder when he thought no one was watching him I assumed it contained a collection of inspiring prayers or psalms . . . '

'And you of course are always keen to read prayers and psalms.' Gweni's comment prompted a burst of laughter.

'All right, I confess, I admit I was curious after catching a glimpse of one of the illustrations,' Catrin conceded.

'So you stole the folder?' Jonnet was clearly shocked.

'I only meant to borrow it. I sneaked it out of the Friar's knapsack when he was praying in the chapel in Elwy's house, but he was interrupted by one of the footmen and picked up his bag before I could replace it. He rode off with Bishop Trefor's party an hour later.'

'When was this?' Gweni questioned.

'A few weeks before Elwy and I were sent to stay with Jonnet's father.'

'Then you've had that folder for months!' Jonnet exclaimed.

'When I saw the pictures I could hardly own up to keeping them. Can you imagine what my parents would say if they thought I'd seen them, and that's without bringing my uncle and aunt into it? Aside from what people would think of me, I'd have run the risk of them thinking I'd drawn them, even though my sketches are nowhere near as good as these. That's artistry I'm referring to not subject matter Here, look.' Catrin thrust a few at Jonnet. 'As you're getting married you may well pick up a few pointers.

Jonnet moved the silver silk gown and sank down on the edge of the bed. She stared at the topmost sketch of a naked man and woman lying side by side on a narrow couch. 'That's . . . ' she turned crimson in embarrassment as blood flooded into cheeks.

Elwy glanced over her shoulder. 'What you and Gruffydd will be doing tonight - and all night - if he's anything like Maredydd.'

'What on earth possessed you to keep the folder, Catrin?' Gweni asked. 'One look at those drawings and I would have . . . '

'What?' Catrin prompted when Gweni's voice tailed.

'Dumped them in the squires' dormitory.'

'And waited for the shouting to start if whoever found them took them to one of the captains?'

'None of the squires would have dared, for fear of being accused of making them. Not that there's anything in those drawings the captains haven't seen.'

'How do you know that, Catrin?' Gweni asked.

'Because soldiers are always talking about what they'd like to do to women. Even monks talk about nothing else.'

'And where have you heard monks talking about women?' Gweni asked.

'In the infirmary in Valle Crucis, when I was helping to crush herbs in the still room. Someone accidentally left the door open.'

'More like you unlatched it,' Gweni suggested.

'Try eavesdropping sometime. I've learned a great deal by listening in on men's conversations. They are always talking about their female conquests and asking others about their experiences so they can compare them to their own.'

'I don't believe you mistook these for prayers or psalms,' Elwy passed her bundle of sketches to Jonnet whose face was still burning like a yule log.

'I confess I was curious when I saw how many positions could be adopted to do the same thing. I always thought that men and women . . .' Catrin fell silent.

'What?' Elwy asked.

'"Made love" sounds wrong when you're talking about dogs and "copulate" sounds harsh when you're talking about people.'

Gweni and Elwy glanced at one another and burst into laughter but Jonnet's colour heightened even more.

When their laughter subsided Jonnet plucked up courage to ask, 'do all men want women to behave as shamelessly as the ones in these drawings?'

'It's not how men want women to behave,' Catrin said authoritatively. 'It's how women behave when they're naked with a man.'

'And what would you know about that, Catrin?' Elwy asked.

'I've spied on you and Maredydd and never noticed any reluctance on your part. As for Gweni.' Catrin winked at her sister. 'She can't keep her hands off Xian any more than he can keep his off her, even when they dine in public.'

'You wait until it's your turn to marry. We'll tease you as mercilessly as you tease us,' Elwy threatened.

'I have waited and am waiting but I'm resigned to spinsterhood.' Catrin's theatrical sigh gave rise to more laughter,

'You'll be resigned to a nunnery if our father sees you with these.' Gweni couldn't resist flicking through the drawings again.

A knock at the door was followed by Konrad's voice. 'Mistress Gweni, my lord is asking if you are ready to walk to the chapel with him?'

'Tell him I will be with him in a few minutes,' Gweni called back. 'Jonnet sit on the bed and pull on your hose and garters. Then stand back on that cloth, all we have to do is slip on the blue under gown and the silver over gown and cotte and your silver slippers . . . '

'And add a touch of rouge and face cream.' Catrin lifted the lids on Jonnet's collection of pots and sniffed the contents.

***

'You look perfect - or at least as perfect as we can make you, Jonnet.' Catrin stood in front of the door and nodded approval.

'You really do look lovely, Jonnet,' Gweni kissed her cheek. 'Gruffydd is a lucky man.'

Elwy gave Jonnet a careful hug that wouldn't crease either of their gowns and followed Catrin and Gweni out of the door.

Non closed it behind them. 'I heard the prince talking to someone at the foot of the stairs, mistress, he'll be here in a moment to walk you to the chapel.'

Jonnet panicked. 'Hand me the glass ... '

'Mistress Catrin was right, mistress. I've never seen you look lovelier.'

'Please, the glass,' Jonnet begged.

Non did as she asked. There was a knock at the door.

Jonnet caught a glimpse of the leather folder and the scraps of sketches lying abandoned on the bed and shouted, 'just a moment.' She grabbed the folder and started collecting the sketches.

'Here, mistress, I'll do it.' Non picked up every one, stuffed them back into the leather binding, hid the folder under the pillows, straightened the bedcover and nodded to Jonnet.

Jonnet took a last look around to ensure nothing untoward was on display, before calling out, 'Come in.'

To her astonishment her parents walked in.

'Father ... ' without giving a thought to her gown she embraced him and her mother. 'What are you doing here?'

Sioned kissed and hugged her daughter again. 'We didn't find out that this was your wedding day until we arrived.'

'The saints blessed the bride by bringing you here, Sioned and Llewelyn,' John Trefor smiled at Jonnet from the doorway. 'Are you ready to be married, my child?'

'I am Bishop Trefor,' she answered.

'I'll escort your mother to the chapel and see you and your father there in five minutes.'

Jonnet clung to her father's arm as he walked her down the staircase. Beset by doubts about Gruffydd's feelings, she looked to him for reassurance. He was smiling. She took comfort in the thought that if Gruffydd did abandon her after the ceremony, at least her parents would have memories of this day to comfort them.

CHAPTER NINETEEN

Glyndŵr's Headquarters Glyncoch July 1401
Crab sang the final notes of the centuries' old wedding song that related the legend of Welsh hero Culhwch's wooing of his beautiful bride Olwen. The flute and harp notes lingered in the air, before being overwhelmed by a burst of applause.

The squires were shouting noisily for more when Owain rose to his feet.

'Tomorrow will bring its own problems. For those riding out on routine patrols, you leave at first light. For those remaining here, Harri has assured me that weapon practice and training will be hard. All captains not out on patrol will meet in the ante room at midday tomorrow for a briefing before leaving the day after. God bless and keep you all. And,' he smiled as he raised his goblet that had just been refilled by Gwilym, 'God Bless the beautiful brides and fortunate grooms.'

***

Footmen moved into the Great Hall to prepare it for the morning. Owain and Margaret invited Llewelyn and Sioned to the ante room, Tudor picked up a wine flask and joined them.

'Do you think Bolingbroke will have reached our brother Gruffydd's house in Llangollen by now?' Tudor filled fresh goblets with burgundy and handed them out.

'He's probably drinking his way through Gruffydd Glyndŵr's well stocked cellars right now.' Llewelyn lifted his cup. 'To you, your captains and your men, Owain. Victory to our noble cause, freedom for Wales and God Bless our royal grandchildren when they choose to arrive.'

'When news reached us of your victory over the Flemings at Hyddgen there was no keeping our sons Adam in Valle Crucis or Morgan at home.' Sioned hadn't intended to complain but there was a hint of criticism in her voice. 'I think even Hova would have joined them if Lowri hadn't been so close to her time.'

'Adam explained why he postponed his plans to take holy orders, Sioned,' Llewelyn reminded his wife.

'Adam was making excuses, Llew. We both know he and Morgan were swayed by tales of heroism at Hyddgen. Neither of the boys would have thought of joining the rebellion if they hadn't heard them . . . '

'I found Adam and Morgan beds in the cottages with the lieutenants. They're probably dicing with Ieuan and the volunteers from Oxford now.' Tudor succeeded in distracting Sioned but not quite in the way he'd intended.

'I hate to agree with you, Tudor, but you're probably right. I didn't bring the boys up to gamble but it's hopeless my pleading with them to desist since they've been subjected to Llewelyn's weaknesses since birth.'

'Jonnet has missed you and Llewelyn, Sioned. She was so happy to have you here on her wedding day,' Margaret broke in. 'Your presence was the best possible present you could have given her.

'It wasn't me who prevented us from coming until now. I've wanted to visit Jonnet ever since Llewelyn sent her here with Elwy and Catrin but he wouldn't hear of it until three days ago when the king sent word that he was visiting Gruffydd's house and would be with us next week. I told Llew then, that he had to bring me here with the boys,' Sioned said triumphantly.

Owain sensed Llewelyn's irritation and glanced at Margaret who rose to her feet.

'I'll show you to your chamber, Sioned. It's close to ours, and,' she lowered her voice as she accompanied her into the hall, 'I've asked the maids put a flask of the honeyed mead you like in there.'

'I'll see you ladies safe through the hall.'

'Don't go on my account, Tudor,' Llewelyn said.

'I'm not, I'm going on account of the squires who'll play fight all night if they're not stopped. I want them and their wits out on patrol tomorrow.'

Owain handed Llewelyn the wine flask. 'Fill our goblets please, Llew. 'A word, Tudor.' He followed his brother into the passage. 'Don't forget . . . '

'I spoke to Morgan. He's already left.' Tudor looked back into the ante room where Llew was filling Owain's cup. 'It's not only the young who'll see in the dawn if they're not stopped. I know two old men who are quite capable of talking all night.'

'Who are you referring to as old?'

'Llew of course.' Tudor avoided Owain's playful punch as he walked out of the front door.

***

'Your wife is a saint, Owain,' Llewelyn handed Owain his goblet when he returned to the ante room.

'I know,' Owain smiled. 'Tudor's useful too.'

'When he's not complaining about my cooking.' Llewelyn referred to Tudor's grumbles about the food he'd prepared when they'd hidden in a cave the previous winter. 'You have plans?'

'I do,' Owain answered Llewelyn.

'I don't want to hear them.'

'That's good because I have no intention of revealing them, especially as Bolingbroke will be under your roof next week. The man is as cunning as a fox.'

'You'll be heading south.'

'Who told you that?' Owain asked.

'No one, but you hold Mid and North Wales. You've beaten the Flemings, so with luck Pembroke will stay quiet for a few years. That leaves the South and East. There are good pickings to be had in both. Am I right?'

'I trust you with my life, Llewelyn, but not the lives of my followers.'

'Wise like your father.' The old man's eyes shone in the lamplight as he looked at the flask. 'Although you're more niggardly with your best claret than he was.

Owain reached for the flask.

***

Jonnet turned her face to the wall as Non stripped the last of her clothes from her. She slid between the linen sheets on the bed and listened as Gruffydd's body servant helped him off with the last of his clothes.

Gruffydd shouted, 'goodnight' to both of them as they left the chamber. He climbed into the bed and lay beside her careful to keep his body from touching hers.

'It's been a long day.'

'It has,' she agreed nervously.

'If you're tired . . . ' He turned on his side and adjusted his pillow, sliding his hand beneath it he pulled out the leather folder the maid had hidden there. 'What's this?'

'Nothing, something I . . . we . . . hid.' She buried her face in her pillow when he opened it.

'Hid, from me?' he asked.

'No - you weren't supposed to see them,' she mumbled, her voice muffled by the feathers.

He rearranged his pillow behind his head, sat up and opened the folder.

'God's navel!' He exclaimed. 'Where on earth . . . '

She lifted the pillow from her head but failed to summon the courage to look him in the eye. 'Someone brought the folder here to show us the drawings . . . '

'Someone? Us?' He closed the folder and looked at the outside. 'If I hadn't opened it I would have taken this for a psalter.'

'I think that was the original owner's idea.' She moved and her bare leg brushed his. She jerked back as though she'd been scalded.

He opened the folder again and thumbed through the drawings. 'Hmmm - someone. Now which someone would have given you this?'

'It wasn't exactly given.'

'You stole it.'

'No!' she protested. It was shown to me . . . '

'You were here with Elwy, Efa and Catrin and the maids . . . ' He shook his head in amusement. 'I sense Catrin's involvement. Did she draw these?' He looked at them again. 'No, they're beyond her skill, and hopefully given the subject matter beyond the experience of a virgin. Did she steal them from a squire?'

Jonnet's cheeks burned as she shook her head.

'Then who?'

'I didn't say she stole them.'

'I'm your husband, Jonnet. You can tell me anything - especially if it concerns Catrin. I love her as I do all my sisters but I have no illusions as to what she's capable of. And, as your husband I promise not to tell a soul anything you confide to me without your permission.'

'Friar . . . '

'Brown . . . ' He laughed so hard the bed shook. 'This is priceless and so like Catrin. She stole them from him?'

'Catrin said she borrowed them.'

'A likely story. Have you looked at them?'

'Some of them,' she admitted.

'Was there one particular position that appealed to you?'

'I . . . '

He stroked the hair back from her face. 'I didn't mean to embarrass you. We don't have to . . . '

'I'm your wife. I know I'm not as pretty as Elwy or your sisters . . . '

'You have your own beauty, Jonnet.'

'I told you I want to be a good wife. I mean it. I will do whatever is expected of me.'

'I don't expect you to do anything from a sense of duty. But I would like to introduce you to the pleasures of married life.' To his surprise he realised he meant it. He had enjoyed his time with Enyd, he'd been besotted by her and for the first time he realised she was right. It couldn't have lasted between them, given the difference in their age and status.

'You were thinking of your lover?'

Too shaken to conceal it, he asked? 'You have the sight?'

'No,' it was Jonnet's turn to smile, 'but I have brothers and I know exactly what an expression like the one you were just wearing means. I promise you, Gruffydd I will be a loyal, faithful and loving wife as long as you are a good husband. But should I ever discover that you have strayed from my bed into another's, I will take it as a signal that I may do the same.'

'But a woman . . . '

'Has to be faithful so the husband knows the children she bears are his?' she challenged. 'Remain faithful to me and I promise you they will be. Go wandering you'll find yourself wondering. And don't you dare laugh,' she added when he smiled again.

'I wouldn't risk it. Since I was a child my father has impressed on me that I am a Glyndŵr, his heir who holds and safeguards the future lineage of the Princes of Wales. It seems to me that I have married a wife who understands that better than I did.' He flattened his pillow and lay beside Jonnet. 'Would you like to discover if we can do better than the lovers the Friar portrayed?'

'I . . . '

He closed his hand over her naked breast. 'It's all right,' he whispered. 'We are married.'

He pressed the full length of his naked body alongside hers, slid his hand between her thighs and kissed her lips.

Llewelyn ap Gruffydd Fychan's house, Caeo Llandovery
August 1401

Llewelyn ap Gruffydd's steward, Ifor, had posted lookouts around his master's estate. The moment he received notice of a sighting, he ordered his assistant to oversee the preparation of the evening meal and rode out to meet his lord and lady.

For the first time since he'd taken a position in his master's household, he spoke to his master without being invited to.

'King Henry arrived one hour ago with his retinue, my lord, my lady. He's taken up residence in the guest apartments in the house. I've accommodated his officers in the guest houses, and his soldiers are camping in the east meadow.'

'Did he say what he wanted?' Llewelyn asked.

'You, my lord.'

***

Sioned left Llewelyn and his squire, Huw, talking in the stables and asked Ifor to follow her into the great hall. Not knowing what to expect after nearly two weeks from home she looked around in relief. The chamber had been swept and fresh rushes mixed with lavender heads and perfumed flower petals were scattered on the floor. Logs burned brightly in the cleaned and polished stone hearths. The tables were laid with pristine white cloths that reached the floor, and her finest red embroidered runner had been set on the cloth on the top table in readiness to hold the choicest dishes to be served to their high ranking guests.

'Everything looks perfect, you have done a fine job, Master Steward.'

'Thank you, my lady.'

'Do we have enough food?'

'The cook has been on his feet roasting meats, broiling pottage and baking pies and dainties in the kitchens since the messenger brought news of the king's visit two days ago. There will be more than sufficient dishes for our guest and his retinue as well as the entire household, my lady.'

'You are sure?'

'The poor have been queuing at the gates since they saw the pigs, cattle and sheep being herded into the slaughtering sheds. They are an excellent gauge of how much food will be leftover to be distributed among them, my lady.'

Llewelyn strode into the room, Huw following in his wake. 'Give me an hour to dress, then show the king and his closest companions into my library for wine,' he ordered Ifor.

'Which casks would you like opened, my lord?'

Knowing how Llewelyn could spin out any conversation on wine with his steward to an hour or more, Sioned interrupted them. 'I will change my gown before seeking out Hova and Lowri.'

'They are both well, my lady,' Ifor informed her.

Sioned smiled at the old man. 'I know, because if they hadn't been, you would have told us as soon as we arrived.'

'They were walking in the orchard a few minutes ago, my lady.'

'I need to talk to my son right away while the king is in the guest chambers. You choose the wine,' Llewelyn said to Ifor.

'Are you sure, my lord . . . ' The steward was shocked. The one skill his master prided himself on was his ability to select and buy the best French wines.

'I'm sure.' Llewelyn frowned. 'For once, I have more pressing problems to consider than whether to serve Burgundy or Bordeaux at my table.'

***

Hova and Lowri were sitting on a bench beneath an apple tree that had ceased to bear fruit a decade or more ago. Llewelyn entered the orchard and frowned at its fruitless branches. He'd frequently threatened to cut it down but every time he did, at least one of the estate children who'd learned to climb on its branches, begged him not to. He always capitulated and as he looked at his son and daughter-in-law sitting beneath it, he was glad he'd left it where it was.

'I prayed you'd return today.' Hova rose and hugged his father.

'If I'd thought the king would cut short his visit to Gruffydd Glyndŵr to come to Caeo, I wouldn't have left you.' Llewelyn sat beside Lowri on the bench. 'Have you seen Bolingbroke?' he asked his son.

'And spoken with him,' Hova said. 'Of choice I would have ignored the man but Bolingbroke is king and Lord Glyndŵr hasn't vanquished him yet.'

Llewelyn looked around to ensure no one could overhear them before replying. 'It is only a matter of time.'

'Bolingbroke told me he wants you to guide him to Lord Glyndŵr's headquarters.'

'He believes I'll betray the prince?'

'He does.'

'Does he know Lowri is the daughter of Tudor Glyndŵr?'

'He knows,' Lowri said quietly. 'He enquired after the health of my father and uncle when I greeted him.'

'What did you tell him?' Llewelyn took her hand into his.

'That I hadn't seen either of them since I married Hova.'

'True enough,' Llewelyn nodded absently. 'I'll plead ill health on your behalf, Lowri.' He indicated her burgeoning waistline. 'There's no need for either of you to join us at the table tonight.'

'Lowri and I want to help and support you, father,' Hova insisted.

'Thank you, but you are too young and trusting to fence words with a double tongued viper like Bolingbroke. Never forget what he did to Richard to take his throne, boy.'

'Father told me Bolingbroke starved King Richard to death,' Lowri said softly.

'I'll not argue with Tudor over that, Lowri. There were sufficient rumours to suggest that's exactly what Bolingbroke did. And that was after he swore a solemn oath not to draw Richard's blood or harm a hair on his head when he snatched the throne from him.'

'Please let us at least sit in the Great Hall with you and mother this evening.'

Llewelyn shook his head. 'No. Everyone knows babies in the womb can hear what their mother hears and I'll not have my grandson exposed to that man's voice. If you and Hova remain out sight there's a chance Bolingbroke will forget your existence. At least for the time he remains here.'

'And if he doesn't, and insists you take him to the prince?' Hova asked.

'I will take him wherever he wants to go. You will stay here.'

'You wouldn't betray our prince.'

Both Llewelyn and Hova knew Lowri hadn't asked a question.

'There are many shepherds' tracks in Snowden. They wind for miles, climbing up and plunging down crags, cliffs and hills.' Llewelyn tapped the side of his nose. 'It takes skill, careful horsemanship and local knowledge to negotiate them. And that's when you reach Snowdonia. The mountain range is more than a hundred miles from here. That's five days travel when the weather is warm and dry, and,' he looked up at the clouds gathering in the northwest, 'I forecast it won't stay that way for long. You can't blame a man for getting lost in rugged country in a rainstorm even when he regards it as his own backyard.'

Hova squinted up at the sky. 'You're right the weather will break by morning.'

'I didn't need Crach to warn me we've seen the last of this year's summer. All the more reason for you and Lowri to stay here, care for the estate and keep warm and dry.'

'And Jonnet?'

'Your sister is safe with her new husband and his family.'

'Then she and Gruffydd . . . '

'Are married.'

'And Morgan and Adam?'

'I've no doubt we'll be hearing from them soon. I'll order food to be sent to your chamber. Stop worrying, boy.' Llewelyn lifted Lowri's face to his and kissed her cheek. 'You too, Lowri. Think happy thoughts for your child. With men like your father and uncle leading us, our cause can't fail.'

Great Hall Llewelyn ap Gruffydd Fychan's house, Caeo Llandovery August 1401

'You know the location of Owain Glyndŵr's headquarters in Snowdonia?' Bolingbroke watched Ifor refill his goblet from a flask of Burgundy.

'Which one, my lord?' Llewelyn asked casually.

'Glyndŵr has more than one?'

'I have heard it said Lord Glyndŵr has as many hiding places in Wales, as you have palaces in England, my lord.'

Sensitive to any comment he suspected of casting doubt on his right to reign, Bolingbroke snapped, 'You cannot compare my rank, authority, or status to that of a barbarian and traitor.'

'Far from drawing comparisons, my lord, I was merely illustrating that when it comes to the wilderness that is Wales, Glyndŵr is as at home among the savages who inhabit this barren land as you are in your English palaces. The man who has never been exposed to the refinements of life cannot be expected to appreciate the benefits of civilisation.'

'Well put, Llewelyn.' Bolingbroke lifted his goblet. 'This contains the perfect example. I hear the traitor's taste buds have been so cauterised by coarse gwisgi they can no longer be tantalised by fine wine.'

'So I have heard, my lord.'

'Yet I have heard that you call the traitor friend and allowed your son to marry the traitor's niece.'

'It was a union that took place before Glyndŵr rebelled against you, my king.' Llewelyn hoped Bolingbroke hadn't yet heard of Gruffydd Glyndŵr's marriage to Jonnet, although he realised it could only be a matter of time before he did.

Bolingbroke looked around the hall. 'Your son and daughter-in-law are noticeable by their absence. Have they refused to eat with me?'

'They sent their apologies for their absence, and mean no offence, my lord. Lowri was taken suddenly ill. We hope for an heir ... '

'The wish for an heir, I understand. The desire to ally your family to a branch of the Glyndŵrs and breed with them, I find incomprehensible.' Henry didn't raise his voice but his glare was razor sharp.

'The family are uncouth, my lord,' Llewelyn agreed, 'but no one who lives in Wales can ignore they are what passes for nobility among the Welsh.'

Bolingbroke continued to glare at Llewelyn. Terrified, Sioned felt that time itself had frozen. Fearful for her husband she watched Bolingbroke from behind her goblet until he suddenly burst into laughter.'

'You are right, Llewelyn. On a scale of rank, Welsh nobility stand a little, a very little,' Bolingbroke moved his thumb and forefinger close together to illustrate just how much of a smidgeon his "very little" was, 'above a gongfermour and everyone knows how much they stink after cleaning out the castle garderobes.'

'Thank you, my lord for forgiving my son and daughter-in-law for their absence and me for my poor turn of phrase.' Llewelyn signalled to his steward to refill the goblets on the top table.

Sioned motioned to a footman while addressing Henry. 'More pork comarye, my lord? Or another slice of game pie? The venison and boar have just come into season. Our cook's crustade is excellent . . . '

'He has a light hand with pastry.' Henry nodded and the footman piled slices of pork and pie on to his trencher. 'Is it true that your household consumes fifteen pipes of wine every year, Llewelyn.'

'That was the year my son Hova married, my lord. The consumption was exceptional.'

'So how many have you consumed so far this year.'

'Fourteen, my lord.'

'And we are not yet in September.' Henry laughed. 'In the interests of saving your cellar and wine bill, I suggest we ride out at dawn's first light in the morning.'

'Ride out, my lord. To where?' Llewelyn strove to remain impassive because he knew the answer to his question.

'To winkle Glyndŵr out of wherever's he's hiding, and confront him, Llewelyn, what else?'

CHAPTER TWENTY

Hills above Cwmhir Abbey September 1401
Owain signalled halt when he saw the sun's red orb slip below the hills that rimmed Nant Clwyedog valley. His men dismounted and his officers gave them leave to eat the rations they carried but not to light fires.

The men unsaddled and watered their horses, stretched their legs, opened their beer flasks and unwrapped the last of the twice baked bread, apple pies and cold bacon that had been packed in the kitchens of Glyncoch.

Owain went over the plans he'd made with the Hanmers, Rhys Coch, Yonge and Dafydd before sitting on a cushion of bracken with Margaret to wait for nightfall. When twilight cloaked the wooded hill in shadow he passed down the command to move out.

The men saddled and mounted their horses and followed Owain to the summit. No one spoke. Their mounts' footfalls fell softly on the carpet of dead leaves beneath the trees and the clinking of their harnesses blended with the hooting of night owls and mechanical whirring of night jars.

Nocturnal animals scattered before them, moving too quickly to be seen in the darkness. When they reached their objective halfway down the hill, the men Dafydd had designated as pickets, handed their mounts to their squires and stationed themselves under his direction. The remainder saw to their destriers before rolling themselves into their cloaks and settling to sleep beneath the trees.

Margaret and Enyd arranged Owain's bed in a copse of willow, but even as they lay the tarpaulin on the ground, Margaret knew Owain wouldn't rest. She sent Enyd to sleep with the other women who'd followed their husbands, made herself as comfortable as she could with her cloak and a saddlebag for a pillow and waited for Owain to return.

He walked round the camp several times exchanging a few words with every man who was awake, before joining her. He lowered himself on to the tarpaulin, wrapped his arm around her shoulders and took the pie she placed in his hand.

'It's apple,' she said when she sensed rather than saw him sniffing it.

'Thank you. As we're too low for moonlight to penetrate, I was afraid you were about to feed me roast beetles.'

'And when have I ever fed you insects?'

'Never to my knowledge, my love.' He pulled her closer. 'I may not be able to see you but it's good to have you with me.'

'Do you mean that?'

'Yes. I would kiss you if I could see your mouth. Now wrap yourself up and try to sleep.' He pulled her blanket to her chin and stared into the darkness.

The future of Cwmhir Abbey and the fate of every man within its walls depended on what he'd find there in the morning. Would the abbot be warm and welcoming? Even if he wasn't, he was sure the man would be apologetic.

But he had one certain way of knowing and measuring just how deep the veins of treachery ran beneath the skin of the Cistercian brothers. Provided his spy remained undetected - and lived. And, provided Bolingbroke hadn't taken it into his head to send armed men there to lie in wait to ambush him.

Cwmhir Abbey September 1401
The bell signalling Prime rang out as Owain, flanked by Dafydd and the Hanmers, rode up to the gates of the abbey. Behind them, the only signs of life were the hawks and kites hovering above the trees that cloaked the hillside and the sheep that grazed the lower slopes.

Dafydd dismounted and rang the bell. A novice ran out and recognising Owain's coat of arms made obeisance.

'Welcome, my prince.'

'I am here to see the abbot.'

'He is at prayer, but I will take you to his quarters, my prince.'

'I know the way, thank you.' Owain rode through the gate ahead of his companions. The novice walked alongside his horse and called out to a lay brother as they approached the stables.

A boy ran out, waited for Owain and his captains to dismount and took charge of their mounts. Owain walked ahead of his captains down the passageway that led to the abbot's library and private quarters. He knocked. When there was no reply, he opened the door and stepped inside.

Rays of morning sunlight poured through stone framed windows, illuminating luxurious quarters for a man who'd sworn a vow of poverty. A wooden chair cushioned by tapestry pillows stood next to a carved stone hearth, long and broad and almost high enough to house a peasant's cottage. A log fire burned cheerfully beneath the chimney.

A lectern held a gold and lapis lazuli illustrated book of the lives of the saints. Next to it a table held a basket of small cakes and butter biscuits and a flask and goblet. Philip picked up and sniffed the goblet.

'Gwisgi?' John Hanmer suggested.

'Excellent Burgundy by the aroma,' Philip answered.

The sound of sandaled feet slapping over stone floors echoed down the passageway.

'It appears Prime prayers have ended,' John said.

The abbot appeared in the open doorway. He inclined his head.

'God speed, lord. Our house is honoured.'

The omission of prince and "my" before lord wasn't lost on Owain.

'God speed, abbot.'

'What brings you here, lord, with your weapons?'

'Private matters have brought me here, abbot. Regrettably we have found it necessary to carry arms in these troubled times.'

'Even inside a holy house of God?'

'Even here, abbot. We have learned from painful experience sharp blades can be hidden beneath a monk's robe.' Owain eyed the brothers crowding into the stone passageway behind the door.

'Your men . . . ' the abbot began.

'Will wait for us to finish our conversation.' Owain turned to John. 'You have your orders.'

'My prince.' John, Philip and Dafydd stood before the brothers.

The abbot stared at Owain. When Owain parried the abbot's glare, the cleric capitulated.

'You may leave us, brothers.'

The monks walked away from the doorway.

Dafydd followed the Hanmers out of the room. He closed the door. Owain knew he'd remained behind it.

'Wine, or would you prefer gwisgi?' The abbot opened a wooden cupboard in the alcove next to the hearth to reveal a row of silver goblets and flasks.

'Neither, thank you,' Owain refused.

'Excuse me. It's cold in the chapel. I need something to warm my blood.' The abbot topped up his goblet, replaced the cork in the flask he'd opened, closed the cupboard door and hesitated in front of his chair. 'Please, sit.' He indicated a bench set at right angles to the hearth.

'If you wish to sit, be my guest, abbot. ' Knowing that in giving the abbot permission he'd relegated him to an inferior status, Owain continued to stand and look around the abbot's library. Apart from the cupboard the abbot had opened, a chest and the table that held food, there was no obvious storage in the room. There was however, a full sized door to the left of the door into the corridor.

The abbot noticed Owain surveying the surroundings. 'Are you looking for something, Lord Glyndŵr?'

'A place that could be used to conceal the treasures of the Welsh nation.'

'What treasures would they be, Lord Glyndŵr?'

'Let us not pretend that you didn't give items to Hugh Burnell to be passed on to Bolingbroke, shall we?'

The abbot reached for his goblet. 'I assure you there are no treasures hidden in Cwmhir, Lord Glyndŵr, nor have there ever been.'

'Never?'

'Never,' the abbot repeated,

'You simply stored valuables here prior to handing them over to Burnell?' Owain questioned.

'I have no idea to what you are referring, Lord Glyndŵr. Worldly treasure does not belong in a house of God where all within its walls have sworn vows of poverty, chastity and obedience. An abbey is no place for the riches and follies of life. The only items we value are those necessary to serve the holy sacrament. You will find them on display in the chapel. They are carved from wood. Christ taught us, it is the sacrament itself and the intention behind it, not the value of the objects used that is important.'

'As you are so certain that there is nothing of wealth belonging to the Welsh nation within these walls, abbot, you will not object to my men searching the abbey?'

The abbot hesitated for so long before replying, Owain anticipated a refusal.

They were interrupted by a knock at the door. Owain opened it without asking the abbot's permission.

Dafydd, hand on sword hilt, bowed. 'The men have arrived, my prince, and are asking for orders.'

'Men?' The abbot repeated.

Owain pointed to the window behind the abbot's chair. The cleric turned his head. As far as he could see the perimeter of the abbey was encircled by a triple row of Owain's soldiers.

'Begin the search, Dafydd. If any of the brothers' protest bring them here under escort.'

'Yes, my prince.'

'This is a large abbey . . . ' The abbot began.

'We are aware of that, abbot. Dafydd, remain in this room. I will station two guards outside the door. Should you require assistance call them.'

'Yes, my prince.'

'My prince.' Llew's son Morgan appeared behind Dafydd. 'Lord Hanmer has found what you seek.'

***

The Hanmers had begun their search of the abbey in the nave under the direction of Morgan, who'd begged the hospitality of the abbey two days ago. Welcomed as a novice emissary from Valle Crucis he'd used the time he could steal from private prayer to search the building as thoroughly as possible without exciting suspicion.

Owain entered the nave and saw two of the Hanmers' largest and strongest lieutenants standing guard in the fourteenth bay. They pushed open a concealed door in the carved wooden panelling as Owain approached, revealing a narrow stone staircase that wound down into the foundations of the abbey. Torches had been lit and placed in the wall sockets on the staircase and on the walls of the crypt itself.

The Hanmers and Morgan were standing next to the tomb of the last sovereign Prince of Wales, Llewelyn ap Gruffydd, who'd been murdered by English soldiers in 1282. Hanmer soldiers were using iron bars to lift the slabs that had sealed the burial chamber. They stacked them against the wall of the crypt leaving the tomb gaping in front of them. Lined up inside were four iron bound chests.

'The monks who buried Llewelyn recorded they only found a torso to bury,' Morgan explained. 'As that shouldn't have taken up too much room I found it odd that his was the largest tomb in the crypt.'

'The abbot gave you the freedom to go where you wanted within the abbey?' Owain asked.

'Not exactly, my prince, but like all Welsh fathers, mine brought me up to be resourceful. There were three full sized slabs sealing this tomb, and when I saw these iron bars were of a size needed to lift the slabs I decided to investigate. Last night I hid beneath the steps and watched six brothers open this tomb and remove a chest. They unlocked it and filled a leather bag with coin from inside before replacing it in the tomb.'

'So Llewelyn's corpse isn't here?' John sounded disappointed.

'Not all of it,' Owain divulged. 'Crach told me his head was sent to London where Edward I had it set up on the city pillory and crowned "King of the Outlaws" with ivy before it was transported on the point of a lance to London bridge. I looked for it when I lived in London but although I met old men who insisted they remembered seeing it displayed when they were children, it had long disappeared.'

'They might have sent it back here to re-join the rest of him,' Philip suggested.

'They wouldn't have bothered. There wouldn't have been that much left after a few years,' John said.

'Skulls don't rot.' Philip never missed an opportunity to contradict his elder brother.

'They become brittle . . . '

'Shall we look into these chests, gentlemen?' Owain suggested.

John nodded to his men who hauled the chests out of the tomb.

'They're heavy,' Philip complained as he helped line them up.

Owain glanced into the tomb. 'There's another slab.'

John and Philip picked up the iron bars and lifted it to reveal the remains of a rib cage and spine poking through rotting sackcloth and a mildewed cloak lined with fur. There was no head, and the arm and leg bones were piled separate from the ribcage and spine.

'It's a sad world when a Welsh prince can't even call his tomb his own.' Feeling as though he had violated Llewelyn, Owain helped the Hanmers replace the slab that had covered Llewelyn's remains.

'Sad only because devil's spawn like that abbot upstairs are allowed to masquerade as Christians. When we chase Bolingbroke back over the border, we can turn our attention to the abbeys Canterbury has allowed to degenerate into cess pits,' Morgan declared.

'Well said, Morgan. I look forward to helping you.' Philip tried the lock on the first chest. It was rusted but strong. 'We need a crowbar.'

'Try this.' John handed him an iron torch snuffer, but when Philip tried to force it beneath the iron bands on the chest it bent.

Morgan left and returned with a stone mason's hammer and chisel. He set to work and after a few minutes succeeded in hitting the lock off the first chest. Owain lifted the lid on a sea of silver coins. He picked one up and took it to the torchlight.

'These were minted in the reign of Hywel Dda.'

'And these are Roman.' John ran his hands through a mixture of coins as soon as Dafydd opened the second chest.

'Gold or silver?' Philip asked.

'Both and copper and bronze by the look of it,' John took a torch from one of his men and squinted at the contents. 'My Latin was never as good as yours Owain.' He tossed him a gold solidus.

'The Emperor Hadrian.' Owain returned it to him.

'You always listened to our tutors in Arundel Castle.'

'You never did,' Owain countered.

'I might have done if the lessons hadn't been so boring.'

They watched Dafydd open the third chest. It contained dozens of solid silver amulets.

'Silver Danegeld.' Owain picked one up.

'How do you know?' Philip asked.

'Because the silver has been fashioned into amulets. The Danes frequently demanded payment from the Saxons in silver in return for guaranteeing the safety of Saxon towns and villages. When they got it, they wore the silver on their arms.'

'You mean the Danes gave their word that they wouldn't attack the Saxon settlements in return for cart loads of silver,' Philip said. 'I recall our tutor suggesting that a Dane's word was rarely kept.'

'They could be relied on to place the welfare of their own breed before others,' Owain agreed.

'Who can blame them if they had treacherous bastards like Bolingbroke to deal with.'

'The amulets were practical. If they wanted to pay anyone for goods or services, they would remove one, hack off an amount equal to the value of what they wanted and hand it over.'

'There's a fair few gold nobles worth there,' John said.

Owain looked at the three open chests. 'The Roman coin was probably hidden when the legions left Britain in the hope they'd be able to return and retrieve it. The Danegeld and Hwyel Dda's coin could have been bequests to the abbey . . . '

'Or placed here for safety during Llewelyn ap Iorwerth's wars with the Marcher lords and purloined by the monks when no one came to claim it,' Philip said.

'And these my prince.' Morgan had knocked the lock off the last chest. 'It was crammed with chalices, patens, wafer boxes, crucifixes, candlesticks and bells wrought in silver and gold.

John picked up one of the gold patens, 'This is inscribed with the name of Cadwallon ap Madog.'

'Unsurprising as he founded this abbey,' Owain said.

'What do you want to do with this treasure, my prince?' Philip asked.

'I want you and John to take the coin and Danegeld to our headquarters in Snowdonia. When the next harvest fails we'll distribute it among the Welsh abbeys so the abbots can buy grain for those in need.'

'And the church silver and gold, my prince?'

'Give it to Abbot David in Valle Crucis to do with as he wills.'

Owain looked up when he heard a step on the stone staircase. The abbot looked down at him in silence.

'You and the brothers have one hour to pack, abbot,' Owain said.

'Where will we go ... '

'To any house that will have you.'

'But I am the abbot of this house. All the other houses will have their own ... '

Owain cut him short. 'One hour, abbot. Packed or not you will be on your way with the goods, chattels, and animals that you, and those of the brothers who volunteer to accompany you, can carry and herd. Do not try to force any who are reluctant to join you. My men will question everyone before they leave and I will charge my captains to see you on your way.'

***

Owain, Margaret, the Hanmers, Rhys Coch and Dafydd sat on their mounts outside the main gates of the abbey. They watched the abbot and his column of monks wend southwards through the avenues of Owain's men who stood, swords drawn, either side of the road.

The abbot, hospitaler and senior monks rode at the head of the procession. Their heads were held high, as if they were on a progress to celebrate a holy day. The faces of the novices who walked alongside the carts filled with clothing and provisions, were damp from tears. The lay brothers and their families who brought up the rear driving the abbey's cattle, sheep and goats showed the most signs of distress.

'We've searched every man and cart, my prince,' Dafydd assured Owain when he saw him eyeing the cavalcade. 'They're burdened with abbey property, and none other.'

'Only because the abbot handed over all the Welsh treasures he was holding to Hugh Burnell months ago,' John commented acidly.

'We've retrieved the most valuable silver and gold pieces,' Philip reminded his brother. 'I'm surprised to see the abbot heading south, I assumed he would head North East to Strata Florida to beg sanctuary.'

'He knows Abbot David supports our cause not Bolingbroke's,' Owain said. 'South he has a plethora of abbeys to choose from, Llanthony, Abergavenny, Tintern, Grace Dieu . . . '

'All of which support you, my prince,' John commented.

'All of which are governed by abbots who exercise Christian charity, which they will extend to their brothers from Cwmhir. The abbot can do no harm to us now.'

Morgan rode up to Owain. 'All the preparations have been made, my prince.'

'Then pass down the order to fire the abbey, Morgan. Tell the men to leave as few stones standing as possible within the time at our disposal.'

'Yes, my prince.'

Morgan rode back to Owain's captains and lieutenants and shouted the order which was repeated and echoed down the lines.

Owain turned his destrier towards the abbey. Smoke was already curling out of the stone windows of the abbot's library. Within minutes flames and black smoke burst from the windows in the chapel, carrying with them the stench of the pitch they had used to coat the wooden choir stalls to ensure they'd burn.

Margaret reined in her mount alongside his.

'I know you disapprove of this,' he murmured too low even for those closest to them to hear.

She rested her hand on his. 'The abbot broke man's and God's laws when he sent Welsh relics to England.'

'That he did.' He beckoned the Hanmers forward. 'I don't have to tell you to exercise caution on your journey or guard those chests well.'

'No, my prince,' John answered.
'God speed.'
'And to you, my prince.'

South of Cwmhir September 1401

Owain, Margaret, Enyd and Morgan drew their mounts to a halt alongside a stream so the horses could drink.

'We have another hour of daylight left, my lord,' Morgan observed. 'Do you want to camp here or press on in the hope of meeting up with Rhys Ddu?'

Owain scanned the surrounding hills. 'We could stay here for ten minutes and wait for Rhys Ddu to catch up with us.'

'You think he's close by, my prince?' Morgan asked.

'I expected a son of Llewelyn Gruffydd Fychan to have keener eyes,' Dafydd joined them. 'Look to the trees on the northern slopes boy.'

As Owain spoke Rhys Ddu galloped out on his destrier, wearing his trademark black armour not a copy of Owain's.

Owain waved to Rhys and pointed to a secluded spot ringed by willows further up the bank. Rhys indicated that his men should join Owain's, spurred his horse and reached the trees before Owain.

'God speed, my lord.' He bowed as much as anyone could bow on horseback when Owain reached him. 'New Radnor is burning. Shortly the name will grace only a smudge on the landscape.

'Your men?'

'Five were injured in the fighting, all were able to ride. I sent them to be doctored at Glyndyfrdwy.'

'With an escort?' Owain checked.

'Of course and under the protection of the same escort I sent the captives we took, mainly English officials who appeared worth ransoming. I ordered the escort to lock them in the prison tower on the estate and stand guard until relieved.'

'You've sent out demands to the prisoners' families?' Owain checked.

'I've given them two weeks to pay on pain of seeing their relatives being sold into servitude. I told the escort to wait four weeks before auctioning them off. I hope the families pay. Most looked as though they've lived off the fat of land too long to bring in a good price.'

'You've done well.'

'You haven't heard it all, my lord. I sent scouts into Montgomery and Welshpool this morning to determine the strength of the garrisons. You chose our next targets well. According to the reports they'll fall easily, and now you're with us we can hit both towns simultaneously, and,' Rhys raised one eyebrow, 'add to your legend and reputation as a magician who can fight in two places several miles apart at once.'

A cloud burst above them and rain began to teem down from the overcast skies.

'As well as control the weather,' Rhys laughed.

'This is one of the times I wished I could do just that. It looks like the night will be long, wet and cold.'

'We've camped in the barns of a derelict plague village, my lord. It's been left to the elements since 1380 or so one of my men told me. They've patched the roofs on the outbuildings so we should remain mostly dry.'

'Mostly?' It was Owain's turn to raise an eyebrow.

'No one wants to be entirely dry inside, my lord and we captured a good few gwisgi flasks and wine barrels before our archers fired their flaming arrows.'

Rhys Ddu's camp, Mid Wales, South of Cwmhir September 1401

'I smell roast pig,' Dafydd sniffed as they rode into the abandoned village.

'In this cloudburst?' Margaret had to shout to be heard above the sound of the rain and the wind. 'You must have the nose of a hunting dog, Dafydd.'

'When it comes to meat, my lady, I have a better nose than any hound, fox or wolf.'

'He's right, my lady,' Enyd said. 'Look.'

As Rhys had suggested most of the cottages had disintegrated into rubble but three old barns and a stable were still partially standing and roofed. A temporary repair at the stable entrance covered a fire that billowed thick whirls of blinding, fragrant smoke. Slung over the flames was a full size boar pig.

'All we've seen for days are sheep,' Dafydd dismounted. 'Where did you find this beauty?' he asked Rhys Fierce who was sitting on a mounting block in front of the fire watching the cooks serve the men.

'Wandering down a side street in New Radnor. It seemed a pity to leave it all alone,' Rhys joked.

'Do you want a slice of belly or leg, my lady, my prince?' Dafydd pushed Rhys's cook aside and tested the meat for readiness.

'Leg I think but in good time, Dafydd. And is that fresh bread I see, Rhys?'

'Baked overnight in Market Street, New Radnor, my lord,' Rhys boasted. 'Fresh out of the oven. We rescued it before we burned the shop.'

'I think I'd like to see my quarters and wash before we start eating,' Margaret demurred.

'Elias, show my lady and her maid to their quarters,' Rhys Ddu ordered, 'and see that food is taken to them when they are ready to eat.'

Bursting with pride at the responsibility he'd been given, Elias bowed before Margaret. 'Please follow me, my lady, mistress Enyd.'

'My apologies, my prince,' Rhys said after they left. 'I doubt that you, or your lady will be comfortable this night, but we have hung a makeshift curtain to add privacy to the driest corner and lined it with straw and wool blankets.'

'Margaret would be angry if you arranged more comfortable quarters for her than any of your men, Rhys.'

'My men would be angry if I didn't, my lord.'

The cook tested the pig with his short blade. 'The fat is running clear, my lords, a slice or two on bread?'

'Would be very welcome,' Rhys Ddu answered, 'send our portions into my quarters.' Rhys took two wooden cups, a skin of wine and showed Owain into the tack room he'd commandeered. They wrapped themselves into their cloaks before lowering themselves on to the dirt floor and leaning against the cold stone wall.

Rhys's squire brought them wooden bowls of meat and bread and a small flask of gwisgi.

'I liberated this from the baker in New Radnor, my lord,' the squire handed Rhys the flask of gwisgi.

'Just the one?'

'Of course.'

'You don't sound convincing,' Rhys shouted after him. He loaded a handful of bread with meat and crackling and bit into it.

'This is good,' Owain said.

'It is,' Rhys agreed between bites, 'You've heard Bolingbroke is in Wales?'

'No, but I'm not surprised. I predicted he'd cross the border at the onset of battle season, but spring was late this year, and then came Hyddgen. Bolingbroke's not the sort to allow his enemies to savour victory for long, even if the heavens hail down a sea or two.'

'That he isn't. The armour of the poor sods manning the garrison in New Radyr was rusting on their backs and they had dry quarters to retreat to unlike the king's men.'

'Did you hear where Bolingbroke was heading?'

'South West, so the captain of the guard in New Radyr told me. He'd spoken to a friar who saw them heading that way.'

'South West?' Owain frowned.

'You expected him to go elsewhere?' Rhys asked.

'He usually stays with my brother Gruffydd when he travels down from Shrewsbury.'

'Perhaps Gruffydd sent him packing.'

'Gruffydd and his wife would kill the fatted proverbial calf, lamb, sow, hens, ducks, geese and fish the largest salmon from the pond for him. My brother is determined not to find himself on the losing side of this war, whoever wins it.'

'And you're still talking to him?'

'Do you have brothers?'

'Point taken.' Rhys finished the last of his meat reached for the gwisgi flask. He passed it to Owain before rising and picking up their bowls. 'More pig?'

'I could manage a slice.'

'So could I, then I'm for bed.'

'Burning towns and abbeys is exhausting business.'

'It is,' Owain murmured, his mind busy conjuring a map of possible targets Bolingbroke could be heading for in South Wales.'

'I almost forgot.' Rhys handed Owain a messenger bag. 'Bolingbroke has written to you.'

CHAPTER TWENTY-ONE

The road from Caeo Llandovery to Snowdonia September 1401

Random thoughts flitted through Llewelyn ap Gruffydd Fychan's mind. The more he tried to concentrate on a single thread, the more it eluded him, slipping away before he had time to consider its implications.

He'd been in turmoil since his last night in Caeo. He'd spent it contemplating his disgust with Bolingbroke, his admiration for Glyndŵr and his support for the campaign to free Wales from England's oppressive rule but whichever way he viewed his future, it didn't portend well for him, or given Bolingbroke's petty vindictiveness, his family.

His introspection had resulted in a frenzy of letter writing in an attempt to settle his affairs in the few hours left he had to call his own.

At daybreak he'd barely had time to grab a hunk of bread and cheese from his kitchen before obeying Bolingbroke's demand that he guide his retinue to Glyndŵr's stronghold in Snowdonia.

After three days of riding from dawn till dusk, during which he'd been hard pressed to keep his wits about him while Bolingbroke engaged him in conversations that bordered on interrogation, Llewelyn had been relieved to reach the foothills of the mountain range.

***

The column of destriers picked their way steadily upwards, as the sun sank over the high peaks on the western horizon. When only a sliver remained, the sky darkened as if a torch had been snuffed. Men shivered as they entered a narrow pass between two peaks. The wind, sharpened by needle thin ice bars, gathered speed as it whistled towards them and blustered into their frozen faces.

'How much longer to our destination?' Henry shouted above the howls of the gale.

Llewelyn looked around for landmarks and spotted a hut in the distance. 'If we're fortunate, less than an hour's ride, my lord. Ysbyty Ifan is halfway up that hill.'

'You sound as though you're choking, man. There isn't an Englishman born who can understand your blasted tongue.'

'Ysbyty is Welsh for hospital, and Ifan is Welsh for John, my lord. It's the name the locals have given the hospice and hostelry of the Knights of St John, who set up the house to care for pilgrims. I have stayed there many times and can vouch for the warm welcome, good food and clean beds.'

'I hope this place that you've sworn to take us to - whatever its name - still exists. I can't even see the hill you spoke of in this murk,' the king grumbled. 'Beaufort!' He called for his brother.

'My king.' Beaufort rode to the front of the column.

'Have the outriders reported back?'

'Yes, sire, and two have gone ahead to notify the Knights of St John of your imminent arrival.'

'The outriders saw the hostelry?'

'They received directions and an assurance of its location from a cottager, my king.'

Henry sneezed. 'Light the torches and send bearers up here. I need to see the road if I'm to get out of this damnable cold before the downpour becomes a flood that sweeps us away.'

'At once, my king.' Beaufort turned back to the column. Within minutes four dozen torches had been lit and bearers arrived to illuminate the road ahead.

They moved off again, only to stop after a few minutes to relight the torches that had been doused by rain and blown out by the wind. It was nearer two than one hour later when their outriders saw the lamps that burned at the door of the charitable order.

Stable boys took their mounts although Huw was careful to follow those who'd been entrusted with his master's horses. The senior brothers escorted the king and favoured members of his entourage into an inner room where food had been laid out and a well-built fire burned in an open hearth.

Llewelyn knew better than to push his way forward to commandeer some of the heat, but Maldwyn, an old friend from boyhood, who'd joined the order early in life, handed him a cup of warm, spiced Bordeaux.

Henry's cloak and boots were taken away to be dried, he was given the most comfortable seat close to the fire and the table was moved within easy reach of his chair. 'Wine, bread, cheese, meat, pies and pastries, the best in our humble house, my king.' The abbot who ruled the hospice bowed before Bolingbroke. 'If you should require anything . . . '

'This will do,' Henry dismissed the man with a flick of his fingers.

'In which case I will oversee the sleeping arrangements for you and your men.' The abbot signalled to the brothers and left Henry and his entourage in possession of the chamber.

Llewelyn stationed himself on the fringe of the group, close to the door with the intention of slipping out, finding Maldwyn and extracting the latest news that had reached Ysbyty Ifan. But his presence didn't go unnoticed by Henry.

'We're in Snowdon, Gruffydd?' Bolingbroke demanded.

'To be exact, Ysbyty Ifan is in the foothills of Snowdonia, my lord,' Llewelyn replied.

'You Welsh are so damned pedantic. How far is Owain Glyndŵr's stronghold from here?'

'I told you, my lord, Glyndŵr has many retreats and sanctuaries in Snowdonia. A few are close to Ysbyty Ifan, most are some distance away. I don't know them all.'

'But you do know their location?'

295

'Of a few, my lord, but it will be more of a guess than a "know".'

'They're within a day's travelling distance of this hospice?'

'One or two are rumoured to be, my lord. Such information as I have is down to gossip. Glyndŵr has never trusted me enough to take me into his confidence.'

'Yet you've entrusted your daughter to his son?'

Llewelyn shrugged and held out his hands in a gesture of defeat. 'My connections to the house of Glyndŵr are no stronger than those of any father who has more daughters of marriageable age than offers for their hands, my lord.'

Henry eyed him for a moment then laughed mirthlessly. 'As king, I've never had that problem.'

'You are truly fortunate, my lord.'

'In the beauty of my daughters or my Divine Right to rule?'

'In both, my lord,' Llewelyn answered tactfully.

'More crowned heads want to ally their houses with mine through the marriage bed than I have daughters. If I'd been forewarned, I would have sired more when I was younger.' Henry kicked a boy who was adding logs to the fire, away from the table. 'Keep your grubby paws from my victuals, boy!'

Not daring to raise his eyes or answer the king, the boy fell to his knees and hung his head before scuttling out of the door.

Henry took a meat pie, bit into it and examined the filling. 'At first light, Llewelyn, you will go out with a scouting party under the command of our brother Beaufort. You will continue to ride out every day until you track down Glyndŵr and bring him to me. Alive if you can. If you can't, his head will suffice.'

'And if we don't find him within riding distance of here, my lord?' Llewelyn asked.

'You will move on, and if you journey too far to return here by nightfall, a night spent out on the mountainside in this weather should sharpen your resolve to find him.'

Bolingbroke spoke softly but there was iron in his voice. 'Make no mistake, Llewelyn, I will have Glyndŵr's head or yours. First light tomorrow, you lead the search under Beaufort's command.'

'As you wish, my lord.'

'I do not wish, Llewelyn, I command.'

Ysbyty Ifan, Snowdonia September 1401

Llewelyn waited until the early hours before sneaking out of the dormitory in the stable loft where he'd been billeted with the sergeants. He threw back the blanket he'd been given and crawled, fully dressed, from the straw pallet he shared with two men from Kent whose snores spoke of too much ale - or possibly gwisgi.

Llewelyn had stayed in Ysbyty Ifan many times and knew the layout of the buildings. He slipped on his shoes when he reached the bottom of the ladder, stole past the Eastern wall of the presbytery of the church, entered the passage that connected to the Prior's parlour, walked through to the cloister and from there made his way down the passage that led into the kitchen.

The appetising aroma of rising bread wafted out to greet him along with the warmth that belched from the ovens. The cook was stretched out, dozing on a settle beside the hearth. Maldwyn was sitting next to him on a stool, leaning towards the fire so he could use its light to read a scroll.

Llewelyn muffled the sound of the latch with his fingers but Maldwyn looked up before he'd closed the door. Holding his finger to his lips Maldwyn pointed to the corridor that led to the pantries and cellar. Llewelyn followed him. Neither spoke until they entered the dairy. Maldwyn looked up and down the corridor, locked the door and retreated further into the still room. He pulled two stools out from beneath the shelves of cheeses, jugs of buttermilk, slabs of butter and bowls of curd and whey.

'I heard Henry threatened to have your head or the prince's,' he whispered in Welsh as he handed him a stool.

Llewelyn nodded. 'How do you know?'

'Lords don't notice the servants who tend the fires. Some of the farmers' second sons sent to us for training have keen ears and active minds.'

'Do you know a walking woman who can travel swiftly and carry a long message in her head?'

'While planning a course south?' Maldwyn guessed.

'Yes.'

'To the prince?'

'To Caeo,' Llewelyn corrected. 'And in case anything goes awry please remember what I am about to say. This is a solemn command to all who know me and hold me in regard. I want no man risking his neck by drawing a blade on my behalf. I am an old man. My time is done. Glyndŵr fights for the future of Wales and all Welshmen including my sons and soon my grandson. I trust him to keep my family safe.'

Rhys Ddu's camp, Mid Wales, South of Cwmhir September 1401

'I can't imagine Bolingbroke has sent you good news, so why the smile, my lord?' Rhys Ddu asked Owain.

Owain folded the letter he'd read and placed it inside his cotte. 'He's offered me, via the intermediary of the De Clares who had the good sense to forward his letter to you, a ransom of 400 marks for Dafydd Gam, which says something for the esteem he holds the man in.'

'Will you take it?'

'Much as I'd like to separate Gam's lying head from his traitorous body, yes. The abbeys in Wales could buy a great deal of grain to alleviate the misery of this year's harvest with that coin.'

'The rains did a deal of damage, other than to your reputation as a wizard, my lord,' Rhys joked. 'And long may it endure. One glimpse of your armour and battle banner is all that's needed to send most of the enemy galloping in retreat.'

Owain rose from the ground. 'You did well in New Radnor, Rhys. You're a loyal friend as well as captain.'

'I have an excellent prince to follow, my lord. Sleep well, there is nothing pressing to be done that can't wait until morning.'

Owain went to the barn and left the door open, so he could use the light of the camp fire to avoid stepping on the captains who were already asleep.

Folding back the makeshift curtain, he fumbled his way into the darkness that shrouded his bed. After feeling his way towards Margaret, he lay beside her pulled her head down on to his shoulder and closed his eyes.

The straw Rhys's men had used to make the mattress poked through the blanket that covered it, pricking his skin. His riding muscles ached, and every time he closed his eyes, instead of the oblivion he hoped for, he found himself reliving the destruction of Cwmhir Abbey, seeing again the flames shooting from the windows and licking around the centuries old carvings that had decorated the walls.

He'd never doubted the intelligence he'd received from Morgan, Trefor and Yonge that had prompted him to attack the abbey. Or the tales of corruption and treachery involving the abbot, prior, almoner and senior monks who'd embezzled the funds entrusted to them to distribute to the poor. Nor could he forget that the abbot had handed Hugh Burnell treasures that belonged to the Welsh people.

But neither could he blot out the guilt that had consumed him when he'd seen the desolation in the eyes of the lay brothers and monks as they'd walked away from the smoking ruins of the abbey that had been their refuge and home.

Did he have the right to destroy the sanctuary of men who'd taken a sacred vow to serve God? Was his desire to free Wales, simply a craving for power and adulation as his enemies said? How many more lives would be lost to add to those he'd loved and buried at Hyddgen?

He remembered riding from London to Sycharth the moment he'd heard Gwyneth had given birth to his first born child. The pride he'd felt when she'd laid David in his arms had never left him. His eldest son who'd loved him enough to follow him to his death . . .

'A Flemish arrow killed David, Owain, not you,' Margaret whispered close to his ear.'

'How do you know . . . '

'That you were thinking of David? I could tell you that I've developed the sight but it wouldn't be true although I feel your pain as though it were my own.'

'You guessed?'

'You whispered his name but I knew you weren't aware you'd spoken it.'

He wrapped his arm tightly around her shoulders.

'I saw what it cost you to fire the abbey, Owain. But you had no choice.'

'Didn't I?' he asked seriously.

'Not if you want to keep Welsh treasures away from the thieving English. Now, other abbots will think twice before handing over our heritage to the English in exchange for coin.'

'You believe I was right to burn Cwmhir?'

'I have no doubt of it.'

'I have started a war . . . '

'I noticed.'

'Do you ever wonder what will happen to our children, our people, our followers and our land, should we lose?'

'We won't.' She moved closer to him.

'But if we should?' he repeated.

'Do you remember the night you left Sycharth for Pont Gweni?'

'I'll never forget it.'

'Or the afternoon you picked up the crown of Elisig in the presence of the Bishop of St Asaph and all our family, friends and your supporters and set it on your own head.'

'Like leaving Sycharth for Pont Gweni, it is a moment ingrained on my memory.'

'And knowing what you do now, would you have acted any differently.'

Owain fell silent but only for a moment. 'No.'

'Then be at peace.'

Before he could say anything more, she closed her mouth over his, silencing him with a kiss.

Snowdonia October1401

After a slow climb, during which his horse twice lost its footing, Llewelyn was glad to dismount and lead his destrier by the reins. They'd been searching the mountains for over a month and hadn't sighted a soul outside of the king's party, or found signs of any recent encampments.

Knowing their lack of progress had infuriated Beaufort, Llewelyn took care to portray a man who was equally exasperated. It wasn't all pretence. Not least because the rain sheeting down from leaden grey skies, had soaked through both his Welsh wool and leather cloaks.

He took his time examining the plateau they'd reached, searching the upward slope for footprints and walking twice around the lake that had formed in a depression half way up the slope.

'Anything?' John Beaufort snapped when he crouched down and examined the muddy bank for the third time.

'There are no signs of a recent camp, but these could be footprints . . . '

'Or sheep tracks,' Beaufort countered. 'I'm cold, wet and starving.' He turned his horse to face his sodden men, 'all of you, follow me to the hostelry. And you?' He wiped the rain from his eyes and glared at Llewelyn, 'you'd better think of somewhere other than these God forsaken mountains to search next. And wherever it is, I'll be complaining to the king if we find neither hide nor hair of the Welsh bastard there.'

Ysbyty Ifan, Snowdonia October 1401

'Be careful who you speak to and doubly careful what you say to any stranger, my lord,' Maldwyn warned Llewelyn when he brought his wet clothes into the washhouse to be cleaned and dried.

Llewelyn dumped his dripping hose and tunic into a barrel. 'What's happened?" he whispered low in Welsh.

'A messenger arrived at noon. He spent most of the day closeted in the parlour with the King. They only emerged to call for food and extra logs for the fire.'

'Did your boy overhear anything?'

'Glyndŵr has been seen in South Wales.'

'South,' Llewelyn frowned. 'Where?'

'Just south. The king has spent the last hour with the almoner and messenger. Plans are being made for the king's party to leave in the morning.'

'Did the king seem angry?' Llewelyn asked.

'I haven't heard him raise his voice, but whenever I've been near, he says few words and they all sound cross. I've never heard him speak otherwise. What are you going to do, my lord?'

'Do?' Llewelyn went to the door. 'Whatever the king asks of me.'

'He asked you be brought to him as soon as you came in. Llew . . . '

Llewelyn smiled and embraced Maldwyn. 'Remember what I told you.'

***

The fireirons glowed crimson in the hearth, propping up the logs so the flames burned fiercely. Llewelyn saw them as soon as he opened the door to the king's chamber. He looked at them, before raising his eyes to the king's.

'You have lied to us and wasted our time.'

Henry waited for Llewelyn to answer, when the Welshman remained silent, he said, 'You don't deny it?'

'Would there be any point?'

'None.'

Llewelyn smiled. 'Then I've saved both of us time.'

Bolingbroke turned to Beaufort who was still shivering although he'd changed into dry clothes.

'The blacksmith is waiting at the forge. Make sure the prisoner's legs irons can be unclipped so he can ride and fastened again when he dismounts.'

'Yes, my king.'

'Lock him in the forge overnight and guard him well. No one, other than you and two of your most trusted soldiers is to go near him. Understood?'

'Yes, my king.'

'We leave at dawn.'

'For where, my king?' Beaufort asked.

'A place where people know this miscreant well, and mistakenly believe they have cause to admire him.' Bolingbroke glared at Llewelyn. 'We are about to teach them and all the Welsh rebels a lesson they will never forget.'

CHAPTER TWENTY TWO

Glyndŵr's Summer Headquarters Glyncoch October 1401
The day was warm, the prisoner sweating despite the chill in the stone flagged, windowless storeroom.

'Torture me to hell and back, why don't you.' The prisoner spat at Elias's feet as he upended a bucket of water over the cell floor.

'Please move so we can wash down this side of the chamber, there's a good fellow,' Joshua could have been addressing one of his tutors in Oxford.

'Here you are. Have a stool, sir, so you can sit,' Peter moved one closer to the prisoner.

'The prisoner picked it up and threw it so forcefully at Peter's head, that the blanket he'd wrapped around himself fell off. Peter ducked and the stool splintered on the wall behind him.

The door opened and Tudor and Xian looked in warily from the safety of the yard.

'There's a lot of noise coming from here,' Tudor commented.

'Our guest objects to having himself and his accommodation washed down, my lord,' Peter explained.

'Given the stench in here I thought he'd be grateful,' Tudor commented.

The prisoner picked up his blanket from the wet floor and shook it out. 'These bastards stripped me, scrubbed me down with lye soap and brushes, all the while mocking, and insulting me. I'm a soldier. A sergeant in Lord de Grey's service ... '

'We know who you are,' Tudor said. 'I was the one who captured you, remember.'

'Three on to one ... '

'A child of two could have caught you, sunk as deep as you were in a drunken stupor.'

'I'd been travelling. Fighting ... '

'Fighting who exactly in a plague village?' Tudor asked.

'My lord's enemies. But that was a fair fight, man to man. Not like having these three beating me ... '

'They beat you?' Tudor interrupted, feigning shock. 'Did you beat this man, Peter?'

'No, my lord, we didn't - but I did ask him to allow me to help him off with his clothes so they and he could be washed.'

Tudor stood back, surveyed the sergeant and shook his head. 'I must admit if you've been beaten, it was cleverly done as I see no bruises.' Tudor sniffed. 'As for the washing, it was sorely needed judging by the reek in here. But now there's the matter of the broken stool.'

'He threw the stool at me, my lord. I ducked.'

'Good move, Peter. Have any of you hit this man?' Tudor asked Elias and Joshua who'd continued washing down the cell by throwing buckets of water over the walls and floor.

'No, my lord,' Elias answered. 'Although I felt like it after cleaning up the disgusting mess he'd made in here.'

Tudor stepped inside and peered closely at the soldier. 'Can you see any marks on this man, Xian?'

'Perhaps they hit him with a pillow so they wouldn't show?' Xian peered at the neat pile the squires had made of the prisoner's effects outside the door. 'There was a tin cup, bowl, empty short and broad sword scabbards, leather gloves, and a lock of hair wound around a pilgrim badge of St John the Baptist's head. Beside them lay a tarnished lead alloy ring.

'Nice pilgrim badge.' Xian held up the effigy of St John's head. 'Amiens cathedral?'

'What if it is?' the prisoner snapped.

'Nice cathedral.'

'You been there?' the prisoner growled suspiciously.

'I've travelled through France a few times.' Xian picked up the ring.

'Keep your paws off that. It was a present from my lord,' the prisoner snarled.

'I see it has the de Grey arms stamped on it. It looks good in lead alloy but it looks better in enamelled silver. Three blue bars, three silver, the top silver bar decorated with crimson circles.'

'You've seen it's like in silver?' The man eyed Xian suspiciously.

'I have.'

'Then you've met one of my lord's bastards.'

Well-schooled in concealing his emotions, Xian nodded. 'He didn't tell me he was a bastard. I assumed he was a captain.'

'Most of the captains are de Grey bastards from one de Grey sire or another.'

'Are they all given rings?' Xian asked.

'In enamelled silver, not cheap lead alloy like mine. They are reserved for sergeants.'

'You'd assume a lord would want to reward his sergeants equally as well as his captains. After all, it's the sergeants who do most of the work.'

'I told our captain that. He said the sergeants would end up selling the rings for gwisgi.'

'Would you?' Xian asked.

'We can be as honourable as our betters.' He stared at Xian for a moment. 'You look funny.'

Xian was used to people staring at his golden skin and narrow eyes. 'No one can help the way they look,' he said without taking offence.

'You're all right for an odd man.'

'Thank you,' Xian offered him his ring.

The prisoner held out his hand and took it . 'As for my honour, that depends on how long it's been since I last tasted gwisgi.'

Xian took the hint. He handed the man his own flask.

'Thank you.'

'Keep it, but don't drink it all at once, it may be a while before you get another.'

'I don't suppose you'll tell me where I am.'

'Wales,' Xian answered.

'How far from Ruthyn?'

'Further than you can walk.'

'In a day? A week?' the prisoner persisted when Xian didn't elaborate.

'You're anxious to return to Ruthyn?'

'I'm anxious to get out of this cell.'

'To serve your lord?'

'The man shrugged. 'Not particularly. Are you about to make me a better offer?'

Xian smiled and walked away.

'Are you about to make him a better offer?' Tudor asked.

'Not now. Perhaps not ever. But it never hurts to know someone who might be susceptible to a bribe.'

Llewelyn ap Gruffydd Fychan's house Caeo October 1401
A moan echoed out of the open window in the upstairs bedchamber. Hova heard it, winced and closed his eyes.

'How much longer can this last?' he pleaded with his father's steward, Ifor.

'Mistress Lowri only went in labour this morning didn't she, my lord?'

'Before sunrise. It was still dark.'

'My wife was in labour three days and four nights on our last, God rest her soul . . . '

'Three days and nights are nothing. My daughter . . . '

Hova left the wooden bench in the orchard turned his back on the washerwoman and Ifor and went to the gate. A woman was walking briskly across the forecourt that fronted the house.

Her woollen dress was covered in dust from the road, her leather shoes, broken and badly laced because the holes that held the laces had broken through.

'You're a stranger to these parts, mistress.'

'That I am, but not to you if you are Hova Fychan ap Llewelyn Gruffydd.'

'You have a message for me, Mistress?'

'You have a ring with your father's coat of arms?'

'The Llewelyn coat of arms, mistress.'

She looked at the hand he stretched out to her and nodded. 'Three passant lions with curved claws and their tongues stretched out. That's what I was told look for.'

'Your message, mistress?'

***

When Hova was certain the messenger had told him all she could, he took her to the kitchens and left her in the care of the cook. After asking Ifor to organise a bed for her for as long as she needed one, he sent a kitchen boy to find his squire, Teg, and another to the stables to ask a groom to saddle his riding horse.

Only then did he race into the house and up the staircase. He winced at every one of Lowri's moans, which seemed to intensify the closer he drew to their chamber. He knocked the door softly, and his mother's voice querulous, irritable answered.

'I said we are not be disturbed.'

'It's Hova ... '

'Can't you hear your wife? You've done enough, boy.'

'Please, mother. It's urgent I have to talk to you before I go.'

'Go where?' Sioned opened the door a few inches and blocked his view of the chamber by standing in the gap.

'It's father,' he whispered urgently.

'What ... ' A cry silence Sioned. A thin high pitched wail that signalled a new life.

Sioned stepped back into the chamber and closed the door in Hova's face.

Agitated, restless he paced up and down the gallery for what seemed like hours before his squire. Teg appeared below in the hall.

'Go pack a change of clothes for me and yourself, and order the kitchens to pack food for both of us.'

'Yes, master. Where are we going?'

'Llandovery.'

A footman crossed the hall.

'We'll talk on our way there, Teg.'

'Yes, master. Do you want me to pack your armour and weapons?'

Hova thought for a moment. There was little he could do against a full complement of the king's guard, but he knew several cottagers between Caeo and Llandovery who would willingly hide his horse and armour if asked. And he would need his weapons if he had to fight his way out of a tight corner . . .

'Pack them. Teg, but on a separate horse and conceal them beneath fleeces.'

'Yes, master.' The squire ran back through the front door as Sioned emerged from the bedchamber.

Pale, trembling, she confronted Hova. 'What's happened to your father?' she demanded urgently.

'Lowri . . . '

'A boy. A fine boy. Mother and baby are well, you can see them after the midwife has finished tending them.' She closed the door, stepped in front of it and whispered. 'Your father . . . '

'A messenger's here, a walking woman . . . ' His voice tailed when he heard Lowri's voice.

'What did this woman say?' Sioned persisted.

'She was hired by Maldwyn, the brother in Ysbyty Ifan father knows . . . '

'For pity's sake, boy, get to the point. What did she say?' Sioned was close to hysteria.

'Father has angered the king.'

'Idiot. He should know better! I knew I shouldn't have let him go . . . '

'Bolingbroke commanded father to accompany him. Father had no choice but to obey. Or would you have had him defy the king by refusing to leave Caeo?'

'The trouble with your father is he can never keep his opinions to himself. Has Bolingbroke confiscated our lands or placed a levy on our estates . . . '

'He's bringing father back to Llandovery . . . '

309

'Then it can't be so awful if father is travelling in Bolingbroke's retinue . . . '

Not wanting to give his mother false hope and realising she was close to breaking point Hova spoke quickly. 'The woman told me Bolingbroke ordered father put in chains before they left Snowdonia.'

'Why would the king do that?' Sioned crossed her arms tightly across her chest as if she were cold, but Hova knew she was trying to stop herself from shaking.

'You heard Bolingbroke ask father to lead him to the Prince of Wales. You know Father would never betray the prince, but I think he'd pretend to do exactly that by leading Bolingbroke and his men on a merry dance around Snowdonia. Bolingbroke's no fool. If he suspected father had no intention of taking him to Glyndŵr . . . '

Hova's mention of the name Glyndŵr hit Sioned like a spark on dry tinder, provoking much the same reaction.

'Llew should have never supported Glyndŵr in his mad scheme of Welsh independence,' Sioned erupted.

'How could father ignore the prince when we're one family, mother?' Hova retorted. 'Lowri bears our name and Jonnet, Glyndŵr's. And even without our marriages our families have been friends forever. Gruffydd Glyndŵr and my grandfather were as close as the prince and father. You know father would die before he'd betray the true Prince of Wales. And it's not just the man, it's his cause. Glyndŵr fights for freedom for us all.'

'You too!' Sioned finally snapped. 'You'd lay down your life for Glyndŵr just as your father would, and gladly. Even now, when your wife has suffered all the agonies of hell to bring your son into this world . . . '

'I wouldn't die for the prince, but I would die fighting alongside him for our cause - freedom for Wales.'

'And what good would your death achieve?'

'Possibly none. But if we have to pay in blood to end our slavery to the English, then I will pay it.'

'Isn't it enough that Adam and Morgan are already with the prince?'

'It's war, mother. Our eyes are open and we fight willingly.'

There was a strength in Hova's words that Sioned knew went past her powers of persuasion. 'What are you going to do?'

'I don't know - yet.'

'You'll need a cool head with you. I'll come ... '

'Your cool head will be needed here, mother. If the king should invite himself here again ... '

'And ask the whereabouts of you and your brothers?'

'We're in retreat in the abbey.'

'Which abbey?'

'Pick one that would take him days to check out, and I'll ask the walking woman to carry a message there.'

'Cwmhir?'

'Strata Florida might be better.'

The door to the chamber opened and the midwife emerged.

'Come to see the result of the pain you caused your poor wife, my lord?' she asked Hova.

'Excuse me, mother, I have a son to welcome to the world.' He pushed past the midwife and went inside.

***

Lowri saw Hova's face and lifted a shawl wrapped bundle high in her arms. She pulled down the fine wool so he could see the baby's face.

Hova kneeled beside the bed and kissed Lowri's forehead then the baby's.

'You ... '

'We're both fine,' she reassured.

The midwife sniffed loudly from the doorway. 'As if any woman could be fine after bringing a child that size into this world.'

Hova rose to his feet and closed the door in the midwife's face before returning to his spot beside the bed. He kissed Lowri again before pushing his forefinger into the tiny palm of the baby's hand. The baby gripped his finger and appeared to squint up at him.

'He knows his father.' Lowri smiled.

'Mother told me we had a son. Do you want to name him Tudor for your father?'

'I thought about it when I was in labour. Tudor Glyndŵr Llewelyn Gruffydd Fychan ap Hova seems a little excessive.'

'That name needs to be shortened and I must go.'

'Where?'

'Not far, just Llandovery.'

'Now . . . '

'I wouldn't leave unless I had to,' he returned her smile. 'It's not enough that your father and uncle have quarrelled with the king, my father has too.'

'Is it . . . '

'Serious? No,' he interrupted her with a lie. 'But given the depleted state of the king's coffers, I expect Bolingbroke to levy a fine. I will be leaving for Llandovery as soon as I have spoken to my father's steward and checked the contents of father's chests.'

She looked into his eyes. 'You will be careful?'

'In Llandovery?' He laughed. 'The only danger is that of attack by sheep in the cattle market.'

'Promise me you'll be careful.'

He saw unshed tears in her eyes, and kissed her. 'I'll be back before you and Tudor bach have time to miss me.'

'We're already missing you,' she murmured as he blew her a kiss from the door.

***

Sioned was on the gallery checking a wooden rocking cradle Ifor and a footman had carried down from the attics. Hova recognised it as the one his grandfather had made for his father before his birth. After it had been used for Llewelyn and his younger brothers and sisters, it had been passed down to his parents for their children.

Sioned had covered a woollen mattress inside it with linen sheets, and was stacking a pile of flannel blankets she'd cut and hemmed.

'I could have carried that into our chamber for you yesterday,' Hova said.

'You could have, but that would have been tempting fate. You know full well cradles should never be carried into birthing chambers until after the birth.'

'The way Tudor Bach was kicking inside his mother we knew he couldn't be born anything but healthy.'

'Tempting fate again.' Sioned smiled when the name registered. 'Tudor Bach after Lowri's father?'

'Llewelyn and Hova are in there somewhere too. I'd appreciate it if you'd help Lowri knock a few names off or people will go to sleep when the boy is introduced to them. To save me talking to Ifor, do you know how much ready coin father has in his chests?'

'As much as you need, boy,' Sioned answered.

'Bolingbroke might ask for everything father owns.'

'If he'll spare his life and those of his children and grandchildren, we'll pay it.'

'And how will we live?'

'We'll throw ourselves on the mercy of Glyndŵr,' she answered drily. 'Those who live with him always look well fed and dressed to me.'

Llandovery Thursday October 8th 1401

'Make way for the king! Make way for His Grace King Henry IV!' The heralds' repeated cries were less effective than the staffs of the king's bodyguard as they cleared a path through the throng crammed around the north gate of the town.

Soldiers were stopping and questioning every trader bringing in goods for Friday's market. They had no compunction about turning away the Welsh who were banned by royal edict from sleeping within the town walls or searching every man, child and woman - especially the young and attractive women - for arms or other contraband.

Hova and his squire hung back towards the end of the tightly knit queue. When Hova realised their horses and clothes especially Teg's livery were attracting the attention of the soldiers, he stepped back even further. If he hadn't seen one of the officers staring at him, he might have tried to disappear into the countryside well away from the town walls.

Llandovery Castle Courtyard Thursday October 8th 1401
Two soldiers pushed Huw aside as he dismounted and ran to help Llewelyn from his horse. One hit Huw's back so hard he fell headlong on to the manure spattered yard.

'You have one minute to disappear.'

'My master . . . '

'Doesn't need an old man to squire him. In fact, soon he won't need a squire at all.'

'He will need me,' Huw argued. 'No one knows my master like me.'

'He won't need anyone. Not where he's going. Push off.' The soldier's harsh London accent grated on Huw's ears, accustomed as he was to the Welsh lilt.

'Go, Huw. Tell your mistress I'm fine and I send her my love.' Llewelyn stumbled, only just managing to regain his balance after a guard hauled him off his horse.

'You won't be fine for long.'

The soldiers burst into raucous laughter at the poor jest.

Huw scrambled to his feet and looked back at Llewelyn who stood impassively while a soldier linked his leg chains.

'I need my horse.'

'Then come and get it.' The tallest and heaviest of the soldiers moved in front of Huw.

Llewelyn saw the soldier square up to Huw and silently mouthed, "Go."

Huw had never felt so cowardly as he ran towards the drawbridge. When he reached it he turned his head and looked back. A soldier had grabbed Llewelyn's cotte and was dragging him towards the gatehouse towers. Llewelyn stood his ground long enough to wink at Huw before turning.

***

Two soldiers stood on the drawbridge. Both stared at Huw as he ran outside the confines of the castle. He saw them watching him, turned sharp right and dived down an alleyway. It was three hours hard walking to Caeo and every step would take him further from his master. But first he had to negotiate one of the town's gates.

Uncertain which one to aim for, afraid of being followed, he looked over his shoulder as a delaying hand gripped his leg.

CHAPTER TWENTY-THREE

Llandovery Town North Gate Thursday October 8th 1401
'God speed, my lord.' Friar Brown hauled on the reins of the open cart he was driving and manoeuvred it alongside Hova's and Teg's horses. The back of the cart was crammed full of young boys dressed in white clerical robes. 'As you see, I've brought the choir from Talley Abbey to sing at the dedication of the new chapel to St Llud, so generously endowed by your family. The bishop, abbot, all the brothers and the choir are gratified that you have condescended to grace the service with your presence.'

Hova knew nothing of any new chapel or dedication to St Llud, but he was aware of the soldiers detaining and questioning everyone who was moving towards the gate. Taking his cue from Friar Brown, he shouted, 'I have come to represent my family, Friar Brown.'

The friar waved familiarly at one of the guards and beckoned him forward.

'Do I know you?' the soldier snarled.

'I'm not sure,' the friar replied boldly. 'All you upstanding fellows look the same in your livery. I carry a pass from the bishop.' He thrust a wooden plaque bearing an etching of a bishop's mitre into the guard's hand but Hova noticed the friar didn't mention the bishop's name. 'These boys are the choir he has sent to sing at the dedication of St Llud's chapel in the church.'

'No one's said anything to me about a choir or a dedication.'

'We were held up on the road and I have to get them to the church urgently, so they can practise for the ceremony tomorrow. As soon as the bishop heard the king was in residence in Llandovery Castle, he invited him to the dedication . . . '

'We've had orders to keep all troublemakers outside the town walls. Glyndŵr ... '

'Glyndŵr!' Friar Brown reiterated theatrically, pouncing on the word for the benefit of the crowd. 'Do I, or any of these lads look like Glyndŵr? I tremble for the safety of everyone in Llandovery if these boys frighten you, soldier.'

Raucous laughter greeted the friar's outburst. Angered at being made to look a fool, the soldier kicked a crutch out from beneath a filthy gongfermour. The man fell awkwardly and heavily to the ground, landing on his knees. The crowd roared even louder, watching impassively as the cripple's equally befouled, stinking fellow workers stooped to assist him.

The friar moved. Suspecting he was about to help the man; the soldier pulled his sword from his scabbard.

'Off with you, friar, before I have you arrested. Not you.' He grabbed the bridle of Hova's horse.

Friar Brown pushed aside the soldier's blade delicately with his fingertips. 'Lord Hova's family paid for the chapel. He's travelled far to see this dedication.'

'Where do you lodge this night?' The soldier demanded suspiciously, eyeing first Hova, then Teg.'

'In the friary hospice, as do we,' Friar Brown replied. 'If you call round tonight I'll make sure the brothers give you a good supper with plenty of ale to wash it down in recompense for any inadvertent insult on my part.'

'And where do I find this hospice of yours, friar?'

'In Friar's court at the cattle market end of Broad Street. It's within spitting distance of the castle barracks. Ask anyone for directions and they'll point it out. Now, if you give us leave, we must be on our way. The boys have to practise. The bishop would be displeased if he heard they were anything but note perfect tomorrow.'

'See you at sunset. Make sure the supper's a fine one, friar.'

'It will be,' Friar Brown replied.

'Get a move on down there!' a sergeant shouted at the soldier.

'On your way.' The soldier sharpened his tone at the reprimand.

Once the cart and horses were through the town gate, Hova and Teg dismounted. Hova looked back. The cripple who'd been felled was on his feet, as much as anyone bent double and dependent on crutches could be.

The soldier lashed out again but the gongfermours' leader, a short stout fellow, pushed their reeking, dripping cart between him and the cripple. Mindful of his boots, the soldier stepped back smartly. The stench of the rubbish collectors, was rank and overpowering as it wafted over the crowd and through the gate.

'The garrison commander sent for us because shit creek is flooding from the extra load the kings' guard has dumped in it,' the head gongfermour shouted, 'I've a mind to tell him the best way to unblock it, is to drop a few of his soldiers in it.'

'On your way,' the soldier snapped.

'Can't wait to be rid of us, eh?' The gongfermour grabbed the cripple's arm. 'Don't worry about getting your own back on this bastard, Iockyn, we'll leave his punishment to our patron saint. St Simon knows how to deal with bullies.'

A judicious shove of the cart sent the soldier sprawling on the muddy ground beneath the cart. The crowd laughed even louder than they had before. Furious, the sergeant marched over and ordered the soldier back to barracks to the delight of the onlookers who pelted him with mud and filth to help him on his way.

Hova continued to watch the cripple who was struggling to move, but realising his own situation was too precarious to burden the friar, Teg or himself with extra trouble, he led his horse behind the friar's cart and headed for the castle that dominated the horizon.

The friar left the main street opposite the castle and slowed the cart as they entered a narrow alley. 'Gates!' he shouted.

Two friars appeared from an outbuilding in the lane that was being used to brew beer judging by the smell. They opened a pair of high wooden gates, beckoned Friar Brown forward and closed and barred the gates the minute the cart was through them.

Friar Brown turned his head to the boys. 'Inside. You'll find food waiting for you.' The boys didn't need a second prompt. 'And, they disappeared as if by magic,' Friar Brown murmured to no one in particular.

Hova saw a man leave the building and stared at him in surprise. 'Huw?'

'My lord.' Tears ran down his father's squire's face.

'Father ... '

'Not here. Inside!' One boy had remained unnoticed in the back of the cart. He rose and jumped to the ground. He wasn't much more than four feet tall but when he folded back his hood it was obvious he was no boy.

Hova, Teg, Huw and Friar Brown followed Crach inside the building.

Hospice Llandovery October 8th 1401

Friar Brown took a tray of food from the cook at the entrance to the small dining room. He laid it on the table before closing the door and pushing the bolt across. There were bowls of boiled eggs, eels boiled in milk, oat and peas pottage, bread and slices of carp. Friar Brown filled wooden cups from a pitcher of small beer and set them out. 'The food here is simple but good and the beds, bug free.'

Crach took charge. 'I suggest we talk while we eat. Huw what can you tell us about the king's treatment of your lord and your journey from Snowdonia.'

'Do you know that my lord was brought here in chains like a criminal?'

'Yes.'

'Who told you?' Huw asked Crach.

'The king is not the only one who has spies in the opposition camps. Messages reached me ... '

'And the prince?' Hova asked hopefully.

'No,' Crach answered. 'He is in the far south. I doubt he's heard of your father's detention.'

'But if the news reaches him ... '

'Friar Brown and I have just come from Valle Crucis. We sent messages to the prince and his captains but we have no way of knowing if they were received.'

'The way my lord is being treated by the most uncouth of Bolingbroke's soldiers ... ' Huw took a moment to compose himself. 'I fear for his safety.'

'With good reason,' Crach said. 'The king has announced your lord will be drawn to the market place tomorrow to be hung and quartered.'

'But I was hoping ... ' Too overcome to say another word, Hova simply stared at Crach.

'To negotiate a ransom?' Crach suggested. 'That was never an option as far as Bolingbroke was concerned. He decided your father's fate before they left Snowdonia,' Crach divulged,

'So I heard but I didn't want to believe it.' Hova rose from the table and went to the window that overlooked the yard. Their meal finished, the boys were practising their song in the barn next to the stables.

'We can't simply stand back and do nothing.' Hova pleaded.

'Look at us, boy,' Crach said, 'we are but four and half men. Bolingbroke has four thousand give or take a few either way according to my spies who watched him ride past on his journey here.'

Hova tightened his hands into fists. 'I have to try ... '

'We can't let the master die,' Huw begged.

'What was the last thing he said to you, Huw?' Crach asked.

'Go, Huw. Tell your mistress I'm fine and I send her my love.'

'He said more to one of the brothers in Ysbyty Ifan. "In case anything goes awry please remember this solemn command to all who know me or hold me in regard. I want no man risking his neck by drawing a blade on my behalf. I am an old man. My time is done. Glyndŵr fights for the future of Wales and all Welshmen including my sons and soon my grandson. I trust him to keep my family safe."'

'Are you saying we should do nothing?' Hova demanded.

'No.' Crach replied. 'But I warn you, given the size of Bolingbroke's retinue, and the garrison of the castle, rescue is impossible. Has anyone here witnessed a drawing, hanging and quartering?' When no one spoke he shook his head. 'It is the cruellest, most painful and degrading death devised by man. Only a devil like Bolingbroke would consider inflicting it on a Christian.'

Hova heard the sound of footsteps in the yard. He turned back to the window, 'The soldiers you invited for supper have arrived, Friar Brown.'

The Friar rose to his feet. 'I knew they would.' He reached into his pocket and pulled out a small stone bottle. He checked the level of liquid in the beer jug, tipped it in and swirled it around.

Glyndŵr's Summer Headquarters October 1401
Tudor was watching the squires load carts outside the stables in preparation for the move to their winter quarters in Glyndyfrdwy. Across the paddock Xian and Konrad were inside the barn Xian used as a workshop, wrapping tarpaulins around barrels of flying fire.

Crab walked out of the archway that led to the kitchen yard with a young man dressed in the robes of a novice.

'A messenger has arrived from the Abbot David of Valle Crucis, my lord,' she said to Tudor.

Tudor looked at the boy. 'I know you, brother, who used to be Stephen.'

'You remembered, my lord.' The novice's eyes were heavy from lack of sleep.

'I do. Given the dust you've collected on your clothes, you look as though you've had a hard journey.'

'I left the abbey three nights ago, my lord, and haven't been out of the saddle for longer than four hours since.'

'Have you the energy to eat before you sleep?'

'I am thirsty more than hungry, my lord, but I carry an urgent message for the prince from my abbot. He instructed me to deliver it as soon as I arrived here and only to him in person.'

'The prince is several days ride away in the south east, so you could have a long wait. You know who I am?'

'Yes, my lord, you are Lord Tudor Glyndŵr, the prince's brother.'

'The prince trusts me. Do you think you could?'

'The abbot's instructions were most specific, my lord. I was to deliver my message to the prince and no one else.'

Tudor didn't argue. He wrapped a heavily muscled arm around the boy's shoulder and walked him back towards the kitchen yard. 'Whatever your message, I see you're in dire need of sustenance. Crab can you ask the cook to find us something?'

'You're hungry as well, my lord?' she asked.

He winked at her. 'You know me, I can always eat.'

***

Tudor took the boy into the ante room. A few minutes later Crab appeared with a tray of bread, cheese, apples, and ale. Tudor whispered in her ear as he took the tray from her and she left, closing the door behind her. After setting the tray in front of the novice, Tudor filled two goblets with ale and sat opposite the boy who'd emptied his goblet before starting work on the food.

'The abbot must have had important news to send you here.'

'He did, my lord.' The boy spoke through a mouthful of bread and cheese. He rose to his feet when the door opened and Crab returned with Jonnet and Gruffydd, who'd proved inseparable since their marriage.

'My lady.' The novice rose and bowed to Jonnet and then to Gruffydd. 'My lord.'

Jonnet smiled. 'It's good to see you looking so well, Stephen. The cloistered life must agree with you.'

'It's proving hard, my lady.'

'May I ask why you have come here, Stephen?'

'Stephen no longer, my lady,' he corrected Jonnet. 'I am a novice and brother . . . I didn't expect to see you here.'

'I am here, with my husband, Lord Gruffydd.' She glanced at Gruffydd who returned her smile.

'I hadn't heard news of your marriage, my lady. My felicitations on your union.'

'Thank you, Stephen. But you still haven't said why you're here.'

The boy blurted out what he couldn't bring himself to divulge to Tudor. 'The abbot wanted me to tell the prince that the king is escorting Lord Llewelyn ap Gruffydd Fychan under guard of his four thousand strong retinue to Llandovery. It's possible they have arrived in the town by now.'

'Why would the king take my father under guard to Llandovery?' Jonnet asked.

'To execute him, my lady.'

***

'No! For the hundredth time - No, Jonnet!' Gruffydd refused. He was packing his saddlebags in their chamber. His squire had taken his weapons and armour to the stables, where his, Tudor's, Xian, Maredydd's and their squires' horses were being saddled. 'An execution is no place for a woman . . . '

'It's no place for a man, woman or child but Llewelyn is my father . . . '

'Exactly.' He buckled his saddlebag and dropped it on the bed. 'Can you imagine his feelings if he knew you were in the crowd watching him being stripped of his clothes and dignity prior to being executed.'

'I thought you were going to Llandovery to rescue him.'

'If we can, my love. But you have to be realistic . . . '

'I don't want to be realistic,' she was crying tears of rage as much as sorrow. 'I want my father.'

'Tudor is talking to Rhys now about how many men we should take. I promise you, we'll do everything humanly possible to save Llewelyn,' he reassured her. 'But you heard the novice. Bolingbroke has over 4000 men in Llandovery. Most of our experienced fighters are south with my father and Rhys Coch. We have barely four hundred here and we can't even take them with us because they're needed to safeguard the women and children.'

'So you're refusing to rescue my father.' She dropped down on the bed as though her legs would no longer hold her.

'If we had no intention of trying to save him we wouldn't be leaving, my love. If we reach Llandovery in time . . . '

'In time? - You think you'll be too late?' Her voice was so expressionless it sent a chill down his spine.

'The novice said Bolingbroke declared in Snowdonia that he would execute your father when they reached Llandovery. The boy was three days and nights on the road. Bolingbroke has fast horses and men accustomed to ride twenty, sometimes thirty or even more miles in a day. They could have reached the town by now.' Gruffydd wrapped his arms around her and looked her in the eye. 'If we leave within the hour and ride through the night my uncle thinks we could reach Llandovery by midday tomorrow. I know you and Gweni and Elwy are good horsewomen but none of you are as strong.'

'So, because we're the weaker sex we have to sit at home and wait for you to send us news of your arrival - or survival - or not?'

'All I'm saying is you would slow us down. As for helping your father - if we can't do anything and he is murdered in a public show of "the king's pleasure" do you imagine he would want any of us to witness it?'

'So what will you do in Llandovery?' Her eyes were dark with imagined horrors.

'That depends of what we find there.'

'And you expect me to stay here . . . '

'My love, Xian, Maredydd, my uncle and I are accustomed to hard riding. We're experienced soldiers and we'll take our weapons. But we're no match for the king's guard, and even if we had more men, a town is no place to wage battle. Please, kiss me goodbye. I promise to return as soon as I can.'

'My father's fate is already decided, isn't it?'

'I promised I would never lie to you. Don't ask me to now.' He took her in his arms and kissed her gently on the lips.

***

Jonnet stepped ahead of Elwy, Gweni and Catrin and pushed open the door of the ante room. Tudor, Rhys, Xian, Ieuan, Maredydd and Gruffydd were sitting around the small table. Ignoring her husband's warning look, Jonnet confronted Tudor.

'Llewelyn is my father . . . '

Tudor glanced up at her, 'I don't recall inviting you, or any of you other ladies to a captains' conference,' he added as they crowded in behind her.

'I need to . . . '

'Do something?' he broke in. 'I know. That is why I am going to give you and Gruffydd a vital task, and please don't interrupt again until I've finished explaining my plans. Given Bolingbroke's superior manpower a rescue attempt in Llandovery would undoubtedly result at best, in disaster, at worst a massacre. Bolingbroke would like nothing better than an excuse to behead every woman and hang draw and quarter every man in your family, and ours, Jonnet. The moment your father breathes his last, Bolingbroke will sequester his house and land, that's if he hasn't done so already. I want you to ride to Caeo immediately with Gruffydd, Maredydd and as many men as Rhys can spare. If you catch sight of Bolingbroke's men, you ride on to Glyndyfrdwy as fast as you can. If they try to follow you, head to Snowdonia on the back tracks. You remember where they are Gruffydd, Maredydd?'

Tudor glanced at his nephews.

'We were hoping to go to Llandovery . . . ' Gruffydd began.

'The last thing Llewelyn needs right now, are headstrong Glyndŵr supporters in Llandovery to antagonise Bolingbroke's soldiers. And don't try telling me that you won't be recognised when you and Maredydd, are the image of your sire. I should have also warned you not to interrupt me as well as your wife,' Tudor said forcefully.

'We all want to help Llewelyn.'

'The realistic among us know and accept that he is past any help we can give,' Tudor said. 'I hate to be brutal but it's time for us to face the situation. Gruffydd, Maredydd, I'm assigning you an important task. To preserve as much of Llewelyn's property as you can for the use of his family, without taking any unnecessary risks.'

'We understand, uncle,' Gruffydd reluctantly agreed.

'Hopefully you will reach Caeo without being troubled by the king's men. If you manage to do so, pack as many of Llewelyn's possessions as you can carry with you. I'd prefer it if you went to Glyndyfrdwy, Jonnet, but I admit you're more likely than any of us to know where Llewelyn keeps his valuables. Take them, your mother, Lowri and your brother Hova - if he's there and not in Llandovery - to Glyndyfrdwy. Tell your father's tenants they're welcome to join us there.'

Jonnet paled. 'And my father?'

'Bolingbroke will be on the lookout for parties of armed men, even small ones. Only Xian will accompany me into Llandovery.'

'You'll be recognised.'

'No we won't and I have friends I can call on to conceal us if necessary. You can trust us to do whatever is possible for your father.'

'I'm going with Maredydd, uncle Tudor.'

Tudor sighed and shook his head at Elwy.

'We'll look after her.' Crab slipped her arm around Gweni's shoulders.

'It's easier to train dogs than women. At least they do what they're told.' Tudor whistled to his mastiff to prove his point.

'I'll need help to get our people to Glyndyfrdwy. You'll ride with me, Ieuan?' Rhys said tactfully, knowing how much the wound in his knee was paining him.

'I will.'

'Then it's settled.' Tudor looked at Gruffydd and Jonnet. 'You go to Caeo to salvage what you can of your father's property and escort your mother, brother and Lowri to Glyndyfrdwy, Jonnet. And you two, Gruffydd, Maredydd, don't under any circumstances leave your women for a moment or attempt to enter Llandovery. Bolingbroke doesn't need an excuse to organise more executions than he has already planned.'

Gruffydd reluctantly nodded and Maredydd followed suit.

'Swear it!' Tudor commanded.

Gruffydd was the first to capitulate to his uncle's reasoning and swear, although he was still smarting at Tudor's refusal to take him into Llandovery. Maredydd managed to comply with his uncle's demand with better grace.

'That's enough time wasted. We ride out in five minutes, Xian.' Tudor left the table.

***

Gweni, Elwy, Crab, Jonnet, Maredydd and Gruffydd stood outside the stables watching Tudor, his squire, Alun, Xian, and Konrad ride into the woodland that crowned the summit of the Southernmost hill.

'We will see them again,' Crab assured them as the stable boys brought out their saddled horses.

'And my father?' Jonnet asked.

'Will be at peace.' Crab reached for Jonnet's hand. 'At the end that is all any of us can hope for.'

***

Hospice Llandovery October 8th 1401

'Loosen the strap on that breastplate. It's too small for you, but then everyone knows soldiers have to take what they're given.' Crach eyed Hova and Teg critically. 'No talking to, or eye contact with anyone especially the king's guard in case they recognise you as your father's son, Hova, or you Teg as in service to the Fychans.'

Crach reached for the clerical robe he'd worn when he'd been driven into the town and slipped it on over his clothes. 'You've told the boys we're leaving for the church?' he asked the friar.

'They're lined up waiting for us at the door of the refectory,' Friar Brown answered.

'Good.' Crach turned to Huw. 'Given the amount of poppy juice that went into their beer, those two soldiers should sleep until sunset tomorrow but don't unlock that chamber for any reason. Not even if they tell you they're dying.'

'I should go with you, sire. My master . . . '

'You travelled from Snowdonia under the same guard as your lord. You might not remember the faces of your escort but they'll remember yours and that recognition could prove fatal not only to you, but anyone with you.'

Annoyed at being excluded, Huw said, 'you told the guards that the choir will be singing at the dedication of a new chapel . . . '

'They will. There is a new chapel. It's not yet finished and when it is, it won't be dedicated to Saint Llud, but none of Henry's soldiers need know that. Friar Brown, we'll need torches.' Crach addressed Hova and Teg. 'As our escort you'll carry them but take care to keep the light from your faces. Look down if you see anyone watching you. Bolingbroke's army is large but soldiers recognise their fellows. One wrong gesture from either of you could betray us. The longer you hide in the shadows the safer we'll be.'

The town clock struck the hour.

'They'll be calling curfew in an hour and we have to be back here before then.' Crach turned to Huw. 'Make sure those soldiers stay locked behind that door. '

'I won't let you down, my lord.'

'Make sure you don't.'

Llandovery October 8th 1401

Friar Brown took a carved wooden crucifix with a particularly bloody effigy of Jesus from the wall of the hospice, held it high and led the choir out of the building and yard. Hova and Teg in their "borrowed" uniforms of Bolingbroke's guards, flanked the procession. Before they reached the King's Road, Crach pulled his hood lower over his face to conceal his wrinkles and whiskers.

Whenever they drew close to one of the parties of soldiers on patrol, Friar Brown prompted the leading small chorister, reminding him to hold up the wooden plaque etched with a Bishop's mitre.

Ten minutes after leaving the hospice they entered the church. The priest had lit the altar candles and stood waiting for them in front of the choir stalls. Friar Brown led his small charges forward, and Hova and Teg sat on the steps that led up to the chancel.

Hova didn't realise Crach was no longer with them until the boys started singing. He looked around but could see nothing beyond the shadows that circled the pools of candlelight. He leaned against the wall and picked up a faint but distinct whisper that seemed to emanate from the priest's robing room. It was too low to make out any words but he heard enough to recognise Crach's unmistakeable gruff tones.

The boys sang two hymns, Friar Brown expressed his gratitude to the priest who in turn congratulated the choir on its performance. Hova and Teg rose to their feet. Crach had reappeared without Hova noticing and was sitting on the step below them. Friar Brown marshalled the boys, shook hands with the priest and led the way out of the church.

The only signs of life in the town were the stray dogs, cats, rats - and the king's soldiers. The guards patrolled the streets and stood in pairs on every corner, tall armed and intimidating. Aside from those, the town was unnaturally quiet considering it wanted a quarter of an hour to curfew, normally a busy time because people used it to run last minute errands.

Hova fought the impulse to shout a protest. Llewelyn ap Gruffydd Fychan was an important man in Llandovery. His family had owned substantial holdings in the town for centuries. Yet his father was imprisoned in the castle, sentenced to be hung drawn and quartered on the morrow and there wasn't a single supporter of the Fychan family to be seen. Not one of the numerous men his father had helped at one time or another and not a single woman prepared to shed a tear over his fate.

CHAPTER TWENTY FOUR

Hospice Llandovery October 8th 1401
Hova waylaid Crach when they returned to the hospice.

'I heard you speak to someone in the church.'

Crach led Hova into the deserted kitchen. The room was large, furnished with wooden benches and tables - and empty. He closed the door behind them.

'Your father is being held in the east tower of the gatehouse. Twenty men, handpicked by Bolingbroke have been detailed to guard him.'

'Then we have no chance of rescuing him.'

'I warned you that we didn't.'

Hova took a deep breath and clenched his fists.

'If it should prove possible for you to see your father for a few minutes would you want to say goodbye to him?'

Hova answered without hesitation. 'Yes.' His voice shook as he added. 'Would I be able to give him something.'

'Like a flask of poppy juice?' When Hova didn't answer, Crach said, 'There are people ahead of you in that thinking, boy.'

'You asked us if we had ever seen a hanging, drawing and quartering. None of us had. Have you?'

'Yes.' Crach jumped down from a bench and opened a low cupboard. He lifted out two wooden cups and filled them from his gwisgi flask before handing one to Hova. 'I was visiting the Hanmers in London in March 1388 when the Lollard Thomas Usk was hung drawn and quartered at Tyburn. Neither the prince - Lord Glyndŵr as he was then - or I had seen such butchery. Not even on a Scottish battlefield. And Highlanders are savages when they set about slaughtering their enemies.'

'Thomas Usk was executed on the orders of King Richard, wasn't he?'

'Yes. Richard accused Usk of misleading him. Usk had fallen foul of a dispute between Gloucester and Northampton. He confessed to being a Lollard, he could hardly deny it given the number of witnesses, but he recanted in prison and received absolution and re-admittance to the one true faith. However his change of heart wasn't enough to spare him the scaffold.'

'Will my father be executed in the morning, or evening?'

Crach sensed Hova wasn't asking for a timetable but hoping he'd prepare him for what was to come.

'The king ordered a sled be attached to a horse at daybreak and taken to the gatehouse. He asked that . . . ' Crach hesitated and decided to refer to Llewelyn as, 'the prisoner,' in an attempt to make it less personal, 'be removed from his cell and tied to the sled mid-morning when the market is at its busiest.'

'The gallows will be erected in market square as usual?' Hova's voice trembled with emotion.

Crach nodded. 'In front of the Town Hall. When the sled with the prisoner reaches the dais the prisoner will be cut free, taken up the steps to the gallows and hung.'

'Will he be cut down while alive?' Hova had heard several reports about hanging, drawing and quartering, although none that he could recall from anyone with first-hand knowledge. Most spoke of it as though it were an entertainment like a mummers' play. But then, he'd never thought it would affect him, or anyone he knew, let alone his beloved father.

Crach spoke slowly, distinctly and unemotionally not wanting to dwell on or repeat anything he'd said. 'The prisoner will be alive and conscious but after being drawn to the place of execution on a sled and hung, his arms and legs may be dislocated. The executioner will strip the prisoner of his clothes, with the help of guards, should it be necessary. He will castrate and emasculate the prisoner by cutting off his genitals. When he has consigned those parts to the brazier for burning, he will open the prisoner's body from breast bone to lower abdomen with a knife. This can be done while the prisoner is still hanging from the scaffold, or after he has been taken down and laid on a table.

'Using the same knife, the executioner will disembowel the prisoner, burning every part as it is removed from the prisoner's body. The organs that remain within the body will be cauterised by hot irons, which delay bleeding and death, and cause physical pain beside any anguish the prisoner might feel at seeing his parts burned while he still lives. The last organ to be removed from the body will be the prisoner's heart. After death the head will be severed and the body quartered. All parts of the corpse will be dipped in pitch and cumin to discourage vermin from picking at it. The head will be sent to London bridge, the quarters to four quarters of the kingdom.'

'The moment of death?' Hova demanded.

'I have heard it said that some prisoners appear to survive briefly after the heart has been removed, but if that is true it could only be for a moment. But I have told you the facts. No words can prepare you for the sight, sound, smell and atmosphere of torture that will pollute market square on the morrow. Once the scent of blood is breathed in - men - women - and children - revert to barbarism. Of all the beasts God created, man has proved the most brutish. As I told you, I have only seen one hanging drawing and quartering. It tainted my life and darkened my days. I prayed to God I would never see another. I didn't envisage your father succumbing to such a foul fate. Unlike many men, Llewelyn ap Gruffydd Fychan has never been anything but kind and considerate in his dealings with me. I respect and love him as I would a brother.'

'And yet he must suffer.' Hova's voice was hoarse with mixed emotion.

'If my contact's plan succeeds, a man will arrive in the stable here in the small hours. He will be dressed in the livery of a senior officer of the king's guard. If it's possible for you to see your father, he will take you to him, but you will not be able to see your father alone. Nor will you be able to intimate by word or deed that you know him, nor will you be able to give him anything. And should you recognise your guide, or recall if you've seen him before, forget his face and never speak of him again. And above all, should you see him again do not betray by word or gesture that you ever met him. 'Here.' Crach handed Hova a parcel.

'What is this?'

'A friar's robe and a crude wooden cross for you to wear around your neck. A priest taking final confession from a prisoner may be given permission to donate it to the condemned as a gift. If so, it might enable you to touch your father's hand one last time.'

'Thank you.' Hova clutched the parcel tight.

'The man who will guide you, hopes to persuade the king to allow your father the comfort of a priest. As your father is condemned for treason it will be the king's prerogative to give his permission, but even if the king should agree, your father will only be given the comfort of a low ranking priest. As you know, there is none lower or humbler than a friar.'

Llandovery early hours of October 9th 1401
Hova did not recognise the young man who entered the stables as the town bell struck twice. Tall, richly dressed, fair of skin, hair and face he pulled the hood of Hova's friar's robe lower over his face before signalling to him to follow.

The sentries standing guard in the street snapped to attention when they passed, as did the guards who unbolted the narrow metal side door set in the portcullis that barred the drawbridge.

Hova's guide led the way into the east gatehouse. Two men were on duty outside the door, four inside. They unbolted an inner door and Hova and the officer climbed up two more floors. All the doors were guarded by four men, two inside, two outside except the last door to the cell that imprisoned Llewelyn. Four men stood outside, broadswords drawn at the ready to beat off an attack. They opened the door at Hova's escort's command to reveal Llewelyn sitting at a table. A book lay open in front of him and Hova recognised the psalter his father took with him whenever he travelled.

He didn't see the sergeant and the guard stationed either side of the door behind him until he stepped into the room and stood between them.

'The king . . . '

Hova's guide interrupted the sergeant. 'Has given permission for the prisoner to receive spiritual comfort in the hope that he will make peace with his maker before he meets him on the feast of St Denis tomorrow.'

'We have received our orders, my lord . . . '

'To guard the prisoner and keep him imprisoned here. Not to eavesdrop on his final confession.'

'My lord . . . '

'You have your duty, which I respect. There is also common decency, sergeant.'

'The length of four Hail Mary's. Not one word more,' the sergeant said.

Hova kept his head bowed until he heard the door clang shut behind his guide and the guards. Only then did he lift his head and look at his father. He held out the cross. His father kneeled before it, took it into his hand and whispered in Welsh.

'Tell your mother I'm sorry for inflicting the sorrow of my end on her. Tell her I love her and God gave me a choice, death or treachery, and despite the sentence Bolingbroke has passed on me I am no traitor.'

'She knows you would never betray our prince,' Hova murmured.

They heard one of the guards snap, 'speak English damn you,' outside the door.

335

They also heard the lord who'd escorted Hova into the tower rebuke him for objecting to a man speaking his native tongue.

'I, and I alone am responsible for my fate,' Llewelyn continued in Welsh, 'care for your mother, tell your sister and brothers I die loving them, and grateful for the love they showed me. Now, go with God, but go. Tomorrow will be hard but it will be impossible for me to bear if you are there to witness my end.'

As his father released his hold on the cross Hova lifted it. Emotion erased all memory of Lowri's suggestion they name their son, Tudor after her father.

'You have a grandson, Llewelyn ap Hova Fychan,' he spoke in Latin, copying a priest's intonation. 'Llewelyn ap Hova ap Llewelyn Gruffydd Fychan.'

'Thanks be to God. You and all my children are a blessing to me.' Llewelyn grasped his son's hand for the last time.

The door opened, Hova removed the cross from around his neck, hung it around his father's and dropped his hooded cowl to conceal his face.

The sergeant and the guard entered the cell with the guide.

Hova made the sign of the cross above his father's head and spoke in Latin. 'May God's goodness and mercy be with you tomorrow, Llewelyn ap Gruffydd Fychan, and always.'

'Thank you, friar, and remember,' Llewelyn switched back to Welsh. 'You have a wife and son. My time is done, my grandson's is just beginning and he needs his father. Trust in God, and I pray that He rains the blessing of dutiful sons and a loving family on you as he has done on me.'

Hova stretched out his hand to help Llewelyn up from his knees. The sergeant hit it aside and ripped off the cross Hova had hung round his father's neck.

Hova took a last look at his father before following his guide back down the circular stone staircase and out of the gatehouse.

East Gatehouse Llandovery Castle Dawn October 9th 1401

Edmund Mortimer walked past the duty guards outside the cell that housed the prisoner. He knocked on the door. A sergeant opened a grill set at eye level and peered out at him.

'My lord, I didn't expect to see you again after last night.'

'I have come to bid farewell to the prisoner.'

'No one has said anything to me about a final farewell, my lord. I have my orders . . . '

'I'm standing next to four stalwart members of the king's guard,' Mortimer said impatiently. 'What do you think that I - one unarmed man can do against four soldiers? Wield a magical invisible sword and fight the half a dozen soldiers stationed on every floor?'

'You have someone with you?' The sergeant looked past Edmund Mortimer and saw a young page holding a tray of food standing behind him.

'The page is not with me. But judging by his load, it looks as though he's brought the prisoner's breakfast.'

The sergeant opened the door and beckoned the page forward. Mortimer followed the boy into the cell.

'Please don't trouble yourself to rise, Llewelyn.' Mortimer set his hand on Llewelyn's shoulder and addressed the sergeant. 'I spoke to the king last night. He is aware I know this man and has graciously given his consent to this visit. The cooks have baked fresh bread and there are cheeses, apples and pottage in the kitchen. If you eat now, you will have finished the same time we will.'

The page set his tray on the table.

'If there's fresh food I and my men will eat it here at our stations. Go, fetch enough victuals for me and my men, and tell the cook not to skimp on our rations,' the sergeant ordered the page.

'Yes, sir.' The boy scurried off.

The sergeant unsheathed his sword. 'You can stay, my lord, for as long as it takes the prisoner to eat but I will not put away my blade or leave this cell or the prisoner alone with you.'

'I understand duty, sergeant. You are to be commended on your adherence to duty.'

The sergeant lifted his sword and chopped the bread cheese and apples on the tray into small pieces. He spooned the pottage out of the bowl on to the tray beside them and examined it thoroughly before returning it to the bowl. He sniffed the jug of ale, and drank directly from it.

'Concerned that the kitchens sent up inferior food, sergeant?' Mortimer asked.

'Concerned that someone might have been tempted to conceal a weapon the prisoner could use to attack us.'

'Or injure himself?'

'It would not do to rob the king of his pleasure,' the sergeant answered.

Mortimer waited for the sergeant to finish examining the food before pulling a stool out from under the small table and sitting opposite Llewelyn.

'Will you take some bread, Lord Gruffydd Fychan?' He handed him the basket of crumbs.

Llewelyn helped himself to a handful, while Mortimer separated two wooden cups stacked on the tray. He filled them both with ale and handed the bottom one to Llewelyn who caught a glimpse of liquid in his cup before Mortimer begun to pour from the jug.

Llewelyn lifted the cup to Mortimer. 'Your very good health, my lord.' He drained it in one swallow.

Friar's Hospice Llandovery Dawn October 9th 1401
Crach sat curled on the sill of the kitchen window of the hospice, his arms wrapped around his legs, his chin resting on his knees. At first glance he gave the impression that he

was staring into the kitchen yard watching the streams of people that flowed past the entrance to the lane that opened in Market Square. But a closer look, revealed his eyes were glazed with a faraway expression that suggested his mind was divorced from his body.

Hova, still dressed in friar's robes joined him and studied the women bound for the traders' stalls. They walked purposefully carrying baskets on their arms. The men who weren't pushing handcarts or driving livestock were dawdling, gossiping, obviously killing time until the execution.

'The market will soon be crowded.'

'It will,' Crach agreed.

The thuds of hammering echoed above the shouts of commerce, exchange of greetings and noise of conversation. Crach closed his eyes and an image of the king's guard erecting the scaffold, a sight he'd seen many times, filled his mind. He frowned.

Could he have done anything more to save Llewelyn? A man he admired, respected and loved almost as much as did Glyndŵr.

'Friar Brown is going to the market to look around before he escorts the boys to the service,' Hova said. 'I thought I'd go with him.'

'As long as he - and you - don't expect the crowd to follow you in some ill-conceived last minute rescue.' Crach beckoned to Friar Brown who was spooning oatmeal pottage into his mouth as if it was the last food he'd ever see.

'I've accepted that rescue is impossible.' Hova's voice trembled.

'You'll keep your friar's hood pulled low.'

'Of course.'

'Both of you?'

'Yes, my lord,' Friar Brown abandoned his empty bowl to join them.

'I would go with you if there weren't so many people who'd recognise me. Both of you, promise you won't do anything foolish?''

'As my father said, I have a wife and son to consider,' Hova answered,

'And I the safety of every man in my order,' the friar added.

'If you should see anyone . . . '

'Like who?' Hova asked Crach.

'Messengers weren't only sent to the abbeys.'

'You think the prince . . . ' Friar Brown fell silent when Crach looked at him.

'I think nothing, because the last I heard, the prince was miles from here. But as we all know he has many followers.'

Llandovery Market Square October 9th 1401

Hova and Friar Brown had to push and shove people aside to make headway through the rows of market stalls set up in the shadow of the scaffold. The Friar made a beeline for "Bakers' Row". When he reached there, he purchased the two largest apple pies on offer and handed one to Hova.

'If you see anyone watching you, push it into your mouth far enough to conceal most of your face. That way you'll be taken for a real friar, not an imposter.'

Hova lifted it to his face but made no attempt to eat. The soldiers had lifted an iron brazier on to the raised dais of the scaffold. They'd stacked it with logs, and packed the space around them with brushwood and lumps of charcoal. After ladling a liberal helping of goose fat over the whole, one soldier struck a tinder and set fire to the kindling, while another nurtured the flames with a bellows.

While they worked on the brazier, two of their comrades tossed a rope over the crossbeam on the gallows and tested it with their weight.

Men and boys shouted ribald jests at the soldiers and one another. Two women wheeled a cart loaded with jugs, cups and flasks close to the dais. After considerable argument which was only settled when the women handed out "free tasters" to the soldiers, they were allowed to set up their beer shop.

'Not hungry friar?' A soldier snatched Hova's pie and bit into it.

Hova turned aside lest the man see his face. Head down he retched, feigning vomiting.

'If he has plague . . . ' The soldier tossed the pie to the ground. A pack of dogs swarmed in on it.

'Too much ale last night,' Friar Brown stepped in between Hova and the soldier. 'I thought the fresh air would cure him. It didn't.' The friar dug a purse from the recesses of his robe removed a groat and flung it at one of the women manning the beer shop. 'A drink so the soldier to wash down the pie while I return my companion to his bed.' He apologised to the soldier before wrapping his arm around Hova and leading him back through the maze of stalls and carts towards Broad Street. He only doubled back to the hospice when he was certain no one was watching them.

Crach was still sitting on the kitchen windowsill but he was wearing his clerical robe on top of his tunic and hose.

'You're going to the church with the choir?' Friar Brown asked.

'I don't want to see what's about to happen but I feel duty bound to witness it, if only to remind myself just how brutally Henry rules this land.' He jumped down from the sill. 'There's a view of the square from the top of the church tower. I will go up there, out of sight of anyone on the dais, the crowd and those who decide to attend the consecration service in the chapel. Although, given what will be happening in Market Square, I doubt any officials will be attending the service.'

'If I may, I'll join you, Crach,' Hova said.

'You could stay here . . . ' Friar Brown began.

'No.' Hova spoke quietly but there was determination in his voice. 'I'll make sure my father won't see me, but I need to watch him until he no longer draws breath.'

Crach nodded agreement. He reached for two sheathed short swords and handed Hova one. 'Wear it under your robe.'

Llandovery Church Tower October 9th 1401
Crach climbed the last few steps of the circular staircase that led to the top of the tower, pushed open the heavy studded trapdoor and climbed outside. The stone battlement offered little protection against the wind that gusted around the open square of the roof. He hitched his robe above his knees, and crawled to the edge of the rampart that overlooked Market Square. Hova followed suit.

The church tower had been built six or more centuries ago to shield the townsfolk who'd sought shelter and sanctuary from marauding Irish, Saxons and Danes. It had survived the ravages of time well enough, considering the years and seasons it had been exposed to the elements. The ramparts were showing signs of crumbling in one or two places, and the cement that cloaked the battlements had fallen away here and there but what remained appeared solid enough. Neither Crach nor Hova had any reservations about leaning against the wall.

The voices of the young choristers drifted up from the chapel as they began to sing the first hymn they'd practised. The beautiful ancient tune soared high, lingering in the air until the sweet notes were drowned in the harsh thuds of drumsticks that emanated from behind the castle walls.

Hova stared at the drawbridge that remained resolutely closed. Crach saw Hova watching the castle entrance.

'The drummers start marking time when the prisoner is led out of his cell to be walked to his sled three floors down. The drawbridge won't be raised for a good few minutes yet.'

Hova clenched his fists and moved back behind the ramparts.

'Watch the eyes.'

'Whose eyes?' Hova looked at Crach in confusion.

'If you are forced to watch someone you love die, concentrate on their eyes,' Crab explained. 'It is the eyes that reflect thoughts, feelings and mirror the God-given soul that lives behind them.'

'You have watched someone you love executed?'

'I have watched many people I loved and will continue to love, pass from this life into the next.' He abruptly changed the subject. 'The drawbridge is opening.'

Hova rolled on his stomach and peered between two upright blocks on the rampart. A single horse drew a sled fashioned from rough planking over the drawbridge. The planking was thin. It splintered as it was dragged over every bump in the road that led to the scaffold. A hush had fallen over the crowd who'd been cursing only moments before as they'd fought and jostled for the best positions from which to view the gallows.

Every sound was magnified by the silence. Hova could hear coughs, sneezes and the sounds of shuffling feet alongside the scrape of the sled grinding over the ground.

'God's nightgown! No!' he exclaimed.

'Quiet!' Crach ordered him sharply. 'We can't do anything to help them. We'd never reach them in time. Pray God cares for them and allows no one to injure them by word or deed.' Crach dropped his voice to a whisper as they watched Ifor part the crowd so Sioned and Lowri could make their way to the front of scaffold. Sioned supported Lowri as she held up her baby so Llewelyn could see him.

'I forgot to look for Huw. I haven't seen him since last night. Have you?'

Hova shook his head.

Sioned and Lowri shouldn't be here,' Crach murmured.

'Look at my mother's face, nothing on God's earth could have prevented them from being here. Father always says if she has set her mind to do something, it will be done.'

Crach's voice echoed in Hova's head as he watched the proceedings unfold.

"The prisoner is removed from his cell and tied to the sled. When the sled reaches the dais the prisoner will be cut free, taken up the steps to the gallows and hung."

Two soldiers dragged Llewelyn from the sled and handed him over to the executioner. From the way they were dragging Llewelyn he appeared to be half asleep. Hova recalled Crach telling him that he couldn't give his father anything, but he also recalled him saying. 'There are people ahead of you in that thinking, boy,' when he mentioned a flask of poppy juice.

"After having been drawn on a sled and hung, the prisoner's arms and legs may well be dislocated. With the help of guards, should it prove necessary, the executioner will strip the prisoner of his clothes."

Hova averted his eyes as the executioner cut the clothes from his father's body and did as Crach had suggested, stared at his father's eyes. His expression seemed oddly calm, as though his father was at peace with himself and the world.

"He will then castrate and emasculate the prisoner by cutting off his genitals. When he has consigned those parts to the brazier for burning, he will open the prisoner's body from breast bone to lower abdomen with a knife. This can be done while the prisoner is still hanging from the scaffold, or after he has been cut down and laid on a table."

Hova didn't know whether to be glad or sorry that the executioner had tied his father securely to the scaffold after hanging him by the neck for a few minutes. He watched his father slowly close his eyes and had the oddest feeling that his father was withdrawing into himself away from the mutilation of the most private parts of his body, just as he was withdrawing from the people around him.

"Using the same knife, the executioner will disembowel the prisoner, burning every part as it is removed from the

prisoner's body. The organs that remain within the body will be cauterised by hot irons, which delay bleeding and death, and cause physical pain beside any anguish the prisoner might feel at seeing his parts burned while he still lives."

Hova didn't know if he could really smell his father's body burning below him and hear the hiss of his organs as they were tossed on the brazier, or if the odour and sounds had been conjured by his imagination.

"The last organ to be removed from the body will be the prisoner's heart."

Sioned cried out when the executioner laid it on top of the other organs in the brazier. She fell to her knees and the silent crowd parted around her to give her space.

'After death the head will be severed and the body quartered. All parts of the corpse will be dipped in pitch and cumin to discourage vermin from picking at it.'

The ominous sound of disapproval rose like a wave, culminating in a crescendo that shattered the silence at the precise moment the executioner tossed the last quarter of Llewelyn into the barrel of pitch that stood beside the gallows. A soldier stepped forward and emptied a bag of cumin seeds on top of the mess and stirred it to the accompaniment of shouts, hisses and cries of "Murdering English bastards."

'Your father died as he lived, honourably and bravely,' Crach said as a fight broke out below them between the soldiers and the townsmen. 'Go down, and ask Friar Brown to round up some of the brothers who can help you bring your wife and mother to the hospice.'

CHAPTER TWENTY FIVE

Charcoal Burner's house, woodland outside Llandovery town October 9th 1401

'The landlord of the King's Head told me Llewelyn ap Gruffydd Fychan breathed his last an hour ago.' Konrad dismounted and tethered the reins of his mount beside Xian's. He walked beneath the roof of the open sided lean to at the back of the charcoal burner's cottage where Tudor, Xian and Alun had sheltered from the wind while waiting for his return

'Then we're too late.' Alun tensed his fists.

Tudor looked up at Konrad. 'Did he suffer?'

'All the tortures of hell according to the landlord, but he said Llewelyn bore every indignity and injury inflicted on him without a murmur of protest, or cry for mercy. He said it was almost as though Llewelyn's mind had already distanced itself from his body.'

'Was he drugged?'

'From the landlord's account he might have been.'

'You saw the king's guard in the town?'

'Everywhere. I can believe Bolingbroke has brought over 4000 men into Llandovery. The king's only been in the castle two days and already food is scarce.'

Tudor gripped one of the wooden poles that supported the roof of the lean to, so hard Xian thought he might snap it. 'After our father's death Owain and I sought Llewelyn's advice and valued his opinion above all others. The news that he no longer walks among us is devastating, not least because of the barbarous way he met his end.'

'Even if we'd reached here before his execution, we couldn't have done anything to save him in the face of Bolingbroke's army,' Xian reminded.

'We couldn't,' Tudor concurred. 'But he has left a widow and children, including my daughter who bears his name and his own daughter who is now a Glyndŵr. We can't abandon them to Bolingbroke's tender mercies. Neither will I allow Bolingbroke to display Llew's head and naked limbs in England for "his pleasure".' He turned to Konrad. 'Did you see anyone you knew in the town?'

'Friar Brown.'

'Did you talk to him?'

'No, you asked me not to draw attention to myself and I didn't think it wise to announce my presence to anyone.'

'Where was the friar?'

'He was with a party of friars who were escorting Lady Sioned, Lady Lowri and Lord Llewelyn's steward, Ifor, into the friary hospice.'

'The one at the back of market square?' Tudor asked.

'That's the one.'

Tudor eyed the charcoal burner's cart. It was piled high with bulging sacks. 'Time to deliver a load of charcoal to the hospice.'

'Do they use it?' Konrad asked.

'If they didn't, they do now,' Tudor said.

Road into Llandovery October 1401

Friendless, solitary by employment, charcoal burners led an isolated existence. Even gongfermours lived and worked in groups. The charcoal burner, ostracised for plying a filthy trade, usually set up home and business in a single hovel in the midst of the woodland that supplied the raw materials he needed. If he chose a spot in proximity to others, his neighbours inevitably moved out of range of the black dust and smoke that contaminated his environs.

If he dreamed of family life, he soon discovered even the poorest, most reviled and destitute of women baulked at becoming wife to a charcoal burner.

His living quarters and workshop were blanketed by a dense layer of black dust that crusted his clothes, his bed and his food. He breathed it, slept in it and ate it. The cart he used to deliver his goods was covered in it, and the original colour of the coat of the nag he harnessed to draw it, lost beneath it.

Crouched on the driver's bench of the cart he'd hired from the charcoal burner, hunched beneath the filthy tarpaulin he'd borrowed to do duty as cloak, and cowl, Tudor rubbed black dust into his cheeks and forehead and flicked the reins in a futile attempt to encourage the horse to quicken its pace.

Xian sat beside him. The white "leper bandage" he carried with him everywhere and wore whenever he wanted people to keep their distance, was besmirched by charcoal and the rags that covered his hands were filthy from his efforts to brush the dust over the rest of his clothes.

Given the horse's inclination to dawdle, Tudor had no choice but to approach the north gate slowly. He scanned the crowd around the gate from beneath his cowl. The sun was concealed behind ominously dark clouds and the wind blasted wintry mountain air down from the north.

The guards on gate duty shivered as they checked the barrows and carts of the queue waiting to enter the town. It was less than a quarter of the length of the snaking horde of traders who'd packed up their market stalls and were heading out for their homes outside the town walls.

'Name?' The guard demanded as Tudor drew his cart close to the gate.

'Cledwyn the charcoal.'

'I know the charcoal burner. You're not him.'

'My brother Carwyn is sick and this load of charcoal has to be delivered to the friars' hospice today.'

'Didn't know Carwyn had a brother or gave house room to a leper.'

'It's called Christian charity,' Tudor mumbled.

'I don't need lessons in Christian charity from a filthy beggar like you. Off with you before you stink out the gatehouse.' The guard slapped the rump of the nag. Tudor flicked the reins and moved off.

'Charming countrymen you have there,' Xian observed in Latin.

'They're English mercenaries, not my countrymen.'
Tudor headed down Broad Street and into Market Square. Soldiers were dismantling the gallows. The boards that floored the dais were saturated with blood and gore.

Tudor turned his back on the square, jumped down from the cart and taking the horse by its harness led it to the gates of the hospice and knocked.

Friar's Hospice Llandovery October 9th 1401
Leaving his borrowed horse and cart with a young friar, Tudor washed the worst of the dust from his hands and face before entering the hospice. Unsure who, or what they'd find in there, Xian didn't unwind his leper bandages. Crach, Friar Brown, Hova, Teg and Ifor were in the kitchen. They were unusually silent, each lost in their own grief as they sat at a table nursing pots of small ale.

They looked up when Tudor and Xian entered.

'My father . . . ' Hova began.

Tudor sat beside his son-in-law and gripped his shoulder. 'No one should suffer the pain and indignity that was inflicted on Llewelyn. He was a man of integrity and stature like no other. I was proud to call him relation and friend.'

'I watched him die, yet I cannot believe he has gone.'

'He will be sorely missed by many, Hova. We set out as soon we received word of Bolingbroke's intentions. I'm sorry we arrived too late to help Llewelyn - or you,- but we're here now and I promise you that your father will be avenged. '

'How can he be now that he is dead?' Hova pleaded. 'What they did to him . . . '

'I have witnessed the ultimate punishment. I know what they did to your father.' Tudor closed his eyes against the pain of remembrance. 'I was told that Sioned and Lowri witnessed his death.'

'How . . . '

'Xian's squire came into the town after the curfew was lifted this morning. He returned to tell us the town was swarming with the king's guards and any rescue attempt would have proved hopeless. Are my daughter and Sioned still here?' Tudor moved to make room for Xian who had filled two cups with small beer and was carrying them to the table.

'They came as soon as they heard Bolingbroke was preparing to execute Llewelyn without trial. I was already here. I didn't know they'd followed me until I saw them in Market Square. They, and my son are resting in one of the upstairs chambers.'

'A son?'

Hova gave Tudor a small smile. 'Born yesterday but it didn't stop Lowri from travelling here today. She wanted to name him Tudor . . . '

'I hope you will name him for his other grandfather,' Tudor broke in.

'I told my father we would.'

'You saw him?' Tudor was amazed.

'A friend arranged a last visit.' Hova didn't elaborate and Tudor didn't ask him to. 'It seemed the right thing to do when I saw him,' Hova continued, 'fortunately Lowri agreed with me when I told her what I'd said to my father. We've decided to name our next son for you.'

'Lowri has agreed to give you another son just after presenting you with this one?' Tudor smiled.

'She's your daughter, my lord.'

'She has more of her mother in her than me.' Tudor looked up as the door opened. A boy walked into the room wearing a clerical robe. He folded back the cowl and Tudor recognised Crach.

'I didn't know you were here, but I'm glad to see your ugly face, old man.' Tudor reached out and grasped Crach's fist as Crach tried to mock punch him.

'Still terrified of my superior strength, I see,' Crach joked. He squinted at Xian. 'That is you masquerading as a leper again, Xian?'

'It is,' Xian answered.

'You've been out making mischief in the town?' Tudor suggested.

'That and looking for Huw.'

'Llewelyn's squire?' Tudor asked.

'He disappeared sometime last night.'

'He must be somewhere.'

'If I knew where, I wouldn't be looking for him.'

'You think he's in trouble?'

'He could be.' Crach looked at an empty spot on the bench beside Tudor and opted to sit opposite him.

'You won't sit next to me now,' Tudor chided.

'I've been told that God appreciates cleanliness and as I owe him a confession or two I need to persuade him to look kindly on me. You're covered in filth.'

'Clean charcoal dust.' Tudor stared intently at Crach.

'What?' Crach asked.

'I sense plots bubbling in your mind like fermenting beer.'

Crach frowned. 'I have a lady friend ... '

'Last time I looked, you had several,' Tudor interrupted.

'This one sits in the back room of the castle tavern when she's not entertaining gentlemen with full purses in her chamber. She was called away from the tavern to amuse one of particular interest to us.'

'If he has information you need and proves reluctant to share it I saw a brazier and pair of pincers going begging on the scaffold when I drove in.' Tudor said grimly.

'The property of the very man in question.'

'She's entertaining the executioner?' Tudor surmised.

'I was sharing a jug of ale with her when he sent for her. I gave her a message to pass on to him ... '

'How tall is the executioner?' Tudor interrupted.

'Six and half feet.'

'Build?'

'Similar to yours.'

'And your friend is delivering a message to him?'

'She is.'

'The message?'

'That he should visit the stables here one hour after curfew to discuss an advantageous assignment.'

'Do you know the whereabouts of Llewelyn's body?' As he asked, Tudor envisioned its present condition and grimaced.

'In a barrel of pitch on the back of a king's guards' cart in the inner courtyard of the castle. It will be sent out to Bolingbroke's designated four quarters of the kingdom tomorrow morning.'

'I see it didn't take you long to martial your spies,' Tudor complimented Crach.

'No spies. Friar Brown took the choristers to the castle gates and primed them to ask where they're taking the remains of the executed man.' Crach answered. 'Soldiers enjoy talking to young boys, because they like to impress them with tales of their strength and prowess. The guards have been charged to deliver the head to London after they've hung the quarters. It appears Bolingbroke has settled for teaching Wales and the marches a lesson. The quarters are destined for St David's, Carmarthen, Shrewsbury and Chester.'

Tudor tapped a drumbeat with his forefinger on the table. 'Your plan?' he asked Crach.

'We have two of the king's guards locked up here in a storeroom.'

'So, we have two king's guards uniforms?' Tudor checked.

'With helmets that cover most of the face. I was thinking Ifor and Huw, when we can find him - but as you're here perhaps Hova and Teg ... '

'I agree. And the executioner?'

'I was about to say you'd fit better size wise than Hova.'

'So, we're waiting on the executioner to show up here?'

'And when he does?' Hova was bemused by the peculiar expressions on Crach and his uncle's face.

'You and Teg change into our captives' clothes and helmets and play at being kings' guards.'

'I don't understand.'

'You will,' Tudor pulled a full purse from his pocket and pushed it across the table to Hova. 'In the meantime go to the castle tavern and ask the landlord to sell you four barrels of his best gwisgi. We'll take them to Glyndyfrdwy to ward off the cold this winter. Ask him to sell you a small cask as well of the same quality and a full sized empty barrel. Never let it be said that Glyndŵr's men diddle a Welshman, so offer him coin for it, as well as the ones full of gwisgi,' Tudor added.

Stable at Friar's Hospice, Llandovery post curfew October 9th 1401

Rain began to fall even before curfew and it escalated to a torrent at twilight. Tudor made a dash from the kitchen door of the hospice into the barn as the town bell sounded the first chime of the hour after curfew.

He dropped the heavy leather bag he was carrying and carried his lamp to the back of the barn. A torch of brushwood spattered with mutton fat hung from a metal bracket on the back wall. He lit it, blew out his lamp, thrust the bolt across the stable door that led to the outside yard and closed the gate that connected the stalls to the barn. He spread the tarpaulin he'd "borrowed" from the charcoal burner on the dirt floor and weighed it down with horseshoes before layering straw over it.

He opened his bag and set out its contents on a stone slab. An axe, two meat cleavers, one small, one large, a bone saw, and four wickedly sharp, pointed knives of various sizes.

He lifted the lid on the empty barrel Hova had bought. It was half full of pitch. Two buckets stood alongside it, both containing the same glutinous liquid as the barrel. The preparations had been made, the planning was complete, all he needed was the subject.

He leaned against the door jam and stared out at the rivulets of rain as they ran from the thatched roof of the hospice, and streaked down over the shutters that covered the kitchen window. The lamp that had been lit to welcome wayfarers, burned weakly beneath the metal grid that failed to keep out the elements, but here and there a crack in the wood gleamed gold from the candles burning inside.

Ten minutes later, he heard the sound he'd been waiting for. Boots splashed towards him through the puddles that had formed between the cracked and broken cobblestones in the lane.

He continued to stand stock still, knowing his figure would be lost in the shadows to anyone approaching from the main thoroughfare. The executioner stepped inside the barn, and as Tudor hoped, headed for the torch on the back wall. He shouted out.

'Is anyone here?'

'I am.' Tudor stepped out behind him.

'You have a job for me?'

'A more merciful one than you gave Llewelyn ap Gruffydd Fychan today.'

Tudor gave the executioner time to draw his sword. He would have considered it cowardly not to.

He killed him with his first quick clean thrust.

***

'God's toes, but this is worse than slaughtering pigs in autumn,' Crache complained as Tudor twined his gloved fingers into the executioner's hair prior to picking up and dropping his head into the barrel of pitch.

'Which is why I spread straw on the tarpaulin to soak up the blood.' Tudor kneeled beside the corpse and set about quartering it. He picked up the largest meat cleaver and brought it down sharply in the centre of the ribcage, splicing it in two.

'What do you intend to do with the straw and tarpaulin when you've finished?' Crach asked. 'You can't leave it here. If the soldiers should find it . . . '

'They won't. I'll pack it.'

'Into what?' Hova, who'd volunteered to help Crab and Tudor with the unpleasant task, asked. The executioner's head bobbed to the top of the barrel and he poked it back down into the pitch with a stick.

Tudor brushed his hair back from his forehead with his wrist. 'The false bottom of the Tudor cart the choir travelled in.'

'And the charcoal burner's cart?'

'Get the choristers to clean it before Friar Brown drives them and you out of town in it in the morning.'

'They'll be pleased. Why can't the friar drive them back in the Tudor cart?' Crach questioned.

'Because I'm commandeering it. Owain named the cart for me because it's not as simple as it seems. Better Xian and I cart Llewelyn's body and,' Tudor indicated the bloodstained straw, 'this mess than Friar Brown, you, and the choristers risk being stopped by curious guards.'

'And if the guards stop and search you at the gate?' Crach asked.

'We have Xian's box of tricks to create a diversion.'

'If that's all you're relying on I pray God looks kindly on you.'

'My knees are sore from my asking him to do just that, Crach.'

'Diversion or not, if the guards find the bloodstained straw and body, you and Xian will be killed. If you're fortunate, quicker than Llewelyn.'

'Better us than a cartload of young boys, you and Friar Brown. And we still have to work out how to spirit, Lady Sioned, Lowri, you Hova, and Huw and Teg out of town.'

'The king wouldn't dare arrest any of us after what he did to father ... '

'I wouldn't have thought Bolingbroke would dare murder your father, Hova,' Tudor interrupted. 'But he did.'

Tudor severed the corpse into two halves at the waist, before chopping down hard on the ribcage with the largest meat cleaver. He severed the quarter of the executioner's body that held the right arm scooped the lung from the ribs, tossed it on to the tarpaulin, and handed it by the forearm to Hova who lowered it carefully into the barrel of pitch.

After Hova poked it down into the pitch he took the left arm and ribs Tudor handed him.

'Don't forget to emasculate and castrate the bastard,' Crach reminded.

'That I wasn't looking forward to.' Tudor picked out a sharp, short bladed dagger. Seconds later he tossed the executioner's penis, testicles and intestines on to the straw. Finally he chopped through the pelvic girdle with an axe.

Hova pushed the last two quarters into the barrel and poured pitch from the buckets on top until the whole was covered and the barrel full to the brim.

'Now what?' Hova asked as he nailed down the top on the barrel.

'I wash, go into the house to congratulate my daughter and see my grandson. Then I return here to dress in the executioner's hood and mask. By which time I trust some kind soul will have dumped this,' he pointed to the tarpaulin, 'into the concealed cavity on the cart and harnessed the horses. After that, Xian, I, and whoever wants to play at being king's guards, will visit the castle with a view to exchanging one barrel for another.'

'I'll go with you,' Hova volunteered.

'I'd rather take Teg.'

'My squire . . . '

'Hasn't the responsibility of a wife and child.'

'I'll tell Lowri you'll be calling on her and Llewelyn bach, we'll argue about this later.' Hova checked the lid of the barrel again before leaving.

Friar's Hospice Llandovery, curfew early hours of October 10th 1401

Tudor washed the executioner's blood from his hands, face and body before scrubbing himself down twice with a coarse bristle brush and lye and wood ash soap. He dressed in his own plain black hose and tunic and left the executioner's mask, hood and leather cotte in the cart for the drive to the castle.

He heard his grandson crying when he went into the kitchen, a soft mewing sound that faded as he climbed the stairs. Hova opened the door at his tap.

'I don't want to disturb you . . . '

'You're not, father.' Lowri was lying in bed, holding the baby in her arms. When Tudor approached she lifted the child.

He took him from her.

'He's a fair size.'

'Half Glyndŵr, half Fychan, he has no choice but to be large.' She smiled as she sat up in the bed. 'Did Hova tell you his name.'

'Llewelyn, yes.'

'Llewelyn Tudor Glyndŵr ap Hova Fychan.'

"Poor child won't thank you for that when the monks teach him to write his name or later in life when he has to sign documents.' Tudor kissed the child's forehead. 'I'm sorry.'

'For what, father?'

'Seeing you there with your son reminded me of your mother. I was there the day you were born.' He took a moment to compose himself. Lowri had only been held by her mother for a few moments before death had taken Elen. 'But I was never there for you when you were growing up.'

'You gave me to Aunt Sioned and Uncle Llewelyn, knowing they'd show me nothing but kindness. And you always visited me whenever you were close to Caeo.'

'In between fighting King Richard's battles, much good it did me - or you.'

Lowri grasped his hand as he sat on the stool beside her. 'I couldn't have wished for a better father.

'You're as kind as your mother ever was.' His voice was hoarse with emotion. 'I'm not much of a one for advice but I'm going to give you two some now.' He looked from Lowri to Hova. 'If the time should come when you're faced with a choice of fighting for what you know to be right or running and hiding with your family. Run! That way you'll live to fight another day.'

'You think my father should have run from Bolingbroke?' Hova asked.

'From what I heard he had no opportunity or choice,' Tudor said. 'Bolingbroke turned up in your home and from that moment set his guards to watch Llewelyn.'

'He did,' Hova agreed.

'All I'm saying to you, boy, is put Lowri's, this boy's and your life first. When you reach my advanced years you will look back and realise there are always rights to be wronged but once people are gone they can never be replaced. Not even by a miracle as wonderful as Llewelyn bach.' Tudor slipped his finger into the baby's tiny hand. 'That's enough philosophy for one night. I'll see you tomorrow.' He kissed first the baby's head then Lowri's.

'I'll come ... '

Stay with your family, Hova. Xian and Teg are already changing into our captives' uniforms.'

CHAPTER TWENTY-SIX

Llandovery Castle night October 10th 1401
The sergeant sat on the only chair in the guard room. His feet were propped on a stool close to the hearth so the warmth of the flames could reach his thighs. A tankard of ale stood on another stool besides his right hand and he was halfway through a steaming beef pie.

Irritated by a knock on the door he shouted, 'What?'

'Executioner, sir.'

'At this hour? Is he looking for spare heads to remove to liven up tomorrow?'

'No, sir . . . '

'Let him in, dolt. It's tiring shouting through a closed door.'

The door opened and the masked executioner bent his head to accommodate the low lintel.

'So it's true?'

'What is?' the executioner asked, confused by the question.

'You don't remove your mask?'

Tudor adopted a fair approximation of the executioner's West country accent. 'A man in my line of work learns to keep his face to himself.'

'Man your size isn't difficult to spot.'

'That depends on the company he keeps. One or two of your fellow officers are of a size with me.'

'True.' The sergeant took another bite out of the pie. 'You're out late,' he mumbled through a full mouth.

'I'm leaving for Bristol as soon as curfew lifts in the morning. I bought a new cart from the friars and I need to pack my tools into it.'

'And your old cart?'

'Is the king's property. His guards need it to deliver the traitor's quarters and head to London.'

The sergeant lowered his feet to the floor. 'Business must be good for you to buy a new cart.'

'The king is generous and I've gone into partnership with my brother. We own a tavern in Bristol. I thought I'd take him a few barrels of Welsh gwisgi. It's not easy to come by over the border. We'll make a tidy profit from what I've packed.'

'I bet you will. And you want me to order my men to pack your cart for you?'

'No thank you, I have all the dogsbodies I need.' Tudor set the small barrel he was holding on the table next to the sergeant's tankard. 'Good Welsh gwisgi. Recompense for the inconvenience. If you have a couple of clean cups we can gauge its quality.'

The sergeant produced the cups. As Tudor filled them he pushed the stone aside on his ring and flicked the contents of the hollow beneath it into the sergeant's cup.

'To the king.' The sergeant touched his cup to Tudor's.'

'And your good health.' Tudor drained his cup.

'You even drink with your mask on?' The sergeant said in surprise.

'Always. Too many relatives bear grudges against me for carrying out the king's wishes. The fewer people who know my face, the safer I remain.' Tudor set his cup on the table. 'And the sooner I pack my cart the sooner I'll stop troubling you.'

'No trouble to me.' The sergeant sat back in his chair. 'Dodric?'

'Yes, sergeant.' A corporal opened the door.

'See the executioner gets what he wants.'

'Yes, sergeant.'

'Thank you and good night, sergeant.' Tudor saluted the man and left.

The corporal closed the door to the guard room and followed Tudor into the courtyard. Dense black clouds blanketed the moon and stars. A high wind had set the flames that burned in metal sconces affixed to the gatehouse walls dancing, projecting weird and wonderful shadows over the courtyard and battlements.

The "executioner's" cart was drawn up on the street side of a small iron door set to the left of the portcullis. Friar Brown, dressed as a labourer with a broad brimmed hat pulled low to cover his tonsure, was standing in front of it holding the horse's head to keep the cart steady.

'If you wheel the king's cart up to the side door that will suffice, corporal. No need to open the portcullis. My men will transfer what I need from one cart to the other through the side door.'

The corporal called out to two soldiers who were shivering in the doorway of the gate house. The three of them wheeled the cart that held Llewelyn's body to the portcullis.

'Thank you, my men will take it from here.' Tudor slipped Doric a small leather flask. 'A taster of what I gave your sergeant. Take ten minutes to share it out of sight with your comrades. We'll watch the gate until you return.'

'I don't know, sir . . . guard duty is guard duty . . . if the captain should come on his rounds . . . ' the corporal watched Teg walk through the side door and jump up on the back of the cart on the courtyard side. He picked up a wooden box and handed it to Tudor who walked through the small doorway and pushed it on to the cart Friar Brown was holding.

'If the captain should come, he'll see us hard at work, and I'll tell him I gave you permission to take a break.'

'Thank you, sir. If you're sure . . . '

'After this day's work, Doric, no captain is likely to be out looking for soldiers to discipline especially at this hour.' Tudor jerked his head sideways. 'Off with you.'

The guard held up the flask, signalled to his fellow soldiers and the three of them disappeared in the direction of the privies.

As soon as they were out of sight, Tudor ran to help Teg and Xian lift the barrel from the executioner's cart and exchange it for the barrel that contained the dead executioner.

While Teg and Xian secured the barrel that held Llewelyn's remains on to the "Tudor cart", Tudor checked around the executioner's cart for Llewelyn's possessions. He retrieved a leather satchel that contained clothes he recalled seeing Llewelyn wear, a psalter and notebooks, quill, and a bottle of gall ink.

A man stepped out of the blackness and confronted Tudor as he reached the small iron door.

Tudor saw the flash of firelight on steel as the man thrust a blade towards him. He sidestepped too late.

Llandovery Castle courtyard the hour before midnight October 10th 1401
Xian jumped off the cart on to the back of Tudor's assailant. He locked his hands around his neck pulled him away from Tudor and pinned him to the ground.

'Careful, a man of his age is delicate.' An odorous silhouette stepped out of the darkness.

'I wondered if you'd be lurking around here, brother.' Tudor ran his fingers over his jaw and grimaced as his fingers slid into a wound and touched raw flesh.

Owain murmured. 'Too late to help Llewelyn.'

'We all were,' Tudor said bitterly.

'You know this man?' Xian rolled over Tudor's attacker.

'Huw's finally turned up. I think he's trying to talk. Hide him between the barrels in the back of the cart. And warn him to keep quiet lest the guards see him and demand I exercise my skills and remove his head.' Tudor followed Owain to the line of carts inside the courtyard. They ducked down between and below them.

'I waylaid Huw earlier today and asked him to help me retrieve Llewelyn's effects,' Owain explained.

'We have them now.'

'I saw. You'll take care of Huw?'

'You don't need to ask. You?'

'I entered the town with the gongfermours. I'd better leave with them in case someone notices the cripple's absence.'

A fox's bark heightened into an eerily human scream.

'Good try but that's no fox,' Tudor declared.

'Let's hope the garrison aren't as bright as you.'

'Brother?'

'Yes,' Owain hesitated.

'Wash before we next meet.'

Owain's smile along with his figure disappeared into the darkness.

Llandovery Castle Wooden Privy over stream flowing beneath South Wall.

Owain opened the wooden door of the privy and stepped back. He'd become accustomed to his own foul stench and that of his fellow gongfermours, but the stinking reek inside the shack closed around him, a cloaking damp miasma of putrefying decay.

The whisper carried, ghostly on the night wind. 'Outside.'

Owain closed the door and trod lightly.

'The air isn't much sweeter here, but it's worse now you're here.'

'Apologies.' Owain crouched down on his heels a yard downwind from Mortimer.

'The gongfermour I spoke to passed on my message?' Mortimer asked.

'I'm here,' Owain murmured.

'Sorry, my brain is fogged from lack of sleep. Your walking woman reached me. She gave me your message but I chose not to pass it on. I know Bolingbroke. He was determined to execute Llewelyn even before he set out to visit Caeo. If you surrendered to him he wouldn't hesitate to slaughter you in the same way. I couldn't stomach watching another friend undergo that butchery.' When Owain didn't answer, he asked, 'Did you discuss your message with Margaret?'

'No.'

'I wondered if you sent it after David's death.'

'I did.'

'You declared war, Owain Glyndŵr. A just war to free your people. They deserve a leader who will fire and guide them to victory, not a sacrificial lamb prepared to take the easy way out.'

'You think Llewelyn's death was easy?'

'Easier than suffering the loss of someone beloved? Yes, I do,' Mortimer replied softly. 'There is no torture worse than knowing a person you love died before their time, especially if you weren't there to comfort them.'

Owain rose to his feet. 'You're thinking of your brother Roger.'

'I miss him.' There was a world of longing and grief in Mortimer's simple declaration.

'If you want me to say I regret sending that message, I admit it. You're right, Mortimer. There is nothing worse than losing someone you love.' Owain hesitated for a moment. 'You did not make a record of what I said?'

'I made a copy so I could understand it. Flur's pronunciation is not always perfect.'

'It isn't. You will destroy it?'

'When I return to Ludlow, yes.'

'Thank you.' Owain began to walk away.

'That's it?'

Owain stopped and turned. 'I'm grateful for what you did for Llewelyn. I watched him die. Some brave soul gave him something to dull the pain.'

'Llewelyn had many friends in Llandovery.'

'So he did.'

'God speed, Glyndŵr.'

'And you, Mortimer. May we never meet on a battlefield.'

'More and more friends seem to be saying that to me these days.'

Owain stopped and turned. 'One last thing. My brother says your fox impression could stand a little work.'

Stables Friar's Hospice lane off Market Square, the small hours of October 11th 1401

'Stop your fussing, Huw. I've had worse bee stings,' Tudor snapped as Llewelyn's squire checked the wine, beeswax and honey poultice he'd used to dress the wound he'd inflicted on Tudor.

'I'm sorry . . . '

'And stop apologising,' Tudor added. 'Just be sure the next time you try to assassinate someone, he isn't already dead.'

'At least you dealt Tudor a good clean cut, Huw,' Xian joked.

'I'm . . . '

'Say you're sorry again, Huw and I'll give you as good as you gave me,' Tudor sniped.

'Here, these are all I could find.' Friar Brown entered the barn with a bundle of rags he handed to Huw.

Xian and Hova had lifted Llewelyn's body parts out of the barrel of pitch, and Hova with Teg and Ifor's assistance was cleaning his father's remains and arranging them on the winding cloth they'd taken from the Friary stores.

'You'll never remove all that pitch,' Tudor warned as he watched Hova attempt to peel off the thick strands that had matted into Llewelyn's hair and beard.

'I know.' Hova sat back on his heels and surveyed his father's remains. 'It's just . . . ' He looked at Tudor. 'I hate the idea of him going into the family tomb like this. He should be laid whole and clean wrapped in fine white linen and laid to rest in a fine carved stone sarcophagus.'

Tudor shook his head and closed his hand over the cut on his jaw when he felt it gape from the movement. 'You do realise you won't be able to lay him to rest with your forefathers in Caeo church. If the king hears as much as a whisper of what we've done, he'll send someone to examine the body parts he commanded scattered in four corners of his kingdom and . . . '

'Arrange to have our body parts hung on various town gates in their place,' Hova suggested.

'I'm sorry, boy,' Tudor sympathised,

'I can't bear the thought of burying father in an unmarked pauper's grave let alone in pieces,' Hova said.

'Let me help,' Friar Brown offered. 'I've laid out so many bodies in winding sheets, I've a fair idea of what goes where.'

'No one who knew your father will allow him to be laid in a pauper's grave, Hova. He was a hero and should rest in peace awaiting eternity among heroes.' Tudor leaned back against a bale of straw. 'But you have to concede it will have to be somewhere secret, off the beaten track, and preferably in ground held sacred by all Welshmen.'

'You're talking about Hyddgen?' Xian murmured.

'For a Seres Chinaman you're astute and more Welsh than the Welsh, Xian. Yes, I'm taking about the heroes' grave we dug at the foot of Hyddgen. But it's for the lady Sioned, you and your brothers and sister to decide, Hova. What do you think?'

Hova swallowed the tide of emotion he felt rising in his throat. 'I think my father would be honoured if he'd known you'd suggest Hyddgen as his final resting place.'

'He'd honour it with his presence.' Tudor rose to his feet. 'But before we can lay him to rest we have to get him there.'

Friar's Hospice lane off Market Square an hour before dawn October 11th 1401

'I'm sorry to disturb you, my lord,' Friar Brown apologised, whispering outside the guest chamber occupied by Lowri, Hova and their baby. 'But there are king's messengers in the kitchen. They say they will not leave until they have spoken with the lady Sioned.'

Hova rubbed the sleep from his eyes, folded back the blanket he'd pulled over himself only an hour earlier and left the chair he'd fallen asleep in. He walked over to the bed and looked down at Lowri and his son tucked up in a shawl beside her. Both were sleeping peacefully.

He opened the door. 'Have you woken the Lady Sioned?' he murmured.

'I didn't need to, my lord, I saw her enter the chapel an hour ago.'

'What time is it?'

'An hour before curfew lifts, my lord.'

Hova went to the bowl on a side table, poured water into it and splashed his hands and face. 'I'll escort Lady Sioned to the kitchen.' He lowered his voice. 'The others?'

'I alerted them, my lord. They're well-hidden and will remain so, but they'll be ready to drive out when the king's messengers have left.'

***

Sioned, hands clasped together, eyes closed, was kneeling before the altar in the chapel. Hova waited patiently at the door for her to finish her prayer. When his mother made the sign of the cross and rose stiffly and awkwardly to her feet, he went to her and offered her his arm. She took it.

'The king . . . '

'Has sent a messenger to speak to me, Hova. I heard the man talking to the Friar in the hall.'

They left the chapel and walked down the passage. Hova ushered his mother into the kitchen. The shutters had been flung wide A tall, fair haired, young man was standing with his back to them in front of the open window. He turned and bowed as they entered.

'My lady, my lord. We have met, Lady Sioned.'

'I recall, Lord Mortimer,' Sioned curtsied.

Mindful of Crach's warnings not to know Mortimer if he should meet him again, Hova bowed. 'We haven't been introduced, my lord. I am Hova ap Llewelyn Gruffydd Fychan.'

Mortimer bowed in return.

Another man was sitting at the table, small, wizened with a pursed disapproving mouth. He did not rise or acknowledge the curtsy Sioned had given him, or Hova's perfunctory bow. Neither did he introduce himself.

'You are Sioned? Wife to the traitor Llewelyn ap Gruffydd Fychan?' he barked.

Hova was about to reply when Sioned exerted pressure on his hand to silence him.

'Llewelyn ap Gruffydd Fychan was my husband, but no traitor, sir.'

'I have been charged to inform you that the estate of Llewelyn ap Gruffydd Fychan, including all money, goods, lands, and buildings owned by him have been sequestered by the king.'

'Our home at Caeo?' Hova stood tall, tight lipped Only a pulse that beat at the side of his temple betrayed his agitation.

'Is now the property of the king. You have until sunset to remove your family clothing and personal effects from the house. No furnishings, jewellery, wine or valuables of any kind of course.'

'Of course,' Sioned echoed bitterly.

'You will not be permitted to take any of Llewelyn ap Gruffydd Fychan's clothes or personal belongings. The king has sent men to make an inventory. They will supervise your visit. These are copies of the king's edicts, made at his expense for you to keep.' He finally rose from the table and handed Sioned a sheaf of papers.

'Mortimer?' the official addressed the young man.

'I will be with you in a moment. Wait for me in the stable.'

'I will wait for you here.' The official picked up his leather satchel, went to the door, opened it and waited.

Mortimer closed the door firmly in the man's face and leaned back against it.'

'My condolences, my lady, my lord.' Mortimer turned to Hova. 'As you said we've never been introduced, Lord Hova, but on the few occasions I met your father he spoke of you with pride. He will be remembered fondly by his many friends.'

'Thank you, for your kindness, Lord Mortimer,' Sioned said softly. The official's harsh unsympathetic treatment had failed to bring the tears to her eyes, that Mortimer's sympathy elicited.

Mortimer bowed again and opened the door. Hova took his mother in his arms as Mortimer's footsteps rang down the passageway.

Stables Friar's Hospice Market Square, dawn October 11th 1401

'We're ready to leave,' Xian called to Tudor who was lying stretched out on bales of hay in the loft.

Tudor stirred himself and crawled to the edge because it was too shallow for him to stand. He locked his right arm around the top of ladder and lowered himself down.

Huw hadn't slept. Instead he'd spent the early hours working on the Tudor cart in an effort to please Tudor as well as assuage his guilt. After polishing the bench seat and wooden bars that secured the barrels roped in the back, he'd cleaned the wheels and finally as day broke, harnessed the horses.

'I could go with you . . . '

'You could, Huw,' Tudor agreed, 'but if the guards decide to take the cart apart and find the Tudor compartment they'll see the body and then they'll have three not two men to hang. As it is, they'll only be able to lay their hands on Xian and me.'

Friar Brown carried a pile of rugs into the stable for the choristers to wrap around themselves against the cold. 'The soldiers finally woke and have left for the castle.'

'Do they realise they slept away an entire day?' Tudor asked.

'I didn't tell them but I dare say their officers in the castle garrison might ask a few questions when they see they're missing some of their armour. As curfew lifted a few minutes ago I think we should leave lest they take it into their heads to return and complain that we drugged them and stole their helmets and breastplates.'

'Is there a queue of people waiting to leave the town?' Tudor asked.

'The usual.' Friar Brown shrugged. 'Half a dozen carts, and two score field workers. I doubt it will take you more than a few minutes to pass through.'

'Unless the guards rip open the fake panel. Let's hope this garb makes them think twice about trying it.' Tudor took the executioner's mask and hood from his pocket and pulled them on before climbing on to the bench seat of the cart. Xian jumped up beside him and covered his head with a soldier's chain mail hood and helmet.

Tudor picked up the reins as Hova walked into the barn.

'I've managed to persuade my mother not to return to Caeo.'

'I know that couldn't have been easy, but I believe you can trust Jonnet to clear your most valued possessions.'

'That's what finally decided mother,' Hova agreed.

'Take the road to Talley Abbey, leave your choristers there then head for to our summer headquarters. We may meet on the road. If not, we'll wait for you there so we can travel together to Hyddgen. If you see us on the road and I'm wearing my executioner garb, give us a wide berth.'

'You don't need to tell me that. Neither my mother nor Lowri will want to go near you looking the way you do,' Hova assured Tudor.

'I'll drive the cart alongside Hova and the ladies' mounts and do what I can to see them safe to your headquarters.'

'Thank you, Friar Brown, and if I were you I'd make sure that Hova, Teg and Huw keep their blades to hand on the journey. Now, if you'll be kind enough to open the barn doors, Huw, we'll be on our way. God Speed to you.'

'And to you my lords.' Hova opened the doors and stepped back as Tudor drove out. He watched Tudor salute a king's guard when they exited the lane into Market Square. He half-expected the man to detain him, but whether the sergeant had passed on the lie about the executioner buying a new cart or not, he simply returned Tudor's salute before turning his back on him.

Gatehouse Llandovery early morning October 11th 1401
'You're up early, sir.' The guard who stopped Tudor's cart looked from the "executioner" to Xian's "guard" and back.

'I've business to attend to in Bristol.'

'Do you mind opening the barrels, sir.'

'You've heard what I'm carrying?'

'The sergeant did mention it, sir,' the guard replied sheepishly.

Tudor thrust his hand inside his cotte and pulled out one of the small leather flasks he'd filled with gwisgi and handed it over.

The guard took it, opened it and sniffed. 'It's good gwisgi, sir.'

'It is.' You're welcome to open the barrels as long as you screw them back tightly.'

'It's not me, sir it's the king . . . '

'Be my guest.' Tudor hauled in the reins, fastened them to the post and waited.

A sharp voice rose above the bubble of voices at the gate. 'Do you think the executioner is trying to smuggle a body out in a barrel? That cart won't be leaving the castle for an hour yet. Let them pass, soldier.'

'Thank you.' Tudor saluted the sergeant, picked up the reins, and cracked the whip alongside the horses.

'Good Journey to Bristol, sir.'

Tudor waved his thanks as drove through the gate.

Road out of Llandovery early morning October 11th 1401
Tudor drove past the queues of carts laden with produce and the Welsh men, women and children who were forced to live outside the town walls but work for their English masters within them.

An hour's journey at a smart trot brought them into the woods that bordered the Caeo estate. Tudor drove off the road and down a path that led to the back of the house.

They smelled the stench of cold fire before they reached Caeo's orchards and kitchen gardens.

Tudor halted the cart under cover of the trees.

'Jonnet and your nephews didn't waste any time. That fire burned out some time ago,' Xian observed as they watched a company of king's guards ride up to the ashes and charred wood that had been Llewelyn's family's home for generations.

Dark eyed, grim faced, Tudor sat back on the bench seat and watched the riders dismount and kick the ashes of the house he'd regarded as his second home and chosen to make his daughter's first, after the death of his wife.

'Caeo was a haven of Welsh hospitality where the welcome was warm and the food and drink the best Wales had to offer. No one, highborn or low was turned back from its doors.'

Tudor emphasis on the word "was" wasn't lost on Xian. 'It can be rebuilt,' he consoled.

'Even if it is, it won't be the same without Llewelyn.'

Realising Tudor was in no mind to be comforted, Xian reached for the bag that held his rags.

When they drove off it was as leper and charcoal burner again, but they'd stowed away their other disguises.

As Tudor observed when he tucked them into a corner of the hidden compartment that housed Llewelyn's shrouded body, 'A man never knows when he might have need of a King's Guard or Executioner.'

CHAPTER TWENTY-SEVEN

Grave at the foot of Hyddgen Mountain October 1401
Owain and Margaret stood behind Llewelyn and Sioned's sons and daughter. They watched Tudor, Maredydd, and Rhys Fierce cut and roll back a length of sod from the mound at the foot of Hyddgen that the local shepherds had already christened "Bryn y Beddau" - Hill of Graves.

Nature had reclaimed the ground in the five short months since they'd battled here. Owain reflected that if he hadn't made note of the landmarks when they'd interred David, he could have passed the spot without giving it a second glance.

Coarse grass, reeds and the occasional clump of heather covered the grave mound, just as it did the neighbouring slopes, concealing all trace of the disturbed soil beneath.

It didn't take Tudor, Xian and Rhys long to dig a bed deep enough to take Llewelyn's body. When they stopped working and stood back at a respectful distance, Hova, his brothers Adam and Morgan and Gruffydd stepped forward.

They picked up the bier Friar Brown had brought from Talley Abbey and carried Llewelyn's remains to his final resting place.

Kites circled overhead, their cries blending with those of grouse, peregrines and snipe. Sheep bleated high on the hills. They were sounds that Owain had associated with his native land for as long as he could remember.

The mood and the moment shattered as the harsh tones of a coarse whisper behind him razored into his thoughts. He recognised Dafydd Gam's whining tone.

'Llew was hung drawn and quartered. That body hasn't been hacked into pieces. It's Glyndŵr trickery. They've replaced Llew's body with another. No doubt someone they've murdered. They won't get away with it . . . '

Tudor glared in Gam's direction and he fell silent.

The king had paid Gam's ransom in a staggeringly short time. As cousin to Llewelyn ap Gruffydd Fychan, Gam had claimed the right of kinship to attend Llewelyn's funeral. Tudor refused to give Gam permission until he watched him sign a solemn declaration, duly and solemnly witnessed by Bishop Trevor, that under threat of excommunication, Gam wouldn't reveal Llewelyn's final resting place to the king, or indeed anyone.

John Trefor, began the funeral service. He spoke and the sky darkened. Dense grey clouds obliterated the sun turning the air grey. The wind whistled as it blasted down from the hill tops. When Trefor uttered the last words of the blessing, Llewelyn's sons and son-in-law lifted Llewelyn from the bier. The novices who'd travelled to Hyddgen from Valle Crucis for the occasion, chanted a prayer as they laid him in his grave.

Jonnet handed her son to Gweni, and wrapped her arm around her mother's waist. Sioned carried a bunch of wild flowers she and Jonnet had gathered on the journey. It was late for blooms but they'd found fern, lady's mantle that still bore gold blossom, and Peppermint and Brome. Sioned dropped the bouquet into the grave and looked down on her husband's remains for the last time.

The baby Gweni had tucked into a shawl she'd wrapped around herself, started grizzling and Jonnet returned to retrieve him. Owain squeezed Margaret's hand, and joined Sioned and Bishop Trefor.

Three white quartz stones marked the perimeter of the area that contained the grave. Owain stepped back alongside one and faced the mourners.

'We stand on Welsh land, watered with the blood of our heroes. None were greater than Llewelyn ap Gruffydd Fychan. He was of my father's generation. A friend to all fortunate to know him. That rarest and most valuable of men. An honest warrior you could trust to watch your back, who could also draw on a lifetime of experience to give you unconditional, impartial advice.

'A man most of you here today knew as a kind and generous host. No one, beggar or lord was sent hungry or cold from his door. A loving husband, father - and the day before he died - grandfather. A man who could have lived a life of ease and plenty in the bosom of his family if he'd taken the gold offered to him in return for betraying me.

'Llewelyn was first and foremost a proud and patriotic Welshman, and it was his love for his country that sentenced him to a brutal and merciless death. A death that has no place in a civilised land.

'Llewelyn ap Gruffydd Fychan's suffering is beyond our comprehension yet he bore it with a courage we can only hope to find when it's time for us to face our end.'

Owain saw tears in the eyes of some of the mourners. 'You may think I am describing a paragon of virtue - a saint, yet as his beloved Sioned and his children knew, he was only too human.

'It wasn't only his wisdom he was willing to share. A somewhat indifferent cook - my apologies Llew - but you were, as anyone who wintered with us last year can attest. He was generous in doling out the questionable fruits of his lack of talent - and quick to admonish anyone courageous enough to leave the tiniest morsel of his cooked gristle on their trencher.'

As Owain had hoped a current of laughter rippled through the crowd. He fell serious when it died down.

'Llewelyn is dead but his soul and ideals live on in his sons, daughter and grandson and in the heart of every Welshman willing to fight for freedom.

'I make this covenant in Llewelyn ap Gruffydd Fychan's, name. I swear to each and every one of you, I will continue this fight for Welsh Independence and I will not cease until the last Englishman leaves this land, or I no longer draw breath. Wales and the Welsh crave and deserve freedom.

'I leave the man I was proud to call friend in this sacred ground with our heroes, and I ride to continue the fight.

'Who is with me?'

***

A defending cheer rent the valley. Dafydd brought Owain his destrier. He mounted and reined in Ariston while he waited for his men to climb on to their horses.

A rider charged up the valley at breakneck speed and headed straight for Owain.

'Someone stick a lighted taper up your mount's ... ' Suddenly conscious of his daughter, Sioned's and Margaret's proximity, Tudor amended what he was about to say, and murmured, 'rear end.'

'Reginald de Grey is five hours ride from our summer quarters with close on a thousand men. He and Henry received word that you were absent from Glyncoch, my prince. They're intent on attack,' Rhys Fierce added superfluously.

'Men at arms to me,' Tudor commanded.

Owain turned to Hova, 'Chose your men, and escort your ladies to Strata Florida and claim sanctuary for them there.'

'I'm going with you, Owain.' Margaret signalled to the boy who was holding her palfrey.

'So am I,' Gweni announced.

'And me,' Jonnet added.

'No time for arguing,' Owain capitulated. 'Tudor go ahead. If de Grey and Bolingbroke know of Glyncoch, the place is no longer any use to us. Fire it.'

'Consider it done, my lord.'

'Gruffydd, Ieuan, Maredydd, scout ahead and help evacuate Glyncoch and the ladies who insist on riding with us to safety. Joshua, Elias, Peter, watch for stragglers in Tudor's rear guard. Friar Brown, you do the same for Hova's party. See them safe to the abbey.'

The mountains reverberated with the sound of hoofbeats, leaving the valley to the kites that continued to circle overhead.

Glyndŵr's summer quarters at Glyncoch October 1401
Mair confronted Ieuan. 'Efa gave birth five hours ago. You can't possibly move her ... '

'De Grey and the king's men are just over the hill,' he began hotly. 'Have you any idea what they will do to you and the other women? And they won't spare the children, not even the babies.'

'Have you forgotten I was a captive of the king's men when you found me?' she retorted furiously. 'You don't have to tell me what they'd do to me. They've already done it!' Mair's glare softened when she looked into Ieuan's eyes. She'd seen him despairing but never angry. She realised he was frightened, but not for himself. 'Where will you take Efa?' she asked.

'Not just Efa, you and all the women and children. My uncle's sending you under guard to a watchtower.'

'And if the English attack us on the journey?'

'They won't! De Grey's men are travelling from the north, you'll be heading south. Gruffydd's squire is slinging litters between palfreys now for the sick and the children too young to ride,' He grasped Mair's arm. 'Promise, you'll take care of Efa for me?'

'Efa is my friend. I don't need you or anyone to tell me to take care of her, which I'll do for her own sake not yours, Ieuan,' she retorted.

'You're strong, Mair. The women will turn to you for help and advice. There'll be enough men to beat off a small attack, but take this anyway.' He thrust a dagger into her hand. 'You shouldn't need it, but I'd be happier if you carried a blade, in case.'

She studied his dark eyes. 'In case of what?'

'In case you find yourself in a tight corner, but if capture is inevitable ... '

Gruffydd's voice echoed up the stairs. 'Ieuan where in Hades are you, and what in God's eyebrow are you doing that's taking so long?'

'Go,' Ieuan ordered Mair, 'I'll carry Efa downstairs.'

'I have to pack ... '

'You have as long as it will take me to settle Efa and the baby in a litter. Only take what your horse can carry. The carts are to remain here. They'd slow you down.'

'But ... '

'You haven't a moment to lose. Thank you, Mair.'

'For what?'

'Taking care of Efa and seeing her baby safely into the world. I know they'll be safe with you.' He smiled at her to soften his impatience, before kissing her lightly on the cheek. Mair ran off.

Ieuan knocked and walked into the bedroom. Efa was dressed and sitting on the edge of the bed. She held up the shawl wrapped baby in her arms. 'You have a son, Ieuan. I thought we could name him, David.'

'Perhaps he should have his own name.' The words were out of his mouth before he realised how much they would hurt her.

' I heard you talking to Mair ... '

'Then you know I have to get you out of here.' He picked up a blanket from the bottom of the bed and shook it out. 'I'll carry you downstairs.'

'I can walk.'

'Not so soon after giving birth you can't.'

Gruffydd knocked the open door. 'You carry one, I'll carry the other. We've prepared a litter for you, Efa. Mair told me you and Ieuan have a son. I take it this my new nephew?'

'He is,' she said shyly, conscious as she always was around Ieuan's brothers, that some of the men still referred to her as "whore" after she'd been sold to a Ruthyn brothel before being rescued.

'You look like a fine fellow in the making. When you've grown a few more inches your uncles will introduce you to gwisgi.' Gruffydd scooped up the baby and settled him in the crook of his elbow before tickling him under his chin.

'You're good with babies,' Efa said.

'My mother wouldn't let me be otherwise given the number of younger brothers and sisters she presented me with.' He turned to Ieuan. 'The litter is waiting, and Rhys is ready to move out, under mother, Jonnett and Elwy's supervision, of course.'

'Uncle Tudor persuaded them to evacuate?' Ieuan was surprised.

'He didn't give them a choice. No one argued after mother reminded them their first duty was to obey the prince's orders just as his captains were sworn to.'

The baby grizzled and Gruffydd smiled down at him. 'Shush now, and stop your fretting. I'll hand you back to your mother when she's safely in her litter.'

'It's cold outside, you'll need your cloak.' Ieuan lifted it from a hook on the back of the door and draped it around Efa's shoulders. 'Your shoes.' He retrieved them from under the bed and slipped them on her feet. He wrapped the blanket around her and lifted her into his arms.

'We will be able to return here, won't we?' Efa asked anxiously.

'You may not want to,' he answered evasively. 'The watch tower is large enough to take everyone here who can't fight, and the kitchens are packing ample provisions.' He hoisted her in his arms, carried her down into the stable yard.

As Gruffydd had promised, a litter had been slung between two palfreys for Efa and the child. Mair was mounted on one, talking to Gruffydd. Ieuan laid Efa on the litter and Gruffydd tucked the baby into her arms.

'I will see you soon.' Efa begged Ieuan.

'You will, and until then you have Mair to look after both of you.' He hesitated. 'David is a good name,' he blurted uneasily, in atonement for his initial reaction to her suggestion.

'May I call him David ap Ieuan?'

'Of course' He knew she was asking him to recognise the child as his. He wasn't proud of his tardiness in doing so. But he couldn't help wishing Lizzie was the mother of his first born son, not her younger sister. No matter how hard he tried, he couldn't forget that she'd prostituted herself. Logic told him she'd had no choice. Not when she'd been forced to service men by the madam and the retired soldiers who "kept order" in Ruthyn's brothel.

Jonnet ran up to Gruffydd. He embraced and kissed her before lifting her on to the saddle of the second palfrey that carried Efa's litter. Rhys Coch shouted an order and the column moved off. Ieuan waved to Efa and Mair and turned his back. He, like his father, had learned to avoid prolonged goodbyes.

'That's nice and convenient for you.'

'What?' Ieuan demanded of Rhys Ddu.

'Having your concubine look after your mistress.' Rhys slapped Ieuan's back. 'There's me having to make do with one wife, who'd emasculate me if I wandered from the marriage bed . . . '

'Emasculate really?' Ieuan questioned sceptically.

'Really,' Rhys repeated, straight faced. 'She warned me she would on our wedding night.'

'As did mine,' Gruffydd smiled.

'I don't believe either of you,' Ieuan said sceptically.

'Sometimes it's easier to say, "yes, yes" and ignore a woman's threats than argue. And then again when was the last time you saw me with my wife?' Rhys questioned.

'Never,' Gruffydd shouted as Rhys walked away.

'You're not serious, about Jonnet, are you?' Ieuan asked Gruffydd.

'Absolutely,' Gruffydd replied.

'Look at your situation from our point of view, Ieuan,' Maredydd said as he joined them. 'It's not easy to stand back and watch your younger brother enjoy the company of two mistresses, one to bear his sons the other to attend to his every whim., when you only have one wife. What is your secret?'

'It's not like that . . . '

'We're not criticising, just envious,' Gruffydd shook his head in mock admiration. 'And even with two women prepared to share your bed, the only woman you can talk about is Lizzie.'

'I'm still looking for her.'

'So we understand from the number of times you mention her in a day, Maredydd said. 'Have you considered what you'd do if she turns up and demands you keep your promise to marry her? Four in a bed is quite a crowd, brother.'

'Is that the voice of experience speaking? If so, I'm surprised your wife allows you ... '

***

Tudor was talking to the archers. He glanced across the yard, sensed a quarrel brewing between his nephews and joined them. 'Konrad and Ulrich are in Xian's workshop, distributing the last of the flying fire that wasn't sent to Glyndyfrdwy. Get some before it's all taken.'

'Has the plan changed since we discussed it when we watered the horses?' Gruffydd realised he'd pushed his joke too far with Ieuan and was keen to change the subject.

'No, but remember my warning. Every man to secure his escape route before "Havoc" is shouted. If the English don't fire this place we will when we use Xian's tricks.'

'You're really going to destroy everything here?' Ieuan asked.

'We couldn't return here now that Bolingbroke and De Grey know its location. And I doubt Hanmer would want it back. The state the main house and cottages are in, I doubt they'll survive the winter.'

Ieuan looked at the tumbledown cottage where he'd lived with Efa, Mair and David. He hadn't realised how attached he was to the place - and its happier memories.

A rider dressed in a shepherd's fleece galloped down the hill. He jumped from his horse when he reached the valley floor and ran to Tudor. 'They'll be on the summit within the hour, my lord.'

'Hide!' Tudor commanded.

***

Tudor ordered twenty men at arms to conceal themselves, battle ready in armour, along with their mounts in the largest barn. More men at arms waited with their destriers behind the closed doors of the stables, two smaller barns and the building Xian had commandeered as his workshop.

Tudor sent the archers to the attics where they found vantage points in the eaves of the house, cottages, haylofts, barn and stables from which they could pick out their targets. Their soldiers hid in the undergrowth of the woodland that bordered the river, awaiting orders from their sergeants to join the battle when and where it raged the fiercest.

Tudor's entire plan hinged on the element of surprise. To that end he issued orders for absolute silence while they waited.

Ieuan had never been patient and he found the half an hour he was shut up in the barn with Gruffydd and his fellow men at arms, irksome. Despite the cumbersome weight of his armour, he left his horse with his squire and climbed into the hay loft.

The thatched roof sloped down to a high bank at the back of the building which would break the archers' fall, "if" or more likely "when" they jumped down. But there was a scant three feet gap between the floor and roof timbers, which didn't leave a man of his size much room to manoeuvre.

He scraped a hole in the thatch, wriggled his way forward between two archers and studied the hill that fronted the main house. The sun had reached its zenith and was beginning its downward descent through a cloudy sky when a lone rider appeared on the crest of the hill. His armour and helmet shone dully in the muted light as he reined in his destrier.

The single rider was joined by half a dozen men at arms, then a dozen more and within minutes a line of horsemen stretched across the skyline from east to west.

'And so they appear,' an archer whispered.

A second line of bowmen on foot stepped out between the mounted men.

'They're carrying lanterns. Just as well Tudor decided to fire this place,' Gruffydd whispered from the other end of the attic.

The enemy archers adjusted their bows, dipped their arrows in fire and loaded them. The command "Loose" was clearly heard closely followed by a line of flaming missiles streaking down the hill. Ieuan and Gruffydd, instinctively ducked, shuddering as their helmeted heads slammed into the low roof.

'Archers, cool heads until you can hit your targets, Men at arms mount,' Tudor growled beneath the whistle of enemy arrows. 'Remember, we surprise them. Not they us.'

When the enemy archers moved forward Gruffydd and Ieuan headed for the ladder. Halfway down the hill, the enemy fired again. The sound of arrows thudding into wooden doors and shutters reverberated, shaking the stable.

'How kind of them to give us fire to light Xian's surprises.' Philip Hanmer reached out with a taper to the flame licking the nearest shutter as the first cry of 'Havoc!' sounded in the yard.

***

Hooves drummed a staccato beat as de Grey men at arms charged down the hill. Screams and cries followed Tudor's order to the Glyndŵr archers to fire upwards. Tudor didn't give the signal to open the barns and stable doors until the mounted enemy who'd survived the onslaught of Glyndŵr arrows reached the courtyard.

The rickety wooden buildings shuddered when the two parties met in the stable yard in a welter of clashing steel and exploding ceramic pots as the Glyndŵr soldiers lit the fuses of Xian's "bombs" and threw them beneath de Grey's cavalry.

Tudor signalled to an archer he'd placed at the highest lookout point of the house. The watchman fired an arrow that thudded high into an oak beside the river. Soldiers ran out from the undergrowth; brandishing spears, hammers and long hooked flails. They set to work unseating de Grey's men at arms.

The advance guard who'd charged down the hill proved easy prey as they'd suffered the brunt of the Glyndŵr arrows fired from the attics. Behind them a fresh second wave of horsemen lined up on the summit of the hill. Tudor watched the line extend two hundred yards and more. A horn sounded and was answered when Bolingbroke's royal banner appeared on a hill to the east.

A third horn sounded long, loud and piercing. The Glyndŵr banner crowned a hill to the west.

Tudor smiled and murmured, 'Thank you, brother.' He shouted, 'To me!' He spurred Satan and led the charge to meet the body of de Grey's second wave of men who, lacking leadership were holding back their mounts.

Ieuan picked his target. Broadsword in his right hand, flying fire in his left, he guided his destrier with his knees and rode towards a helmed man who sat high on his saddle. His armour was steel, plain with silver embellishments and of enviable quality.

The target saw Ieuan and heaved on his reins intending to turn his mount, but Ieuan struck a flint, lit and tossed a flying fire "cup". The horse reared on his hind legs. Unbalanced, the rider clung on. He rocked. One of Glyndŵr's soldiers hooked a flail around his neck and heaved. The man toppled and fell prey to half a dozen of Tudor's spearmen. He landed on his back on the straw and manure coated cobbles while Welsh foot soldiers swarmed in, hacking at the joints in his armour like kites pecking a sheep to get at the flesh beneath the fleece.

Ieuan saw two of de Grey's men at arms bearing down on Gruffydd. He dug his knees into his mount and lashed out at one who was wearing dark grey armour. The knight parried Ieuan's blow, lost his balance and fell.

Horns sounded again and a fresh party of men carrying his father's banner charged into the chaos.

One voice rose above all others. 'I yield.'

'My Lord?' A foot soldier addressed Ieuan.

Ieuan lifted his visor and looked down at the man in silver embellished armour. He was pinned to the ground by the foot soldier's spear. A second soldier kicked open the visor of the downed knight who continued to lie on his back, as impotent as an overturned beetle.

'As I live and breathe,' Owain dismounted and walked towards the man. 'Ieuan, meet Reginald de Grey. His men killed your mother, burned your home, kidnapped your betrothed and murdered your neighbours. De Grey, you'll have to beg a deal louder - if you want my son to show you mercy.'

Ieuan lifted his head and looked up to the hills. There was no sign of Bolingbroke's banner - or his army.

***

Sheep and bullock carcasses had been impaled on makeshift spits, slung over fires fed by the wooden doors, furniture and tapestries of the cottages while flames continued to lick at and flicker around the stone walls.

De Grey's men had been stripped of their weapons and horses. The ranks who weren't worth ransoming had been escorted across the river by Philip Scudamore's cavalry. Grateful to be alive they'd run east, the same direction the king's party had last been seen heading in.

As no building had been left standing near the house, Reginald de Grey and those of his captains wealthy enough to pay for their freedom had been bound hand and foot and relegated to what had been the kitchen yard.

***

Ieuan walked with Tudor and Xian as they spoke to each captive in turn. Gruffydd stood behind them, noting the estimates Tudor made of each man's worth on a slate, before calculating a fair ransom price.

Aware of a sudden eruption of angry shouts coming from the latrines Tudor looked up. 'What's going on?'

'This is going on.' Rhys Fierce and Philip Hanmer hauled de Grey and his squire forward and pushed them towards the other prisoners. 'We caught them trying to escape from the latrines.'

'Bastards, knocked three of our boys out cold before we stopped them,' Hanmer added.

'Where's his armour?' Ieuan asked.

'Here. It's now yours as he yielded to you.' Philip Hanmer tossed a bulging sack at Ieuan's feet. 'His squire was carrying it, presumably so his master could run faster.'

Tudor eyed de Grey who'd fallen on the ground. 'Your leg is bleeding.'

'I stuck my best dirk in it to slow him down,' Rhys Fierce frowned. 'Bastard moved and the blade snapped. So if there's a dirk among his weapons . . . '

'It's yours, uncle,' Ieuan offered.

'You're all bloody savages with no idea of the rules of warfare or chivalry . . . ' de Grey snarled.

'But we do have a sense of fairness. I have no need to ask your worth, given the size of your castle and estates,' Tudor said brightly. 'It may be problematic to separate your holdings from those you have stolen from your neighbours, but hopefully your fellow landowners will be able to assist us when it comes to marking out the boundaries.'

De Grey glared at Tudor but made no comment.

'That is a fine looking ring you have there, My Lord.' Xian crouched down beside the Baron. 'May I take a closer look at the coat of arms?'

'So you can steal it? No you may not.' De Grey jerked his hands away from Xian but as they were tied he couldn't move them from Xian's reach.

'Etiquette, my lord,' Tudor chided. 'Weren't you taught to be polite to those inferior in rank.'

'I assume the arms are those of your house, my lord,' Xian continued. 'It's fine silver and blue enamel work. I admired one like it not so long ago,'

'You would not have seen one like this,' de Grey insisted. 'This was my father's.'

'But I assure you I have seen a similar ring worn by a knight. Your brother perhaps?'

'My father had but one ring which he gave to me. There are no other unless . . . '

'Unless?' Xian prompted.

'There are none, I tell you.'

One of the knights on the periphery of the group nodded to Gruffydd and whispered in his ear when he approached.

'I warned you,' de Grey shouted at his men, 'if you value your lives, do not speak to the Welsh.' He spat out the last word as if it were an insult.

'He has a wound that needs tending, Lord Grey.' Gruffydd waved to Dafydd who walked over to the man.

Tudor took the slate from Gruffydd and scanned the figures. 'Nephew?'

'Uncle?' Gruffydd supressed a smile at Tudor's formal address.

'Haven't you placed a somewhat low value on Baron de Grey's ability to ransom himself? Only 10,000 marks for such a lord . . . '

'Equals 20,000 gold nobles, uncle.'

'Still - a man of his worth could afford to lose at least 40,000 gold nobles from his purse in my opinion, and not even miss them.'

Ieuan supressed a smile as his brother and uncle continued to wrangle for the benefit of the captives whose grimaces cut deeper as the estimates of their ability to pay grew higher.

Xian didn't smile, preoccupied with de Grey's enamelled silver ring he'd pulled out one of the ivory tablets he used to make notes and was busily sketching the coat of arms on it.

***

At dusk, feeling exhausted and depressed as he had done after every battle and skirmish he'd fought, Ieuan sat with his father, and the other captains. They were eating scorched mutton and beef, and drinking the ale and gwisgi

Tudor had retrieved from the caves where he'd hidden it before the battle.

Owain squinted up at the sky. 'You say the women and children have everything they need in the south watchtower.'

'They'll be comfortable enough for one night,' Tudor assured him. 'Even your new grandson.'

Owain smiled at Ieuan, 'Efa had your child?"

'Early this morning. We named him David.'

'We must toast his arrival and that of your grandson, Tudor. Gruffydd, pass round the gwisgi flask.'

Xian opened his purse and dropped a ring into Ieuan's lap.

'Ieuan picked it up. 'You persuaded de Grey to part with his ring?'

'Not de Grey, that ring was taken from the hand that was closed around your sister Gweni's leg when she rode into Sycharth to seek help the night de Grey's men attacked Pont Gweni.'

'Then who ... '

'Other than he must have been related to de Grey to have a similar ring I couldn't say. But that,' Xian nodded to the ring, 'coupled with the need to deliver the ransom demand for de Grey could open every door in Ruthyn castle.'

'Allowing me to search for and rescue Lizzie?' Ieuan murmured more to himself than anyone else.

Ieuan looked so happy at the prospect neither his father, uncle nor brothers had the courage to remind him that they had no proof she was still alive.

CHAPTER TWENTY-EIGHT

Glyndŵr's Headquarters Glyndyfrdwy October 1401
Owain and his army arrived at Glyndyfrdwy after a two day ride that had been hard but bearable because no Glyndŵr man had been killed at Glyncoch and none so badly wounded that they had to be left behind.

Margaret had managed to organise what Tudor called "a fitting welcome home feast". After everyone had eaten and the dishes cleared, Owain rose to his feet and lifted his goblet.

'Thank you, every one of you, who safeguarded our families and saw them safe from de Grey's men by escorting them from Glyncoch. Thank you, all who fought valiantly to win our victory there. Thank you, all who remained here and cared for our families in our absence.'

After the toast had been drunk, Tudor said. 'Now all we have to do is find a new summer headquarters for next year.'

'Pick your castle, Uncle Tudor,' Gruffydd joked from the table where he was sitting with his brothers and their ladies, 'and watch the youngsters capture it while you take your ease and rest your old bones.'

'Why stop at one, nephew. I choose Caernarvon as a winter residence.' Tudor mentioned the largest and strongest of the ring of iron castles Edward Longshanks had commissioned James of St George to build in North Wales to control the unruly Welsh.

'And for a summer retreat?' Gruffydd asked.

'Harlech or Aberystwyth,' Tudor answered decisively, 'a man should summer by the sea in case he fancies a dip.'

'No need to take any castles this week,' Owain declared when the laughter died down. 'De Grey's men won't give us any trouble until they've raised the ransom we've demanded, for fear of us harming a hair on his head. And it will take them a while ... '

'Two, three or even ten whiles,' Tudor interrupted.

' . . . to gather the marks Tudor wants,' Owain nodded to Tudor. 'If we're fortunate Bolingbroke won't stop running until he's crossed the border and returned to England to lick his wounds.'

'With luck he'll winter there and leave us in peace,' Tudor added.

'No king, prince or man could ask for better followers. Now we can rest and spend time with our families - and,' Owain smiled, 'sweethearts. When I return from delivering our ransom demand to Ruthyn, we'll plan next year's campaign and pray God gives us strength to add to the glory you have blessed our banner with this season.'

Owain's speech met with an outburst of approval. He left his seat, walked over to his sons' table and sat on the end of a bench next to Ieuan.

'You don't need to ride to Ruthyn with us tomorrow. Stay with Efa and get acquainted with your son.'

'It's never too soon to begin teaching boys the rudiments of sword play and gwisgi drinking. Your David is the right age to start.' Tudor joined them and, ignoring Gruffydd's frown, filled his goblet with the last of the wine on the table.

'For two years all I've heard of Lizzie are rumours. I have to know . . . ' too choked by emotion to say any more he fell silent. 'If she were dead . . . I'd feel it. I know I would,' he blurted.

'When two people are as close as you and Lizzie, neither time nor distance can separate them,' Owain said. 'If you're set on riding to Ruthyn, you're welcome to join us. We leave at first light.'

Owain reached out and held gripped Ieuan's hand. When he released it he turned to his brother. 'Tudor you'll take charge of things here?'

'You've no need to ask.'

'Send ten men at arms and their retinues to relieve Rhys Fierce. I want the guards changed at the prison tower every four days to prevent them from growing bored and careless.'

'The hawking and boar hunting are good in the hills around there so the men will have no excuse to get bored, and the tower is secure. Don't worry, brother, our pigeons will remain safely shut in our coop until their ransoms are in our coffers.'

Owain looked around the table. 'I suggest those who ride with me in the morning find their beds lest they end up riding with a hangover.'

'One last toast to the victors.' Tudor reached to the table behind him and checked their wine jug.

'It's always one last toast where you are concerned, Tudor,' Margaret smiled. 'But this time I agree with you. Ladies,' she rose to her feet, lifted her goblet and looked to the women and girls, 'shall we raise our cups to our lords, sons and protectors.'

When the toast had been drunk Margaret left the table. She stopped behind Ieuan's seat and placed a hand on his shoulder.

'God speed tomorrow. I hope you find your love.'

Ieuan covered her hand with his but failed to answer.

Ruthyn Castle Steward's Quarters October 1401
Lizzie lay curled on the cot at the foot of the steward's bed. Her head ached and she felt sick, hardly a surprise as she was with child again. She didn't want to think about the coming baby any more than she wanted to consider the child she'd already borne. His care and upbringing had been entrusted to a nursemaid the steward had engaged. He, the housekeeper and his daughter Mary played with the child during his "wakeful times". She avoided looking at him and hadn't held him since the day he was born. Fortunately the steward and his housekeeper had desisted from trying to persuade her to take him.

Whenever she considered her feelings towards the child she was beset with a mixture of outright loathing rooted in the rape that had resulted in his conception and odd cold shivers that were far removed from love or caring .

"The child" - she realised she never thought of it as "her child" - but then it wasn't. It was the steward's child, and she had too many things to resent her master for - raping her - taking her virginity - stealing the life she had planned to live with her beloved betrothed.

The steward had caged, raped, abused and constantly belittled her as well as killing all her hopes for her future. He had stolen the children she had dreamed of bearing for Ieuan that would never be born. In confining her to his apartment within the castle and setting her to work on the accounts twelve hours a day he'd robbed her of freedom, not just of movement but time to think. In using her the way farmers used their brood mares and cattle, he'd enslaved her body. And worst of all, whenever she'd tried to fight back he'd threatened to use the castle guards to constrain her until she complied with his demands.

She tossed restlessly on her thin mattress and attempted to retreat to and take comfort in the imaginary world she'd created. A world that existed in day dreams and half remembered fragments. A world where Ieuan's mother still lived and presided over the village of Pont Gweni.

She knew from the invoices she wrote for the steward that it was October. If the autumn had been mild the last of the roses would be blooming around the doors of the cottages. The barns and storerooms would be full of vegetables and grain they'd harvested to see them through the winter. The pigs they couldn't feed over winter would have been slaughtered and sides of bacon and ham would hang smoking over every hearth, so slices could be cut when the men came in hungry from hunting.

After work was done for the day there'd be singing at supper, and on feast days and birthdays, dancing in her mother-in-law's kitchen. Ieuan would look across the room at her ...

The image faded when she failed to conjure Ieuan's face. Not quite two years since she had last seen him on the eve of what should have been their wedding day and she'd forgotten what he looked like.

Her throat constricted and she sobbed.

'Lizzie?'

She swallowed hard and tried to speak, but her voice was faint and all she managed was a faint squeak.

'Lizzie, are you awake?'

'Yes, steward.'

'Get into my bed.'

'I'm ill, steward . . . '

'I ordered, not asked. Get into this bed, girl.'

'Yes, steward.'

'Now!'

She left the cot, rose and went to his bed. He reached out to her and pulled her in beside him.

'On your back.''

She complied and he rolled on top of her. She cried out as a sharp pain accompanied a tearing deep inside her.

'This won't take long. He thrust hard and she screamed.

'Quiet! You'll wake the household.' He slid his hand down the bed. 'You've wet the bed . . . it's soaking . . . it's . . . ' he held up his hand. Moonlight shone through the window illuminating dark stains that could only be blood.

Lizzie tried to protest but the image she'd worked so hard to conjure earlier bloomed into life. She took the hand Ieuan offered her and stepped out of his mother's house into their garden . . .

Ruthyn Castle October 1401

Owain rode at the head of his men through the streets of Ruthyn. Dafydd, Xian, Gruffydd, Ieuan and Maredydd rode behind him, followed by forty of their men at arms. Maredydd carried Owain's battle banner, Dafydd the white flag of parley and truce.

Owain halted in front of the castle to give his retainers time to line up behind him before crossing the drawbridge.

When they were in place Owain's page blew his horn and Owain walked Ariston over the drawbridge into the Upper Bailey behind the castle walls.

Reginald's eldest surviving son and heir, fourteen year old John de Grey, stood on the steps in front of the Great Hall in the Upper Bailey with his mother Margaret, his father's liege men and the garrison that manned the castle.

Gruffydd dismounted, took a sealed missive from the leather satchel he carried, advanced, bowed and presented it to John. 'Your father is in good health and well cared for.'

'Thank you. The king has asked me to forward your ransom demand to him. I will send you his reply when we receive it.'

Gruffydd bowed and returned to his horse. Ieuan dismounted and took Gruffydd's place. He removed the ring Xian had given him from his glove, walked to John and offered it to him.

John stared at it, but it was his mother Margaret who took it from Ieuan. She turned it over and looked up questioningly at him.

'Where did you get this?'

'I will tell you, and anything else I know pertaining to this ring on condition you take me to my betrothed.'

John took the ring from his mother. 'Your betrothed. What is she to do with us?'

'My betrothed, Lizzie ferch John was brought her after your father's men burned and sacked Pont Gweni and killed my mother, other members of our family and neighbours. Shortly afterwards we heard Lizzie had been taken into your father's steward's household but we have heard nothing of her since.'

John turned to the steward. 'Is Lizzie ferch John the girl you have working in your household?'

'I don't know, my lord . . . '

'Is her name Lizzie?'

'Yes, my lord.'

'Bring her here.'

'She is ill, confined to bed, my lord.'

'My mother and I need to know whatever news this man can give us of my brother Thomas's fate. Bring her here.'

'She can't walk ... '

'Captain!' John snapped in a fair imitation of his father's gruff tones.

The captain stepped forward.

'My lord.

'Go with the steward. If the lady can't walk, carry her.'

***

Ieuan remained standing between John de Grey, his mother and his father's mounted men while the steward and captain entered the castle. A cold wind blew inside the upper bailey rattling the thatch on the stable roofs, and scattering the straw that covered the cobbles.

Owain's men and their horses moved restlessly behind him. Just when Ieuan assumed that neither the steward nor the captain would emerge from the gatehouse, the captain stepped out, carrying a body wrapped in a rough, military cloak.

Ieuan stepped forward. The captain flicked back a corner of the cloak and Ieuan looked down at Lizzie. Her eyes were closed and her body fell limply into his arms.

'She's alive.'

Ieuan turned and saw his father standing at his elbow.

'We'll find a doctor.'

John stepped forward. 'You said you'd tell me how you came by the ring.'

'I gave it to him.' Xian who was wearing his helmet visor down so it covered his face dismounted.

'That ring belonged to my brother. It is engraved with my father's coat of arms. It never left his hand. Where did you get it?' John demanded.

'From a severed hand.'

'Lift your visor so I may see your face?'

'No.'

'Why not?'

'Because I am a leper,' Xian lied.

'Did you kill my brother?'

'No. His hand and only his hand was closed around my wife's ankle. I did not see him or any other part of his body. My wife told me the owner of the hand had attacked her there was a fight and the hand was severed by a blade. A blow that saved her life and honour.'

'Then my brother is dead?' John asked.

'I only saw the hand. Not the man who wore the ring, or the fight that resulted in the severing of his hand. That is the truth. I swear it on my honour as a knight and on the blood of Christ.'

'My brother's body?'

'When I found my wife she was in shock. I removed the hand from her leg. I have not spoken of the incident to her since for fear of provoking memories of a time when she almost lost her life.'

'My brother's grave?'

'I have no knowledge of a grave, if there is one or not. Or even if the owner of that hand still lives. I have told you the truth, I cannot tell you more.'

Ieuan carried Lizzie to his horse. Gruffydd took Lizzie from him. When he'd mounted he handed her up to him.

'We need to find a doctor,' Ieuan pleaded.

Owain turned back to John de Grey. 'You have the ransom note. The friars will deliver a message to me. We will wait to hear from you.'

'But . . . ' John looked on helplessly as Ieuan turned his horse and rode back over the drawbridge.

Xian mounted and faced John. 'Keep that ring as a reminder of how some men can sink low enough to attack a defenceless woman for amusement. Even those who pride themselves on being highborn.'

CHAPTER THIRTY

Inn outside Ruthyn October 1401
The midwife bustled down the stairs of the inn and knocked the door of the private room. Gruffydd opened it but Owain reached the passageway before his son.

'God willing she will live, my prince, but I wouldn't advise moving her for a week or more. I live nearby. Should the pains return in the night call for me, if not I will be back in the morning.'

'Thank you,' Owain handed her a purse.

'Thank you, my prince.'

Owain walked up the stairs to the rooms they'd rented, knocked and waited for Ieuan's permission before entering. Ieuan was sitting on the bed next to Lizzie, holding her hand. Her eyes were open and they were gazing at one another as though they needed nothing and no one else in this world.

Owain recalled the day Ieuan and Lizzie had ridden to Sycharth from Pont Gweni to ask his permission for their betrothal. If only the world had remained as quiet and peaceful as it had been that day?

He pictured Gweni's grave in the ruins of the church in Pont Gweni. David and all the men who had fallen alongside him at Hyddgen lying beneath the sod at Bryn y Beddau. The grave that had been dug for Llewelyn's mortal remains next to them. People he had loved and lost who he would never see in this life again.

'My lord,' Lizzie murmured. 'Ieuan told me you are truly a prince now.'

'And you are soon to be my daughter.' Owain kissed her forehead. 'The midwife said she will come in the night if you need her.'

'I want to go to Glyndyfrdwy with Ieuan ... '

'I think not,' Ieuan interposed. 'You heard the midwife. You need to rest for a week or more ... '

'The midwife doesn't know me or my strength. I won't slow you down. When you leave here, I'll ride alongside you.'

'Lizzie . . . ' Ieuan looked at her and forgetting the argument he was about to have with her, smiled.

Owain gripped his son's shoulder. 'I see you've found yourself a wife fashioned from the same cloth as your mother, sister and your brothers' wives. I leave you to your argument.'

'My prince.'

'Yes, Lizzie.'

'Will you allow women to fight in your war for freedom for the Welsh?'

Recognising her need to fight back after what had been done to her, he answered, 'Anyone, man or women is welcome to join our fight for freedom for Wales, Lizzie. But I want no one to fight beyond their strength or capabilities.'

'You have found yourself another soldier, my prince, she said softly.'

'One who needs love and healing. Look after her Ieuan. Welcome to our family, Lizzie.'

***

Owain was aware of a disturbance at the door of the inn. He went downstairs to see Xian still in his armour, with his visor down standing in the open doorway.

Owain's hand instinctively closed over the hilt of his sword as he sensed a crowd of men outside.

He stepped forward and saw fifty or more men all in the uniform of the garrison of Ruthyn castle.

'They are calling for you, my prince,' Xian said.

Owain stepped outside, Maredydd and Gruffydd were talking to their captain.

'My prince.' The man drew his sword, laid it at Owain's feet and bowed. 'Today we saw the manner in which a true born Christian knight deals with his enemies.'

'I could never afford to purchase a knighthood, even when King Richard offered me one.' Owain revealed.

'But you are the prince we want to follow, my lord.'

'Then you need to learn to drink. Go inside the lot of you.' Dafydd ushered them in.'

He waited until the last one was inside the tap room before lowering his voice, and whispering in Owain's ear.

'You can't blame them for changing sides. They only want to sit at the best supplied table, and after the de Greys' have paid for their lord's ransom it won't be in Ruthyn Castle.'

'So you want me to recruit mercenaries now?' Owain asked.

'They want food, drink and the spoils of war, we want freedom, why quibble if our journeys have led us on to the same road, my lord.'

'My Lord, my Prince,' Yonge rode up to the inn door, a man slumped over the saddle in front of him. 'They said in Ruthyn I might find you here. Thank God I have.' He dismounted and lifted off the man who was dressed in a novice's robes. When Yonge stood him on the ground, Owain and Dafydd saw that the man's eyes had been burned out.

'Bolingbroke has occupied Strata Florida Abbey, my prince. He has taken Llewelyn ap Gruffydd Fychan's wife son, grandson and daughter-in-law hostage, stabled his horses in the sacristy, stolen the plate and murdered every monk who tried to protect the church.'

The novice fell to his knees. 'I beseech you, my lord, Bolingbroke spares no one. Not child, woman, man, monk nor cleric.'

Dafydd helped the novice up from the ground. 'What was that you said about a restful winter spent with family and sweethearts planning spring tactics, my prince?'

EPILOGUE

Snowdonia May 30th 1421

'1401 that was the first full year of the war and it changed Glyndŵr. He was never the same afterwards.' The old man leaned against the wall of the cave and handed his companion the bag of bread and cheese the landlord of the inn had packed for them.

'In what way?' his young companion asked.

'It was as though a piece of his soul had been torn from him.' The old man sank his head in his hands as though the memories were too heavy to bear. 'That year took a toll on all who followed the prince. We learned to harden our hearts against loss and suffering. It's one thing to talk about killing the enemy, another to look into the eyes of a man as you thrust a sword into him.' He spoke slowly, haltingly, reminding his companion just how long he'd lived alone in the cave. 'Hyddgen . . . '

'The Prince's first great victory. Fought and won against impossible odds of ten to one,' the young man broke in.

The old man shook his head. 'You've been listening to the bards. It was three to one. I was there.'

'Even so, three to one must have been daunting. My brothers told me they charged downhill into the enemy camp in full sight of, and within target of their archers. That takes bravery.'

The old man's eyes grew misty in the smoke from the fire. 'Bravery?' He gave a wry smile. 'Or gwisgi.'

'You were drunk?' the young man was astounded.

'I can see you've never fought a battle.' The old man drew closer to the fire. 'Every one of us, from the prince down to the youngest squire, drank their fill from the gwisgi flasks before we drew our swords. Tudor saw to that. He handed out enough spirit for us to forget that we were about to die, not only at Hyddgen, but before every battle. If he hadn't I doubted we would have ever won a victory.'

'Are you saying soldiers need drink to stiffen their sword arm?'

'Only a madman or drunk would ride willingly into a slaughterhouse.'

'Whenever I asked my brothers what battle was like they never took the question seriously. I thought they were trying to downplay their bravery.'

'The only way a man can live with sights and sounds that can never be forgotten is by making light of them. Whenever I hear a priest mention hell, I picture a field of broken men and limbs soaked in blood. Not just the ones we fought on during the prince's war for independence, but those your father and I shed blood on for King Richard.' He shook his head as though he were trying to shake off nightmare memories. 'Hyddgen was different because we were fighting for something we desperately needed, our freedom. We were all grateful for Tudor's numbing liquor. Even the prince warned us the battle was lost before we mounted. I remember the speech he gave us.' He closed his eyes and murmured, '"I do not command, but beg. Sell your lives dearly this day, and if God chooses to deliver our death, let us meet it like Welshmen. Sword in hand, stout in heart ready to deliver to the enemy what he would deliver to us if we allowed. No quarter".'

He blinked and looked at his companion as though he was surprised to find himself in the cave and not back on Hyddgen.

'I wish I'd been there.'

'To taste sheer terror like the rest of us?' the old man smiled.

'You lived to taste victory.'

'I and a few others.' the old man mused. It came at a high price. We left 200 of our own beneath the field.'

'I've seen their final resting place on Bryn y Beddau - the hill of graves at the foot of Hyddgen.'

'It breaks a man's heart to look at the spot where his own kind lie buried.' The old man poked a stick into the fire and stirred the flames.

'I was five when he was killed.'

'Do you remember him?'

'Yes,' the young man answered. 'I miss him.'

'As do we all. He was a fine warrior, brother, father and man. Another lies beside him who was too old to fight at Hyddgen. Llewelyn ap Gruffydd Fychan should have died peacefully in his own bed surrounded by his children and grandchildren. The Prince never forgave Bolingbroke for ordering him to be hung drawn and quartered in the public square of Llandovery market.'

'My father often spoke of Llewelyn and the influence he had on his life.'

'Your grandfather, Gruffydd Glyndŵr, died when your father was ten. Afterwards Llewelyn looked out for Gruffydd's wife and children and your father was his favourite godson. He and the prince were closer than most fathers and sons. Llewelyn didn't deserve the agonising death Bolingbroke sentenced him to. It almost broke your father when he heard of it, but at least Tudor Glyndŵr spared Llewelyn the ignominy of having his head displayed on London bridge.'

'Did Bolingbroke ever discover Llewelyn's body had been replaced by another?'

'I heard he suspected it, but he had no proof.'

'Do you know whose body replaced Llewelyn's?'

The old man smiled. 'Your uncle Tudor knew and trusted the secret to a few people. None ever talked, that I know of.'

'Not even you?'

The old man took a hunk of bread. Lost in thought he stared at it for a moment making no attempt to eat. 'The Prince took every humiliation Bolingbroke inflicted on the Welsh to heart. He blamed himself for the pain and suffering that they caused. I watched him wrestle with guilt all through the summer and autumn of that year of 1401. And then came Strata Florida . . . '

'I was six years old, training to become a squire. No one would tell us much, other than the sights there were heartrending.'

'They were. The loss of our men at Hyddgen and Llewelyn ap Gruffydd Fychan to the scaffold, turned your father's heart to stone. But it was Strata Florida that truly closed his ears to English pleas for mercy . . . '

BOOK 1
GLYNDŴR THE FORETOLD SON
BOOK 2
GLYNDŴR GLORIOUS SHALL THEIR DRAGON BE

COMING IN 2021& 2022

BOOK 3
GLYNDŴR III MY CHILD'S CHILD TO WEEP
BOOK 4
GLYNDŴR IV WHEN WARRIORS GO TO DIE

AUTHOR'S NOTES

The idea for the Glyndŵr series of books originated in a meeting with the CEO of Tanabi Films, Euros Jones Evans. I'd worked with Euros when he brought my script of my crime novel By Any Name, starring Cengiz Dervis and Samira Jefferies to the screen of Amazon Prime. Working with live people is a luxury for a novelist. It was humbling to see the work actors and crew put into bringing characters born in my head to life, but initially I was less than enthusiastic about the Glyndŵr project.
Some years ago an editor suggested I write about him. I did some perfunctory research and decided I had reservations about a man who'd abandoned his wife, and family in Harlech Castle to be captured by the English and incarcerated in the Tower of London.

Three years ago, I began researching again. I began by reading as many translations of original medieval documents that mentioned Owain Glyndŵr or Oyen Glendourdy (or any of his other misspelt names) that I could lay my hands on, along with those that mentioned his contemporaries.

Llewellyn ap Gruffydd Fychan, an elderly Welsh noble was hung drawn and quartered in Llandovery market by Henry IV for supporting Glyndŵr. Owain's fellow soldiers, and friends, Hotspur and Edmund Mortimer, fought for Henry IV (as Owain Glyndŵr once had) before switching allegiance and joining Glyndŵr. Owain had powerful arch enemies, Reginald de Grey, scheming Welsh noble Dafydd Gam, and, Kings Henry IV and Henry V, whose claims to the English throne were weaker than Glyndŵr's own grandson, Lionel Mortimer.
The most moving document I read was Owain Glyndŵr's "Pennal Letter", which revealed so much of Glyndŵr's character, proving he was centuries before his time in statesmanship and compassion. I discovered no

contemporary records had survived of the siege of Harlech, and felt that Owain Glyndŵr had fallen victim to Winston Churchill's adage, "History is written by the victors."

"Sometime in the early fifteenth century, an unknown reader, sitting in the choir of the abbey of St Albans in Hertfordshire, was so anxious about a particular entry in the chronicle manuscript he was reading that he defaced the page with the following jotting:
Christ, Splendour of God, I beseech you, destroy Glyndŵr."
(A carefully crafted expression of fear, written in dactylic hexameter, scribbled at the foot of the historical narrative for the year 1403 in a chronicle attributed to Thomas Walsingham (d.c.1422))

Given the distance between Owain Glyndŵr's sphere of operation in Wales and along the Welsh Marches and St Albans I take the inscription as proof that Henry IV commanded the services of a far better medieval publicist than Owain Glyndŵr.

A devoted husband, father, family man, highly educated linguist, fluent in English, Welsh, French, Latin and Greek, Owain Glyndŵr was in turn, soldier and warrior, a lawyer who practised in London's Inns of court, politician, country squire, charismatic leader of men, and courtier but above all a Welsh noble of Welsh royal lineage, and like all Welsh nobles, despised by the English nobility of Norman extraction.
Three years spent reading about his victories and defeats, visiting his haunts in Wales, and speaking to those who revere his name, convinced me that he was the greatest Welsh patriot, military tactician, politician and philosopher who ever lived.

The wealthiest Welshman in Wales in 1400, Owain Glyndŵr could have settled into comfortable old age in his homes surrounded by his wife, children, friends and bards, instead he sacrificed everything he valued, his family, estates, wealth, life and the lives of his sons, daughter, granddaughters and friends for Welsh freedom. His thinking was centuries ahead of his time. Six hundred years ago he dreamed of a Welsh Parliament, two Welsh universities one in the North and one the South, and a Welsh church free from the corruption of Canterbury. If he had been victorious, England and Wales would have become very different countries.

The third book is underway, it only remains for me to thank the people who have helped bring this book to life.

My brilliant and incisive editor Mary Loring.
Steve Jones for his continuing support and brilliant book jackets.
Julian Lewis Jones, consummate actor and perfect Owain Glyndŵr who agreed to be photographed for the jacket.
Euros Jones Evans for involving me in the project.
John and Ralph Watkins for tolerating me when I was physically with them and mentally in medieval Wales.
All the Welsh too numerous to mention who so generously shared their Glyndŵr stories with me in every corner of Wales. You know who you are.

Catrin Collier was born and brought up in Pontypridd. Visit her website at www.catrincollier.co.uk

Historical by Catrin Collier

Book I Glyndŵr The Foretold Son
Book II Glyndŵr Glorious Shall Their Dragon Be

Hearts of Gold
One Blue Moon
A Silver Lining
All That Glitters
Such Sweet Sorrow
Past Remembering
Broken Rainbows
Spoils of War
Magda's Daughter
Bobby's Girl

Swansea Girls
Swansea Summer
Homecoming

Beggars & Choosers
Winners & Losers
Sinners & Shadows
Finders & Keepers
Tiger Bay Blues
Tiger Ragtime

One Last Summer

Long Road to Baghdad
Winds of Eden
Scorpion Sunset

The Tsar's Dragons
Princes and Peasants
A Dragon's Legacy

CRIME (as Katherine John)
Trevor Joseph series
Without Trace
Midnight Murders
Murder of a Dead Man
Black Daffodil
A Well Deserved Murder
Destruction of Evidence
The Vanished

By Any Other Name
The Amber Knight
The Defeated Aristocrat

MODERN FICTION (as Caro French)
The Farcreek Trilogy
Lady Luck
Lady Lay
Lady Chance

QUICK READS
Black eyed Devils - Catrin Collier
The Corpse's Tale - Katherine John

SHORT STORIES (as Catrin Collier)
Poppies at the Well
Christmas Eve at the Workhouse
Not Quite Leningrad

SHORT STORIES (as Katherine John)
The Ghost before Christmas

No writer writes a book, especially a historical book alone and I am indebted to all the authors whose books I have devoured so avidly. Thank you.

The Revolt of Owain Glyn Dŵr published by Oxford University Press. 1997. ISBN 0-19-285336-8. Professor Sir R.R. Davies'
Owain Glyn Dŵr - Tywysog Cymru translated by Gerald Morgan
Owain Glyn Dŵr - Prince of Wales, Professor Sir R.R. Davies' published by Y Lolfa. 2009. ISBN 978-1847711274.

Professor Glanmor Williams, *Owain Glyndŵr,* University of Wales Press. 1993. ISBN 0-7083-1193-8.

Owain Glyndŵr – A Casebook, by Michael Livingston and John K. Bollard. Liverpool University Press. 2013. ISBN 978-0-85989-884-3.

Dyddiau Olaf Owain Glyndŵr, Gruffydd Aled Williams. Y Lolfa. 2015. ISBN 978-1-78461-156-9.

In Search of Owain Glyndŵr, Chris Barber Blorenge Books. 2004. ISBN 1-87-2730-33-7.

Owain Glyn Dŵr & the War of Independence in the Welsh Borders, Geoffrey Hodges. Logaston Press. 1995. ISBN 1-873827-24-5.

Glyn Dŵr's War, G. J. Brough. Wales Books Glyndŵr Publishing. 2002. ISBN 1-903529-069.

The Rise and Fall of Owain Glyndŵr, Gideon Brough. I.B. Taurus. 2017. ISBN 978-1-78453-593-3.

Glyndŵr's First Victory – The Battle of Hyddgen 1401, Ian Fleming. Y Lolfa. 2001. ISBN 0-86243-590-0.

Owain Glyndŵr – The Story of the Last Prince of Wales, Terry Breverton. Amberley. 2009. ISBN 978-1-84868-328-0

Owen Tudor Amberley Publishing Terry Breverton

The Mystery of Jack of Kent & the Fate of Owain Glyndŵr, Alex Gibbon. Sutton Publishing. 2004. ISBN 978-0-7509-3320-9.

Owen Glendower, J.E. Lloyd. Oxford University Press. 1931.

A Brief History of Wales, Gerald Morgan. Y Lolfa. 2008. ISBN 9781847710185.

A History of Wales, John Davies. Penguin Books. 1990. ISBN 0-14-012570-1.

Owain Glyndŵr and the Last Struggle for Welsh Independence. 1902. A. G. Bradley,

Owen Glyn Dŵr. 1934. J. D. G. Davies,

Land of My Fathers, 1974. Gwynfor Evans,

The Fifteenth Century. 1961. E. F. Jacob,

Owain Glyndŵr. 1962. G. A. Jones,

The Royal Policy of Richard 11. 1968. R. H. Jones.

Henry 1 of England. 1970. J. L. Kirby,

Owen Glendower. 1931. J.E. Lloyd,

Welsh Records in Paris. 1910. T. Mathews,

The Fourteenth Century. 1959. M. McKisack,

Medieval Welsh Society. I1972. T. J. Pierce,

A Selected Bibliography of Owen Glyndŵr. D. R. Phillips,

South Wales and the March, 1282 - 1415. 1924. W. Rees,

Owain Glyndŵr, Prince of Wales. I. Skidmore,

Richard 11 and the English Nobility. 1973. J. A. Tuck,

When was Wales. 1985. G. A. Williams.

Some Secret Supporters of Owain Glyn Dŵr. Ralph Griffiths

Memoirs of Owen Glendower (Owain Glyndŵr) with a sketch of the history of Ancient Britons from the conquest of Wales by Edward I to the present. 1822. Thomas Rev Thomas

Mortimer History Society

Eluned. Anthony Griffiths (landscape photographs)

Owain Glyndŵr. Aeres Twiggy Gomer (children's book)

National Redeemer. Elissa P Henken

The Revolt of Owain Glyndŵr in Medieval English Chronicles. Alicia Marchant York Medieval Press

Printed in Great Britain
by Amazon